The Rose in Darkness

The Rose in Darkness

An Adepta Sororitas novel

Danie Ware

BLACK LIBRARY

A BLACK LIBRARY PUBLICATION

First published in 2023.
This edition published in Great Britain in 2024 by
Black Library, Games Workshop Ltd., Willow Road,
Nottingham, NG7 2WS, UK.

Represented by: Games Workshop Limited – Irish branch,
Unit 3, Lower Liffey Street, Dublin 1,
D01 K199, Ireland.

10 9 8 7 6 5 4 3 2 1

Produced by Games Workshop in Nottingham.
Cover illustration by Jan Drenovec.

A CIP record for this book is available from the British Library.

ISBN 13: 978-1-80407-629-3

See Black Library on the internet at

blacklibrary.com

Find out more about Games Workshop
and the worlds of Warhammer at

games-workshop.com

Printed and bound in the UK.

For more than a hundred centuries the Emperor
has sat immobile on the Golden Throne of Earth.
He is the Master of Mankind. By the might of his
inexhaustible armies a million worlds stand
against the dark.

Yet, he is a rotting carcass, the Carrion Lord of
the Imperium held in life by marvels from the
Dark Age of Technology and the thousand souls
sacrificed each day so his may continue to burn.

To be a man in such times is to be one amongst
untold billions. It is to live in the cruelest and
most bloody regime imaginable. It is to suffer an
eternity of carnage and slaughter. It is to have cries
of anguish and sorrow drowned by the thirsting
laughter of dark gods.

This is a dark and terrible era where you will
find little comfort or hope. Forget the power of
technology and science. Forget the promise of
progress and advancement. Forget any notion of
common humanity or compassion.

There is no peace amongst the stars, for in the grim
darkness of the far future, there is only war.

Prologue

Kamilla stood alone.

Around her, the cathedral's immense, exquisitely carved walls were in ruins, their oriels and archways broken, their glassaic hanging in shattered, lead-lined shards. Statues of saints stood headless, and great spars of steel stuck up like flagpoles, catching torn prayer-scarves that flapped in the wind. If she turned, she could see down, down, all the way down, through the streets of the Inner Sanctum, Opal's Holy of Holies. She could see the three main roads, the three Martyrs' Archways, all of them thronging with the incoming horde. Despite the cathedral's destruction, the deep, iridescent glitter of the stonework seemed alive with joy and wonder. And the people *sang*.

Saint Veres comes!

They were a sea of faces, a thousand, a million, a billion of them, all gazing rapt at the sky. Kamilla wanted only for them to join her, to feel their joy as her own, share it. Her eyes followed where they were looking, saw the great, turning vortex of cloud, the opening void at its centre. It was a gift, it was a god, it was a saviour. It was their only hope and future.

Believe in me, it said. *Believe in me and I will bring you hope. I will bring this precious world of Opal to its new dawn, its new life.*

Yes, she said to it, tears pouring down her face. *Yes! We are broken and we need you! Come to us and take us from the darkness!* Hymns reached her, crystal in the cold. *Come to us and take us to the light!*

Somewhere in the Capital's streets, bells rang from unseen shrines. Peals of music, clarion and hymnal, herald and glory. As the vortex grew and the prayer-flags flapped like live things, frantic, the bells rose in volume and vehemence, a celebration of–

Silence.

It was so sudden, so utter, that Kamilla almost staggered. She heard her pulse pound hard in her ears. She felt her heart, the lifeblood that beat through her veins. It felt like appetite. Like *hunger*.

Saint Veres comes!

And there – *there!* – a shape, like some huge, organic creature. It was beautiful, incredible, a bearer of miracles. The vortex grew further, whirling stone-dust, making her blink and rub her eyes. The struggling prayer-scarves tore free, tumbling over and over as they were sucked up into the sky. Struggling to see, she stumbled again, and clung to the edge of a half-crumbled wall.

Bless me, she cried silently. *For I am but the least of your followers. O holy Veres, warrior and hero, saint and martyr, bless me with your sacred heart, with your courage that faced the heretic!*

The shape came no closer, yet it seemed to touch her, sending a shudder down her spine. Amid the whirling clouds of dust, she could make out Opal's lone ring, visible day and night and shining with the light of her star. It was the world's halo, her blessing and her symbol. The Emperor Himself had placed it there, or so said the legends.

For we are Opal, Gem of the Segmentum Border, Home of the Million Saints. We are blessed by the God-Emperor, He touched our very stone with His shine. And yet… A stab in her heart, like the point of a bayonet. *And yet still, we are broken, and we need your help.*

Even as she watched, the vortex grew bigger, filling the entire sky. Rock by rock, tiny satellite by tiny satellite, Opal's halo was fragmenting, being eaten alive. And there, at the vortex's heart, there was something else. Was that another shape, and another? More? Half-seen, half-imagined, tumbling spheres of deeper black, like darkness within darkness…

The touch became a feeling, fatherly and gentle. It said, *There is no need for fear, child.*

For I am Veres returned, and I am here to heal your soul.

Kamilla woke with a jolt, like she'd fallen from some unknown height. For a moment, she had no idea where she was, or what had startled her to wakefulness. Her breath was short, her body tense with stress. Her eyes seemed full of grit and sand.

Had she been dreaming?

Deliberately calming herself, she listened.

Saint and Emperor, guard me while I sleep, and bless each day as it begins…

But the cadets' barracks were quiet, familiar. They were square and ordered and home. Slants of ring-light tumbled down through the windows, catching the drifting dirt. Soft snores came from the other bunks, rhythmic and oddly comforting – the previous day, the cadets had been on a punishing schedule and they'd come back exhausted, almost too tired to make the mess hall. In the bunk below, Endre muttered and snorted. Kamilla recognised Tibor's wheeze, and the regular burble that was Petra, further down. They made her smile. They were more than comrades; they were family, brothers, sisters. Orphans all, they'd been raised together from children.

A second prayer touched her lips, warm and reassuring. Firmly, she told herself: *He is with us.*

She checked the barracks' chrono, was about to turn over and go back to sleep when below her, Endre said, 'Saint Veres comes.'

The words were like a shock. Called back from the darkness, fragments of dream-images spiked at Kamilla's mind: massive, ruined walls, a vortex in the sky.

What was *that?*

She froze, listening with every nerve, but the words did not come again. Endre grunted, and his snores grew deeper.

She didn't move. She lay there, staring out at the ring-light and asking silent questions, as was her unintentionally blasphemous habit. Were dreams heretical? How did you know if they came from the Emperor, if they were holy and pure? The cadets attended a pre-dawn service, in full uniform as was proper, but the sermons told only of courage and duty, of obedience and faith, of Opal's historical saints. Anything else was fanciful, and would incur a significant penance. Perhaps, if she did well enough in her bouts tomorrow, she may gain a boon, and be permitted to see Father Arkas. He was the closest thing she still had to family, and he listened and did not judge.

At the far end of the barracks, Benedek suddenly snorted and muttered aloud. Another voice joined him, wordless and pained, and the winter wind breathed chill through the window frames. The glassaic rattled and dust-ghosts stirred across the floor.

Tangled in her potential heresy, Kamilla shivered.

Carefully, not wanting to wake the others, she leaned out of the bed and rummaged through the tiny standing locker at its side. Her combat fatigues, clean and pressed, hung where she'd left them, their disruptive camo pattern all square angles and pale greys, like Opal's walls. But they weren't what she wanted. Fumbling deeper, her hand came out with a tiny talisman: a brass compass, hanging from a chain. It had belonged to her uncle, and if she moved its rings and slides to the correct time and date, it would point at the Sol System, at Holy Terra and His light.

At the heart of the segmentum.

Hunkering back down in the bed, she pulled the scratchy blankets almost completely over her head. Carefully moving the markers, she watched the compass settle, taking her thoughts with it.

Saint and Emperor, she prayed. *Grant me clarity. Grant me a warrior's life and warrior's death. Grant me the holiness of Opal herself...*

Kamilla carried no grief for the deaths of her parents; she didn't remember them. Only her Uncle Jakob, her mother's older brother, who'd raised her until she was seven. He'd been killed in food rioting at the Outskirt, trying to help the starving people, but she remembered his smell and his great strength. The sensation of being engulfed by his arms, and by safety.

Distinctly, Endre repeated, 'Saint Veres comes.'

Startled, she dropped the compass, her heart racing. A wash of adrenaline broke over her, a sickening fusion of fear and exaltation, of revulsion and wonder.

Was he having the same dream? Was that even possible?

Saint and Emperor, protect our humble lives!

With a silent prayer, she told herself firmly to stop such blasphemous wonderings, made the circle-symbol of Opal with her thumb and forefinger – the plea for the saint's protection. This was a good world, a sacred world, a world of hymns and tocsins, of prayers and pilgrims, and of the proud, resounding bellow of the organ loft...

Below, Endre whimpered, turning in his sleep. Dream-images lingered half-seen, like pieces of a broken window. Tension still knotted in the back of her throat, Kamilla retrieved the compass. Holding it in her hands, she resolved to win her bouts, and to speak to Father Arkas. Because he understood, and if she had questions, he would always find the time to answer them.

Part One

Dreams and Portents

THE STAR OF VICTORY

The freighter hung still, a tiny silhouette against the vast, striped curve of the planet's ring. Along both sides of her underbelly, glitters of lumens showed her saviour pods, their rail-gun launchers silent. In rows above, the hydraulic doors of her gunnery decks were sealed tight against the void. The light of Denar Alpha caught her vox-antennae and flashed briefly from her oculus deck, revealing the scarred and serious face of her captain. Had it penetrated further, following the patient thrum of the frigate's engines, gliding smoothly along her access tunnels and companionways, down past her hatches and ladders, it may have reached the deepest, darkest recesses of her belly. Not her fusion reactor, burning still as it blessed the great ship with life, not her chapel and its holy statues, but the dark bilge of her inner hull, and the things that floated within.

Here, it might even have paused, touching the marching ranks of ferrocrete pillars, the rusted walkways, the broken wires and tumbling sparks. And it may have stopped completely at the sound of a sacred hymnal, echoing harmoniously out across the water.

'A spiritu dominatus

'Domine, libra nos...'

Wading through the icy stillness, there came an arrowhead of five red-armoured figures, each with weapon in hand. Five suit-lights shone outwards, angled through the darkness, and at their head, a single auspex glimmered green. Black-and-white robes trailed behind each one, making ripples upon the water's surface and soaking up the filth. It had been twenty-five Solar years since the schola, but still Sister Superior Augusta Santorus felt a fierce and holy joy at the advance of her squad, and at the purity of the Sisters' battle-hymn.

'From the lightning and the tempest...'

Around them, almost too deep to hear, hummed the chest-shuddering echoes of the ship's void-engines. The *Star* had travelled safely from the Convent Sanctorum on Ophelia VII and Augusta thanked Him for the frigate's strength and spirit.

And for the blessing of this, their newest mission.

'Our Emperor, deliver us.'

A flare of excitement, a prayer of pure wonder. For the first time in over a decade, the *Star* carried her not outwards, to planets of invading xenos or the heave and slobber of the Foe, not to worlds of chemical darkness and death all overgrown, not even to ruined cathedrals and their horrific and bloodstained depths. Not this time.

This time, He called her inwards, to the closest outskirts of Segmentum Solar and to Opal, a world of shrines and light.

'In His name, Sister Superior,' her canoness had said, 'you have striven hard, and well. You have fought His enemies in every segmentum, and you have returned with honour. You have faced loss, and grief, and bloodshed, and horror. And now, He has a different task for you.'

Elvorix Ianthe had a soul of pure courage, and the austere restraint of the lifelong warrior. But – unless Augusta had imagined it – she had almost been smiling.

'A task,' she had said, 'that will surely speak to your heart.'

The *Star*'s engines rumbled as she shifted slightly, aligning herself with the planet's orbit, and settling to her place. Soon, the Sisters would disembark, attaining planetfall by mid-afternoon. Their mission was brief, and should conclude within the day; they would find few enemies here.

No, here, they would find only Him – and the skull of Saint Veres, most blessed hero and martyr. He who had cast down the traitor ecclesiarch, and saved his world of Opal. The skull dated to the Age of Apostasy itself, and, due to reports of rising unrest in the planet's Capital, Augusta must retrieve it for safekeeping.

On the other side of the formation, Sister Viola Taenaris, always the hothead, muttered an unseemly curse.

'Where are they?' she said, over the vox. Her thrice-blessed heavy bolter, its barrels inscribed with a filigree of sacred prayers, glimmered in the dying sparks' light.

On point, Sister Caia de Musa shook the auspex, and twitched a shrug. 'They are staying low, I think.'

The air was cold and dark and bitter, frosting like crystals on Augusta's pauldrons. It creaked with titanic emptiness, with odd, cold resonances that made her skin prickle. Things bumped at her legs: rotting things, eyeless things. In places, the dripping sparks spat like irregular rainfall, each one glinting briefly then fizzling to a soaking end. Some struck her scarlet armour, flashing brilliantly as they died. Others hit her bolter, the chainsword at her hip, or made tiny char-marks on the roses of her robe.

'They will be ahead of us,' Augusta replied. 'If they came down the delta quadrant ladders, then the auspex will pick them up.'

'Maintain your vigilance, my Sisters,' said Sister Alcina Leiva, the squad's second. From Viola's far side, she sounded curt and wary. 'They cannot be far.'

'Sister Melia,' Augusta said. 'Watch the rear.'

'Yes, Sister.' Next to the Sister Superior, Sister Melia Kaliyan gripped her flamer, and turned her suit-light to the darkness behind.

Caia moved forwards slowly, Augusta and the squad following. The water dragged at the Sister Superior's shins and her mag-fastened chainsword, but her hands on the bolter were steady.

'From plague, temptation and war...'

'Hold.' Caia stopped, the light of her auspex glinting. Exposed and with no cover, Augusta dropped to one knee, ordered the others to do the same. The five of them knelt in silence as the thick bilge stirred and slapped.

'Our Emperor, deliver us.'

Things turned to the surface, bobbing and bloated things, but they were dead – they were of no matter, and Augusta took a full three seconds to scan her surroundings. The space was almost incomprehensively huge: a monstrous hollow, its walls and roof unseen. Grey pillars stood soldier-like, endless ranks of them, dwindling into the distance. Some still spilled light, tiny pools from half-broken lumens that reflected in the water; others had shattered panels, or broken screens. Still more had rusting ladders and sagging metal gantries.

Ideal lines of sight for the undetected foe.

'Sister Caia,' Augusta said. 'What is our situation?'

Caia moved her auspex through a one-eighty scan. 'Nothing, Sister. Nothing that looks like the enemy, and no sign of an incoming threat.'

'Scan again,' said Alcina, her tone grim.

Caia repeated the action, with the same result.

'Still nothing, Sisters,' she repeated. 'And the spirit of the auspex works truly. I can only assume that they are out of range–'

'Or they are stationary,' Viola said.

Alcina gave a faint, thoughtful snort. 'We know they are here,' she said across the squad-vox to Augusta. 'But we do not know how they are deployed. Or how they will attack.'

Augusta did not respond. Under her helm, sweat itched on her fleur-de-lys tattoo.

'From the scourge of the Kraken…'

She tightened her grip on her bolter. Its weight felt *good*, like strength and reassurance. The weapon was as much a part of her as her prayers, her faith. It was His presence in the darkness, waiting to thunder its song.

'Our Emperor, deliver us.'

Flicking on her preysight, she watched the gantries, but there was nothing. No heat, no warmth. No tell-tale ruddy shimmer to show the enemy's location. The sparks flashed brief and glorious, dazzling, but the great ship's belly was empty, an endless stretch of almost uniform cold.

Viola made an impatient noise. 'Your orders, Sister?' she asked. 'May we continue the advance?'

Still Augusta said nothing, only continued to pray, and to scan. The enemy could still be anywhere, down here, lurking silent and unseen. They could have taken cover behind a pillar. They could be watching the Sisters' advance, tracking the faint glitter of the auspex, measuring the moving ripples. They may even be under the water, still and silent, their heat concealed.

Eyes seemed to watch them, from every angle and shadow.

'Sister Superior.' Viola had the heavy bolter at her shoulder, was moving it through watchful arcs. 'Your orders?'

'We know that they are clever, and well aware of our armaments,'

Alcina said, still thoughtful. Her voice was quiet, but all warning, bleak and considered. 'They also outnumber us.' She paused, let out her breath, then said, 'Sister Augusta, may I recommend that we proceed?'

'Sister Caia,' Augusta said. 'You have the location of the target?'

'Yes, Sister.' The auspex glinted again. Sparks fizzled and fell, dripping like orange raindrops on Augusta's armour. One struck her robe, and there was a tiny curl of smoke.

'We will follow your lead,' Augusta said. 'But be watchful. Under no circumstance do we allow the enemy to get behind us. Viola, take point.'

'Yes, Sister.'

'From the blasphemy of the Fallen…'

The ancient battle-prayer swelled once more, and Sister Viola rose to her feet, wading forwards through the bilge and allowing Caia to fall back. Augusta and the squad moved out, still in arrowhead formation. Their motion stirred the swollen things, blue and white and rotted. Despite herself, the Sister Superior glanced down, remembering her very first mission from the schola, when she'd been an unblooded novice. Just like they had been then, the things were lost, bloated and half-eaten, or rusted to pure corrosion. Some of them still had eyeholes, and they stared reproachfully; others had mouths ever-open, now flooded with filth.

But she was Augusta Santorus, and she had seen worse.

Seen worse, and slain it.

'Our Emperor, deliver us.'

Alcina's strong contralto sang out, both faith and focus. The squad sang with her, and moved steadily forwards.

Still, they saw nothing.

The darkness loomed massive, filling with phantom sound. The faint, distant rumble of the ship's engines, like some great, slow heartbeat; the soft creaks of her life and movement. Down here, the Sisters were away from her metal veins, her walkways and tunnels; they were below even her gunnery decks, and those ever-patient saviour pods. The *Star* seemed almost like some huge living, breathing thing, groaning as she settled into place.

'Hold,' Caia said again. The auspex was still in her hand, though it showed no motion. 'Sisters, we have reached a crux-point. Pillar two-four-seventy is a marker, and shortest route to our target means moving straight ahead. Or, we can turn left and follow the hull, but the route is longer. Sister Augusta, what is your direction?'

'We will take the shorter route,' Augusta replied. 'We have left Sister Akemi alone, and we are running out of time. Akemi, do you have line of sight on the enemy?'

'*No, Sister.*' From the far end of the empty hull, the voice of the youngest Sister, Akemi Hirari, was firm in Augusta's ear. '*Should He bless me with such a sighting, I will raise the alarm.*'

'Very well,' Augusta said. 'Then, in His name, we will proceed. Shortest route.'

'Sister.' Following Caia's auspex, the squad moved on, walking under the towering pillars like tiny, scarlet specks.

Still they saw nothing. Only the pools of the pillars' light. Only the sockets of the floating dead, as the Sisters kicked the corpses from their way. Augusta flicked her preysight in and out, scanning as she moved. She was sure that she was missing something. In the great and echoing space, their movement was loud, they sang, and they made splashes that resonated like bugle-calls: *Fear us, for we are here!* Why had they not been assailed? Had the enemy gone for Akemi, after all?

'*From the begetting of daemons...*'

She waded onwards, taking cover by the pillars where she could. Her mission was clear – and, as ever, failure was not an option. If they did not gain their target and bring down their enemy, then they would damage the honour of the squad, their reputation, and the reputation of the Order of the Bloody Rose...

'Our Emperor, deliver us.'

Caia said, 'Still nothing.'

In her gauntlets, Augusta's hands were starting to sweat. She gripped the bolter like her faith, like strength and retribution. She knew the enemy was down here, knew the Sisters had to locate them. She had made the decision to leave Akemi alone, rather than further compromise their advancing strength. Was that enemy, even now, laying an ambush in the darkness, and waiting for the Sisters to come closer?

'Sister Melia?' Sister Alcina was still softly spoken, but there was a crack of command to the word. Her tension, too, was palpable, even over the vox.

'From the curse of the mutant...'

'Still nothing, Sister,' Melia said. 'I suspect they have gone to ground. Finding them, in this–'

'He is with us,' Augusta responded, undaunted.

'Wait!'

The voice was Caia's, a soft bark of urgency. The green glow of the auspex was clear, now, far brighter than it had been. A myriad flickers winked on its surface – a distance away, but clearly not things floating.

'Lights out!' Alcina's order was sharp.

Instantly, the suit-lights shut off, and Caia dropped the auspex into its mag-fastened case at her belt. The hymnal paused, hung on a breath, as the five of them stopped as one.

Listening.

For a long moment, Augusta could hear nothing – nothing that sounded like movement. The vox seemed to fill with an unfelt wind, the hull's slow, metallic creaks were almost musical, gentle as the great ship settled. The thrum of her engine had softened, now, to a faint and beating pulse.

There – was that a splash?

Something out there *was* moving. Searching. It was creeping forwards, almost silent despite the water.

Into the squad vox, Caia said, 'I can see lights. Distance five hundred and fifty yards. Heading one-six-five degrees... They are behind us.'

'Throne!'

Viola cursed, but Augusta said only, 'Caia, the pillar to your left. Up the ladder, out onto the gantry. I want a clear heading, numbers, trajectory. Tell me exactly where they are.'

'They are heading for Akemi's location,' Viola said. Augusta had ordered Akemi to hold the rearguard position – needing a strong spearhead attack to secure the target.

'I would agree,' Augusta said. 'But we must be sure. I want a full sweep, and a full head count. I want to know where every single one of them is, what they are armed with, and precisely where they are going.'

'Sister.' Caia ran for the ladder. It was rusting where the water lapped at it, but she grabbed the higher rungs and pulled herself up until her feet could rest on solid metal. A moment later, she was up on the gantry, which creaked at the weight of her boots.

'Sister Akemi,' Augusta said. 'You have incoming.'

'*Understood, Sister. Direction?*'

'Straight ahead of you,' Caia said. 'Two minutes. With the Emperor's blessing, we shall achieve the objective first.'

Akemi's sung prayer chimed in response.

'*Our Emperor, deliver us...*'

Metal graunched and ripped, and Caia loosed a curse – the platform was tearing free. She scrambled, got back on a solid footing. Sparks tumbled past her, making her scarlet armour flash like some erratic beacon.

'Your scan, Sister,' Augusta said.

Caia said, 'Sightings confirmed – three locations. A guard at the target, four of them. And there are two moving patrols, one behind us, stretched out to cover the ground. The other is waiting at an ambush point, right on the edge of my scan.' She paused. 'It is a good location, but they have made their mistake. They expected us to follow the hull. I suggest we do not engage – we should round them, and achieve the objective.'

'How many?'

'Six in each patrol.'

'Very well,' said Augusta. 'Caia, Viola, with me. We will continue forwards. Avoid the scout patrol and go straight for the target. Keep the auspex hidden unless you have no other option. Melia and Alcina will go back, and eliminate the patrol behind us.'

'Is it wise to split our strength that much, Sister?' Alcina asked. 'Akemi is already alone.'

'We are Adepta Sororitas,' Augusta responded flatly. 'He walks with us, and we are enough.'

'Understood.'

Swinging down from the ladder, Caia landed with a splash, her bolter in hand. 'We should shift heading by another ten degrees,' she said. 'Just to be sure. Quiet as we can, and follow the pillars. They are His markers and they will show us the way.' Augusta could almost hear her grin. 'And four guards? They should have posted twenty.'

The Sisters moved quietly.

'A *morte perpetua*...'

Their hymnal was outwardly silent, now, but the music still

flowed over the vox, bringing coordination, devotion and unity. Pushing onwards through the water, Augusta moved with an alert smoothness, Caia and Viola with her.

They passed a rusting servitor, still upright, its sensor array twitching and broken. One of its eyes was half-alight, an eerie glimmer of sentience. A maddened mutter came from the thing, repeated over and over. They passed a shattered grav-tray, more hole than steel. They passed a slumping body, faceless and half-eaten. And the pillars marched ever onwards, like endless ranks of Titans.

Slowly, the ship's creaks faded to nothing, and there was quiet. Even the engine noise had gone. There was only the sloshing of their legs through the water. Only the vox-borne prayer.

'*Domine, libra nos…*'

Augusta was about to order another scan, when Akemi suddenly barked, '*Contact! Six of them, incoming on my location. They are moving slowly, but they know exactly where I am.*'

The three Sisters paused.

From a distance, Alcina responded, '*We have them, Akemi. Your incoming patrol is in our sights.*'

With the suddenness of a thunderclap, a single bolter shot roared through the darkness. There was the sound of it striking ferrocrete, a detonation of rubble and dust. Across the vox, Akemi's voice bawled prayers.

Augusta said, 'We must secure the target. Run!'

The three of them ran, splashing through the water's drag, kicking the floating monstrosities out of their way. To one side of them, there came sudden shouts, but the Sisters' heading had been good and they'd missed the scouts completely. Caia tripped, lurched, kept running. Viola's ammo belts rattled.

Across the vox came Alcina's contralto bellow: '*That thou wouldst bring them only death!*'

'There!' Caia extended an arm, her vambrace gleaming red.

And there it was, ahead of them: their objective. Tiny, and visible only in the circle of light that tumbled from the pillar above...

A flag.

The blazing-sword flag of the *Star*, only the size of a pennon, but proudly and defiantly placed. Before it, four Naval guards, each one with rifle in hand. Skirting the light-pool, the three Sisters spread out, Viola at the centre.

Behind them, more noise erupted. The slashes of scarlet were more frequent, now, blazing across the darkness like some night-time celebration, some festival of His light. Akemi shouted again, the clarion courage of a prayer. Alcina snapped orders.

But Augusta and the others were there, right on the edges of the light that barred their way...

Then one of the guards pointed downwards. The Sisters' ripples were visible, like arrows, indicating clearly their positions and headings. Well disciplined, the guards raised their rifles.

Akemi was still shouting.

Augusta said, 'Viola. Cover me.'

Not waiting for Viola's response, she leapt into motion, rolling fast through the water on one shoulder and coming up in the soldiers' midst like some bright red manifestation. The guards started, yelled, but she'd had the sheer force to send them tumbling.

One, the lieutenant by the pip on his shoulder, retained enough discipline to bring his rifle up to bear, but confronted by the muzzle of the bolter, by the faceless, Sabbat-style mask of a Sister of Battle, he fell back, dropping the weapon and raising his hands. His fellows, white as ghosts, did likewise.

'We have the flag,' Augusta said. 'Time check, oh-nine-thirty-two, Solar time. In His name, that is a victory.'

THE FESTIVAL OF SAINT VERES

In the wide, dirty base of the combat-pit, Kamilla bounced on her toes.

Under her laced-tight military boots – done with molten polish and shined until she could almost see her face in them – the ground was grey sand, rough and already stained with fluids. Her breath steamed in a chill she did not feel; her shoulders were bare and sweating. Opposite her, fists raised, her barrack-mate Endre had burst lips and one eye already swollen and closing. Kamilla had split her knuckles, hitting him. Thin lines of scarlet trickled down her hand and wrist, but she paid them no attention, just jabbed in with another left hook.

Endre ducked back, and she missed.

Around the pit's edges, the standing audience gave a collective gasp, a noise like the hissing of steam. They leaned down, shouting, encouragement or bloodlust; they called and whooped and cheered and sang. Here and there, there were jingles as gamblers placed bets upon the outcome, or upon the time that the combatants would last. The odds had been long against Kamilla at the start – Endre was strongly built, with a much better reach.

But Kam was fast. And lucky, or so the rumour went.

Lucky – and *blessed*.

The two of them circled, and the shouting grew.

'Go on, short stuff! Punch him!'

Kamilla grinned. Her world may have dwindled to the pit, and to the dart and strike of her opponent, but somewhere up there, out beyond the faces and voices, there were other sounds – the rising harmonies of the festival's opening hymnals, the celebrations and greetings, the constant rounds of bells. They'd started even before the cadets' morning muster: the chime of the hourly tocsins and the steady, bass clanging of the Saints' Cathedral, vox-cast across the Capital. The outer combat-pits were a distance below the Inner Sanctum, but still the festival's call was strong, demanding faith and reverence from all.

This is Opal, it said. *Our saints laid down their lives for you. Our warriors saved your worlds. And this is how we remember them, in His name.*

Endre came in hard, aiming for her temple – but the move was slow and he'd left himself open. Quick as a whip, she cracked him in the face.

The crowd roared, bawling approval as scarlet splashed from his nose. The cadets didn't usually fight to the death, but broken limbs and heads were common – and injuries were sacred to Saint Veres and the Three Martyrs, inflicted for the God-Emperor Himself.

This is Opal. Our saints laid down their lives for you…

Kamilla's energy was high, her nerves humming. Endre was faltering now, his fists not as tight as they had been, his focus not as strong. She'd fought him before, many times in training, occasionally in public, and she knew his weaknesses. Despite his size, or perhaps because of it, he tired easily.

Then a single, clear shout came from a warden at the pit's edge, and there was a flash of thrown steel. Endre flicked a quick glance. Instantly, Kamilla aimed a punch for his ear, but he ducked away, picking up the metal things that had landed in a puff of sand.

Knuckle-dusters, spiked ones. Bloodstained from a previous bout.

Saint and Emperor!

The crowd's roar grew. The jingle of coins became louder.

Concentrating hard now, Kamilla considered her next move. If he clouted her with those things, she'd spend the rest of the festival in the hospice. If she got up at all. And this was Opal's greatest moment, her highest joy, the thing the cadets had been training for for *months*. Kamilla wanted, more than anything, to earn her place at the Sermon of the Hero, and to see that sacred, golden skull for herself.

A flicker of dreams, like a drifting phantom: *Saint Veres comes!*

But Endre had made his mistake: he'd paused, split second, to pull the dusters on.

Kamilla moved, ducking in, jabbing left right left. His hands busy, Endre caught all three blows to the side of his head. He staggered, dropping the dusters and reeling back. Quickly, she dived, rolled past him, picking them up as she went, but she didn't bother to put them on. Instead, she just gripped them firmly, and walloped him, as hard as she could. The metal caught him smack in the teeth.

Blood and enamel flew. The crowd howled. Hymnals and bells still rang. *This is Opal! Our saints laid down their lives!* Kamilla's adrenaline surged.

With a crash like a falling statue, Endre went over.

Not stopping, she pounced after him. Dropping one of the dusters, she pulled on the other and landed, knees first, smack on his chest. Ribs cracked. For one second, he focused on her, eyes both widening, then the duster smashed him full in the face. A second time. A third.

He slumped boneless, out cold.

Raising her arms, Kamilla shrieked a prayer, the noise of it absolutely primal. In response, the crowd's howl grew. They threw things down to her: food, creds, relics purchased from the holy markets. Hymnals sang on, exultant and oblivious. The bells rang, perfect. Everything was noise.

Her head spinning, Kamilla lurched to her feet, her bloody hands still aloft. Figures were running onto the sand – medicae, retrieving Endre's fallen form. From the control box, the pit-master was bellowing her name.

'Kamilla! Kamillaaaaah! Her first fight of the morning! She may be small, pilgrims of Opal, but she be fierce! Witness her skills! The God-Emperor blessed her as a babe, and here we see her fighting for His glory! For our hallowed, haloed world! For Saint Veres *himself!*' The man's voice was a perfect goad, spiking at the audience, making them react. 'Say it with me – in His name!'

Eagerly, the crowd picked up the roar: 'In His *name!* In His *name!* In His *name!*' It became a solid, regular stamp, powerful and rhythmic, a blood-lusting.

Kamilla turned round, slowly. She let the adulation wash over her, let it buffet her, side to side. She'd beaten Endre before, but never like this, never in front of *this* many people, never with this sheer *rush*… And the festival was only on its opening day! There were three more days after this one, and there would be many, many more fights. Not just the cadets, but the Blades of the Holy Interior, Opal's regular planetary defence – and not even just fights, but displays of combat techniques and marching formations, of manoeuvres and disciplines and even *music*–

'You okay, Kam?' a voice said at her side.

'Fine.' Opening her eyes, letting her arms drop, she saw a dark-skinned young man, his expression concerned. He bore a medicae's armband and was examining the bloodstains up her wrists.

'Not mine,' she told him with a wink. But the noise was fading now, taking with it her vitality. Her sweated vest was sticking to her, uncomfortable and chilly. She shivered, realising there was sleet on the wind–

Saint Veres comes!

A shudder went through her, leaving her staring at nothing. The dream-phantoms passed again, a ghost of pure cold in their wake. She could almost remember, *almost* recall what she had seen.

A vortex in the sky. A cathedral in ruins…

She stood there, shocked to the core, frozen to the spot. *What had she been dreaming about? What–*

Then something metal touched her fingers and she jumped, the recollections gone. She blinked. A canteen of water had been thrust into her hands. She stared at it, confused.

'You fight like a fiend,' the medicae was saying, chuckling. 'Thing your size! Get some water down you, you'll feel better. Was blessed by Father Istavan, up at the Shrine of Saint Nemes, only this morning.'

It brought her back to the fight, the sands, the bright chill of the air. The pain in her knuckles.

'My uncle taught me,' she said, almost reflexively. 'Taught me to punch when I was a kid. Because I was little.' She frowned and took a sip of the water. It was icy, and it made her shivering worse.

'Here.' The medicae had picked up her combat jacket. He passed it over and she shrugged her way back into it, checking for the compass in the pocket.

The pit-master was still shouting, promising bigger fights, and opportunities for the pilgrims themselves to face Opal's warriors, if they so dared. The heats would last for the next two days, culminating in the full-on death matches in the machine pits of the Inner Sanctum. The small scattering of Opal's red-cloaked adepts had been consecrating them for days.

'Come on,' the young man said. 'Let's get you off the sands before they start the next one.' He winked at her, impish. 'And we can make sure you're in good shape for this afternoon, huh? Keep fighting like that, kid, you're going to be busy.'

The hospice was an old underground bunker, attached to the side of the combat-pits. It had few patients, at this time of the morning, but it was still an hour before the medicae would let her escape. He kept her at Beneficia Minor and whispered at her that, if she wanted to make some extra creds, the combatants' blood was being bottled and sold.

At last, she managed to assure him she was fine, really, and went to drag herself away – but not before he'd pressed a stimm-pack into her hand. Winking, he whispered, 'Give you an edge for the next one. I'm counting on you!'

Annoyed at his petty avarice but smart enough to keep the advantage, she shoved the thing in the pocket of her combat trousers. Pausing only to check on Endre, who'd regained a somewhat rueful consciousness, Kamilla headed to the far end of the tunnel complex, and back up the steps to the main street.

'Cadet.' The duty Blade, his angled grey camo just like her own but overlaid with a polished white chestplate and pauldrons, nodded as she passed. His head was bare and he had a single dagger painted on his left shoulder, marking him as rank-and-file. 'Nice fight. Would put a wager on you myself, if I wasn't on duty.'

But Kamilla barely heard him. She was gawking at the roadway. And at the *people*.

By the Light! She'd known the Festival of Saint Veres would be busy, but this was bigger than any celebration she'd ever *seen*...

Beneath the sloping holiness of the Inner Sanctum, the streets of Opal's Capital were usually sedate. A few priests, the occasional soldier or scholar. Servitors, human and mechanical both. Administratum staff attending their regulation sermons. Workers, diligent and humble. Groups of worshippers, carrying personal offerings, self-flagellating, or begging for alms... Even at dawn, as the cadets had been at muster, it had still been comparatively quiet.

But no longer. The Festival of Saint Veres took place once every eight hundred years – every eight hundred and four – and now, the road was absolutely *heaving*. People trudged and pushed and shoved, heading inwards and upwards. In keeping with the planet's military pride and history, many carried banners, or wore simulacrums of the local camo, or of Militarum or commissarial garb. Some were even more daring, imitating the armour and markings of the Sisters of Battle. It made Kamilla goggle – legend said there were indeed Adepta Sororitas among the planet's saints and martyrs, but still, she wasn't sure if the costumes were veneration or heresy. Other figures wore robes, in modest brown, or covered in sewn-on devotions. Entreaty scarves wrapped heads and hair; people's faces were painted, or daubed in blood or ash. Some carried knotted, already-bloodied flails, or had symbols newly engraved in their cheeks and foreheads. Still others had tattoos, sore about their edges. Here and there, a Mechanicus adept's red robes flickered in the mass.

And the *noise!* Not only the vox-cast of the cathedral's great bells, high at the Inner Sanctum's peak, but the hubbub of constant prayer and conversation, the sound of a million throats. The clamour of sermon and preacher, of kettledrum and marching band. The call and banter of the up-sprung holy markets, selling artefacts and sacred souvenirs. The bellow of the wealthy, the imperious or the impatient, demanding that everyone get out of their way.

At the cadets' briefing, Spear Takacs, their commanding officer, had warned them about this. Thousands of ships, he'd said, were achieving geostationary orbit. In their turn, they were birthing numberless flotillas of shuttles, ferrying people to the space ports – the sky was still alive with the things, like buzzing clouds of flies. And every one of them was dropping the pilgrims who owed Opal their lives, those whose worlds or cities or families or supply routes had been saved by the planet's saints.

Kamilla had understood the theory, of course, but the sheer *weight* of humanity present was just absolutely staggering. Some of her fellows were on more regular duty, standing guard at noted corners or running errands for the Blades. Since she had been actually fighting, upholding the planet's honour, she was able to gain special boons – like a chit permitting her festival food.

Real food.

Thank you, Saint and Emperor.

The grumble in her belly was enough – with a prayer, she stepped out into the morass. Immediately, she plunged below its surface, was shoved back and forth and sideways. She almost lost her footing, found her face full of bags and packs, and gaudy replica weapons emblazoned with icons. Everything was thick with smells, with body sweat and perfumes, with incense and machine oil and the copper tang of blood. Ducking and twisting, leading with her shoulder, she was small enough to move swiftly. She caught sight of a furtive figure, even smaller than herself, hands in everyone else's pockets, but they were gone before she could grab them.

Shrines and temples towered, a mass of arches and domes and spires. Statues vox-recited stories of saints and saviours and galactic wars, some of these on plinths and rearing fifty feet and more above the streets. Between them, running cable-cars hummed on their wires, laden with faithful, bright with banners and dispensing holy blessings to the crowds below. *Repent,* said one. *Donate,* said another. A third *Sacrifice,* a fourth, *Duty.* Coloured ribbons fell from their bows and sterns, each with a sacred message. And everywhere, strung along the roadsides, there were lines and lines and *lines* of human skulls, their teeth all brown and yellow. They dangled in loops between the street-lumens and watched the worshipful revellers, their eyeholes as black as death.

These were more of the planet's soldiers. Not those who had saved other worlds, but the Blades who had saved this one, and been slain in His name–

A vortex, turning in the sky.

That same ice-like shock hit her, and she found that she'd stopped; was holding up the flow. People tripped over her, cursed. Someone stood on her foot, jabbed her ear with an elbow, but she didn't move. She was semi frozen again, trying to gasp the dream-phantom before it faded, sublimating to steam and smoke, and wisping away.

A touch, like a fatherly blessing.

'You! Don't just bloody stop!' Behind her, a figure was bawling abuse. With a stagger like an apology, Kamilla started moving again, heading upwards, towards the markets and some lunch.

Saint and Emperor! What had got into her today? What were these images, eating at her mind? She was *definitely* going to see Father Arkas, once her bouts were over.

Clutching both compass and chit, she forced herself onwards.

Before long, the streets began to widen and the crowds spread out, moving more slowly. She had come upwards, now, almost as high as the Wall of Glory, the decorous, scalloped series of balconies that separated the Capital proper from the blessed boulevards of the Inner Sanctum. Under the wall's shelter, there were plazas, each named for an Opal hero and centred on a sparkling font, or some gloriously carved basilica. Whatever they were, every one was now filled with ranting preachers, with roped-off display-squares where the Blades played pipes and drums. On some corners, ancient camo-painted Tauroxes stood silent guard, plaques at their forefronts explaining their history. On others, there were great, metal-limned scars in the ground – stone sockets for missing weapons, and for the arcs in which they'd turned.

Kamilla stopped by one of these, its rusting steel cold. Beside it, there rose the exquisite carved and flying buttresses of the Abbey of Saint Zalan, each wrought with bas-reliefs of rifle-pointing soldiers holding monstrous enemies at bay. Between them, stall-holders had lined up to offer their wares. The air was thick with scents and sizzles and her belly grumbled again.

Early morning combat really made you ravenous.

Pottery amphorae were popular, here, and judging by the unsteady reel of a few celebrants, they held more than holy water. Grifters promised that *their* finger bones and fragments of fabric had come from the Three Martyrs themselves. Kamilla got a censer, smoke and all, almost right in her face and jerked her head to one side, coughing–

Stone-dust. A great vortex storm.

This time, the dream-flash was so powerful that she almost fell; her head pounded with the savagery of the recollection. The same cold had sheeted across her body, and she stared, transfixed, at mid-air...

Black shapes, like darkness against darkness.
Saint Veres comes!

There was an odd taste in her mouth, like a silty layer of fear. And just for a split second, she knew – she *knew* – that this whole festival meant nothing. It was hollow, a farce of greed and blasphemy. It made coin, nothing more. And she knew that if she pushed at it, or tore at it, it would peel back to emptiness, its charred decorations all burning away and revealing only the skulls' eyes, their stained teeth, the writhing monsters in the stone, like some terrible, bone-stark truth–

'Just for you, lady!' The voice was right beside her, making her start. 'Bullet-cases taken from Opal's most ancient battlefields!'

She turned to frown at the stallholder. He was a little man, grinning like a fiend. His table was layered with cloths and shining with empty brass casings. Hanging lines of them jingled prettily, like pure mercantile enticement.

'All proceeds to Opal's most holy church.' His gesture was broad and unabashed. 'Tell me which one you'd like, lady.' With perfect, innocuous subtlety, he tapped the most costly, nudging it and drawing her attention.

'And which battlefields were those?' Smarting from the dream-phantoms, and from the chillingly serendipitous pitch, Kamilla was half-tempted to discipline him 'Opal's last real war–' She stopped herself, quickly looking around. If anyone had overheard her say that...

But the stallholder was still smiling, apparently oblivious. 'Or how about this one, lady?' Another shell-case, much larger. 'A genuine bolter round, from the Adepta Sororitas themselves, and blessed by the Arch-Deacon Janos, at the Ceremony of the Coming Conjunction just last week. I've only two of them left. To you, as you're in uniform, forty credits...'

'I'm on duty,' Kamilla told him, glaring.

'Right you are.' Shameless, he turned to the next eager pilgrim, and began his patter again.

A little later, her food secured, she sat in the shadow of the abbey wall, her eyes absently exploring the carved writhe of warriors and grotesques that swarmed about the stonework. Sermons told that the soldiers were real, Opal sinners, walled up to die and screaming forever, though Zalan himself had been a senior Astra Militarum officer, dying for his Emperor on some far-flung hellscape world. His banner flew from lines of flagpoles, flanking the far side of the square – a proud figure in officers' dress, all frogging and shining threads.

In his honour, his throng of pilgrims bore similar garb – their jackets and trousers were good cloth and fine embroidery, with colours bright and buttons glittering. Some carried sabres, others wore caps, or bore gifts and offerings worth more than everything Kamilla had ever owned. Many of them were kneeling, in lines on the steps before the doors. Some carved sharp blades over their own skin, offering sacred wounds. They were waiting for the abbey dean's opening sermon, one of hundreds that would take place at mid-morning.

A sudden burst of shouting made her look round. The air was chill and still sparkling with sleet, and a glut of people had gathered at the plaza's opposite corner. Their garments were much less ornate, and charm-hung silver chains were looped about their necks.

From the rumblings of Zalan's faithful, they were not welcome. *Saint and Emperor.*

The cadets had been warned about this. Ramming the last piece of lunch into her mouth – she wasn't going to waste it – Kamilla ran. But voices were already jeering.

'You! You're not welcome! Don't you bring your heresy here!'

'This is the officers' quarters, son, you can't come through!'

'Zalan was a gentleman, you slime. You go round!'

'Go back to where you belong!'

Laughter.

Kamilla swallowed, nearly choking herself in the process, then cleared her mouth and yelled, 'This is *Opal!*' She roared it at them, making them listen. 'She belongs to *all* her pilgrims. You will let them past!'

There was bristling and unrest, mocking and jeering. At the very front of the silver-chain pilgrims, a larger man had come to the fore. He had callused hands and an unshaven jaw. His stance was defensive and his eyes wary.

'Easy,' Kamilla said to him. 'You–'

'We're not looking for trouble.' The man looked her up and down, then gave a curt nod of thanks. 'The Path of the Thousand Humble goes through here, and we're just following the Path, as decreed by the Soldiers' Doctrine. We walk where our faith takes us–'

'You're not stepping here, you *grunt.*' The faithful of Saint Zalan were hands on sabres, moving now to block the area. Kamilla was getting shoved aside like no one had even noticed her.

'We're following the *Path,*' the man said, squaring his shoulders. 'The Thousand Humble, the Opal soldiers who died for our worlds!'

'You reek, mate. Go have a wash!' More laughter.

'All right, enough!' Kamilla was yelling. Right now, she *really* wanted to be taller. 'You! Stand down. You! Back off. This is a place of His faithful and we all stand the same. The Path of the Thousand Humble leads from shrine to shrine, all over the city. Its pilgrims are gifted free passage, in His name. And you shame your saint with your behaviour. You will *get out of the way!*'

Zalan's faithful laughed outright at her. 'How old are you, little girl? Should've given the job to a grown up!'

'Last chance,' Kamilla snarled at him. 'Stand back, and let them through.' She balled her fists, came up on her toes.

The faithful of Saint Zalan eyed her like she was a bug, incredulous – but cadet or no, she was still in uniform, and grumbling, they backed out of the way. As they moved, the large man led the Path pilgrims onto the forecourt.

'You lot are a disgrace,' sneered the Zalan follower as they passed. 'Look at the state of you.'

'Better an honest soldier than an overstuffed shirt.'

'You snivelling grot–'

The crunch was his nose. Kamilla's heart sank.

All at once, the people were bunched up and shouting. They surged forwards, lashed out; they fell in heaps, punching and kicking and struggling. They pulled scarves and tore garments. They ripped caps from heads and bags from hands. Sabres flashed, new blood slicked the stone. Silver chains hung broken, their charms scattered.

Wading in, Kamilla used her boots and fists. She punched one in the back of the head, hauled him upwards and threw him aside; punched a second in the ear and kicked her off the pile–

Saint Veres comes!

Again, the image swamped her, flooding through her like pure chill. Again, the strange taste in her mouth. This time, it was so powerful that she staggered forwards, fell beneath the faithful.

What? In His name, what–

Then someone landed on top of her, more bodies on top of them. She coughed, her chest crushed. Regular boots thumped somewhere at the edge of her awareness, a voice was bellowing orders, but that image... *Why* did she keep seeing that image? The ruin? The whirl of storm?

Saint Veres comes!

The bodies over her lightened as people stood up, moved. She shook herself and regained her feet. An errant elbow cracked her jaw. Wincing, she grabbed the retreating arm and twisted it, forcing the woman to the floor. The struggle was becoming a full-on brawl, more and more people throwing themselves into the fray.

She bawled orders, was ignored. The crowd grew and surged and eddied, crushing offerings and donations. Duty Blades had started shouting, and their thumping boots sounded close. She was half-tempted to go and find them, but she stood her ground, still roaring at the mob.

Then sudden bells rang loud, drowning everything else. Not just from the abbey, but all across the Capital.

The opening sermon.

Kamilla saw a collective shudder go through the people, but they didn't stop, their righteous wrath was just too strong. And then, appearing right over the top of the scuffle, the thirty-foot image of the abbey dean. With her long robes flawless, and Zalan himself embroidered on her chasuble, she manifested like some apparition, a haze of hope in blue. The bells rang their final round and echoed to a stop.

'By the saint!' In the moment's quiet, Kamilla was on her toes, yelling at the top of her lungs. 'You will stand and *listen!*'

The faithful did not care. Even as the dean raised her vox-cast voice, praising Him, praising Saint Veres and the Three Martyrs, Zalan and his most holy sacrifice, the Thousand Humble and their lives both dedicated and modest, they were still spitting and kicking and fighting. Determined, Kamilla waded back in, punching one man in the kidneys, hard enough to drop him to his knees.

'I said, *enough!*'

Drowning her out, the dean called for the blessings of the saint. She thanked everyone for the festival, for their generous donations that allowed the Imperial Church to continue His blessed work. But Kamilla was not listening; they were all round her now, wavering in the light of the hololith's robes, fighting and swearing and cursing. Grinding each other's offerings to a bright and holy dirt.

More orders tangled the air – the Blades had arrived, with fists and bludgeons hammering. Kamilla heard them shouting, dragging the brawlers apart.

Oblivious, the dean began to sing, and her praise floated skywards amid the faithful's agonised screams.

iii

THE GOLDEN SKULL

'With respect, Sister Superior, your request is more complex than you realise.'

Resting like a nestled prayer at the heights of the governor's palace, the audience hall was both impeccable and ornate. The floor was a huge marble mosaic, showing the stylised stripes of Opal's most holy halo. One long wall was windows, currently open to the winter's chill. Sleet danced through them, shining like gems. Along the wall opposite was an elaborate tiled frieze, *The Last Triumph of Saint Veres*. In a caricatured version of the Blades' uniform, he watched the long table – real wood – with eyes as cold as glaze.

But Sister Augusta's attention was aimed at the table's head.

Planetary Governor Vass Mihaly was a slim, dark-skinned man, his short hair faded to grey. Framed by Opal's hanging banner, a ringed globe held aloft in a great, gauntleted hand, he sat forwards in his chair, long fingers tapping on the tabletop. To one side of him sat a frowning, silent woman in the now familiar Blades uniform: Tamara Kozma, the planet's military commander. She bore three sets of crossed swords on her polished white pauldron. To the other sat an aide, scowling at a data-slate. A quartet of dress-uniformed guards lined up along the rear wall, their jackets' frogging shining.

'My lord governor,' Augusta said. 'As I have already explained, I am here in the God-Emperor's name.' The Sisters' welcome had been considerable – honour guard, full escort – but the squad had now been in here for more than an hour, and already the conversation had gone in a circle. 'And it is not a request.' Her tone was straightforward, showing no hint of her ongoing frustration.

Grant me patience, O Emperor. This battlefield, I do not relish.

The governor continued tapping. 'Please.' He gave a gesture of weary patience. 'Will you not take seats?'

None of the Sisters moved. In their scarlet armour, black-and-white cloaks fluttering faintly, any one of them could have broken the slender man in half. Sternly, Augusta held both her place and her temper, and tried again.

'My orders come direct from my canoness, Elvorix Ianthe herself,' she said. 'Meaning no insult to your festival, governor, commander, but the skull of Saint Veres is a relic most holy. There is turbulence amongst your people, and it is not safe. It cannot stay here.'

Tamara Kozma eyed Augusta with a threatened, complex antipathy. 'Sister Superior,' she said. 'Opal is a world of warriors. Across the last five millennia, billions of our children have gone on to fight the Imperium's wars. They have carried His banners all across the galaxy, just as you have done. They have bled and perished in His name, just as you have done.' Her voice was hard, her eyes cold. 'Veres himself, with the three survivors of his spear of Blades, cast down the heretic Bakos, even as Bakos sought to align this world with *Vandire*.' The word was a barb. 'Surely, this is a subject that speaks to your heart, Sister of the Bloody Rose?'

Augusta exhaled, keeping her face calm. *I am His daughter, my faith and weapons unquestioned, unquestionable; war is my craft and my study…*

At the table's sides, likewise on their feet, her squad shot discreet looks at one another, though they made no comment. The training stains had been cleansed from their armour and robes, and they stood still, at parade-ground ease, as if inspected by the canoness herself. They'd left Augusta the place opposite the governor, at the table's foot, and had arranged themselves with Caia and Melia on one side, one as blonde as the other was dusky and standing like twins, and Viola and Akemi on the other. Alcina stood at Augusta's shoulder. In full scarlet armour, she cut a broad and imposing figure.

Across the squad vox-link, Sister Caia said, *'Be vigilant, Sister. Her words are honest, but she takes great pride in both her world and her role.'*

Augusta did not react. In truth, she would rather face a thousand orks than she would navigate the pitfalls of the administrative table – but she was here by His will, and would face whatever test He set. She drew in a breath, let it out with a silent prayer.

'I respect your culture of soldier-saints, commander, but the safety of the relic cannot be compromised.'

'It is not just a culture, Sister Superior.' Kozma sounded faintly insulted, though her tone remained calm. 'Our soldier-saints are our faith, our' – the pause was infinitesimal – 'tithes, our gifts to Him. This festival is their origin and their celebration. I train my Blades very well, and can keep our relic perfectly safe.'

'Commander, please.' The governor gestured, and Kozma quietened. 'Sister Superior, perhaps you would permit me to elaborate.' He spoke politely, his tone chiming clear with the outside bells.

'The skull of Saint Veres is the very heart of not only our festival, but of our reputation, our faith, our society and economy – *millions* of pilgrims have come to see it. At the festival's height, at dusk on the fourth day, this system's three outer planets – Kira, Ava and Sara, named for our first governor's daughters – will be in perfect conjunction. All across Opal, the bells will sound and the people will *sing!* Celebrating the very moment that Veres slew the heretic, the blessed will file into the Saints' Cathedral to attend the Sermon of the Hero, and to behold that holy skull for themselves. They will praise the life and the sacrifice of he, our most hallowed son.' His fervency was powerful, touching. 'Their souls will be lifted to *battle*, Sisters, they will take up arms in His wars! They will be inspired to slay the heretic, the witch and xenos, all across the galaxy! *This* is our purpose, Sister Superior, not only the purpose of our culture, but of the very relic itself. It is the crux of our strength and honour, and it belongs *here*. With Veres' world, with his people, with his sacrifice and history. With his courage and leadership.' He held her gaze, emphatic. 'I understand that you have orders, but would taking it not bereave us? Bereave us of both our saint and our highest and most holy purpose? Of our place in the galaxy? Of our future warriors – and His?'

Almost despite herself, Augusta found her heart touched by his passion, by his love for Veres, for Opal and for the Emperor Himself. By Kozma, too, though the commander did not have the governor's loquaciousness. Kozma's love for her world was that of a soldier, and the Sister Superior understood.

But her mission remained. 'Governor,' she said. 'I hear you. But my orders from my canoness remain.' Her tone had eased slightly but still, she would not be refused. 'The relic is threatened by dissidents, and must be secured.'

'"Dissidents", Sister Superior?' The new voice was sharp.

Behind her, the double doors had banged open, revealing a

larger man, tall and powerful. He was younger than either the governor or the commander, but his shoulders were broad and his self-assurance palpable. Layers of rich robes swished as he walked and rings flashed on his fingers.

A server scuttled behind him, censer in hand.

'Arch-deacon.' Augusta's tone was carefully respectful, but she was not about to back down. 'Your eminence, it is an honour.'

'And you, Sister Superior, Sisters Militant. My apologies for not welcoming you in person. I have a great deal to manage, as I'm sure you can imagine.' His smile was pure benevolence and he moved like he owned the place, his authority palpable. The long room seemed to shrink around him.

'I understand, milord.'

'Of course you do.'

Alcina's armour creaked as she shifted, and Viola's green eyes flicked dislike at the newcomer.

Under her breath, the Sister Superior murmured the Litany of Divine Guidance. *Show us, our Emperor. Show us to the Light.* She caught Viola's gaze, warning her to stay silent.

The deacon had stopped at the governor's shoulder, turning smartly on his heel and standing there like some great and beneficent guardian. He had the square jaw and good cheek-bones of some heroic illustration, but his eyes were as blue and as cold as the winter sky outside. The censer-holder swung the chain, and scented smoke wafted through the room, tangling with the sleet and winding gently out of the windows.

'In the name of the God-Emperor,' the deacon said. 'In the names of Saint Veres and of the Three Martyrs, I am delighted to welcome you to Opal, and to our most holy festival. The attendance of the Order of the Bloody Rose is an… unexpected privilege.' His smile spread, blessing them all. 'Some of our planet's highest daughters have gone on to join the Adepta Sororitas,

47

and I would be honoured if you would accept a… ah… central role at the Sermon of the Hero. With your Order's following of Saint Mina, it would seem most appropriate.'

Outside, a hymn had gathered pace. It was a distance away, down beyond walls and gardens, but its music was hopeful, a sound of sincerity and faith.

'*In the morning, soldiers muster, bringing faith and hope to all.*

'*In the morning, prayers are lifted, lest those soldiers fight and fall…*'

'Thank you, milord,' Augusta said carefully. 'But we cannot stay. My orders are quite specific.'

'Sister Superior.' His radiant smile didn't change. 'Surely your canoness would understand? We are His shrine world, after all. Our pilgrims must see you, and a role at our festival's height would be perfect – indeed, I already have something in mind.' He beamed, his teeth very white. 'You are, after all, warriors of legend yourselves. What could be more suitable to the tale of the heretic's fall?'

There was a glint to the words, something not quite sardonic. Closing one gauntleted fist and letting the metal bite painfully at her fingers, Augusta cast a further glance at her Sisters. Akemi, small and slender and with her hair shining black, had a faint line between her brows, and Viola, freckled and red-haired and always impatient…

Forestalling any lapse in discipline, she answered, 'Milord, I cannot compromise my orders.'

'But surely, her eminence the canoness must be aware of Opal's reputation?' His beam hadn't faded. 'We are the blessed among the blessed, the most sacred of shrine worlds and touched by His grace. Or perhaps your briefing did not fully cover our history?'

Augusta caught her breath, set her expression in ferrocrete. Twin spots of high colour had appeared on Viola's freckled cheeks and Akemi's frown was growing.

But Sister Alcina could stand it no longer. 'With all due respect, arch-deacon,' she said. 'To imply insult—'

'I imply nothing of the sort, Sister—'

'Enough.' Again, the governor gestured, bringing quiet. He had an edge of authority to him now, a need to both steer and moderate the situation. 'Arch-deacon, the Adepta Sororitas are here to secure the relic's safety, which is of paramount importance to us all. And it is true that the festival has caused some… unrest upon Holy Opal.' He twitched a frown. 'Our pilgrims fight amongst themselves, and there are areas of the outer city that do not embrace the saint as we do. The celebrations are only just beginning, yet already, they rumble with discontent.'

His tone was respectful and dignified, and again, Augusta found herself warming to the old man. He was perceptive, his diplomatic skills considerable, and some part of her was genuinely curious, wanting to see his world of soldier-saints for herself. Singing floated from the outside, and occasional bursts of laughter.

'My Blades,' Kozma repeated, 'are in complete control of the situation, governor.'

Mihaly glanced and she subsided. He said, 'Sister, please understand. The skull is His guiding light. Without it, our festival loses its heart, loses something truly sacred. Perhaps you would consider staying, as the deacon has requested? It would be our honour to have you here, and surely, no threat can come to the relic while the Adepta Sororitas stand sentinel?'

The deacon beamed, bestowing his benevolent smile back upon the Sisters. 'I couldn't agree more, governor – surely, it must be His will that the Sisters are here at all. And I would be delighted if you would attend the Mass of the First Martyr, Martyr Cae, at sundown this evening. It will give you the chance to behold the Saints' Cathedral for yourself. Truly, it is one of His wonders.'

Augusta looked at the three of them – the deacon's smile,

the serious face of Mihaly, the flicker in Kozma's gaze. Yet they were united in their love for their world, and in their zeal for the coming celebration.

Her heart whispered a prayer – *guide me, my Emperor* – and her eyes strayed to Veres upon the wall, his head haloed in light. For a moment, she seemed to see him face the heretic, even as Mina had faced Vandire himself.

Perhaps He really had sent them here, to behold this sacred remembrance.

'Very well,' she said.

The governor blinked. Viola and Akemi exchanged a swift glance. Alcina shifted again, her armour creaking. Kozma's expression frosted over, as if Augusta had offered her some insult, but she said nothing.

'Sister Augusta.' Mihaly came to his feet. 'Truly, you render me speechless. That you would do my world, my festival, the honour of offering it your strength.' He saluted hands across his chest in the sign of the aquila. 'We are humbled.'

'We will stay,' Augusta told him. 'But we will not merely stand sentinel. We will seek out these dissidents and eliminate them, ensuring the skull's safety for the festival's duration. At its end, however' – her tone was all warning – 'the skull will come with us, to the reliquary upon Ophelia VII.'

Kozma's gaze tightened, though she still said nothing. The deacon continued to beam his benevolence.

'I understand.' The governor nodded slowly. 'Sister Superior, we can return to the discussion of the relic once the festival is over. Perhaps it can be kept safe upon Ophelia VII, and brought back to Opal, with a suitable guard of honour, in eight hundred years' time.' A gesture, and the aide had a finger to his ear, was speaking softly over his private vox. 'I will secure you suitable quarters.'

Augusta said, 'I must speak to the *Star*, my lord, and send a message to the Convent Sanctorum.'

'Sister Superior!' On the squad vox, Alcina's voice was livid. 'This is outrageous! We do not presume to interpret our orders, we follow them to the letter.'

'I do not take this decision lightly, Sister.' Augusta replied. 'But this world of warriors, of saints and martyrs – it speaks to my heart, and it does so in His voice. We will stay.'

'Wonderful.' The deacon was still beaming. 'The matter is resolved.'

'The matter is not resolved,' Alcina commented, her tone acid. She took a step forward, stood firm at Augusta's side. 'You will give us your oath that you will surrender the skull–'

'Desist.' Augusta's voice was only for Alcina's ears. 'When the festival ends, we take the skull. I believe the governor to be an honourable man, but whatever their politics, they will not be permitted to gainsay us.'

Alcina shot her a single, blazing look, but moderated her tone. 'It is His relic,' she said, glaring at the three of them. 'Do not think for a moment that we will leave without it.'

The deacon caught Augusta's gaze, his eyes amused. 'You permit your squad an unusual level of freedom, Sister Superior.'

Augusta glared. 'My squad have fought His enemies in every segmentum of the galaxy and I am proud of each and every one of them.' With a certain military self-assurance, she returned the arch-deacon's smile. 'We will be privileged, of course, to behold your Saints' Cathedral, and to attend your mass this evening. And, in due time, we will secure the relic.'

The deacon's expression did not change, but it was the governor who replied, 'Truly, you bless us. And as holy warriors yourselves, I'm sure you will find the festival to your liking.'

* * *

'Sister Superior!' Behind closed doors, Sister Alcina finally released her outburst. 'Our orders are very specific–'

'I have made my decision.' Augusta had no time or tolerance for disagreements. 'We will stay for the festival. And if you ever undermine my authority in public again, you will be doing penance.'

The chamber they'd been offered was a neat stone dormitory, a small and patterned window at one end. Three sleeping pallets flanked each side, and a set of steps led to the outer grounds of the palace, lying beside the Saints' Cathedral and at the height of the Inner Sanctum. The walls were plain, grey stone, all with Opal's distinctive glitter, and the room smelled faintly of cleaning fluid.

Alcina glowered. 'Sister.' She made an effort to calm her tone. 'We are not here to take part in some re-enacted–'

'The matter is closed.' Augusta did not raise her voice. 'We have a little time before this evening's mass, and I wish to scout. We should discover everything we can about this world, its festival, and about these reports of dissent.'

'Yes, Sister Superior.' Alcina said nothing further, though her glowering expression did not fade.

'Akemi,' Augusta said. 'You have been studying the data. What have you learned about the festival's history?'

The squad's youngest member glanced up from the slate in her lap.

'I can add little, Sister,' she said. 'Veres was an Opal Guardsman, dating from the Age of Apostasy. He and his three surviving spear-mates did indeed bring down the Ecclesiarchy traitor Bakos. There was a colossal detonation – the wrath of the Emperor, according to legend – and they were slain in their turn. The legend also agrees that the outer planets' conjunction marked the date, and that the Capital, including the Sanctum and the cathedral, was built – rebuilt – in Veres' honour.'

'And the world has celebrated his sacrifice, ever since,' Augusta said. 'Every eight hundred years. Eight hundred and *four*.'

'In terms of dissidence,' Akemi said, 'there are indeed a myriad different pilgrim factions, each of whom believe that *their* saint and saviour is the one true path, and that the others are heretics. Scuffles are very common.'

'Scuffles are not the problem.' Viola was angry, sitting down and shaking a stone out of her boot. 'The serious matter is, will they let us take the skull at the festival's end?'

'I believe Mihaly to be a good man,' Augusta told her. 'Honourable, and strong in his faith.'

'I do not think Mihaly is the issue.' Beside them, Melia checked her medical case, supplies and sanguinators. 'It is more about the pilgrims themselves. Whatever their faction, they have come a long way, and their loyalty to the planet's saints is strong. They may be fanatical. And they may not wish to see the relic leave.'

'It cannot remain here,' Alcina said. 'For all its military posturing and venerated saints, this world has but a basic defence force. And, despite Kozma's claims, the Blades of the Holy Interior seem more like performers, with their bands and their marching. They appear–'

'Inexperienced,' Augusta finished. 'I agree with you, Sister, Opal's defensive soldiers like their pomp, but I do wonder when they last fought a true enemy.' She rattled gauntleted fingers on her bolter, thinking. 'All the more reason to face these "dissidents" ourselves, whether they are within the Capital or without. Akemi? What of the outer city?'

'Lore regarding the Capital's outskirts is somewhat thin, Sister. Our report identifies it as an area of poverty, and suggests a possibility of organised rebellion – particularly against the festival, since it displays great wealth.'

'Very well,' Augusta said. 'Then we must scout the area, and silence such heresy before it has the chance to spread, or become a threat.'

'Yes, Sister.'

Alcina unfastened her bolter and began to strip and clean it. 'And what of the deacon's mass, Sister Superior? Do we attend this also?'

'We must do all of these things,' Augusta said. Still tapping her bolter, she was pacing, thinking. 'We must send this world – her pilgrims, her rebels, and her *rulers* – a very clear message. We are the Adepta Sororitas, and we tolerate no disrespect, no dishonour.' She paused, looking round at the others. 'As the responsibility is mine, I will first send our message to the *Star*, and on to the canoness. Sister Alcina, Sister Akemi, you will attend the librarium, and gather what lore you can, particularly about the city's outskirts and any potential rebellion. Sister Melia, Sister Caia, you will walk the festival.' The two Sisters were close, and had better social awareness than the rest of the squad. 'And while you walk, you will pay attention to the people about you, and learn what you may about these celebrations, about their factions and tensions, and about the saints and pilgrims of this world. Not all data can be gathered from slates, and I wish to know all there is.' Her tone was pointed, making sure her Sisters understood. 'You will also ensure that you are *seen*.'

'By the governor?'

'By the governor, and by the faithful,' Augusta said. 'We will show Opal's festival that the Sisters of Battle stand here.'

'Yes, Sister.'

'Viola and I will attend the service, and then move to the outer city.' She wasn't letting Viola out of her sight. 'Sisters, I understand that I have decided to change our orders, and there may well be repercussions. But I do believe in the holiness of this festival. It belongs to Him, and to Saint Veres, and our reverence must be complete.'

Viola flushed, her skin as red as her hair, and looked down at the floor.

'Yes, Sister Superior.'

'We have walked upon many worlds,' Augusta said. 'Worlds of darkness and terror, of xenos and psyker, of the ancient Archenemy. And many times, we have seen our Sisters lay down their lives.' She looked around at her Sisters, meeting the gaze of each one. 'I will say to the canoness and I now say to you – in many ways, it is for them, as much as it is for Opal, that I have decided to stay. Martyrs and warriors should have their names ever upheld, in His light. So let us take a moment to remember Sister Kimura, Sister Felicity, Sister Jatoya, lost to orks and daemons upon the far-flung jungle world of Lautis. Sister Nikaya, and those of our Order who fell upon the rusting platforms of Lycheate, to the Heretek Vius' corrupted Mechanicus force.' Faces filled her mind and she paused, tracing the shape of the fleur-de-lys on her armour. 'They have served Him, and stand now at the Throne, their trials done. Blessed be their memories.'

The Sisters recited together, their heads bowed, 'Blessed be their memories.'

A moment of quiet, of hearing the Capital's hymnals on the sharp, chill breeze. Jatoya's face, particularly, filled Augusta's mind and while she understood that her Sister – her second for ten years – had perished in honour, facing the might and terror of the Lautis Bloodthirster, Jatoya had nevertheless left a hole, a place of both grief and poignancy. And some part of Augusta still felt responsible for her death.

Blessed be her memory.

'However.' The Sister Superior brought them all back to the room, drew every Sister's eyes. Her gaze had stopped on Alcina, the squad's new second, who stood now in Jatoya's boots. 'We will maintain our vigilance. We will identify and remove every threat to the relic, and to the festival – be they heretic, pilgrim, dissident or rebel. So let us stand strong, and let us maintain both honour and alertness, in His name.'

Outside the Sisters' dormitory, the great slope of the Inner Sanctum was divided by three main boulevards, named one for each Holy Martyr – Cae, Nemes and Kis. Along the sides of these, there hung ranks of exquisitely wrought steel cages, many of them still with rotting skeletons within, now dangling half-out of the bars. Ribbons and prayer-scarves adorned them like offerings, a flutter of brightness and colour.

Above these towered massive statues in warlike poses, colossal archways engraved with endless battle scenes, temples that blazed with song and light and wealth, with braziers and gargoyles, and with the names of the endless saints.

Walking the festival, Sister Melia kept her hand upon her flamer, and scanned for unnamed threats. The massed crowds made her almost claustrophobic, and the flamer was a comforting presence. Blessed by Him, it was something that still made sense.

Over her vox-bead, she said, 'Forgive me, Sister, but I find this place unsettling.'

Caia chuckled. The two of them had known each other from girls, had been through the schola together, and had taken their Oaths of Ordination at the same time. Melia would not have voiced her doubt to any of her other Sisters, but Caia was different.

She said, 'It feels...'

'Prosperous,' Caia said. The word was a judgement.

She was right, Melia realised – there was a coiling stink in the air, a reek of costly fragrances, of rich spices and fine wines, of precious metals and money. It wafted strongly from overbearing figures, ostentatiously dressed or carried on palanquins. An entourage of servitors, with a capital and personal guard, followed many, scattering precious offerings as they came.

Caught between fascination and horror, Melia was trying not to stare. 'Why do they wear these... costumes?'

Many of the sanctum's affluent pilgrims wore mock-uniforms, gilded and embroidered, or frogged in real gold. Some even had bloodstains, sewn in with scarlet thread, or bullet- or las-holes carefully marked out with black silk.

'They buy them here,' Caia answered. 'They get caught up in the war-legends of their own worlds, and they come laden with coin, offerings for their souls and for the futures of their planets. Look.' She nodded sideways, and both Sisters saw a line of elaborate boutiques, each one hung with costly jackets and trousers, with prayer-decorated simulacrums of lasrifles, with great flags and standards. 'We use our history to learn, to understand honour and death and warfare and sacrifice. Opal, it seems, uses hers to generate wealth.'

'It is inappropriate,' Melia said. 'Exaggerated to extreme. The commander called this "a world of warriors", yet none of these people have ever seen a real battle.'

In places, pilgrims' servants were crowding at the tables, holding out handfuls of creds and squabbling to grab the ephemerae of a particular saint. Saint Jona, the Holy Martyrs of Csill, the Sacrificed Nine at the Walls of Andreas, their names seemed endless. Others picked up the symbols of Opal's own defensive force – the crossed swords of the Blades of the Holy Interior.

Some of them, Melia saw, apparently aware of the Sisters' arrival, were already selling red roses, singles and garlands, crafted from fabrics and beaten metals.

In your name, she thought. *This is like no holy festival that I have ever seen!*

As they passed, heads turned. People nudged each other, pointed. Many stopped to stare, or showered them with new red petals. Some fell to their knees, begging for forgiveness, blessing, absolution, punishment. Others reached out to touch, as if barely daring to believe. A couple even started to sing, echoing the Sisters' sacred battle-hymn – though where they had even learned the words...

At this, Melia rounded on the singers, her hand on her flamer. They fell back, silencing immediately. Mutters broke out as they vanished back into the crowd.

Caia said, still over squad vox, 'Be wary, Sister. We must do no harm. We cannot bring disgrace onto the squad. Or onto the festival.'

'Disgrace?' Melia's word was a detonation. 'Look at all this... frippery!'

'Sister.' Caia stopped, caught her elbow, made her listen. 'We are here to scout, are we not? We must recall what we observe and report it back to the Sister Superior. If there is to be judgement, or retribution, then it will come at her orders, and at His command.'

Melia glared at her, then subsided. 'Very well,' she said. 'Let us behave as befits warriors. But I dislike this, and somewhere in my heart...' Tailing off, she frowned. 'Somewhere, He tells me that these threats may be more than we realise.'

THE CITY'S SHADOW

As dusk gathered on the first day, and the bells for the Mass of the First Martyr rang out over the Capital, Kamilla's pit-fights finally ended.

She had done well, winning her bouts and her ongoing place in the pits – and with nothing worse than scrapes and bruises. The cadets were technically still on duty, but Kamilla's success had earned significant honour for her barracks, and more than just a food-chit for herself.

'Three hours,' Spear Takacs had told her. 'You're permitted to walk the festival, attend the services, and praise our most blessed and holy saint. But you'll be back here by Final Prayers – I want you fresh and ready to fight in the morning.' He'd fixed her with a beady gaze. 'Our reputation is resting on you, Kam.'

'Yes, sir. I understand, sir.'

'Make sure you do.'

Three hours was going to be tight, Kamilla thought, grabbing the stimm-pack and carefully steaming her camo jacket and pants before returning them to her locker. She was half-tempted to just take her fears to the cadets' pastor, the old soldier-priest who lambasted them with their daily rhetoric, but if she talked about 'dreams' to him, she'd be cleaning boots for a month. And she needed to understand.

So many questions, my little one, her Uncle Jakob had once teased her. *You always have so many questions.*

Jakob had died when Kamilla was seven, but he'd been a devout man – and he'd left her two things. One was her compass, His guide to her answers.

The other was Father Arkas.

As Kamilla left the barracks compound, she found the Capital's streets still packed and the intensity of their mood high. The wine was flowing freely now, and the hymns – and the squabbles – were many and drunken. Suspended in long lines, the skulls' jaws hung lax or broken and their electro-candles were just starting to shine, making their eyes glow. A million bony sockets watched her as she slipped quietly along one carved and prayer-hung wall.

A group came past her, loud and raucous. They carried a coffin, complete with skeletal occupant, borne aloft and covered in garlands. Silver chains representing the Path of the Thousand Humble hung round their necks, a multitude of charms jingling. One man eyed her garments – her uniform now replaced with basic civvies, all covered by a big, hooded coat. He sneered at her, his breath stinking, and she glowered as she passed.

Her dream-flashes were still haunting her, lurking at the back of her thoughts – whorls of cloud and towering ruins, the touch of that familiar mind. She wished she could remember them more clearly, could understand why they kept recurring, and why her barrack-mates had dreamed them, too.

So many questions, my little one.

She thought back to her uncle, a big, bearded, booming figure who she remembered as a noise, and as a warm smell of vellum. When her family's hab-block had collapsed, he'd been in his cubicle, untangling some pile of Imperial paperwork. Kamilla had been a baby, and the only survivor of the disaster. She didn't know why, but the God-Emperor had seen fit to spare her tiny life, that day. They'd called her 'lucky' ever since.

Lucky – and *blessed*.

She put a hand to the compass, its curved edges hard against her skin. With its metal as her anchor, she tried to pray as Jakob had taught her, but the words, like the dreams, felt tangled.

What was the *matter* with her?

Laughter rose, bursts of song and worship. The people were happy, exultant, radiant with His blessing. They sang hymnals to Veres and to Cae, the First Martyr – not in tune, but full of passion and sincerity. Music rose, ribald and holy, to the red-tinged sunset skies. But the sinking sun sent darkness angling, and the shadows of towers and spires, of moving and swinging cable-cars, were cold. In her mind, the music turned sour and dissonant, and she swiftly hurried away, as if trying to escape it.

Were her very questions blasphemous, in a world that taught only duty, only the holiness of obedience? Certainly the barracks' pastor would have told her so.

Struggling with her thoughts, she turned a corner, another, and the crowds grew steadily thinner. The mass bells rang their final summoning, and stopped. Released from their endless clamour, she began to breathe more easily. The glitter in the stone, the thing that had given Opal her name, was more visible here. Legend said it was warriors' souls, the very foundations of the planet's sanctity. It was said that the Capital's very streets, all the way up to the Wall of Glory, the Gate of the Martyrs, and the Inner Sanctum itself, had been built of the bones of the slain, those who'd perished in Bakos' detonation...

The thought made her shiver, but she kept moving – three hours really wasn't enough time and she couldn't afford to dawdle. Picking up speed, she broke into an easy jog. Soon, she came to the outermost limit of the Capital proper and the second, lower wall, this one the Wall of Diligence. It reared high and merciless, covered in prayers, and dotted with the massive, round towers of Opal's orbital batteries, as neglected as her Tauroxes and Chimeras.

Beyond here, the festival did not spread and the hymnals thinned to silence. Instead, on the wall's far side, there waited a series of straight, dark valleys, short roads flanked by tight, sprawling tangles of habs, manufactories and warehouses. Here, generations of servitors wove flags and embroidered prayers, crafted offerings and sewed souvenirs. In places, carved aquilae glittered with Verses of Industry, acclaiming hard work and blessed rewards. On their far side, the sinking sun glowered, sullen and massive like some red and lidless eye.

And beneath the sun's light, shining like molten steel: the River of Saint Varadi the Drowned. Like both walls, it was a barrier – but of a slightly different kind.

Kamilla's heart pounded. She glanced back over her shoulder, but no one had followed her – no one would. The Capital's blessed denizens did not come this far; they had their eyes and hearts focused inwards, upwards, towards the Inner Sanctum and the Saints' Cathedral at its peak. They had no need – no desire – to wander these common roads.

She turned back, her hand on her compass.

Because there, down *there* on the water's far side, was the thing that wealthy, perfect Opal ignored. It was the dark underbelly to the planet's bright holiness, the ignoble stain upon her faith and reputation.

A shiver crept across Kamilla's skin, and she moved to the

edge of the wall. From here, she could see it in the water: that other, older city, all upside down. In the stillness of the river's oily gleam, it was rooftops, spires, towers and domes. It was statues and cenotaphs, porticoes and basilicae. It was the Capital's shadow-sibling, its echo, lost and ruinous. Some called it only 'the Outskirt', though most did not care to call it anything. There was too much light in their eyes.

Her heart thumped louder, timpani in her ears. Jakob had always believed that the Emperor dwelt in the Outskirt, that He was a figure of mercy and safety. Most of the pilgrims, she thought, would disagree. If they even cared.

A rustle made her jump, but it was only a rat, scurrying away from her feet. Now the festival had begun, the factories' servitors were needed elsewhere and many of these buildings were empty, leaving plenty of wind-blown trash.

Gathering her courage, adrenaline thumping, she hurried to find the steps, to move down and into the tangle. Her boots seemed so noisy, she was sure that someone would find her, hear her – but she reached the riverside safely, and stopped again.

She tried to pray, but could find only ashes and fear. In the fading sunset, the water gleamed like blood. Two long, dark bridges spanned its width, their arches cracked and weed-grown. Martello towers dotted the nearer ferrocrete bank, though the closest was a distance away. A second planetary defence occupied these – the Blades of the Holy Exterior, tainted by the nearness of the faithless.

But Kamilla had her own route, a stinking, somewhat leaky foot-tunnel, grown with weeds and all but forgotten, its defensive metal grilles long since rusted away. She'd found it by accident, many years before.

After all, to her, the Outskirt was home.

* * *

At last, the sun set completely, leaving the cold sky stained with its going. On the far side of both tunnel and river, Kamilla came to a stop before a sprawling, half-tumbledown cathedral, its stone softened with age, its quadrangles of cloisters all crumbling and overgrown, its grounds filled with a myriad slumping outbuildings. Much of it was graffiti-daubed, the symbols and sigils of a hundred backstreet gangs, and everywhere clusters of people were gathered about oil-drum braziers, their hands outstretched to the heat. Some sat hunched and muttering, leaning against ancient gravestones. Others loitered in at the wall-sides, like streaks of threat and watchfulness. Broken street-lumens glittered, casting shadows like pits.

Kamilla ran up the steps, nodding at the grey-robed verger in the doorway, a solid, middle-aged woman with square and callused hands.

'Eszter.'

Eszter nodded back, and continued watching the grounds.

Kamilla found Father Arkas at his table, frowning and oddly restless.

'Working too hard?' she asked him, by way of greeting.

'Kam!' Arkas was in his forties, tall and lean, his long brown hair tied back, his short beard greying at the edges. At the sight of her, a broad smile spread across his face, creasing the lines at the corners of his eyes. 'Shouldn't you be punching something?'

'Did well enough to escape.'

She glanced round, taking in the scruffy assortment of stalls, stone and trash and rusting metal, some pieces of real wood rescued from the river. These were places of backstreet trade, of help and information; some of them offered soup or gruel or basic medications. Instead of pews, the surrounding floor was covered in sleepers, drifters, people injured and hopeless. And instead of incense, lho-smoke drifted in the air.

'I… I need to ask you a question.'

Arkas raised an eyebrow. 'Tell me you didn't sneak out?'

'I like my guts on the inside.'

He eyed her for a moment, as if validating the truth of her words, then chuckled, stood up and came round the table.

'You're always welcome, you know that. When did you last eat something?'

'Lunchtime. Don't mother me.'

He spread long hands, claiming innocence. 'Wouldn't dare. So, what's the matter, that it brings you all the way out here?'

'I…' Feeling suddenly self-conscious, she blurted it before she could second-guess herself. 'Does the God-Emperor send you your dreams?' It came out like a confession.

'Dreams?' For a split second, Arkas gawked. Then he seemed to remember himself, and carefully schooled his expression. Behind him, broad altar steps rose to a statue of the saint, his stone flak and camo as age-softened as the building's headless walls. To one side of these, the lectern spread its aquila wings. To the other, a second verger was telling a story to skinny, cross-legged children.

'I'm sorry,' she said. 'I knew it was a stupid question. I shouldn't have bothered you.' She flushed, feeling idiotic – a little child, jumping at shadows. Jakob would surely have teased her.

Yet the dream still turned   the vortex, the call of that gentle, paternal touch.

Saint Veres comes!

Arkas said, his voice tense, 'What dreams?'

'I dreamed…' The words stuck in her mouth, tasting like ashes.

I dreamed of ruins, much bigger than these. I dreamed of a mighty whirlwind, and of the saint coming to bless us all…

He hadn't moved, and she realised she was standing there with her mouth open, her words caught in her teeth. She shrugged, struggled to speak.

'I dreamed of Veres,' she said, almost dismissively, playing down the importance. 'And of a… a storm.' Her cheeks were flushed, she could feel it. 'It sounds so petty when I actually say it aloud. But it's just been haunting me. And I need to know – why is this bothering me so much? Have I had some sort of vision? Or is it heresy? Can it even *be* heresy, here on Opal? How would I know the difference?'

Arkas was staring at her, his face absolutely unreadable. He said, his tone carefully flat, 'The festival is a tense time, Kam. You've been training for months–'

'That's not what I asked,' she said. 'I want to know what these dreams are. Because I'm not the only one having them.'

The storm. The hole in the stars.

This time, the recollection was almost vivid enough to drive her to her knees. Her mouth tasted strange again. Her pulse was hammering, her breath short. She could feel the sweat on her skin.

'Kam?' Arkas had caught her elbow, steadying her. His brown gaze was searching her face, her eyes and cheeks and jaw, almost as if he was looking for something.

Staring back at him, she said, her voice a whisper, 'What *are* they? What do they mean? Why do they keep coming back?'

His grip was intense, almost painful. 'They mean nothing,' he said. He was telling her almost like he was telling himself. 'They just mean you're tired. They're not some sacred vision, and they're not anything heretical.' He managed a smile, but she still stared back at him, searching him as much as he was searching her. 'They're only dreams. That's all.'

'You've had them too,' she told him, with a sudden shiver of realisation. 'Haven't you? The vortex? The thing in the sky?'

A spark crossed his gaze, and was gone. 'A lot of people are having them,' he told her, with conscious sincerity. 'Kam, you grew up here – you know what the festival means to the Outskirt. We're desperate and hungry, sick and dying. We watch those we love suffer, and we can't help them. We watch our children starve, our parents die. Watch people dwindle to nothing as they lose themselves in the lho – and why shouldn't they, if it offers them comfort? We can hear the festival's bells, and hymns, and praises – sometimes we can even smell the incense and the food – but we can't touch it. Taste it. Reach it. It's not for us. If we tried to enter the Capital, the Blades would gun us down, no questions, no challenges. No mercy.' He glanced up at the statue, the remains of the window behind. 'Yet Saint Veres was a poor man, or so they say – he came from the Outskirt himself.' A short sigh, aware of the bitter irony. 'I do what I can, Kam, what I always have. I give my people what hope I can muster. I try to give them back their faith, the faith that the Capital denies them–'

'But surely, faith is about fighting,' Kamilla said. 'This is *Opal*–'

'That may be,' Arkas told her, with a flex of firmness. 'But not out here. If He is all things to all worlds, if He can manifest to each and every planet in the way that they choose to see Him, then He can manifest to me, to this sanctuary, to the Outskirt itself, as a figure of compassion.'

He smiled and touched her cheek, paternal and gentle. For a second, the touch of the dream came with it.

'Jakob believed, all his life, that the Emperor could be kind. And I have worked, all of mine, to bring what blessings I can to the people I can reach.' His smile spread, warm and genuine. 'I'm no fighter, Kam. No saint. No leader. But I do my best.' His eyes crinkled. 'Do you trust me?'

He was family – and he could still touch her heart.

'You know I do. My uncle used to call you the last true holy man on Opal.'

That made Arkas chuckle, fond with memory. 'Then please, Kamilla, don't worry. I know there's tension in the Outskirt. Envy. Anger. Resentment. And it's only to be expected. The Capital may celebrate the festival as Opal's greatest blessing, but here… well, the bells ring sour. But what can I do?' He shrugged. 'I offer counsel, and peace, prayer and faith, food and medication. As I have always done.'

She stared at him for a moment longer, but his odd sense of tension had faded – he was back to being just Arkas. Her guardian, her guide, her friend.

'Then the dreams…' she said. 'They're just… anxiety.'

'That's as good a word as any,' Arkas said, his smile gaining a hint of mischief. 'We worry about things, and they invade our unconscious minds. And that's all.'

But they seem so real…

She didn't say it aloud. How could she? He had told her not to worry, and she had just told him she trusted his judgement. To question it now would be a rejection of that.

He said, 'You should eat something, and then get back to your spear. Eszter was making soup – can I get you some?'

Many of the slumped figures on the floor had their hands wrapped round battered metal mugs, their faces bathed in curling white steam. It wasn't festival food, not here – it was probably corpse-starch, or something – but at least it would be warm. She sighed, her questions still circling her like flies.

'Go on then. And then I should go. Otherwise Takacs'll hang me up by my intestines.'

'I don't think he would, Kam. Not really.'

Kamilla snorted. 'Yeah. You think you've got problems.'

THE SAINTS' CATHEDRAL

The Saints' Cathedral was a wonder.

At the very peak of the Inner Sanctum, rising massive to the winter sky and to a shining, central dome, the building offered three huge carven doorways, each flanked by twin bell towers and defended by a martyr's statue. But its interior...

Standing upon the central doorway's steps, Sister Viola had never seen its like. Three wide, vaulted aisles led to a central pulpit, but these were not what pulled her attention. Instead, she found herself looking up, up, all the way up, at the dome's interior, and at its huge glassaic panels, arranged like gleaming slices. As the sun finally set, so they bathed the whole place in the most incredible plays of dancing, coloured light.

By the Throne!

'Is Segmentum Solar all like this?' she asked, over the vox. 'It's so... *clean.*'

She half-expected some severe response from the Sister Superior, but Augusta only said, 'It feels like another galaxy, does it not?' Her words were oddly thoughtful. 'So many worlds of darkness, one forgets how to stand in His light.'

'Sister.'

The pews were in four triangular sections, quiet and still mostly unoccupied. Drifting servitors, both human and metallic, acknowledged the Sisters but did not pause in their duties. After the surge and bellow of the racket outside, it seemed incredibly serene.

'In His name, Sisters, welcome.' A robed aide had appeared at their flank, his face pale but his manners flawless. 'The archdeacon will be with you presently.' He glanced behind them, as if expecting something. 'Only the two of you?'

Augusta levelled him with a look and he blanched, cleared his throat. With only the slightest hesitation, he continued.

'The Mass of the First Martyr is a small service, attended only by the governor, a select few of the city's families, and by some of our more... notable guests. To be here is a great honour.'

'We are privileged to attend.' Augusta's words were courteous, empty.

Viola said nothing. She was discovering a whole new feeling: social politeness. Etiquette was not something that she had ever encountered, or remotely comprehended – and she *hated* this nebulous sensation of being constrained. These lists of invisible rules that they had needed to navigate – the whole thing seemed somehow dishonest. It felt like some damned minefield, and Viola liked an enemy she could identify, one she could face and fight...

With your grace, I shall know discipline...

'Please,' the aide said, gesturing for them to precede him up the aisle.

Reflexively, the younger Sister looked for the servitor with its offered brass tray, but there was nothing. Bright though it was, this whole place was increasingly disconcerting. But... maybe Segmentum Solar *was* all like this.

With your grace, I shall stand strong, whatever trials you may place in my path...

The aide walked with a show of confidence, gesturing at their surrounds. 'Built on the site of Veres' last stand, Sisters, before Bakos' fall detonated the explosives that killed them all, and that levelled the city. His final heresy left a crater, and Opal's people offered penance as they rebuilt both Capital and Sanctum. Living with his deceit had shamed them. As you can see, the exact location is noted.'

As they came towards the dome, Viola craned her neck and saw that the panels depicted a battle scene, a man in the uniform of Opal's Blades facing a dreadful, robed figure, with a cloud of rising darkness at his back. Beneath the dome itself, there was a circle of choir stalls, all occupied by grey-clad singers, slates in their hands. At their very centre, there rose a tall, curling spiral of steps and a circular, metal-limned pulpit, all likewise constructed from glassaic. These colours, too, were absolutely exquisite, yet Viola's sense of unease was still growing.

Across the vox, she said, 'Sister–'

'Keep your thoughts quiet and holy,' Augusta commented. 'We will speak of everything once we are regrouped.'

The aide was still talking, explaining the Three Martyrs and their histories. He paused as the deacon came to meet them, striding forth from the back of the building.

'Sister Superior,' the man said. He was in full, official robes, now, all gold thread and gems glittering. Rings like jewelled knuckle-dusters shone on his fingers, and an embroidered prayer-chasuble hung around his neck. 'Are the rest of your squad delayed?'

'They are attending the festival, milord.'

He eyed her for a moment, measuring the response. 'Ah. Then please follow me.'

Garments shining as the glassaic's colours slid over them, he stalked back the way he had come. Something about the man's attitude made Viola smart, and long to punch him, hard, in the back of the neck.

But then her attention was taken by something else. A distance behind the pulpit, oddly shadowed from the glassaic's shine, there lay the high altar. It had a wide, proud set of steps, electro-candles gleaming upon every one, but it had no great window. A statue stood at its head, but it bore no sword...

She felt Augusta tense, realising the same thing: the statue was not the Emperor. A long, exquisitely embroidered grey banner hung behind it, with the globe-in-hand emblem of the planet, and three smaller statues, all in the same garb, were ranged about it, but the highest honour of Opal did not belong to Him.

It belonged to Saint Veres.

'Your cathedral is fascinating,' Augusta commented, her tone edged. 'Its veneration of the saint is particularly unusual. We should explore the reliquary, assure ourselves of the skull's safety, while we are here.' Viola knew her Sister Superior, and understood that it was not a request.

A clattering came from the organ loft as a young man seated himself before the keys. Pedals rattled as he settled his feet. The choir shuffled and cleared its collective throat.

'I'm afraid we're out of time, Sister.' Reaching the foot of the pulpit steps, the deacon spun on his heel, and smiled like the rising sun. 'And the skull is locked in the crypts. For security, I'm sure you understand. You've said yourself that it is under threat.'

The words were mildly spoken, but the rebuff was like a slap and Viola's jaw dropped. Stealing a sideways look at the Sister Superior, she saw that Augusta's stance was pure stone.

Had the deacon just outright *refused?*

Drowning her astonishment, the organ blared its opening notes. People were filing through the other three doors, now, stopping to talk or dispersing neatly out to the pews. Every one of them was elaborately dressed, wealth and gems shining.

'Praise the saint and praise the martyrs!' sang the choir. 'Praise the warriors, heed their call!'

'Say nothing,' Augusta voxed, her tone livid. 'We will attend this service, and then we will move to scout the Outskirt, and assess its incoming threats. But his behaviour will not go unanswered, and I will tolerate no attempt to prevent us taking the skull. Sister Alcina–'

The vox shut off, and Viola guessed that Augusta was using a private channel to speak to her second.

'Praise our holy world of Opal! Praise her halo, ringing all!'

'Now,' the deacon said. 'Sisters, you will kindly flank my position in the pulpit for the duration for the service. And when we reach the Sermon of the Hero, upon the festival's final day, please do make sure your squad is in full attendance.' He was smiling and nodding, greeting the arriving notables. 'And then, of course, I will be delighted to show you the relic.'

By the Throne!

When the service was over, Augusta walked. She stormed, or as close to it as she would permit herself. Helm off and chin up, down from the Inner Sanctum's slopes, down past the Martyrs' Arch, down to the Capital proper.

About her presence and armour, the crowds parted. People fell back, startled and pale-faced. Some bowed their heads and made the sign of the aquila, begged her for punishment for their sins, or just forgot themselves and gaped. Augusta should have stopped and spoken to them, demanded that they control themselves – the Sisters may be His warriors, but they were still human, and to goggle at them was unseemly. But she was angry. Blisteringly, savagely angry – angrier than she'd been in a great many years.

Were he an enemy, I would sing as I cut him down!

The deacon's behaviour was staggering. To refuse her request was tantamount to outright blasphemy, unthinkable, a disgrace beyond words. She fully expected him to try and stop her taking the relic, come the festival's end.

And for that, she would not stand.

She wished that she could face and fight him, decry him as a heretic, as she had done the fallen Inquisitor Istrix, upon the rusting world of Lycheate. Take the skull *now*, and obey her orders to the letter, after all...

But this was Opal, holy shrine world of His saints and warriors, and the issue was more complex than that. Insulting though the deacon's behaviour was, both the governor and the festival had earned her respect.

I would rather face a thousand orks... Bless me, my Emperor, show me to the Light.

Her litanies rang rhythmic to the stamp of her boots. Beside her, Viola kept pace, likewise helm off and chin lifted. The younger Sister, too, was fuming. In the swelling light of the skulls' billion eyes, Augusta could see the spots of high colour on Viola's freckled cheeks – always a danger sign. The last thing she needed, in the middle of all this, was Viola's temper.

With your grace, I shall banish my unworthy thoughts...

'Sisters.' Over the vox, she called the squad. 'Report. What is your situation?'

'*Melia and I walk the festival,*' Caia responded. '*We find ourselves unsettled by this place, Sister, by its shamelessness and wealth. It seems the governor was correct when he said that the festival – and* the skull – are the heart of Opal's economy, as well as her faith and culture.'

'We are still at the librarium,' Alcina responded. 'Information on the city's Outskirt is erratic, but we have found reports of illicit trading, of assaults on known buildings, and of river barges recently going missing. Heretical communications have been reported, though we do not yet know their content.'

'We will end them,' Augusta said. 'Viola and I are on our way to the river. We will establish a muster point and you will join us there.'

'Yes, Sister.'

A passing worshipper scuttled from her path. Staring at her like she'd risen from some legend, the young man clutched his prayer-scarf and backed away, muttering words of awe and shock. The crowds thronged thickly, younger now, many loud with wine. Among them, there were a myriad preachers, upright on walls or plinths, some of them on the fronts of the standing Tauroxes, their hands and faces raised rapt to the sky. Their voices rippled outwards, a hundred prayers, a thousand, overlapping at their edges. Every corner and junction seemed to have another one, telling the tale of an Opal saint.

The praise was constant, yet Augusta now found it dissonant, rather than harmonious. Despite the chill, a sheen of sweat soon gleamed upon her brow. It itched like restlessness, like a desire to fight.

With your grace…

Lost behind the crowd, servitors attempted to clear up. They wore uniforms in the governor's colours and were grubbing about on the flagstones and in the fonts, retrieving trash and wasted food and lost offerings.

'Sister,' Viola said suddenly. 'To our left.'

And there, towering high over the heads of the throng, a single, standing column, a great hooded skull engraved upon its front. They were deep in the Capital's outer streets here; the buildings were tall and narrow, the people more tightly packed and their clothes less garish. They were still pushing, weary but elated, and almost all going the same way. They tripped over their feet and each other, still singing.

'This must be the Path of the Thousand Humble,' Augusta said. 'The arch-deacon mentioned it in his sermon. This is where Opal's more… modest pilgrims come to pray.'

'Look,' Viola said.

Before the column, the queue had come to a clustered standstill, each waiting for their fellows to kneel. Some of the worshippers wore Opal's distinctive, grey camo, though they were clearly not soldiers themselves. But all held long silver chains looped about their necks and wrists, and from these chains there hung hundreds of tiny fetishes.

Beside Augusta, there was an older man, his head bald and his skin liver-spotted. Held in shaking, arthritic hands, his chain caught the ring-light, glittering like a blessed thing. It took Augusta a moment to understand what she was seeing.

Bones.

Every tiny, silver charm was a bone, splintered or fractured or broken. The Path of the Thousand Humble must celebrate how every one of these warriors had died.

The realisation was as clear as His touch, calm through the heaving chaos: this was Opal. It was His world, His festival and these were His warriors. They were true, and strong, and her choice to stay was well made. It made her shiver, more powerful than any petty rage. He had told her clearly: *this* is where you will find your serenity, and Opal's holiness. Not amid the wealth and the gemstones and the presumptuousness of her deacon, but here, among her true martyrs.

'We will pay our respects, Sister.' Taking Viola with her, she moved towards the shrine.

A mutter went through the crowd, and they fell away, flattening themselves against the sides of the road.

The preacher at the shrine paled, but she kept her feet. The column towered over her, twenty-five feet and more. It was square in section, the hooded skull on each of its four faces. From each skull's mouth, clear water ran down the stone, filling a round pool at its base, and the pool shone with small coins and trinkets, each gleaming like a promise. Above the skull emblem there was a skeletal hand, its bony fingers clutching a standard-issue military knife.

Stammering, the preacher said, 'Welcome to the shrine of Aron, three hundred and forty-seventh of the Path of the Thousand Humble. A daughter of Opal, Aron was stationed upon the Temassian border, where the Archenemy touched her mind. Rather than allow such taint within her soul, she offered her life to Him, and she cut her own throat.'

'A deed of great courage,' Augusta said. 'Blessed be her memory.'

Viola echoed her and the words flowed out among the gathered people.

'You have no chain, Sisters,' the preacher said. 'Would you accept them, in the name of Aron's sacrifice? In the name of the Thousand Humble and of all of Opal's slain?'

'We would be honoured.'

Taking the silver-link chain, Augusta looped it about her pauldrons. Viola did the same. Her hands trembling, the preacher attached to each one a silver, skeletal hand, complete with blade.

'Continue the Path in His light,' she said. 'A billion soldiers' lives are sacrificed, all across the galaxy, but all are gathered to His side. Ave Imperator, Adepta Sororitas.'

'Ave Imperator.' Augusta gave the young woman the sign of the aquila and she reddened, dropping her gaze. 'You do His work, sister,' Augusta told her gently. 'And you may stand secure, knowing that He watches you, as He watches us all.'

'Thank you, Sisters.' She looked back up almost shyly, but there was a glow of real warmth to her words, a catch like gratitude. 'Thank you for understanding.'

'We are all but warriors, and we stand in His light.'

Augusta gave the woman a courteously stern nod, then moved away, taking Viola with her. The streets were still busy and snatches of drunken hymns rose on the chill wind.

They moved on through the crowd, letting the passing glances and exclamations roll off their armour like Opal's melting sleet. Soon, they came to a quieter road, a place where the wind blew with greater freshness, cold and sharp after the heat of the heaving people. Augusta lifted her chin, letting it touch her skin like His grace. She heard a faint and final burst of singing, somewhere behind them.

They had come to the heights of a massive wall topped by the rearing towers of orbital defences. On the wall's far side there was a sprawling, scruffy maze of hab-blocks and on the far side of those, the gleam of a great river. This was the Varadi, shining like steel and reflecting the great arc of the planet's ring-light.

And down there, across the water, lay the Outskirt, a scatter of lights and fires. With her magnoculars, Augusta could explore their patterns; see the lines of still-occupied streets, and the glimmer of illuminated windows. The Capital's Outskirt, it seemed, was far from empty.

'What do you see, Sister?' Viola asked.

'A beginning,' Augusta answered. 'On the far side of the closer bridge, there is a large building, the ruin of a great cathedral. And gathered about it, there are many fires.'

'You think this is the rebellion?'

'Whether it is or not,' Augusta said, 'it is a good place for a muster. Let us move, and learn what we may.'

THE MARK OF THE CHOSEN

Once Kamilla had bolted her still-hot soup, Arkas shooed her from the building.

'You have people to punch,' he told her. 'Go on, before you get into trouble!'

Her dreams still nibbling at her like rats at a corpse, she put her hood up and slipped carefully past Eszter at the door. She trusted Arkas, of course she did, yet somehow her heart was still unquiet, and the vortex of the dreams still hovered, filled with strange potential.

You've had them too. Haven't you?

What *did* they mean?

Outside, it was cold. Between the steps and the lych-gate, the cathedral's half-dead outbuildings loomed pale in the ring-light, their opaline stonework glittering. In the Capital, the shine was holy and pure, a mark of Opal's grace; this side of the river, it just looked spectral, like times lost and names forgotten. Around the listing, moss-limned tombstones, braziers flared, casting odd, flickering shadows. Massive sarcophagi stood like markers, their inscriptions unreadable with age. Many had been daubed in markings, garish and nonsensical, or bitter and blasphemous. Others had been broken completely, cast down and left there, in a mess of shattered fragments. A fountain was choked with green slime, its waters long gone.

Kamilla shivered.

Far away, the other side of the river and looking like a different world, the Inner Sanctum rose in perfect, wordless mockery, the cathedral's glorious, holy shrine at its peak. A spike in her heart made her turn away – it seemed so utterly unreachable, reminding the backstreets only of their own unholiness.

Saint Veres comes!

Why had Arkas been so... so blasé, if he'd had the dreams himself? Was he trying to protect her from something? Perhaps Kamilla should ask the barracks' elderly pastor, after all.

She walked the path through the graveyard, thinking. At the braziers, people glanced up, eyeing her with a suspicious wariness and she pulled her coat-hood further over her face. If they identified her as a Blade, cadet or no, they may react badly.

As she reached the lych-gate, however, a movement made her stop. In the deep shadow of the gate's overhang, there stood a figure, his clothes dark, his face almost hidden by a broad-brimmed hat. As she passed him, he lifted his chin and tipped the hat back, revealing pallid skin and an undernourished look. His eyes were dark as pits, and his face was etched in symbols – gang-marks, she thought.

'Hello, Kamilla.'

She stopped and stared at him, her fists closing. 'Where the saint did you come from?'

The man smiled. He had the typical look of the Outskirt, hollow-cheeked and thin, but his gaze was burning with fervour.

'Lots of places. I'm here to see Arkas.'

'Why?' She eyed him warily. 'How do you know my name?'

'You're well known down here. The local girl who made good – or is it bad? The one who betrayed her childhood, by going on to be a *Blade*.'

Kamilla glared. 'You know nothing about me.'

At the fires, the people were shifting, muttering, some of them looking up. Whispers flowed, one huddle to another. Glancing at them, Kamilla saw the gleam of newly drawn weapons. She came to her toes, ready.

The man clocked the movement, and his smile deepened. He said, 'Which side are you on, Kamilla? Which side of the river? Do you know? Because you're going to have to choose.'

She glared at him, her closed fists rising. 'Who are you?' Cold was prickling up her arms, now, up her back.

'Come away, Kam.' Behind her, Father Arkas had appeared at the cathedral steps, Eszter at his shoulder.

Kamilla stayed exactly where she was, glaring at the man. 'I asked you a *question*.'

'Don't you know?' The man's smile hadn't faltered, but he jerked his chin at Arkas, on the steps. 'He does. I'm the future. I'm courage. I'm *hope*.'

'You're a lunatic,' Arkas said. 'I welcome all to my church, Henrik–'

'But not me?'

'Kam, I said, come *away*.' Arkas' expression was thunderous.

By the fires, the people were rising fully to their feet, gathering into clusters. They stared at the newcomer, fascinated or appalled.

Expansive, Henrik turned to them. 'Yes, my friends, I am back!' He called it like a clarion, like a trumpet that opened some fateful gate. 'Back to bring you strength, belief. A reason to go on.' Brazier-light flickered on his face. 'Back, to fulfil my promises and to bring you a future.'

'You bring nothing of the sort.' Arkas was coming down the steps now. 'You just bring trouble, Henrik, as ever. And I've warned you already–'

'Opal wallows in wealth!' Walking to meet Arkas, Henrik still spoke to the graveyard. 'While we languish in destitution, lurk ever in the shadows. Saint Veres *himself* was but a poor man, he was one of us – he was *all* of us! And yet here we cower, thus forgotten! In faith and in hope, in Veres' name, in the name of the holy visions we have all shared… the saint is almost come!'

Whether they knew him or not, the people were utterly silent, staring. Kamilla too, found herself caught – she could almost hear her own breathing.

The man called louder, every eye now following him.

'And I say – he will greet us as our saviour! We will have clean water! We will have medicines, and food, and proper shelter! Our children will no longer go hungry, our mothers and fathers will no longer perish in illness and in pain!'

In Veres' name, in the name of the holy visions…

It took Kamilla a full second to realise he meant the dreams – the vortex, the darkness. The dreams she'd shared with her barrack-mates, with Arkas himself. Cold iced up her spine. *Did* they mean something, after all?

Saint Veres comes!

Which side are you on, Kamilla? Which side of the river?

Caught between doubt and certainty, between home and duty, between the two sides of Opal's life, she stared at Henrik, half-mesmerised, her heart thundering. Trying to shoulder her way through the questions, the clarity of his call, she pulled out the compass, shifted its markers, let it drop on its chain. It turned and settled, pointing at Terra, so far away.

Show me, she told it, like a prayer. *If you are my guide to His will, then help me. Show me to the truth. Show me what these dreams really mean!*

'Yes! We remember you!' The people had started shouting, some angry, some hopeful. Figures were moving away from the braziers and gravestones, coming to Henrik. Some of them were half staggering as though not used to movement; others had sleepy children with them, carried, or being pulled along by their hands. Some looked diseased or terrified, resigned or anxious. Others looked exultant, their eyes full of stars. A few raised old electro-torches, their pale lights glittering.

And they were shouting, 'We have *seen!* The visions have touched us! Lead us, and we will follow! The saint is coming! We will be *saved!*'

Kamilla glanced at the closest – a young woman, a bundle of rags in her arms that might have been a babe. Heeding the cry, the woman raised her own voice with it, a sudden, triumphant madness, a banishing of her own fear.

'*Yes!* We have seen the truth! Saint Veres comes!'

Had they *all* had the same dreams? The idea was terrifying. But Arkas was angry now. Robes swishing angrily at his ankles, he strode down the path to block Henrik's route.

'These people are under His protection, and mine. I will not have this heresy here.'

The man raised an eyebrow, as if surprised. He said, 'Heresy, you call it? Ever the coward, Arkas, preaching acceptance and victimhood.'

'You try to assail the Capital and they will gun you down, every last one of you. I am trying to save their *lives*, as well as their souls.'

'Poor, misguided Arkas.' The man's tone was whetted. 'The saint is almost upon us. And we will know our new beginning!'

Murmurs of agreement were rising. Shaking herself free from her odd fascination, Kamilla ran to catch the man up.

'You'll know no such thing,' Father Arkas said. 'You'll know only las-fire–'

'You're craven,' the man said. There was a certain savage humour in the remark. 'A lone yellow-belly on a world of warriors. We will rise up! We will be *free!*'

More echoes, more voices joining the cry.

'Don't listen to him!' Arkas stared round at his people. 'What have I taught you? Spent years teaching you? The Blades will tolerate no invasion...'

But Henrik was right in Arkas' face, his followers now all round him. 'Arkas, you've seen the visions. The saint has spoken to you, too. Join me. *Lead* your people to the light.'

'Don't you touch him.' Angry, Kamilla had reached them, and she shoved herself between the two men, her back to Arkas, glowering at Henrik. 'I'll break your face.'

'Will you, child? Or have you seen them too?' He smiled at her. 'I think you have.'

Her cheeks burned. Doubts and dreams and recollections, confusions thrown back at her like weapons.

Saint Veres comes!

'What do you want?' Against the flare of his charisma, her question sounded small. Hollow and ridiculous.

'I've told you – hope.' The words were not loud, but they blazed with power. 'First to rise, and first to lead, and first to fly the saint's new banner. As was foretold, Veres will come again, and he will greet us, not as some archaic hero, but as a living, breathing champion. He knows our suffering and he will *help* us.' He turned back to Arkas. 'We will not perish, Father. The saint's messages are heard throughout the Outskirt, and his voice is clear in the vox. He will bless our uprising, and we will be *victorious!*'

Arkas was frowning, and Kamilla shook her head, still trying to clear her thoughts, focus. But the dream-images were back, surrounding her completely now, storm-wings beating at her head. On some level, she knew this, had *felt* it.

Victorious!

Saint and Emperor, could it even be true? *Could* this man lead the poor from the Outskirt? Was that the answer to her dreams, the one she had come seeking?

Which side of the river?

'Yes! Help us!' More figures were stumbling from the tombstones. 'We have heard his voice! He will bless us!' they cried. 'He is our true redeemer!' One, no more than a lad, shoved past Arkas and Kamilla both, and tumbled to his knees. Tears streaked the dirt upon his face.

'Please!' he said, weeping. 'Please!'

'Soon,' Henrik said, laying a hand on the boy's hair. 'Very soon, the moment will come.' But his attention was still on Arkas, burning with intensity. 'Behold, Father – the mark of hope and victory, the mark of Veres' chosen!' With a flourish, Henrik tore open the neck of his shirt. 'It means we can *win!*'

On his throat, there was a black burn-mark like a coiled worm. He offered it like a bribe, or a prompt, like some wonder both glorious and irrefutable.

'That mark's all over the Outskirt,' Arkas said. 'And it doesn't change anything. You won't draw me, or my people, to some reckless, pointless death.'

The man's eyes flared with feeling – anger, wariness.

'So be it, then,' he said. 'If you will not join me...' He gestured, and the cluster of people moved. Not with the rough, haphazard violence that Kamilla had seen in the city; this was slower and had a mean, dark edge. The weeping lad was on his feet, his expression twisting, his eyes filling with zeal. He had a blade in his hand, serrated and rusty, and the look he carried was genuinely terrifying. Not angry, but rich with fanatical belief.

He was younger than Kamilla, but she moved without thinking, bringing back one elbow and slamming her closed fist, full-force, into his face. He rocked back on his heels, blood streaming from his nose. Grinned. Arkas, furious, shoved her sideways and out of the way.

'Kamilla, get out of the–'

It ended in a cry. The lad's blade had gone straight into his belly, stabbing upwards and under his ribs. With an astonished, bloody splutter, he clamped both hands to his gut and went over.

'Arkaaaaas!'

Screaming, Kamilla lunged for the lad, grabbing his wrist and twisting his arm, forcing him to drop the weapon and driving him to his knees. The verger Eszter was shouting, moving, shoving, but not fast enough; everything was a blur.

They were surrounded, the preacher's faithful now filling the lych-gate's space. They closed like some awful, dark net, but she didn't care. She barely saw them, didn't care about her own safety; she dropped the boy and fell to her knees beside Arkas, seeing his bloodied hands wrapped round his stomach, his robe staining to a thicker, glistening black.

'Nonononononono.' The words were a prayer, a plea, a denial. Eszter was keeping the people back, her robe dirty white amid the rising dark – but what could she do? A red bubble burst on Arkas' lips as he tried to speak.

'Saint and Emperor, please.' Kamilla was praying, kneeling, applying pressure to the wound; she was up to her wrists in his blood. The crowd was still closing round them; two more vergers had reached her side.

'I gave you your chance,' Henrik said. Amid the humming in her ears, his voice sounded oddly distant. 'You didn't listen.

You've betrayed your people and your saint. Our rising will come, and *soon!*'

'We've got to move him,' Kamilla said, glancing up. 'We've–'

Arkas tried to lift his head. 'Kam–'

'Shhhh,' she told him. 'Don't try and speak.'

A hand grabbed her hair, tugged.

Coming to her feet in a rush, she howled, 'Leave him alone!' She lashed out, downed one, kicked a second in the knee, ducked under the clumsy punch of a third and came back with an uppercut, knocking the wind out of him and sending him flying backwards. It felt unreal, almost like the combat-games, back in the pit.

But these were street people, not cadets. They were untrained. And she knew this, knew this like her own pulse – she did not fear them. Rage and grief were pure fuel, driving her on.

A belly-wound. She knew what that meant.

Still howling, she kicked another, lashed out at a fourth. She felt white-hot. It felt *good*. A fist hit her temple and she staggered, rounding on the man and slamming him in the throat. A punch caught her in the shoulder, knocking her sideways. Blood sang in her ears, her pulse hammered like the city bells.

I will finish you all!

'Get him inside!'

Eszter was shouting, putting up a decent fight of her own; more people were emerging from the cathedral, spilling down the steps. There were yells, cries.

And then, in the haze of motion and sound, Kamilla heard something else – the thunderous report of some monster sidearm. It wasn't a lasrifle; it was ballistic and *loud*. There was a detonation; the coughing rumble of falling masonry. People shouted and screamed. Cried abuse and epithets. She couldn't hear Henrik, any more, and wondered where he'd gone.

Instead she heard a voice, female and hard with authority.

'You! In the name of the God-Emperor, you will *stand down!'* The colossal pistol fired again.

Kamilla wanted to get up, wanted to help carry Arkas, wanted to know who the newcomers were, but the people were all still round her. A foot hit her chest and she went over, a sharp shock of pain in her ribs. She gagged, couldn't breathe.

Above her, a figure, its face in a rictus grin. She saw the boot, lifted. She saw it come down.

And then, she saw nothing else.

THE INSURRECTION

'You!' Augusta bellowed. 'In the name of the God-Emperor, you will *stand down!*' She let off a second shot with her bolter, straight up into the air.

Before her was the tumbledown cathedral that she'd seen from the wall, its grounds streaked with shadow and lined with ancient gravestones, its outbuildings derelict and rundown. Sleet fell, weapons flashed, voices screamed and shouted; there were boots and elbows and blades. Some of the braziers had been knocked over, and smoking coals were scattered across the flag-stones. People tumbled, and heat hissed on cold skin. Screams and cries followed, and the smell of burning flesh.

At the forefront, a heavy backstreet figure threw itself out of the fighting, leering at the arriving Sisters with a face full of eagerness and half-demented rage. A single shot removed most of its chest.

'Desist!' She was still walking forwards, weapon aimed at the mêlée. 'By the God-Emperor, I said, that is *enough!*'

As she drew closer, the Sister Superior saw that the brawl was centred on something, two somethings, lying motionless on the ground. Around them, a scatter of slightly grubby, pale-robed figures was fighting to retrieve the fallen.

'Viola!'

Viola gave a curt nod, roaring orders. 'By the Golden Throne!' She aimed her bolter over the heads of the brawl and pulled the trigger, letting off a five-round burst. The noise was shocking. 'You will stop this *now!*'

Some of the figures stopped, falling out of her path; others hurled themselves at her, spitting and swearing. She lowered the weapon's muzzle and it barked, barked again – clean, single shots that missed the hovering vergers completely. In the midst of the madness, Augusta thanked the Emperor Himself for Viola's accuracy.

Snarling now, the crowd pulled back. Faced by two fully armoured and righteously furious Sisters of Battle, they muttered and grumbled, and started to slink away.

And there, at the bottom of the pile, were the two figures, both limp. One was a girl in an oversized black coat. She looked no more than about fourteen, her dark hair all but shaven, her skin bloodless-pale around her smashed-in nose and teeth. The other was a robed, bearded man in his forties, quite slender, and slumped in a pool of gore.

'Watch the road.' Mag-fastening the bolter and pulling off one gauntlet, the Sister Superior dropped to one knee.

Both the man and the girl were breathing.

'Who are they?' Augusta looked up at the closest hovering figure, a solidly strong middle-aged woman. Her grey robe was bloodstained, some of it her own.

'Father Arkas, our priest.' Her tone was bleak and both sets of her knuckles were bruised and scraped. 'The child is Kamilla.

Please, Sister, we should take them inside. We do have some medical facilities, but–'

'What caused the riot?'

'A local troublemaker.' The woman – a verger if Augusta had to guess – looked round, but the street was now almost empty. 'He's been stirring the people for some time, talking about the festival, about how we should rise up and storm the Capital.' Her expression closed, she gestured at some of the others to retrieve both the priest and the girl. 'But we are not rebels, not here – such would be utter folly. It's the Emperor's will you came, Sister.'

A skitter like His blessing flickered down Augusta's back.

'Keep your eyes open,' she told Viola over the vox.

'Sister.'

Standing up, partly to check the road and partly to let the hovering vergers retrieve their fallen, Augusta said, 'Tell me what happened.'

The skitter down her spine was growing stronger. She could still see dark figures skulking, keeping their distance, but not retreating completely. Whatever it was they had wanted, they had not given it up – merely withdrawn for the moment. They'd left a scatter of their own dead and broken, and though Augusta looked at the fallen carefully, she could see nothing unusual, no emblems of heresy or of the Ancient Foe.

'His name is Henrik, Sister, and we've seen him before. He tries to trade arms at our tables, or recruit our people to hit-and-run raids. He broadcasts rhetoric from what vox-casters remain, rallying support for his cause.'

Augusta said, 'We will find him.'

'Yes, Sister.' The verger nodded her head in agreement. 'We are a peaceful house, here, offering His grace and sanctuary, and help where we may.' Two figures were picking up Arkas and carrying him inside; two more carefully lifted the girl. 'But it is true that the festival has made things... difficult. The people watch it with envy, like starving canids straining at their leashes. And Henrik plays upon their needs. I fear many already follow him.'

'Did he bear banners, or flags? Symbols of any kind?'

Was he the Foe?

'Several.' The verger looked pained, like Augusta would bite her head off any minute. 'Inked into his skin. One was a curl, another a skull, still more were weapons and names – though most were of the Outskirt's backstreets, and long familiar.' She offered a slightly apologetic shrug. 'May I suggest, Sister, that we move inside? The Father, and Kamilla – they need our help most urgently.'

'Of course.' Spinning on her heel, Augusta headed for the steps. Into the vox, she said, 'Sisters, we muster at the Outskirt cathedral, at the far end of the Varadi's eastern bridge. In His grace and wisdom, He has shown us to a dissident leader, who must be located and slain, his insurrection silenced, before he can assault the festival. We will secure the relic, and the safety of Opal herself.'

The replies came back to her: *'Yes, Sister.'*

'And praise Him, for He has shown us swiftly to the truth!'

'In His name,' Sister Alcina responded.

In His name.

After the frustrations of the bureaucratic table, Augusta thought, the anticipation of combat was like a blaze of faith in her heart.

Along one outer side of the cathedral cloisters, there lay a long room that may once have been a chapter house. It had a single door, close to one end, and its walls were lined with narrow alcoves, each one holding the remains of some ancient statue.

Glassaic windows lay high along its outside, some of these broken. And under them, there waited a line of eight simple, steel-frame beds, rusted but intact.

A modest hospice, but a hospice nonetheless.

Eszter's strong hands had treated Arkas and the girl, Kamilla, and had laid them in two of the beds. Viola's imposing red shape had taken a defensive position in the cathedral's doorway, watching the road. And Augusta herself now prowled the nave like an angry predator, eyeing the verger, who sat on the altar steps. From the transepts, gazes followed the Sister's movements, tight and wary; she felt them as if they were wires, tugging at her back. Her mind had caught on a single thing, a memory she could not let go.

Eszter had said: *a curl*.

She was remembering another mission, another great glassaic cathedral. Another alignment of worlds. She'd been much younger then, yet she could still hear her Sister Superior, Veradis' final order, commanding the martyrdom of her squad-mate, Sister Pia. Pia had closed with the great xenos, preventing it from moving, and given the command...

Leona, fire!

But Pia, too, had been caught in the barrage of Leona's heavy bolter. The noise of it echoed down the years like the peal of sacred bells. Was Opal's glassaic cathedral itself some kind of message, a sign from Him? Or was the conjunction? Had He guided the squad here to confront a great xenos enemy?

Or was she just needing a fight? A focus for her frustration, her reaction to the deacon's presumption? Rebellion, from such disadvantaged streets... It may be no more than it seemed. And wishing for such things, here upon Holy Opal, was surely heresy.

Guide me, my Emperor.

'My squad are incoming,' she said. 'They will not be long. I need to know where Henrik has gone, where these vox-casts originate. Would the Father or the girl offer further information?'

With faint reproach, the verger said, 'Sister, Father Arkas is my friend. He is not a great man, but he is a good man. He is known to all of the Outskirt as a man of gentleness and goodwill.' She spoke as if Augusta's efficiency was somehow disrespecting the man's injury.

'My squad are blessed with many skills,' Augusta said. 'And if the God-Emperor wills it, we may assist with Arkas' healing.'

The verger's gaze sharpened. 'You can save him?'

'Not I.' Her tone was composed, almost gentle. 'For I am not a medicae. Warfare is my grief, my faith, and my privilege. But some among my Sisters have additional gifts.'

The woman stared at her for a moment, then flushed faintly, dropped her gaze. 'I'm sorry, Sister, I misunderstood. I've just... just known him a long time.'

'Then pray for him, pray for them both.' Augusta permitted herself the indulgence of looking up at the statue at the head of the steps. Here, like in the Saints' Cathedral, it was not the God-Emperor, but Veres.

Again, that skitter down her back.

In your name... Her prayers were silent. *Is this just some local uprising? Do I conjure some terrible foe, seek battle where there is none? Or is there truly something sinister here?*

Somewhere in the back of her thoughts, there lingered the dreams of the Lautis daemon, terror and fire and hunger and violence...

Angry with herself, with the recollection, she said, 'When my Sisters arrive, we will offer you what assistance we can. And we will halt this insurgence, whatever it may be. Such things threaten this world, and our mission, and cannot be permitted to take root.'

* * *

'A *spiritu dominatus*,
  'Domine, libra nos...'

In the ring-lit streets of the Outskirt, the Sisters moved with a perfect, smooth efficiency. The squad had mustered at the Outskirt cathedral for a briefing, though Augusta's orders had been curt – they would find this insurrectionist leader. Now, with Viola at their head, and Melia at the rear, they shared the words of the litany across the vox.

Eyes tracked them like beacons, but the lingering local denizens made no reaction – not to the fully deployed wrath of the Adepta Sororitas.

From the Sisters' reports, their separate missions had been achieved: Akemi and Alcina had completed what research they could, while Caia and Melia had attended the festival, as ordered. Melia had also tended to Arkas and to the girl, though she had roused neither to full consciousness. By His blessing, Arkas' heart and lungs had remained intact, but the damage to his upper bowel was significant. The girl, Kamilla, was closer to wakefulness, and Melia had assisted with her also, carefully resetting her nose. The girl bore a good wound, a combat wound – a novice at the schola would carry such injury with pride.

''Ware,' Augusta said into the vox. 'Maintain your vigilance, my Sisters. This Henrik... he may yet surprise us.' Sternly, she reminded herself that this may yet be just a simple mission, nothing more than local rebels.

Yet caution was surely His blessing.

In the streets, the sleet had stopped. The great arc of the planet's halo was still partially hidden by the clouds, and visibility was poor. The Sisters moved from shadow to shadow, cover to cover, running and kneeling in that so-familiar skirmish manoeuvre that was as much a part of them as their armour, their bolters, their faith. Fragments of lumens still shone from broken doorways, pools of pale and erratic light that made the stonework glitter with phantoms. The perfect shine of Opal's Capital seemed far away, here, and the walls were lined with ancient gravestones, with ghost-pale weeds that were growing in their cracks. Ancient gargoyles grimaced as they passed, fangs bared.

Softly, Akemi said, 'The streets here are much older than the Capital – they were distant enough to withstand Bakos' detonation. Legend says that their population gave their lives to the reconstruction of the Capital, the Inner Sanctum, the walls and the Saints' Cathedral. Their bones are said to be the Capital's foundations, though their actual gravestones lie this side of the water.'

'Sister Caia,' Augusta said. 'How close are we to the next location?'

Eszter had briefed the Sisters on Henrik, on what she knew of his vox-casts, and of his known haunts and lairs. Akemi had commented on several of these, the ones that had turned up in her research as known areas for trouble. This had given Augusta a list of likely targets and now the squad had paused, kneeling in cover at the nearer end of a great stone bridge. This one did not span water; instead, its towering archways carried it across a patch of waste ground, buildings long tumbled to rubble. Twisted girders stood stark and skeletal, and there was a lone and rotted Chimera still standing guard at one corner.

'I have movement,' said Caia. 'Focused to our left, thirty degrees, approximately half a mile. Of the vox-cast locations, this is one of the largest. May He bless our scouting.'

'He will surely not be far from Arkas' cathedral,' Alcina commented. 'If Henrik does wish to assault the Capital, it is a good muster and staging point. Not only close, but a secure location in itself. And it has medical facilities.'

'There will be no muster,' Viola commented grimly.

'Estimate of numbers?' Augusta asked.

'Two hundred,' Caia answered, without hesitation. 'Though they will not be armed as well as the Blades. They will bear only what they have scavenged.'

'Eszter told us that Henrik was trying to trade arms,' Augusta commented. 'So be wary, my Sisters. Follow the steps, and let Him be our guide.'

'Understood.'

'That thou wouldst bring them only death…'

Softly, the litany flowed over the vox. Not the full bellow of battle-rage but a sound much softer, wary and sharp. It still whetted Augusta's nerves, made her hands tighten on both bolter and chainsword.

Walk with me, my Emperor.

They moved forwards, downwards. The steps were slippery beneath their boots, the stone worn to dips by long millennia. They reached the bottom, and stopped.

'Hold!' Caia's vox-cry was quiet but insistent. On point, she and Viola had crept forwards, stopped at the edges of the space – an old market square, perhaps, its mosaic all shattered and broken. A huge statue stood ancient guard, one arm uplifted, its cupped hand holding a ringed orb. It was the same image as on Vass Mihaly's banner, and it felt like a signpost, like He had brought them to the right place.

'Guards,' Caia said. 'Two of them, at the base of the statue. They have not seen us.'

'Then He is with us,' Alcina said, her tone unpleasant. 'We have achieved our first target. We wish to know the full size of his insurrection, its plans, and in how many places it lurks. Sisters, we will retrieve one of these alive.'

'Agreed,' Augusta said. 'Viola. You have line of sight?'

'Yes, Sister,' Viola said. There was a thrum of impatience in her tone. Augusta knew exactly how she felt.

'The rest of you, stay in cover. Caia, keep your auspex to hand. If anything else moves...'

'Yes, Sister.'

That thou shouldst spare none...'

At the base of the steps, the squad paused, still singing. Augusta heard Viola's armour rattle, heard her boots scrape as she ran forwards, across the mosaic. She heard the scouts as they challenged her, then the echoing thunder of the heavy bolter on a full suppression.

Alcina snapped, 'Viola! I said alive!'

Caia commented, 'That woke them up. The whole gang is coming this way.'

'I think this one's still breathing,' Viola said. 'I'll bring him back.'

'*Sister* Viola.' Augusta was angry with herself, angry for letting her hold on her squad slip, angry for letting her need for battle overcome her good command structure and sheer common sense. 'We have no time to dispense medical aid to an enemy. We muster for full combat immediately.' Anger edged her every word, but she would deal with Viola later. For now, the squad needed unity. 'Melia, join Caia on point. Viola, you, Alcina and Akemi will take secondary positions. We will cauterise this entire area, and save the questions for afterwards.'

Viola was back, the scout over her shoulder, his arms swinging like meat. Alcina and Akemi stayed down, in cover. Augusta came to the fore, with Caia on one side of her and Melia, with the flamer, on the other.

'Sister Caia?'

The auspex blipped green with incoming dots. 'They move like a rabble, no discipline, but there is one, very clearly in the

lead. The God-Emperor continues to bless us, Sister Superior –
it seems that Henrik will confront us himself. Whatever this
rebellion really is, I think He is about to give us its message.'

Henrik, Augusta saw, was barely twenty. Under a broad-
brimmed hat, he had night-dark eyes and white-pale skin, all
etched in a multitude of marks, and he walked tall, his step
light. There was zeal to his stance and an unruly gaggle of his
faithful behind him.

He showed no sign of any curling symbol, though his shirt
was buttoned to the neck. He came to a halt, facing the Sister
Superior absolutely fearless, as if he had the power to defeat
her, if he so chose. Melia and Caia at her shoulders, she eyed
him like a bug.

'We are the Adepta Sororitas,' she said. 'And you preach heresy,
here upon Opal's very streets. For this, we do not stand.'

The young man smiled, his expression beatific. 'Welcome,'
he said. 'I confess, your appearance is… somewhat unexpected.
And I – we – needed some time to think.' He gestured, as extra-
vagantly confident as if he stood within the palace itself.

Augusta's bolter was trained on him; she wanted only to pull
the trigger. But she didn't know, not enough, not yet.

That thou shouldst pardon none.

'You have no time, heretic. You seek to raise insurgence, and
your life is forfeit.'

The man laughed, soft and musical. 'Sister, I am the bringer
of a greater truth, not some petty protestor. And you are perceptive, are you not? In your piety, you must have witnessed
Opal's lies. Its popinjay folly and the emptiness of its pipes
and drums.' His eyes glittered, absolutely compelling. 'Opal is
no gem, Sisters. It is a falsehood, celebrating only glories long
lost. Wars forgotten. But I…'

He had not raised his voice, but his charisma was tangible.

'I am blessed. I am *called*. I can return this world to her full glory, deliver her from her pain.' He had dropped his tone to a thrum, a note like a plucked string. 'And you – you can stand at my side.'

Augusta raised her bolter. 'You stand against Opal, and against her holy church. You threaten the very relic that we are here to secure.'

Undaunted, the man smiled wider, radiant. Focused intently on Augusta, he said, 'And that must be the skull of Saint Veres. Did you know, Sisters, that Veres had nothing, only his courage and his honour, when he faced the ecclesiarch traitor? He faced the *heretic*, Sisters, just as you did, so long ago. He faced the Deacon Bakos, just as your own Saint Mina faced Vandire himself.'

The word *Vandire* sent a cold shudder across Augusta's shoulders. Everything in her was poised, tight as a drum.

'Your orders, Sister?' Alcina's tone was almost rasping. 'We must silence this heretic.'

The man stepped forwards, looking right into Augusta's visor. 'I'm not your enemy.' His words were still soft; there was no force to him, no rage. 'I'm your ally, your friend. You who are the very soul of Opal's honour, surely you are here to help me. Help *us*. Help the people, the *true* faithful of this world. In the name of Veres and Mina both, you can bring Opal *back* to her magnificence.'

All round them now, the people were singing, wordless and beautiful, a ululation that was as coaxing as the man himself.

'Picture the glory, Sister,' Henrik said. 'The wonder of the Saints' Cathedral. Picture a man in the pulpit, but not some wealth-saturated preacher – he's a warrior, in Opal's uniform, with flak-plates in white and a dagger on his pauldron. His face shines with a light of its own, like his very skull is golden, and glowing through his skin. *Veres.*

'With him are three other figures, one man and two women. Each of them gleam, serene and radiant, and they bear great trays laden with food and medical supplies. With icons and blessings. As they once faced Bakos, so now they walk, one down each of the aisles, and they hold these trays out to the people. Bringing them hope.

'"Trust me," Veres says from the great, glassaic altar. "For I am returned. Opal need suffer no longer."'

With his last words, Henrik opened the neck of his shirt, and revealed the curling mark.

Seeing it, Augusta was jarred from his compulsive performance. She felt that same flash of memory – that other great glassaic cathedral, far across the galaxy – heard the words of Sister Pia the Martyr.

'But lo! From the unsanctified places of the Emperor's tunnels there came forth darkness unendurable, heresy manifest in claw and tooth, in hunger given form. And, though the humble servants of the Emperor's mines gave battle with great bravery, the beasts were a seethe of cruelty beyond their ken, and thus, they were slain.'

It was a message as powerful as Truth, as His touch in the centre of the Outskirt's battered streets. As compelling as His call that had brought her down here, as His light in darkness of her questions...

Truly, this was a fight, indeed.

'I know you.' The words were a knell, though her heart sang with a fierce, holy joy. 'Xenos.'

The man blinked, fell back a step. For the first time, he looked unsure, glancing from side to side as if to gain support from his followers. But they were too enraptured by his vision, by its hope and future.

We beseech thee, destroy them!

'You cannot hide from Him, traitor. Or from the Adepta

Sororitas. We have seen your kind before, and we will not be fooled by your rhetoric. We *know* your call, your insidious influence.' The litany blazed from her heart, her soul, its words like relief, like potency and clarity and a pure and cleansing flame. 'You are no saviour, no follower of ancient saints. You are not the Archenemy, and you are not some idle rebel. You are something else completely. You are the mouthpiece of a power most terrible. You are the herald of the Great Devourer, the jaws that will eat all, and I say, you will *perish*.'

Faltering, Henrik looked at her, insulted, almost bewildered. 'No, Sisters. I am the way and the truth. I am the lightbringer. I bring ascendance – and surely, you are here to join us! Guard our walk to glory, our passage across the Varadi, our meeting with the saviour!'

'You are a fool, gutless and anile. You and your followers have been deceived. For when your saint comes, he will not be human, and he will not be your *redeemer*.'

She felt a savagery that was almost joyful, a discovery of something that she could face, and fight.

'Sister Melia. Burn them all.'

viii

THE WISDOM OF THE GOVERNOR

In the stark lumens of the audience hall, Augusta's armour shone like pure, incarnadine fury. Despite the sharp, late-night cold, the windows were still open and she was helmet off, her breath steaming. She stood at the long table's foot like an icon, like the pure and righteous anger in her soul.

Watching her from the table's head, Governor Vass Mihaly was seated and frowning, his grey hair pale against his dark skin, his expression unreadable. His garments were plain, and, other than a single camo-clad guard, he was unaccompanied – no aide, no commander, no deacon. Rolling, drunken hymnals floated upwards from the streets below.

'Sister Superior,' he said, in a tone of wary patience. 'The festival cannot be just… stopped. We have countless millions of pilgrims here. They have come to Opal with considerable expectations, and they will not simply accept–'

'It is important you do as I say, governor.' She glared, refusing to back down. 'This is a call to arms. The dissident threat in the

Outskirt is far, far more serious than you realise, and in His name, you must stop the celebrations and muster.'

'Sister, I cannot.' His tone was regretful, and his words emerged in puffs of warm air. 'If I even made the attempt, the results would be utterly catastrophic. I would have rioting in the streets. And you say yourself – this threat is the other side of the river. It can be contained.'

'Governor, you do not understand the sheer severity of this matter.'

'Whatever it is, Sister, I have complete faith in you. You have executed its leader, have you not? And we have the necessary forces in place to prevent any... leftover invasion.' His voice was calm, but he was clearly used to being obeyed. 'I fear that you do not fully comprehend the sheer *momentum* that the festival has gained. It is a juggernaut, eight hundred years in the making, and one that will not just halt.' Standing up, he scraped back his chair. 'Sister Superior, I leave the Outskirt in your highly capable gauntlets. Thank you for your time, your strength, and your striving on behalf of my world. Ave Imperator.'

Taking a breath to steady her temper – she'd had more than enough of bureaucracy – Augusta said, 'In His name, governor, its momentum will not matter.' There was a whip-crack in her voice now, the tone she used to errant convent novices.

'Sister, with my sincere apologies, I cannot halt the festival. If I even try, the tensions between the pilgrims will detonate. We will have death in the streets. And you are here to protect the relic, are you not, rather than endanger it further?'

'This is larger than the relic, governor.' Strangling her rage, clinging to it by will and faith alone, Augusta snarled at him, 'If we do not contain this uprising, your whole *world* will perish!'

'This is Opal's highest moment,' the old man told her. 'The God-Emperor is with us. Resistance from the Outskirt was already anticipated, and has now been beheaded, thanks to the skill of the Sisters of Battle. I will ensure that the bridges and towers are fully defended, and offer you additional troops, if you deem them necessary. Surely, Sister, with the Sororitas here, there is no reason to disrupt the Capital?'

With a prayer of rising impatience, Augusta closed one hand, once again letting her gauntlet bite at her fingers. The pain was good, giving her focus. Far below, the drunken hymnals still sounded, cheerfully tuneless and so utterly, shockingly naïve.

'Governor, you must heed me.' She took a moment, composed herself. Outside, the hymnal scattered into laughter and then started again, louder.

Emperor, teach me patience. Teach me observation. Teach me the knowledge of my enemies… That I may understand fully the nature of your foes, and that I may bring them to your justice…

Letting her faith calm her – whatever the governor's polite obstinacy, he was still here – she said, 'Permit me to tell you a tale of my youth.'

The governor eyed her; the guard looked like he wanted to be anywhere else.

'Please, continue.'

'Many years ago,' Augusta told him, 'when I was new from the schola, I attended a service at another great glassaic cathedral.'

The old man leaned on the table. Ignoring this, Augusta went on.

'The service was assailed by a great beast, crashing down through the cathedral's roof. A beast we faced unarmed.' She'd had her punch-dagger, but such things were not mentioned outside the Sororitas. 'Sister Pia sacrificed herself, but she enabled us to slay the xenos.'

'Your point?'

'You tell me Opal is proud of her warriors, her festival. If this is so, then when He calls for combat, it is your holy duty to answer that call. Not to beg Him to save you, or to dishonour yourself as you sit and do nothing – but to take up arms, and to face your foe.' She paused; let the old lesson sink home. 'At the schola, we are taught, He defends those who defend themselves. And those that wait for the Archenemy will soon feel the closing of its teeth. My lord governor, in His name and in the name of Saint Mina, she who faced the heretic…' She didn't say his name. 'This is not just some rebel incursion – this is the greatest threat your world has ever seen.'

With a certain conscious theatre, the governor drew in a breath, released it again. He stood back upright, eyeing her down the polished length of the table.

'Sister Augusta,' he said, matching her tone exactly. 'You have lived a life of warfare. Your name is known, your reputation considerable. You have fought upon worlds of darkness, of horror, of strife and of faithlessness. But you are clearly unused to complex matters of planetary administration.'

I would rather face a thousand orks…

Augusta said nothing. She would not utter a falsehood, but to agree with him was to give his argument weight – and she had a feeling she knew exactly what was coming.

The governor went on, 'I understand that your squad did not fully muster for the Mass of the First Martyr? Sister, the arch-deacon was… disappointed by your implied disrespect, and this has placed me in a difficult situation.'

Augusta prayed, held down her temper. She said, 'There was no disrespect, governor. My squad had duties.'

'I understand,' he said. 'But the arch-deacon takes his role upon this holy world very seriously.' The guard leaned forward to say something in his ear, but Augusta did not hear what it was. He waved the guard away. 'Please, try and put yourself in my place. You arrive with little warning. You demand our holiest relic, and during the very festival that celebrates it. You question my world, my military, my defences. Are you not undermining my festival, Sister Superior, that you may retrieve the skull of Saint Veres and achieve your mission?'

Her jaw almost dropped. 'In the name of the Emperor Himself! You accuse me…!'

'Not accuse, Sister, you would simply be following your orders, as any other good soldier. You told me yourself that they came from your canoness.' The words were gentle, but he dealt them like some winning ploy. 'Are you not simply seeking to… ah… facilitate the situation?'

Livid, Augusta inhaled, clenched her fist harder to focus her temper. The man was a politician to his fingertips: manipulations and subterfuge, intrigue and control.

Sharply, she said, 'Tell me – how will Opal defend itself against a full genestealer uprising?'

'*What* did you say?'

That one caught him off-guard. His measured tone was gone and he was staring at her like she'd uttered some unthinkable heresy. The guard blinked, his face paling.

Augusta rested her knuckles on the table, metal scraping against wood.

'Governor, this is the message that I have come to deliver, *if* you will finally listen. Your Blades could be the best-trained troops since the fall of Cadia, or they could stand back and throw their kettledrums at the enemy – neither will remotely matter. The cultists are rising in the Outskirt. They have probably been there for years, breeding, making nests, stealing equipment, building caches, cultivating agents and sympathisers.' She glared at him, forcing him to face the full truth. 'If we do not eliminate this entire infestation, and do so *now*, then your festival, your whole world – *everything* will be devoured alive. Devoured screaming. Denizens of the Outskirt, your own population, your pilgrims in their millions, your cathedrals and basilicae. There will be *nothing* left. Opal will be turned to acid and digested. So, in the Emperor's name, you will mobilise everything you have, you will move your troops to the Outskirt, and you will do so now. You must eradicate every last *sign* of this xenos insurrection.'

This time, she saw the old man falter, saw the fight go out of him. His shoulders sagged and he fell back into his chair, his years suddenly heavy upon him. A burst of laughter came from outside, and the drunken singing continued. Flakes of sleet drifted in through the windows, glittering like tumbling gems.

He said, 'You… You are sure of this?'

'It is why He brought us here.' She held his gaze, thanking Him that she had finally made the old man listen. Then, pressing her advantage, she said, 'The rebel Henrik said "soon", and we have seen that the cult are well established, that they have been working for a considerable time. The hive fleet may already be on its way. Tell me of your planetary defences, governor, your orbital batteries. Can Opal muster warships? I need not remind you how many defenceless vessels are still hung above this world.'

Mihaly gripped the table, his knuckles bone-white. His expression had congealed – horror, grief. His voice catching, he said, 'Only one of our orbital batteries is still operational, Sister. The one at the Saints' Cathedral.' A faint note of bitterness, of self-deprecation. 'It has been maintained down the millennia to… to fire a fusillade at the festival's height.'

'A fusillade…?' She stared at him like he'd grown another head. 'By the Throne! How has Opal become this powerless?' Her words ran away with her now, any hint of politics had gone. 'This arrogant? So full of its own holiness that it has forgotten even the simplest of His commands? What of the ones at the Wall of Diligence?'

Under her onslaught, the governor crumpled. The guard watched him, expression aghast. A breath of wind made one of the windows bang.

Staring at his fingers, now spread flat on the table, Mihaly said, 'They will... need to be repaired, re-blessed.'

Augusta was still staring at him, everything else forgotten. As if the Emperor Himself had told her, she understood like a shock – the governor *knew*. He *knew* how vulnerable his world had become, how empty its pipes and drums. Perhaps that's why his denial had been so emphatic.

By the Light!

Prayers shot through Augusta's thoughts, prayers of focus, prayers of strength and courage. Prayers of realisation, of the tangle of adrenaline that was both eagerness and dread, of the dawning, colossal comprehension of what they really faced. Such prayers had few words but powerful music, and they wove one through another as she watched the old man's expression, watched the guilt and fear that settled upon him like a cloud.

And everything was coming sharply into focus – the Capital's vulnerability, a full cultist infestation. How long had Henrik been working the Outskirt? What plans were already in place? Where were his cells, his claws, his vox-casters and weapons caches? What sabotage had already been committed, or set up? She wanted to rail at Mihaly that they didn't have time; she wanted lists of his troops, his Blades, his artillery, his orbital fleets, but the pain of his expression held her.

The window banged again.

Her voice a growl, she said, 'Why, Vass Mihaly? Why have you let your defences crumble? Become this... pageant?'

His face spasmed – sorrow, regret. 'It has been thousands of years, Sister – the fault lies with numberless generations. Once, our soldiers were the pride of the segmentum border, and they defended the Imperium, in His name. But decades passed, then centuries and millennia, and so does their truth become tale, their tale become myth, their myth become legend.' His tone was layered with both pride and shame, with memories. 'Truly, Opal has... drifted from what she was. She has become a smaller world, a minor world, and the Imperium pays her no mind, not really. We pay our tithes, of course, but it has been a very long time since we have seen a war. Have seen xenos, such as you describe.'

'But you still trade for credits on your past glories. You march, and you sing, and you toot your little bugles.' Watching his expression, Augusta said, 'Governor, we must locate and exterminate the cult in the Outskirt. Every cultist we kill will make their beacon that much weaker, and, if, by His grace, we remove both patriarch and magus, then they cannot send the beacon at all. In this way, we may yet prevent the hive fleet's arrival.' She exhaled, blowing steam like a slowing engine. 'If it is too late, and the fleet is already closing in, our objectives do not change – we still remove the cult, and its leaders, so we do not face a war on both fronts. Either way, it is still your responsibility to draw Opal's weapons. Yours – and mine.'

The old man glanced up, letting the hand drop, and she saw his eyes glimmered with tears.

'Yes, Sister Superior, I hear you. I am no hero, I fear, but neither will I disgrace His name, or our long-ago saints. I fear I may not be able to halt the festival, but I will begin the rearming of Opal. Of *all* of her forces.

'It is time to find our honour anew.'

Deep night had fallen on the Capital. Hung in strings, the skulls' eyes shone cold, watching the last of the revellers. The market stalls were closed, now, though their lumens still glittered. At many of the shrines, hololiths shone with memory: lists of soldiers' names and dates that flowed endlessly round domed roofs. And above it all, the planet's ring shone perfect, like some single, cosmic halo.

Drenched in anger and irony, surrounded by trash and scurrying servitors, Augusta had stopped by the same square pillar, the one from the Path of the Thousand Humble, where she and Viola had been given their silver chains. She had kept hers with her, tucking it inside her armour.

The palace astropath had sent a second message to the Order's canoness, Elvorix Ianthe, back on Ophelia VII. While the convent world was close, traversing the warp was timeless, subject only to its own whims, and to His. Augusta could only pray that the Order would reach Opal, and soon. Because the full might of the hive fleet...

By the Throne!

Her joy for the coming fight had ended, leaving her chilled through and cold with comprehension. There were six of them – her Sisters and herself – to remove an entire genestealer cult, and to locate and eliminate its leaders. The size of the task was like some towering edifice, threatening to tumble over and bury her, but Augusta stood at the shrine, square-shouldered, praying for the strength to accept the burden. Coins in the water glittered, like remnants of the festival's innocence.

Her Sisters were still in the Outskirt, under orders to locate the genestealers' mustered cells – *claws*, she reminded herself. She had sent a message to the *Star*, requesting the ship's three shuttles to make planetfall. As well as his promise to mobilise, the governor had turned over a full sword – three spears, or approximately a company – of the Blades of the Holy Exterior to her command. Unlike their marching and drumming comrades, the 'Blex', as they were usually known, had genuine combat experience.

In your name! The prayer was almost a plea. *How can we, a single squad and a company of soldiers...*

She silenced the internal cry – it was unworthy. It was not that Augusta feared death, far from it. To perish in His name, to kneel before the Throne, at last – such was every Sister's ultimate aspiration. But this – this was bigger than simply offering her life. If the Sisters perished with their task uncompleted, if they could not exterminate every last nest, then Opal would be gutted like some devoured and hollow corpse. Millions of His pilgrims would die.

Not a fear of death, she thought, but a fear of failure. Of the ultimate dishonour.

While I may walk worlds of darkness and terror, there you shall walk with me. I shall know no doubts, no fears, in your name.

Turning from the shrine, she began walking, then running, smooth and swift and merciless, her armour rattling and her thoughts and prayers in turmoil. Scuttling servitors scrambled from her path; occasional drunken partygoers slumped in corners, or napped against His walls. Forgotten treasures, scarves and scrolls and promises, blew cold on the wind. She passed a huge and automated cenotaph, clanking loudly in the ring-light – it bore lines and lines of tiny, rigid steel soldiers, all rattling upwards round a newly oiled and blessed rail track. As they reached its peak, they fell – down, down to the water below. Then they righted themselves, got back on the track, and rattled upwards once more.

Endless, repetitive. Death both imminent and inescapable.

May we walk with the Emperor, and carry His light into the very darkest reaches of the galaxy.

By the Throne, this was just inappropriate. She was not some unblooded novice. She had stood fast in the face of xenos, of daemon, of psyker, of inquisitor, of heretek. She was permitted no fear, would indulge no fear. She would achieve this task, no matter how huge, or she would perish in her best attempt. Her honour – and her *faith* – required nothing more, and nothing less.

He promised that He would grant us strength to face our enemies, the weapons of all who hate us…

She had no time to indulge such foolishness. She had a world to defend.

'And so,' she said, 'that is our situation.'

Back at Arkas' sanctuary, she spoke again to her Sisters. The Father's health was poor, but the injured cadet should regain consciousness any moment. Augusta needed to speak to the girl, but the briefing of the squad came first.

'The governor confirms, Opal offers almost no operational orbital defences. No air force to speak of. And most of her mobile artillery has been repurposed as *ornamentation.*' The word was scathing. 'He commands full repairs, but such will not be swift. The Blades of the Holy Interior have never seen active duty, though their faith is strong and their training, certainly, has been thorough. He will not be moving them from the Capital, as they may be needed to control or defend the festival. The Outskirt is guarded by the Blades of the Holy Exterior, who are the only troops to have seen actual combat. They defend the bridges and towers at the Varadi, and will repel any invasion. We have a sword of these Blades, approximately three hundred individuals and with a solid and experienced commander, mustering at this location.'

Around them, the old cathedral was quiet. A scatter of vergers still drifted around the floor, but the tables were unused now, covered by cloths, and long snores came from many of the bundles on the floor. The squad were gathered at the base of the altar steps, and were talking in hushed tones – less because they were unwilling to wake the sleepers, and more because they did not wish to be overheard.

'The shuttle – all three of the shuttles from the *Star* – will commence an overflight of the Outskirt area, focusing on the points that Akemi has already identified.' Again, that feeling of toppling ferrocrete. 'Sisters, by His grace, He has given us some time – the fact that the astropath was able to send the message means that the hive fleet is not yet in the system. But may He guide our scouting, as the ground we have to cover is *huge*.'

Viola said nothing, though her green eyes flashed. Caia and Melia stood with weapons in hand, helmets at their belts and almost identical expressions of concern. Akemi was frowning hard, her fingers twitching like she missed her little fetish.

'The cult is throughout the Outskirt?'

'Without question,' Augusta said. 'If they are almost ready to rise, then they are long established. And their battle plan seems clear – they will advance across the bridges, invading the Capital to meet their incoming saint. This, we must prevent. The governor does not wish to halt the festival unless there is no other option, and the Capital must remain secure.'

'We should question the cadet,' Melia suggested. 'She will know more about the world, and the area. She can suggest locations for nests, and the possible identities of the cult's other leaders.'

'She's only a novice,' Viola commented.

'But she knows Opal well, and we do not.' Augusta looked at them, each face in turn. 'Very well. For now, we will hold this location – the shuttles will bring our pallets across the river. Once here, we will deploy the vehicles to scout critical locations, and upon the arrival of our Blades, we will move out. We will locate and eliminate each and every claw. And if it lies within our blessing, we will save this holy world.'

The five Sisters said nothing, though Augusta could feel their questions.

She said, 'Speak them aloud, my Sisters. You have worthy experience, all of you, and your wisdom is welcome. We will face this together, in His name.'

Glances shifted across the ring of faces, but it was Melia that said, 'The Order is on the way?'

'The message has been sent.'

'What happens if the xenos reach Opal first?'

'Should He face Opal with this test, then the *Star* is armed and on alert,' Augusta said. 'There are others, a small number of frigates and destroyers, escorting the wealthier pilgrims' transports. These are armed also. Their crews are mustering, and they know to prepare for an assault.'

'What of the unarmed vessels?' Melia said. 'Are they moving away?'

'I have commanded them to stay,' Augusta said. 'If the worst happens, we may need to order an evacuation.'

'But...' Akemi blinked. 'There are *millions* of people...'

'And if they carry the xenos taint?' Melia asked.

'They stay on their ships,' Augusta answered. 'Or they are moved to some remote moon until the necessary screenings can commence.'

Viola swore, an epithet that made Alcina glower.

Caia said, 'What are your orders, Sister Superior? If the hive fleet does arrive?'

'We serve Him,' Augusta said. 'To our last prayer and breath. To the last round in our chambers, and beyond.'

The snores and mutters of the injured continued, loud in the vaults of the ceiling.

'For as long as the threat is this side of the river, then the

Capital, and the festival, are safe. And, with His grace and blessing, we can stop this before the xenos even arrive.'

Part Two

Pilgrims and Warriors

ix

THE FIRST CLAW

Tangled in memories, Kamilla stirred.

She was a child, her uncle swinging her up and around, a broad grin on his bearded face. Arkas was with him, with his smile of light and hope. It was a good image, but even as she remembered it, it charred through like scorching fabric, and behind it lay only ash-stained, chattering skulls, their teeth yellow and rotting.

'You are awake.'

The voice was soft, contralto, female. Unfamiliar.

Struggling through a headache that encompassed her whole face, Kamilla tried to open her eyes. They were swollen, painful, bled tears from their corners, but she blinked repeatedly and managed to clear her vision. Half sitting up, she put her hands to her cheeks, her mouth. There was something – two some-things – shoved up her nose, and they hurt.

'Yfth…?' She got no further. Even her teeth felt wrong.

'Stay still, child.' The same voice, gentle. 'You are sorely injured but I have administered a mild stimm, and it will ease the pain. Here is water. Drink it carefully.'

A canteen was pressed into her hands, but she paid it no attention. She'd focused on the speaker and had stopped, gawking.

'You...' She tried again, but her mouth still moved funny. A touch of her tongue told her that teeth were broken, their jagged edges cut and hurt. She wanted to ask what had happened, but was still staring at the woman.

No, she couldn't be. Not here.

The figure was dusky-skinned and dark-eyed, possibly in her mid-thirties. Her dark brown hair was cropped short, sticking up in the haphazard spikes of someone who'd recently removed a helmet. There was a distinctive fleur-de-lys mark on her cheek, and her *armour*... It was beautiful, ceramite and blood-red, shining almost with a light of its own; it clattered as she shifted in place. Its strength and colour seemed to gleam from the stone, to bathe the walls and alcoves in reflected light. Kamilla had no idea how the woman could move in it, let alone move so easily, like she wore it all the time.

'Take slow sips,' the woman said. 'You are dehydrated and will need the fluids. But do not make yourself sick.'

Kamilla was still staring. The woman put a hand on the bottom of the canteen and pushed it upwards. 'Drink.'

'You're... you're Sororitas.' The words were almost unintelligible. Trying to frown, wincing, she took a sip of the water and swilled it carefully round her mouth before swallowing it. It stung in the scabs on her lips and gums, but she tried again. '*Sororitas.*' That was better, though she had to concentrate on speaking. She hadn't meant to insult a genuine – saint and Emperor! – a *genuine* Sister of Battle.

She thought of the simulacrums she had seen, and almost blushed. They looked absolutely nothing like this.

'I am Sister Melia Kaliyan,' the woman said. 'I am a Sister Militant of the Order of the Bloody Rose, but I trained for a time with the Order of Serenity. I have been caring for you.' Slants of light from the windows made squares on her pauldrons. Her robe was black and white, embroidered in roses, and the flamer at her hip was one of the most fearsome weapons Kamilla had ever seen. Kamilla was used to lasrifles, and that thing looked like it could torch half a city.

Lasrifles... Oh no...

Spear Takacs would have no idea where she was, or what had happened to her. She'd be cleaning boots for months, if he didn't open her back. With a crusty yank, she pulled the whatever-they-were out of her nose, wiped at the leak of fluids, and tried to stand up.

'My spear–'

'Stay where you are.' Melia's voice was gentle, but she was absolutely used to being obeyed. 'Cadet, you are now under the command of the Adepta Sororitas, and of the Order of the Bloody Rose. Eszter tells us that you know the area, and we require your assistance. She has sent a message to your barracks.'

Eszter? Where's...?

It took a long, poised moment for the memory to crystallise, but when it did, she was dropping the canteen, and all but throwing the blankets aside. Injury or no, Kamilla was looking about her, seeing the bed next to her own, the pallid and sweating face of the man that lay upon it, his chest like wax, a bandage tight round his belly.

Her heart contracted in her chest. *Arkas!*

'Oh no...' She couldn't bring herself to say it, to make the possibility real.

'The Emperor has not yet called the Father home,' Melia said gently. 'I have done what I can, and he rests.'

In her mind's eye, Kamilla saw the serrated blade, saw it stab and cut. She whispered, like horror, like penitence, 'He's the only family I've got left.' Everything else forgotten, she buried her hurting face in her hands.

Melia said, 'Be at ease, little one. He does not suffer.' Kamilla could feel the woman's dark eyes on her skin, searching for something, some information or answer. 'I must ask you questions, child. Henrik, the man with the mark–'

'He wanted Arkas to join him,' Kamilla mumbled through her hands. 'Arkas refused. He attacked us, caused a riot...' Sobs heaved in her chest. Water flowed freely down her face. Her nose hurt like fire and her cheeks felt broken. Carefully she touched her own skin, wincing at the pain and the damage both.

Arkas!

The upward cut of the blade, the priest falling, the hard slam of the boot, coming down on her like some black and falling rock...

Suddenly, she wanted to ask for a mirror, but it felt disrespectful and she did not want to seem vain. Instead, she closed one hand on the compass, still tucked inside her garments.

There was the stamp of boots, and a second armoured figure in the doorway.

'Sister Melia.'

Looking up, still wiping her nose and blinking tears, Kamilla had to stop herself scrambling out of the bed, leaping to attention as if at some surprise inspection. This Sister was older, grim-faced and grey-haired, lined with years of discipline and severity. Her scarlet armour was equally as well worn, filling the doorway with its blood-red command. She bore a pistol every bit as fearsome as Melia's flamer and a huge, chain-toothed blade.

She carried age and authority like an aura, and had a tangible sense of presence.

'You are well, cadet.' The words were not a question. 'Can you stand?'

An order like that… She was weak as a newborn, but Kamilla didn't argue. She turned sideways, put her bare feet on the cold floor. Her head spun, but Melia held her elbow and she steadied, the dizziness receding. She swallowed a mouthful of bile, pulled a face.

'Ack.'

The older Sister gave a brief, approving nod. 'You have courage. That is well. We have need of you. And swiftly.'

'But–'

The grey-haired Sister raised an eyebrow and she shut up. She blinked, hard; her eyes were puffed up and still streaming. Beside her, Arkas lay silent, his chest rising and falling. Despite the quickness of his breathing, he just looked so serene. Her breath caught on a sob. She didn't want to cry in front of this austere, grey-haired Sister; it made her feel ridiculous, like a child with a scraped knee.

But the Sister said only, 'I am Sister Superior Augusta Santorus, and you will accompany me. Arkas rests in His grace, but our battle is only just beginning. And you…' She eyed Kamilla with a careful, assessing glance. 'You will need your wits about you, child.'

Kamilla nodded, then regretted it.

'Good. I have a spare vox-bead for you, and Sword Mezei has found you a laspistol. You will stay by me at all times, and I will preserve your life. Do you understand?'

Kamilla nodded again.

The Sister Superior eyed her. 'I said–'

'Yes, Sister,' she hurriedly answered.

'Better.' Her expression advised, *remember that.* 'My shuttles are few, and their scouting spread thinly. They require guidance. And so do I.'

* * *

'This is the old Munitorum depot, Sister,' Kamilla said, over the new vox-bead. 'It's the biggest of its kind, dating far into Opal's past. People do use it as refuge, but it's not been operational for centuries.'

The building was a hulking grey mass, falling in at one end. Its grounds were weed-cracked and its wire fences long since dissolved to rust. An ancient shuttle-pad sat silent, its landing lumens caked in old dirt. Half-crouched against the nearest wall, Kamilla could feel her heart pounding, one hand curled round the laspistol. The sprawl of streets was denser here, darker and heavily industrial. They were deep in the Outskirt's badlands, tiny figures among a towering of cranes and ancient, tangled metal. Even the shrines had fallen away, and there were no more hab-blocks or cubicles. Instead, there were crumbling steelworks, filthy and clustered with ladders. There were vehicle graveyards, broken haulers, cable-cars corpsed and rotting. There were warehouses, massive and abandoned, their roofs falling in. And here and there loomed overhead bridges, stark silhouettes against the planet's ever-visible ring.

It didn't much look like a halo, out here.

'In His blessing and grace, may He guide us truly,' Sister Augusta said. Her helm was on, making her faceless and even more intimidating. Her voice came only over the vox as she said, 'We have already observed that people live in the Outskirt. Do they work in this industrial area? Or is it all ruined?'

'Mostly ruined, Sister Superior,' Kamilla said. 'After Veres' death, when the workers rebuilt the Capital and the Inner Sanctum, Opal abandoned her attempts to be self-sufficient, relying instead upon her faith – and upon her faithful – to sustain her.' She said the words hesitantly, not sure how the Sister would react. 'To bring her luxuries and foods.'

'And soon, she depended upon such imports, having little

further need for her own industry or labour,' Augusta said. 'Thus leaving it to rot.' She paused for a moment, then said, 'Very well, then. We know that the enemy will have targeted critical sites – power, water, infrastructure, armaments. Communications. We will locate and eliminate each claw, cutting critical lines as we advance, and removing any threats of sabotage. And, with His blessing and guidance, we will encounter the cult's leaders, or clues as to their whereabouts. Once they are identified, these deaths are our main priority.'

The Sister Superior's certainty seemed both pitiless and invincible. Augusta bore her bolter in both hands, still carried the massive, toothed sword at her hip. Kamilla barely reached the woman's shoulder – and felt almost like she scuttled in her shadow.

Saint and Emperor!

Her other hand touching the compass, still tucked in her shirt, she tried to dismiss both her nervousness, and the ongoing pain in her face.

Carefully, they moved towards the building. Two more of the Sisters were with Augusta, one with a prayer-carved heavy weapon that looked capable of levelling a mountain, the other with an auspex that she moved in steady arcs. Spread out from this, and accompanied by three more of the Sisters' squad, was one of the spears of Blex – one hundred members of the Blades of the Holy Exterior, deployed to an extended line and bristling with wariness and lasrifles. Their commander, Mezei, was a swarthy, dark-haired man with a long scar down one side of his face. He was older, and faintly familiar – from the combat-pits, Kamilla thought.

Above them hovered a single shuttle, stubby wings and a nose-mounted cannon. Two more shuttles, blockier and less well armed, flew wider, scouting Kamilla's recommendations to discover the other... What had Augusta called them? Claws.

A further spear of Blex walked with each of these, spread out to cover as much ground as possible.

By the Light, she thought, slightly irreverently. *Please don't let me make too many mistakes!*

Gently, their harmonies crystal-pure and eerie in the emptiness, the Sisters began to sing.

'A *spiritu dominatus...*'

It was uncanny, beautiful – filling the metal emptiness with sound. Kamilla found her anxiety steadying, taking courage from the Sisters' absolute faith, and from the presence of the Blex, the reassuring familiarity of their communications and manoeuvring. She was remembering that she'd done missions like this one – in training at least – many times. The sound of their boots was the bass-line to the Sisters' hymnal, and it was the rhythm of her whole life.

'*Domine, libra nos...*'

As if it had heard her, the auspex began to blip.

'Your area knowledge is good, cadet,' Augusta commented softly. She held up a fist and the formation stopped. The shuttle lifted, a whine of engines and a hard blowing of dirt. Kamilla didn't see where it went. The Sister Superior indicated her two Sisters, then pointed. They ran, fast and low, following the specified direction.

Smoothly, the Blex dropped into cover. Kamilla did likewise, ducking down beside an overhang of collapsing metal crates. She held her breath, felt her pulse bang in her ears, in the pain in her cheekbones. She was trying not to touch her broken teeth with her tongue – she'd already cut herself once and filled her mouth with that familiar copper tang. Above her, a murmur came from Augusta, standing like some blood-red carving.

With a shiver, Kamilla understood: she was still singing.

'*From the lightning and the tempest...*'

Her voice was contralto, thrumming now like pure courage and the cadet's heart lifted further, her anxiousness catching fire and becoming adrenaline. The pound of her pulse increased; she tightened her hand on the laspistol, reached again for the compass.

Arkas! The thought was half-prayer, though she knew that was wrong. *Please, don't die. I'll do anything...!*

'Our Emperor, deliver us...'

Intricate harmonies filled the vox. Seconds became minutes. Minutes stretched to agonising lengths. Rusting steel towers soared silent around them, all balconies and walkways. The sleet had finally stopped, and the planet's ring arced above it all, ghostlike and pale.

'From plague, temptation and war...'

Beside where Kamilla knelt, there was a great knotted tangle of cables. Caught by the ring-light, it looked like some massive crawler, a many-limbed creature, scuttling–

The hole in the clouds. The void against the darkness.

This time, the dream-recollection hit her like an electrical charge. She could see it, feel it, *taste* it. Her heart thundered at its closeness. She felt sick, spat blood and froth and copper. Heard herself say, 'It's an ambush.'

Augusta's faceless helmet turned to her, paused for a split second, then turned back. Over the vox, she barked, 'Pilot, floodlights!'

Stark streaks of white sliced down through the darkness, and the shuttle's engines snarled as it lifted, spreading them to a wider beam. Her blood racing, Kamilla wondered why the Sister had heeded her – but she had no time to think on it for long. From somewhere ahead, there came a weapons-bark – not the slash and sizzle of las-fire but something much bigger, the boom and thunder of a Sister's heavy bolter. It was accompanied by a cry of prayer – more a shout than a hymn.

The hairs on Kamilla's arms were standing on end. *The void, the hole in the stars. The charisma of the pallid man, Henrik, telling of hope for the Outskirt. That fatherly touch in her dreams.* She gripped the pistol, asked herself what on Opal she thought she was doing, out here with *real* Sisters of Battle...

Which side are you on, Kamilla? Which side of the river?

'Viola!' Augusta, in the vox. 'Do you have line of sight?'

'No, Sister.'

'Got them!' Another voice – it must be the Sister with the auspex. 'They're all around us. They... By the Throne. They must have known we were coming.'

'They will have seen the shuttles.' Augusta's words were aloud, and Kamilla could hear the battle-rage in them, hear the edge of pure tension that was the fusion of the Sisters' faith and fury. 'It matters not, they will still perish.'

Another Sister cried, 'They are behind us!' The voice sounded young, barely older than Kamilla herself. 'They are *everywhere!*'

'Full suppression! We are here in the Emperor's name. We tolerate no xenos, we tolerate no rebellion!'

'Our Emperor, deliver us!' Another bolter barked and thundered.

'Caia, give me a description.' Augusta's tone was firm. 'We must know what we are dealing with. Pilot, do you have locations?'

'Beyond any final doubts, Sister,' Caia responded, her tone grim. 'There are hundreds of them. We have found their first claw.'

'From the scourge of the Kraken...!'

The Sister Superior's hymnal was a roar.

The air filled with dust and rust and noise, and Kamilla was still crouched in cover. She couldn't see their attackers, not yet. The floodlights of the shuttle slashed backwards and forwards, making streaks from the smoke and sending shadows scudding swiftly across the ground. In the passing glare, Kamilla saw the

Sister with the heavy weapon run and then kneel. With perfect smoothness, she tucked the massive thing against her shoulder and opened fire.

Bullet casings flew. Stone and metal shattered under the onslaught.

Beside her, the Sister with the auspex was shooting one-handed, half her attention still watching the instrument's screen.

Then the floodlight was gone again, and everything was darkness. Muzzles and las flashed, shuttle engines whined. Clouds of muck billowed. A moment later, there was the colossal boom of a cannon and the squeal of falling steel.

Crouching as small as she could manage, Kamilla struggled to work out what was happening. This was not like training, clean and smooth, with known ground and good lines of sight and clear and perfect orders, this was *mayhem* – or it seemed that way. Hard barks of bolter fire came from round her; there was the cough and whoosh of the flamer, the scarlet slash of the Blex's lasrifles. And there were other noises – stubbers and handguns, screams and shouts, and the clanking of heavy chains. With her tiny laspistol, she could do nothing, but she had no time to think about it. Sister Augusta was moving; commands came over the vox. Kamilla scrabbled upright and followed her.

Engines roared close, and the floodlight passed them again, dazzling. Metal creaked and spanged. From somewhere, there was a howl as someone fell from an unseen height, then a horrific, screeching tear as one of the towers came down. It hit with a terrific crump, then the tinny, echoing impacts of multiple smaller pieces.

Dust billowed, choking, and the floodlight was gone.

Stopping herself swearing, Kamilla blinked her still-swollen eyes. She was struggling to make sense of it all.

But Augusta bellowed, 'With me!' and the young woman ran as if pulled. She knew the theory, knew the commands and hand-signals, knew what she was supposed to do, but how could you fight if you could not see? Her gaze was full of smoke and grit and she was coughing; her whole face still hurt. Still had no real idea where these 'cultists' even were.

And Augusta was running, her boots bang-banging with enough force to shake the ground. Caia was still following her auspex, the glimmer of green that led them on through the maze. Viola, the Sister with the heavy bolter, was still shooting, roaring prayers like defiance. The huge weapon bellowed like some loosed and holy beast.

'Our Emperor, deliver us!'

They ran, stopped, ducked, ran again. Kamilla's lungs burned, her face pounded. She'd bitten her tongue again and there was more blood in her mouth. Coughing harder, she spat scarlet.

Caia shouted, and Augusta barked in the vox, 'Mezei, to your left! Forty-five degrees! Kill every last one you see!'

'Sister!' Shouts came back through the murk. There were cries, yells, screams. More shrieking, the appalling, ground-shaking smash of a tower going over. One throat-ripping yowl that didn't even sound human. A lot of harsh, military swearing.

Kamilla could do nothing but run, keep her head down and pray, one hand on her compass. Dust-specks stung. She blinked, rubbed her eyes. Regretted it.

Somewhere ahead of her, a Sister stopped, a red blur. Viola. The heavy bolter was still in her hands, and she stood utterly fearless, as if she could deny this entire infestation – whatever it even was – passage through the streets if she so chose.

She was still shouting, words of prayers and rage; the other Sisters echoed her, Augusta between barks of orders.

Behind them, a voice cried out, a prayer like a shriek, a noise of pain and absolute fury, and then went silent.

'Akemi!' Augusta's cry was edged, livid with horror. 'Akemi!'

Another Sister said, her tone bleak, 'Sister Akemi is fallen.'

Kamilla felt, rather than saw, the terrible shudder that went through Augusta's frame. The cadet half-expected some howl, some enraged loss of control, but the Sister Superior said, with snarling, ice-cold venom in every word, 'Sister Akemi stands at the Throne, her life given in honour, and we will *not* disgrace her memory, or her martyrdom, by failing in this mission. We *will* attain the objective. Mezei, advance by sections, lay down covering fire. When you are in position, give the word. Sisters, you will await my command. We will enact our vengeance for Akemi's death. *From the blasphemy of the Fallen!*'

At the head of the formation, Viola bellowed, echoing the prayer. Her bolter thundered; it blew rust and shards from the metallic tangles ahead. Another tower bent under the onslaught and came down; there were whoops and cheers from the surrounding soldiers. And then...

And then, the floodlight passed them again – and Kamilla saw the enemy.

And stopped.

She wasn't sure what she had been expecting. From the Sisters' use of the word 'xenos', monsters, perhaps. Beasts of legend with fangs and claws and glowing red eyes. Gargoyles, like the ones on the buildings. This figure had none of those features. She was in her twenties, wore the standard, scruffy-drab clothing of the Outskirt, and carried an old stubber in one hand. She was blonde, dirty, her teeth rotted, but no more than any other Outskirt denizen. And Kamilla was sure that she'd seen the woman before. Maybe at Arkas'?

Then her face was gone, exploding in a shower of gore.

Shaking, the cadet swallowed. Hard. Tried to ignore the quiver in her knees, the cloud vortex that was now, apparently, turning in her belly. That had not been a monster! That had been...

'Third or fourth generation.' Augusta's tone was brutal, like some pitiless icon of death. 'He is with us, His wisdom has guided us truly. We will avenge our Sister. And you,' she said to Kamilla. 'You will tell me how you knew of this ambush.'

The cadet was still reeling, still trying to encompass what she had seen, the suddenness, the sheer *viciousness*, of the woman's execution. Again, she swallowed blood and bile. Her stomach roiled.

'I...'

Saint Veres comes!

Viola's heavy bolter clattered empty. She uttered a shocking curse-word and reached for another belt, feeding it into the weapon. Caia had come forward and was covering her, shooting into the mass of rust and filth beyond. Lasrifles still sang from the flanks, to be met by an eerie sing-song howling, a sound of threat and menace. The shuttle's floodlight was there and gone again, replaced by the whine of engines and a harsh downdraught of dirt.

Kamilla struggled, still blinking. Death and music surrounded her, and the vortex turned in her head. The Sisters seemed so brutal, so overwhelming and terrifying. Creatures of scarlet murder...

Saint Veres comes!

She couldn't focus. The dreams filled her with hope and light and love. Through their blur, there were more figures, and more. And more. And they were as human as the woman had been, old ones and young, just the normal people of the Outskirt with little armour, fewer weapons. They looked like the people that Arkas helped, the hungry and the hopeless, the lost and the unwell.

Struggling to comprehend, Kamilla wanted to ask, 'This – *this* – is your xenos cult?' but she had no idea how to frame the question. Augusta was more than human – or less. Merciless and terrible. An executioner.

Over the vox, Melia said, 'We are fully surrounded.'

For a heartbeat that lasted forever, Sister Augusta did nothing, seemed poised on the edge of some decision, some precipice. Had she made a mistake? Kamilla wondered. Would she spare these people after all? But her shoulders were both broad and armoured and she stood to her full height, the muzzle of the bolter not moving.

Over the vox, she said, 'Mezei, are you in position?'

'Yes, Sister.'

'We will advance on the Munitorum depot, move through the objective, and reform on the far side. Spare nothing and no one, every one of these people is xenos-tainted and must die. On my mark and on the double. And *move!*'

Following the Sister's cloaked and armoured back, Kamilla ran, her mind clamouring.

She ran helter-skelter, headlong but ducking and weaving as best she could. Bolters boomed and roared, lasrifles crackled and spat. Slashes of scarlet sang through the rising dirt. The cannon boomed again, and there was the rumbling topple of ferrocrete. The cadet was dimly aware of the Blex, their line now with Augusta at its centre, their Opal-grey camo showing up as if they were ghosts themselves. They shouted as they ran and she shouted with them, mustering her courage with the force of the yell.

At the head of the full-on charge, the Sister Superior ran like a stampeding grox, her boots as loud as drums. Bolters and voices sang. Bodies shredded and tore, tumbled, exploded. The stench was incredible – hot and sick and coppery, like the taste that still lingered on her tongue.

Ahead of them was the Munitorum depot's main building, its hangar bay doors rusted open.

'From the begetting of daemons!'

'There!' Augusta's roar was loud.

Through streaming, swollen eyes, Kamilla could make out the factorum's inside – metal shelves, lathes and wheels, trucks and conveyers, its floor all stained with oil. Ring-light tumbled through a broken roof, enough to make out...

Saint and Emperor!

Those shelves weren't empty. They weren't full, but still, they carried stock. Everything from small-round ammo boxes to rows of waiting shells. That and the bright, clean glint of machinery in recent use. And there, at the very rear, stood a single figure. He was tall, lean, clad in the full, pale camo of the Blex. He had taken control of the central diagnostic screen, and was flicking the switches and dials. Seeing them, he laughed and the throng laughed with it, one sound, one mind.

'You are foolish, refusing the saint's glory. You are also too late.'

'The Emperor is with us,' Augusta returned, her voice still cold with rage. 'You will not succeed.'

'Against six – five – of you? And your grunts? I don't think so. Saint Veres comes, and he brings exoneration to the people of the Outskirt! He brings not only food and water and medicines, but new *life!* New *existence!* He will save us from Opal's cruelty. And from yours!'

'Saint Veres will eat you for breakfast and wear your entrails as a hat,' Augusta said. 'Your blindness will be your ending. The ending of your *world.*'

'And your arrogance will be yours.' The figure tapped the screen, still laughing.

Sister Caia suddenly shouted, 'Clear the building. Get *out!*'

And Kamilla saw only red ceramite as what remained of the roof came down.

X

THE INFESTATION

'The orders were mine,' Augusta said, her voice grim. 'I take full responsibility for Sister Akemi's injury.'

On the hospice bed, the youngest Sister's eyes were closed and her resting body was hooked to an emergency drip-feed, set up by Sister Melia. Akemi's ribs were badly broken, but He had not yet called her to the Throne – her armour had been dented but not split, and her organs were not damaged. The youngest Sister's battles, it seemed, were not over.

Yet still, Augusta heard that final cry in her ears, and in her heart. Heard it like some chapel bell, tolling accusation…

Dying, dying, your Sister lies dying…

Seated at the bed's other side, Sister Alcina said, 'Sister Akemi yet lives. And we have removed their ammunition supply. This is well done.'

'But we have not yet encountered their leaders, and we have lost – *I* have lost – one of our Sisters. We have so little time, and such attrition, such poor judgement, is not acceptable.'

The image of the depot collapsing into a pile of ferrocrete was haunting her, and she found no words adequate. She ended on a silent prayer.

Guard her, O my Emperor. Guard my choices and my commands. I cannot continue to make such errors.

Vergers rustled past the open door, but kept their faces lowered. Alcina sat with her heavy shoulders rounded, also praying for the life of the youngest Sister. She had carried Akemi, armour and all, away from the battle site – a feat of both strength and determination.

'Akemi is Adepta Sororitas,' Alcina said, sitting up to look Augusta in the face. 'Trained and strong, and fighting in His name. Her life, and her death, rest with Him, Sister Superior, not with you.' Akemi's jury-rigged diagnostic beeped to the rhythm of her heart. 'We have no space or time for doubt.'

Augusta removed a gauntlet, and laid her hand on Akemi's forehead, the gesture like a blessing. The memory of the training-battle in the belly of the *Star* floated in the back of her mind – Akemi left alone, the Sisters split up, outflanked by the Naval soldiers. Now, it felt ominously like a warning – a warning that she had failed to heed.

'Our return to Lautis was her first mission,' Augusta said. 'Facing the horrors of the daemons in its depths.' She remembered, very clearly, Akemi and her little silver fetish, the feather that represented her novice training with the Order of the Quill. 'She is still so very young.'

Seated between the beds, Alcina replied, with the faintest hint of rebuke, 'She lives, Sister. And she is strong. We have achieved much. We have information. We have scouts and shuttles and local knowledge, and the cadet has identified more likely sites for cultist nests – the hauler stations, the construction yards. She has told us of the old vox-towers, and where they may be located. Our Blex are deployed throughout the Outskirt, with Caia and Viola to accompany.' Sister Melia had returned with Augusta, to treat the fallen Akemi. 'Caia's scans will locate the clusters, and Viola–'

'Will wreak His bloody vengeance upon them,' Augusta finished, with a twitch of a smile. 'The encounter at the Munitorum depot has taught us that the cultists will be armed with only basic weapons – what military hardware they could steal or manufacture, mining tools, simple vehicles.'

'Opal has few mining tools, Sister,' Alcina said. 'And any that still remain will be in a state of disrepair. Sister Viola will eliminate anything she encounters with a volley of both faith and fury.'

'Agreed. She is… fearsome.'

'She…' Alcina stopped herself, frowned.

But Augusta knew, had heard the warning in her second's tone. The warning that was Viola's temper, and her unpredictability. It tangled with Augusta's concern for Akemi, with her failure to protect the youngest Sister, with everything they had still to achieve. Yet they were Sisters of Battle, icons of combat, fighting in His wars. They were supposed to be above reproach. *She* was supposed to be above reproach.

With your grace, I shall banish doubt…

With your grace, I shall banish weakness…

She focused on her prayers – for her Sisters, for Arkas, still lying in another bed. For what was to come, and for Opal's future. It was imperative that she locate every last nest, the lairs of the cult's leaders, the patriarch, the magus… with one of their number already fallen.

By the Throne!

Again, images of that collapsing Munitorum building threatened to overwhelm her – now a nightmare heap of corpses that would bury them, herself and her squad, cover them without a trace, without hope...

With your grace, I shall defy both fear and shame...

No, to despair was blasphemy. Faith permitted her death, provided she strove with honour, and gave her best. To die for her duty, what could be holier? This fear was entirely her own – in her more than twenty years of service, she had never felt such a thing. And it was *sacrilege*.

With your grace, I shall know both defiance and rage!

Something in her movement must have given her thoughts away, because Alcina glanced across the bed at her, her gaze measuring. With no preamble, she said, 'Why am I here, Sister Superior? You said you wished to speak about Akemi, yet there is a burden upon your thoughts. I feel it as I would feel my own. And we are Sisters, are we not?'

Augusta paused. Had her second been Jatoya, she would have trusted the woman without question, but Alcina was a more recent addition, placed in the squad by the canoness after their encounter with Istrix, the corrupted inquisitor, upon the heretek world of Lycheate. Alcina, Augusta knew, had had orders to observe the squad. And Augusta did not know if those orders yet continued.

But still, she had to trust someone, and to doubt her own second was as much blasphemy as succumbing to this terrible sense of futility.

'Sister–'

Akemi's biosign monitor pulsed, and both Sisters jumped, looking down at their injured comrade. Under her eyelids, her eyes were flickering, back and forth.

'She dreams,' Alcina commented.

A shock of cold went up Augusta's back – it felt like warning, a perfectly timed message from the God-Emperor Himself: *you must not fail.* Her hand still on Akemi's forehead, she prayed for her sleeping soul. After moment, the youngest Sister muttered and settled.

Taking a steadying breath, Augusta chose to admit her weakness. 'I seek counsel, Sister Alcina.'

Alcina blinked. 'He is ever your guide and solace, Sister Superior.'

'He is ever my guide and solace,' Augusta agreed. 'But this… this is like nothing I have ever encountered. Sister Akemi lies injured, and we know not if she will recover. The Order comes, but we know not when. The enemy multiplies, but we know not where. We have spoken of Viola's temper. Opal's Outskirt may be overflowing with the faithless. With xenos in their millions. And her soldiers…'

Alcina twitched big shoulders, a stolid, military shrug. 'Sister Superior, as I have said, we have no time or space for doubt. This is a battle like any other, and you conduct yourself with honour, fighting until you cannot. I believe that your decisions have been good ones – Opal's forces are mobilising, the Blades of the Holy Exterior stand full guard upon the bridges, and Sword Mezei moves in good formation, taking with him our strongest, and our most observant. The Order is on its way, and will bring force enough to eliminate the xenos threat. And if we do fail,' Alcina said, her tone steely, 'then Opal will feel His final wrath, that of Exterminatus. Faith bears no qualms, Sister Superior. It is absolute.' Alcina studied her, her face an admonition. 'You have said this yourself, have you not?'

'It is not my faith I doubt,' Augusta said, looking down at the youngest Sister's silent form. 'For the first time in my life, I find I doubt my decisions.' The admission was painful, almost as if speaking it aloud gave it life. 'Akemi is fallen, and I doubt my commands, my leadership.'

'Do not,' Alcina told her shortly. 'Opal cannot afford your

doubts. If you bear the fate of this world upon your shoulders, Sister Superior, then you stand tall and you carry it proudly, in His name. And pray, like the lives of a billion pilgrims are dependent upon your strength.'

'E morte perpetua!'

Heavy bolter at her shoulder, its muzzle flaring in continuous fire, Sister Viola thundered the words of the litany. In the shadowed desolation of the old construction yard, the noise was incredible, and flying shell casings jingled and sang. Over her, colossal, towering cranes creaked in metallic harmony; a thousand ferrocrete corners hid threats without number. Under the hammering onslaught of the thrice-blessed heavy bolter, girders groaned and dust and stone-chips flew.

The yard was the fourth location they'd stormed, and the second with an enemy presence. The raid on the munitions factorum had ended with heavy casualties and many soldiers unaccounted for – but the job had been done, the threat eliminated. The old generator, however, had been deserted. The Sisters had seen rows of forgotten capacitors, rusted to barely skeletons, and a startled local vagrant who'd promised to give up the lho and find Him. And that had been all.

But Caia's instincts were telling her that if the cultists were massing anywhere, then it was going to be here, at the construction yard. If they truly intended to storm the bridges, then they would need vehicles as well as ammunition.

The wind was cold, still billowing sleet. To one side of her, a pile of containers was rusted through at one corner, listing precariously. To the other, tangles of warehouses and admin blocks were half-tumbledown, their fence-wire rusting, thick weeds growing from their walls. Their windows were empty and broken, and the threat of snipers lurked behind every one.

'Let's keep this steady.' Mezei was relentless, sharp-eyed and fierce. His Opal-pale camo was grubby with use, something that the Sisters found faintly reassuring.

He gestured, and the line moved forwards, the Sisters at its centre. Viola's bolter muzzle tracked back and forth; the auspex in Caia's hand showed occasional tiny blips, but no more.

Under her breath, she muttered, 'Come out, you faithless bastards, and face the Emperor's wrath.'

Viola muttered a curse. 'Where *are* they? Why are they not here?'

The yard's expanse was silent. The place seemed unfeasibly vast, its floor stained by ancient oil, its roof broken and leaking. Crew pits gaped like maws; tumbles of stonework lay piled in haphazard heaps. Loops of barbed wire snagged shreds of blown fabrics: the tattered remnants of the Capital's prayer-flags, blown across the river. A pile of half-constructed dirtcycles lay rusting, tangled and dead. Above them, a vast winch stood watch, the sky behind it now puce with the rising sun.

The whole place felt like it was waiting. Unbothered by her lack of sleep, Caia could feel its jaws about her, eager and hungry. *Guide me, my Emperor.*

'Anything?' Viola said. There was an itch in her voice, an itch like an impatient trigger-finger.

'Conserve your ammunition, Sister,' Caia said. 'You– *There!*'

A fleeting blip, a scurry of shadow.

Both Sisters reacted without thinking – a single shot from Caia's bolter, a neat, five-round burst from Viola. Mezei barked, 'Move!' and the Blex broke for cover. They moved swiftly and well, diving behind the piles of stone, reappearing with their rifle muzzles ready.

In a moment, the two Sisters stood alone, instinctively back to back, both scanning the cold, sleet-filled murk of the empty ferrocrete floor.

Nothing.

And then: a second blip, a third. A fourth. Viola shifted the heavy bolter, watching. Her armour squeaked as she flexed on her toes; Caia could hear her agitation. But the blips weren't coming closer, they seemed to be flitting, dancing, circling just outside the Sisters' lines of sight.

Rats? Scavengers?

No, there it was again – a running shadow, crossing right at the limits of their vision. Once more, they both reacted instinctively, muzzle flashes bright in the pre-dawn gloom, but the flicker was already gone.

'They think to play games?' Viola growled, half-incredulous.

'We must teach them their folly,' Caia said. 'Mezei!'

With a gesture at the Blex to follow, she and Viola advanced once more. Slowly, weapons ready, shoulders twitching all the way, they crossed the open expanse of the yard. Beyond, they would cross into the tangles of warehouses proper, many collapsed, many still full of debris.

'Walk with us, O Emperor. Bring us your rage, your light, your truth.'

Caia prayed aloud, her voice across the vox. Viola echoed her, stanza by stanza. Behind them, the coarser voices of the Blex joined her, though they did not know all the words. The Sisters did not stop them.

'Your rage, your light, your truth.'

They reached the far side safely. Here, the walls closed in, sifting the formation to a double file, the Sisters at its head. Broken doorways were covered by sheets of corrugated steel, sagging at their corners, rusting into holes. There were no lumens, not out here, and the early light gave everything a fiery, orange glow. Caia flicked her preysight; saw the tiny scurries of rodents.

'Domine, libra nos.'

The litany came from Viola in words of tight impatience.

Still they moved on. Still the blips circled, but didn't come close. Soon, the walls started to show marks – graffiti, daubings, crude stylisations. Here, the mark of a familiar spiral. There, images that may have been Veres himself, and the Three Martyrs. Pictures of *stars*.

Like the prayer-marked walls of the Capital itself, the cultists celebrated their gods–

No, not gods. Caia caught the thought and squashed it, a prayer of penitence upon her lips. There are no gods, only the Emperor, He who walks at our backs.

Your rage, your light…

Auspex still scanning, they moved on.

And they walked right into the ambush.

It reminded Caia oddly of Lycheate, of the Sisters' first encounter with the tainted Mechanicus world. But these were not machines; they were people, dirty and poorly armed, yet savage with heretic zeal.

A voice blared over unseen voxmitters. 'For the saint! For Opal and her future!'

Viola reacted instantly, the thrice-blessed heavy bolter bawling its song of death. Caia's own bolter took one, two. A cultist with a lasrifle fired back. The hit caught Viola in the shoulder, but the sizzle hissed only to steam, leaving a hole in her robe and a round, black mark on her pauldron. She swore, with some creativity. The voxmitter was still shouting, zeal and rhetoric.

Mezei was shouting orders. *'I'll take the left flank. Lilla, break right. And go!'* Scattering, the Blex angled down side roads, running to get behind the attackers.

'Straight ahead,' Caia said to Viola. 'But be vigilant. We do not yet know their numbers.'

Ahead of them, the narrow roadway opened out to a tight, dark square. Prayers of industry and diligence were carved within its stonework, and it had a fountain, a circle of open-mouthed gargoyles long since choked with dust.

Snorting, Viola walked out into the centre of the space.

'*...wouldst bring them only death!*'

The rocket took her straight in the chest, denting her armour and sending her backwards. With a curse to make a hardened soldier blush, she hit the wall like an industrial wrecker, sliding to the floor and struggling to keep her grip on the bolter. Dust hissed and trickled. Running out, bellowing prayers, Caia saw a makeshift defence, a pile of rubble and wire. A skull, its open jaw showing the speaker within. A crack and sizzle missed her as she rolled to one side.

'Praise Saint Veres! We will ascend!'

The skull blasted words, goading. Behind the barrier, someone was bellowing frantically, telling Erik to reload, to reload *now*, but Erik, it seemed, wasn't fast enough. Regaining her feet, roaring the battle-hymn, Viola ran forwards, still firing, battering the barrier with rounds. Caia moved with her, taking snap-shots as she ran.

Weapons boomed and thundered; the whole square echoed with the noise.

'For the Emperor!'

With a shout, Viola jumped straight on the top of the barrier, smashing the skull as she landed. Hands clawed and people tried to jump at her, but she kicked them away, shooting them straight in the face. Leaping into their midst, she cracked the butt of the heavy bolter into the face of the rocket-launcher user, sending him over, his neck broken. The rest of them, a ramshackle group with no leader that the Sisters could see, threw themselves forwards with an assortment of small-arms and blades.

Unable to fire – they were too close, now – Viola used her feet and elbows, screamed prayers at the biggest ones, knew no hesitation, no fear.

'That thou shouldst spare none!' The litany came from her in pure, furious fervour. Behind her, Caia was calmer, more focused, but equally deadly.

The attackers were many, but they were not enough. And it was all over far too fast.

Bodies lay cooling, steaming; the floor was red and slick, dust congealing to sludge. Voices moaned for help, for hope, for blessing. Single shots silenced them for good.

'Mezei,' Caia said. 'Report!'

'We have secured the rear,' Mezei said. *'The defenders' barrier has come down and we are incoming. Hold your fire.'* There was a thrill to his tone, almost as if he was finally realising Opal's ancient dream – truly fighting for his world.

Viola chuckled, rapping her knuckles on the dent in her armour. 'If this is the best the cult can do,' she said, her grin audible, 'then we will tear down every last one of them.'

'Let us hope so,' Caia said. 'In His name.'

The rest of the yard was deserted. No cultists, no resistance, no leaders or monsters. No demolitions or charges. The dawn wind blew cold and the great cranes creaked, echoing and eerie. Looking round her, Caia had a rising feeling of unease. There was graffiti, more of the leering, voxmitter skulls, but the cell was no longer there.

Viola said, 'Nothing.'

There was a note of disappointment to her that almost made Caia smile – but this was far too serious. Sleet touched her visor and hackles chilled down her back.

Carefully, they continued to walk the site.

Where had they gone? What were the Sisters missing?

Behind them, the Blex moved cautiously, rifles in hands.

'This isn't over,' Mezei said. *'Keep 'em peeled, people.'* He had a magnocular, was scanning as he walked. *'I see nothing, Sisters.'*

The tension in Viola's form was palpable. Prayers jagged in the vox, all words of frustration. Caia moved her auspex, searching.

There – a single figure, hunched on a corner, asleep or dead. Another, a little further away; another, rocking and muttering to herself. Could they be spies, already infected? Or were they just local denizens, going about their–

By the Throne!

In a flash somewhere between realisation and sudden white-cold fear, she understood. Understood as if He Himself had told her...

You are too late.

'We are in error.' She spoke like horror, like penitence. 'They may have been here once – but they have gone.'

Both Viola and Mezei turned to stare at her.

'The cultists *have* been hiding here – look at the markings – they have probably been hiding here for years. But they are not here now...'

She tailed off. Viola's helm was turned towards her, and Caia could imagine her Sister's expression. She didn't need to say anything, and the vox was silent, crackling as if assimilating the new knowledge.

'The Munitorum depot...' Caia was thinking aloud, now, her words spilling from her like understanding, like His voice in the chill and the dark. 'They had been using it, certainly, but its work was done. Whatever they were doing, it is complete.'

'Then they must surely be gathering,' Viola said. 'Readying for their "ascension"–'

'Or for combat.' Caia's tone was grim.

The two Sisters were staring at each other, helms faceless but their gazes intense. Caia's skin was prickling with absolute horror, and her robe-hem fluttered in the cold wind. Mezei was looking from one red figure to the other, catching up, but his expression was still puzzled. He looked like he wanted to ask them what was going on, but couldn't quite bring himself to speak.

But Caia was still thinking, pulling threads from theories, trying to see the whole picture. Sister Viola and the Sister Superior had interrupted Henrik at Arkas' sanctuary – whatever riot or assault or operation he had been starting, they had prevented it.

Voicing her thoughts aloud, she said, 'But why would they place defences at the sites they were no longer using?'

'To keep us busy,' Viola growled. 'While they form up somewhere else.'

'Dominica's *eyes!*' Opening a vox-channel, Caia said, 'Sister Superior.'

'*Sister Caia.*' Augusta's voice. '*What is your situation?*'

'These sites are clear, Sister. The construction yards had a token resistance, but that was all.' She paused. 'We believe that the cultists have moved. Perhaps they anticipate the fleet's arrival, or perhaps they move to a muster – perhaps both.'

There was a long pause, the background sound of a quiet, regular beeping. In her heart, Caia whispered a prayer for the fallen Akemi, and for Melia who tended her.

Viola said, 'There are still objectives to check, and our shuttles are still scouting, taking with them the other two spears of Blex. The enemy must have gone somewhere.'

'*We must find them,*' Augusta said. '*If they move to muster, then we are running out of time. Tell Mezei, his troops are to run full reconnaissance, taking every location we have identified, grid reference by grid reference. For every one secured, he will leave a vox-operator*' *in a stealth position. You and Viola will return here.'* There was a note to her voice that Caia had never heard before: a thrum of strain, of trepidation.

Of fear.

The Sister Superior had faced a greater daemon and prevailed. Whatever this was... But Caia's heart knew – it already *knew* – that Augusta had reached the same conclusion. The Sisters had failed; they were chasing shadows.

Somehow, the main force of cultists had already crossed the river.

THE OUTBREAK

They hit the Capital at dawn.

The Day of the Second Martyr, Martyr Nemes, was commencing, and the festival was already busy. There was a throng of early risers, singing and praying, offering penitence and flagellation, and attending the sunrise services. There was a scatter of drunken carousers left over from the previous night. The corner pastors were up and out, preaching Opal's vox-cast rhetoric; the stallholders were starting to trade. But whoever they were, whichever saint or path they followed or role they fulfilled, it did not matter. They died in a ringing of screams.

The attacks were swift, lethal. Clamouring figures, bearing banners and howling Veres' name, boiled from sewer openings, or launched assaults from lingering shadows. Every attack was brutal, cruel – and then gone, leaving mess and horror in its wake. The festival's vox-cast prayers and bells were silenced; they all crackled to a hissing emptiness, then were replaced by a powerful broadcast, praising the name of the saint and exhorting his followers to violence.

'Saint Veres comes!'

For the first time in five millennia, the streets of Holy Opal were bathed in heresy, and in her pilgrims' blood.

But the deaths were only the beginning. As the assailants withdrew, disappearing as swiftly as they had come, the broadcast fell from the air, leaving a ghost of laughter behind it. Panicked, the people rounded upon one another, hurling abuse and blame and accusations of sacrilege. Still recoiling in shock, some tore at their clothes, punishing themselves or smothering their skin in the still-warm blood of the slain. Others swore wrath and retribution, and turned upon their apparently sinful fellows.

Already present tensions exploded into full-on viciousness, and the Blades of the Holy Interior were swiftly out of their depth. Overwhelmed by the pilgrims' numbers and ferocity, they struggled to keep order.

All over the Capital, people sobbed and wailed, telling tales of horror and rebellion and mourning their friends and families. In some places, Opal's faithful, fuelled by the world's history and by the spirits of its long-dead saints, formed angry gangs and chased down the tunnels after the attackers. None of them came back.

Dread and terror and rumour and panic all detonated, rippling outwards through the streets.

And the day had only just begun.

By the Light!

At the Blades' command centre, Sister Augusta gleamed in furious scarlet. As the first attacks had struck, she and three of her squad had leapt into the shuttle and headed back over the Varadi. Bathed in sunrise, they had prayed for Opal, trying to assimilate the sheer level of death and destruction.

And what it meant.

'My city reels, Sister Superior,' Commander Kozma said. Her camo jacket was pressed and perfect, her flak as white as the planet's ring-light. 'Opal's pride and history stand disgraced and smeared in blood.' Her breath steamed in the early chill. 'You were supposed to keep the threat in the Outskirt.'

'I failed,' Augusta said. The words were raw, like a stain on her soul. Still, she stood tall, made no plea for understanding or circumstance, and Kozma offered no word of support or empathy. If the Saints' Cathedral was this world's heart and faith, Augusta thought, and the governor's palace its leadership, then this squat, no-nonsense building was surely its courage. And it still believed – completely – in the light of Opal's righteousness.

'And now, the festival is in ruins,' Kozma said. 'We have tens of thousands dead.'

Augusta controlled a flare of ire. She was angry – angry with herself for her mistake, angry for not forcing the governor to listen to her, angry for feeling overwhelmed, for her inability to protect Akemi or the Outskirt or Opal herself. Angry with the commander's mouthing of the obvious.

'May I remind you,' she snapped back, 'your bridges were supposed to be guarded.'

'They are,' Kozma said. She held the Sister Superior's gaze, just long enough. 'The assault did not come across the water.'

Augusta blinked.

'It came from beneath.' Turning, the commander indicated the huge hololith map of the Capital now projected upon one long, whitewashed wall. It was a somewhat ragged isosceles triangle, underlined by the Varadi at its base and peaking at the apex of the Saints' Cathedral. Three main roads started at the Wall of Glory and the three gates of the Inner Sanctum, ran down through the Capital itself, then branched out further as they passed the Wall of Diligence, about two-thirds of the way down. Elaborate networks of dotted lines were the cable-car routes and stations. And everywhere, a multitude of blips flared, marking the locations of the attacks.

'Long ago, before even the time of Saint Veres,' Kozma said, 'the Varadi was known to burst its banks, swollen with spring rains.' She indicated the long, slow loop of the river, the two lines of its bridges. 'Beneath it, there are ancient flood defences, though these were sealed when the workers rebuilt the Capital. The Capital's ground is higher, sloping up towards the Sanctum, and it had no further need of such things.'

And you did not care if the Outskirt flooded. Augusta did not voice the thought aloud. Instead, she studied the map, the marks indicated by Kozma's blunt, trigger-callused finger.

'The cult are long established,' Augusta said. 'They will certainly have had time to remove the blockages. These large spaces.' She indicated marks at the riverside. 'They are ideal grounds for proliferation. Why was I not informed of these?'

'They were blocked,' Kozma repeated. 'Other than a single maintenance tunnel, suitable only for servitors.'

'You are the military commander of your world.' Augusta clenched one fist, holding down her explosion – rage aimed as much at herself as at Kozma. 'I may have erred, but your lack of oversight is also to blame. You will *tell* me of these attacks. Of the failure of your communications. If the cult is rising – and rising *now!* – then we will muster everything we have.'

A bellow of orders came from outside. The command centre was at the outside of the Inner Sanctum, its grounds wide enough for a central barracks, an armoury and training areas. Someone out there was already delivering a briefing.

'The assaults on the Capital were very carefully placed,' the commander replied. 'They struck at our most populous areas.' She indicated several of the blips. 'The death toll is already in the tens of thousands, and the hospices do not have enough beds. My people quail in terror. Sister, the festival–'

'The festival is over,' Augusta told her. 'Get the people off the streets, or you will have rioting. I have sent a message to my ship. The *Star* will monitor astropathic communications, and will tell me if they fail. If the cult are indeed at muster, then the hive fleet must surely be incoming.'

'Xenos!' Kozma's comment was almost disparaging and her expression was lit with a new, bright eagerness. 'Surely, we have been blessed, Sister! We will fight and die as befits this, our most holy world, our saints and martyrs! We have nothing to fear from these creatures.'

Augusta's jaw muscles jumped. Kozma was the very manifestation of her world's lack of combat experience, its empty pipes and drums. And yet, on another level, she completely understood the commander's ardour and wanted nothing more than to reflect it. To throw herself forwards into martyrdom, to banish her own doubts with a blaze of combat action. Her faith, her fire, her fury, demanded no less.

But she could not. She had to think.

From the desire to be extolled, O Emperor, deliver me.

Somewhere, hymns were ringing, harmonies on the wind. They seemed far away, from up here. Frail, somehow, desperate and backed by the after-echoes of screams. Out there, the servitors were even now washing the blood from the stone. The preachers were offering consolation and confession, the injured were being taken to the hospices – or their lives ended, in His mercy.

I would rather face a thousand orks...

The memory came with a feeling of sudden, very personal guilt, almost as if she had wished this foe into being, after all.

You know, our Emperor, the secrets of our hearts!

'...will assay a pre-emptive strike.' Kozma had turned back to the map and was already laying plans, sweeping her hand across the shining lines. 'I have never faced such a challenge as this, Sister, and I will honour Saint Veres, the God-Emperor and Opal herself! I will engage my streetrunners, my scouts. They can locate these cultist nests – these "claws", as you call them – find them in the sewers. And a full force of my trained Blades can surely eliminate them.' She spoke with assurance, no doubts in her tone. 'We shall celebrate Opal's splendour with each and every one we destroy, and then offer our thanks at the festival's height.'

Augusta drew in a long breath, let it out again. Carefully, she said, 'Commander, the festival is destroyed. Thousands have already died. And as the hive fleet approaches, the dread and terror among the people – your Blades included – will be like nothing you have ever seen. Your primary objectives are to secure your starports, your infrastructure and your communications arrays, and to prepare the Capital for a full evacuation.'

'Evacuation!' Again, Kozma turned, this time almost gaping. 'You, Adepta Sororitas? Augusta Santorus *herself*, quailing from a fight? I confess I am surprised. And more than a little disappointed.'

'I do not quail from the *fight*.'

The words were a snarl. This was her own question, her own doubt, come back to shadow her – was she enough to face this? Could she lead her Sisters to victory, when she had failed Akemi? Left Melia alone in the Outskirt? Surely, their task was to simply throw themselves forwards to their deaths... But this was too complex, there was too much at stake. Opal depended upon them, upon her.

'We cannot attack unplanned – to do so would be madness. We would perish with the task unfinished, leaving your people aban-doned, and your world unguarded as the hive fleet descends. And is such a death truly honourable, if it just leaves Opal defence-less? Permits the cultists to rage loose in the streets, the xenos' acids to melt and digest both them and us? We will not only die, commander, we will *fail*. We will perish, laden with sin. And we will never attain the Throne.'

Almost offended, the commander said, 'My force numbers more than fifty thousand, fully trained Blades–'

'And how many locations must they defend? How many sewers must they traverse? How many nests must they locate?' With an effort, the Sister Superior kept her tone flat, and gestured at the map. 'It is not only your starports and infrastructure, but also your central reactor, your cable-car stations, your water, your power... All of these things are under the threat of cultist sab-otage, and they must be secured. And your Blades are already stretched, just keeping order in the streets.'

With a harrumph, Kozma told her, 'My Blades are very highly trained. They are more than a match–'

'*Commander.*' Augusta cut across her again, needing her to understand the severity of the crisis, her naïveté, the naïveté of her troops. 'Your Interior Blades perform well in a combat-pit, against each other or some weapon-whirling servitor. Their presentation is flawless and their ability to march is impressive indeed. But against a slavering, stink-breathed enemy, tearing their fellows to pieces while it bares its blood-slick fangs in their faces... that is a different matter. Your soldiers have never seen *anything* like this. They have no experience of following orders while under fire, of seeing, hearing, *smelling* their closest companions losing their guts, shitting themselves and perishing in a welter of prayers and howling. Of crawling on broken legs, firing with broken arms. They have no idea what is in wait for them. You must prepare to evacuate.'

And only fifty thousand of them! Like the unused tanks and

batteries, the planet's infantry numbers had surely declined with its long peace.

'They are not children, Sister,' Kozma said. 'They have full experience of live-fire exercises. Of facing injury and death.'

'That is not the same thing!' Augusta was pressed hard now, praying to keep herself calm. 'You *must* prepare–'

'Sister, I cannot. The arch-deacon has insisted that the festival continue.' Kozma was getting angry, her map haloing her in white light. 'We are Opal! We are enough to face these xenos!'

Augusta glowered, staring the woman down. Kozma was a good soldier, with a healthy measure of Opal's pride – but she needed more. She needed wisdom, needed humility, needed to understand the difference between legend and reality, between her neat and shining rulebook and the blood that soaked her streets.

Needed to understand the full and terrible horror of what she was facing.

Gesturing at the hololith, Augusta said, 'Observe your map, commander. There could be a hundred, a thousand, a million individual claws.' Bells clamoured from outside, and she waited for them to pause before continuing. 'And we have no idea how much time we have left. Defeating an attack from the Outskirt would at least have been straightforward. But this...' She rallied, raising her chin. 'Commander, your people are panicking, not only because the cult is on the move, but because they may already feel the approach of the hive fleet too. You will halt the festival, secure the starports, and make plans for the evacuation. And you will do so now.'

The commander eyed her, a gleam to the woman's expression. Augusta was a direct threat to her authority, and to Opal's legendary past, and her faint glimmer seemed edged with either triumph or anger.

'You sound like you are admitting defeat, Sister. We are *Opal*, and the God-Emperor is with us. Our forces walk in the boots of saints! They carry His strength, His blessing, His fire in their hearts. We can just attack.'

Augusta's own question again, her own tangles of both duty and responsibility. Throwing oneself into combat, fearless and sure of one's own death and blessing – that was a clear path, simple and honourable and strong...

'Attack *what?*' With a snap of ire, Augusta stamped forwards. 'This is no tale of ancient heroes. There is no legendary fortification that you can assail, can cast down in some great and banner-waving conquest. This is *war*. It is wrath and agony and suffering. It is a brutal and screaming death. If the hive fleet is upon us, we must do only one thing – secure the streets against every line of assault, both upon the surface and from orbit. We will not attain victory, but we will get as many people clear as we can.' She glowered, making sure the woman understood, making sure she herself understood. 'It is very easy to celebrate a war when you have never seen a real one.'

That made the commander flush, furious. 'Sister Augusta.' She came forwards now, glowering. 'I can *exterminate* this infestation!'

'Commander.' Augusta held the woman's gaze. 'You stand strong amid the lives of your saints, this is well. You carry courage and honour, this is also well. But we are talking *death*. The deaths of millions. Your precious Opal, dissolving in acid!' A pause, to drive the point home. 'You cannot fight this battle from the text. You must observe, act, react, think upon your feet and follow where He leads. To thunder ahead, unknowing and unaware, would be utter madness – you would perish in your thousands. You would leave millions of your pilgrims – Opal herself! – to perish. We must *think*. Your pilgrims' lives depend upon us and we must consider both tactics and strategy. And that is not easy, against a foe who shows so little of either.'

Kozma had stopped, was eyeing Augusta with a narrowed gaze, assessing – but whether it was the Sister herself or her words, Augusta did not know. After moment, she said, 'You have said yourself that these cultists are armed only with the most basic weapons–'

'Weight of numbers will kill anything,' Augusta said. 'Even as water drips through stone. The cultists have had access to both munitions and to transport manufactories. They have assaulted your communications. And when the tyranid swarms fall upon the people–'

'Then what do you *suggest*, Sister Superior?' A snap, cut short by more church bells. 'You tell what I am not, what I cannot do – what should I do in its place? Look at this!' She turned back to the map, gesturing at the various blips. Lines had connected them now, one to another, where she had been seeking patterns or triangulating locations. 'Tell me where these cultists are!'

'They are everywhere,' Augusta said, like a knell.

The room went quiet. Kozma blinked, faltering for the first time. 'Then–'

'Your forces must hold the starports, secure the vox-arrays, and prepare to move the people.' Her gauntlet scraped against the wall, and the city's lines curved suddenly over her vambrace. 'After that, the central reactor is your main priority. It must be secured against potential sabotage.'

Kozma frowned. 'The central reactor is… difficult, Sister. It is in the sewers, beneath the city.' She tapped the map, close to the centre of the Wall of Diligence. 'Here. And it is…' She paused, her frown deepening. 'Cursed. Many legends are told of its origin–'

'We do not have time for superstition, commander. If you wish to save your people, your starports will need power. And the reactor must be secured against assault, or potential detonation. If necessary, I will go down the sewers myself… by the Throne.'

Even as Augusta said the words, she understood the combat-plan as if the God-Emperor Himself had shown it to her, all etched in lights on the map.

'The sewers,' she said. 'They warren all through the Capital?'

'Right down to the Varadi, and beyond.'

'Flood them.' Augusta was thinking now, looking at the map herself. 'Flood the old defences completely, drown anything below the waterline and render it uninhabitable. Flood the sewers of the entire Outskirt, the interlinking tunnels, everything you can...'

Even as she spoke, she realised that this last detail was not possible – Kozma had already said that the ground of the Capital sloped upwards from the riverside towards the Inner Sanctum. But that didn't matter; her tactical mind was working, now, and her plans were absolutely clear.

'Simultaneously, have your sappers and adepts seal every sewer entrance in the Capital itself, and stop the cultists attacking again. Leave a few open, right down by the waterside, here and here.' She indicated points at the Varadi's nearer bank. 'Place Blades at these points.'

'And where will you be?'

Augusta was almost grinning, her heart lifting with a ray of genuine hope. 'Three of my squad patrol the streets, seeking insight and offering courage and solace where they may. Another lies sorely injured and my medicae has stayed with her, to guard her life, and to secure the Outskirt.' There was still something snagging at her thoughts about Arkas and his cathedral, and about Henrik – something that had remained important, though she did not yet understand what it was. 'I have all three of my ship's shuttles flying search patterns, and three spears of Blades still on patrol, but at the moment they can tell me little.'

Kozma was watching her now, the woman's expression tight.

Her arms were folded and she had an air of expectation, as if she was waiting for some gem of faith or wisdom.

Augusta offered her hope. 'I will take my Sisters, and whatever force you can spare, and we will penetrate the sewers at their highest point. You will seal the entrances behind us. And we will fan out, driving the cultists downwards, ever downwards, towards the flooding and the last open exits, down at the river.' She scanned the map, thinking. 'They will be forced up, out, onto the streets. And there, you will slay them all. And, as we progress...' She tapped the map. 'So we will also secure the reactor.'

Kozma was nodding, her eyes on the map. 'Yes, Sister.'

'I agree with the taking of decisive action.' Augusta was still thinking. 'But we must be aware – this attack is a calculated risk, as we do not yet know where the cult's leaders are located, or where their greatest strength may lie. They may become aware of our advance, and detonate the reactor anyway.' Prayers rose in her thoughts – prayers for guidance, for clarity. 'But He tells me, in my heart, that this is the right step to take – it will secure Opal's power, and thin their numbers, that we may better face what remains.'

'I understand,' Kozma said.

Augusta was beginning to think she meant it. 'Opal has her sins, commander, but He has not abandoned you. He still offers you a chance at survival.' Bells sounded, underlying her words with His grace. 'Take hope from one fact – such cultists as these would usually remain unseen, undetected, only to rise at the very last moment and overrun any resistance with sheer weight of numbers. Yet we are blessed, for they were not expecting our presence, or our resistance, and this has brought them to a war footing. We still have time, if only a little. This is His gift to your world, that we may save your people.'

Kozma raised an eyebrow.

Augusta said, 'The cult sought to take an early staging post, and by His blessing we discovered them, and foiled their plans.' She spoke to Kozma as if she was telling herself. 'In this, He has given us both time and hope.'

The commander had lowered her gaze. 'I hear you, Sister.'

'My ship will command basic orbital security – such as can be offered. There are a small number of frigates and destroyers that will rally to Opal's defence. When the hive fleet arrives, these vessels will not survive, but they will buy us time to evacuate as many as we can. We may offer our lives in His service, commander, but let us not do so recklessly.'

'I hear you,' Kozma said again. 'I will mobilise my street-runners. My sappers will have the demolitions rigged within the hour. My adepts are already working with the mobile artillery, and with the other orbital batteries.' She caught Augusta's eye, though her expression was grim. 'I understand you, Sister Superior – dying for the Emperor is an honour, but dying and leaving Opal to suffer... that is more complex. If it lies within my might and resource, I will help you save my people.'

The abbey forecourt was a mess. Servitors were bustling, still scrubbing blood and viscera from the steps, but the stains – and the stench – were all too recent. Opal's holy glimmer had been dulled by a welter of gore. Sister Alcina stood at the outermost corner, surveying the wreckage of a row of market stalls. Scatters of loose bullet casings rolled about in pools of drying vomit; there were sodden, fouled fabrics, and the hysterically crushed remnants of food and pottery.

'There,' Sister Caia said.

On the far side of the forecourt, a small storm-drain entrance was still open, and a swirl of blood and other fluids was washing down to the depths. The penitently scouring servitors paid the three Sisters no mind as they moved closer, Caia's auspex glowing green.

A pair of duty Blades nodded at them, and stepped back. They stood tall, but had a haunted look about them, like a shadow across their souls.

'Nothing,' Caia said. The screen showed the scattered blips in the square, but no lingering muster. No force lying in wait just below the surface.

Viola, the heavy bolter in both hands, made an ugly noise.

'Desist,' Alcina told her. 'The canoness comes, and she will be less tolerant of your foolhardiness than I.'

Her shoulders still angry, the younger Sister subsided.

On the square's far side, taking shelter below the abbey's massive buttresses, a cluster of people were still huddled, one of them sitting with his arms around his knees. The biggest of the bullet casings was still clutched in his hand like a talisman, and he was staring into nothing, his lips moving as he prayed.

Alcina approached him, her boots splashing. 'Tell me. What did you see?'

The man did not react, continued his muttering. Next to him, a woman looked up, her face streaked with tears.

'Why, Sister?' She was sobbing, her breath catching as she spoke. 'Why did He punish us?'

'Because you have sinned,' Alcina told her, as if it should be obvious. 'Opal...'

Caia's gauntlet on her vambrace stopped her. 'Easy, Sister.' Crouching down, she said to the woman, 'We are here in His name, to purge the xenos and the heretic. You must tell us what happened.'

The woman sniffled, wiped her nose with the back of her hand. 'They came out of the ground,' she said. 'Hundreds of them. Broadcasting heresy.' She put the hand on the rifle at her side – it was a poor simulacrum, its barrel blocked and its workmanship crude, but the hand-and-globe of Opal still decorated its side. 'We prayed, but He has forsaken us. My brother... he tried to pray for them, but they gutted him and just left him to die.' She gulped a sob. 'The rest of my party... followed them. Down to the dark. But there were others' – her breath caught – 'others who were saying they'd had a *vision*...'

The three Sisters exchanged looks. 'Did they say anything else?' said Caia, still crouched. 'What was this vision?'

'They'd had dreams, dreams of the saint!' The woman shook her head, confused and overcome. 'But why? Veres is Opal's hero, why would he punish us so? Why would the God-Emperor turn His back upon us? You who are His daughters, help us understand! Are we sinners? Why would this happen to us?' She dissolved into hiccupping sobs, and her closest friend gripped her shoulder.

Viola twitched the bolter. 'We will purge every last one of these accursed creatures.'

'Sisters.' The duty Blade, crossed spears on his pauldron, had joined them. 'The attack commenced as the forecourt was at its busiest, filled with pilgrims waiting for the dawn mass. The dean, she...' He glanced at his comrade, who nodded encouragement. 'She came out to offer her courage, and was slain. About her, the faithful of Saint Zalan were slaughtered almost to the last man and woman. And yes, many people did follow the cultists back down the tunnels.'

'To slay them,' Alcina said.

'Reports are confused,' the soldier answered her. 'Some were war parties, certainly. But others seemed caught up by the broadcasts. They went to seek the blessing of the saint.'

'They're still recruiting,' Caia said. 'By the Throne.'

'They never stopped,' Alcina commented, her words like rock. 'We must silence their communications, lest the whole Capital fall to corruption.'

Viola was still covering the drainhole. It was not big enough for a person to fit through, but the squad's second contemplated it anyway, praying for guidance, for clarity as to their next move. It was very clear that the younger Sister wanted to loose her frustration in a battle-rage of bolter rounds, and Alcina was tempted herself. Like her Sisters, she would welcome the rush of combat.

'Sister Superior,' she voxed. 'We believe that the cultists are still actively seeking new members.'

'*Understood.*' There was an edge of aggravation in Augusta's voice. Briefly, the Sister Superior explained her plans, explained how the commander was structuring the city's answer to the assault.

Alcina snorted, thoughtful. A red-cloaked adept bustled about the plaza's lone Taurox, praying and blessing it with holy oil, but it didn't seem to be moving. She kept her scepticism to herself.

'*Proceed to the Wall of Glory, between the Capital and the Inner Sanctum, and to the Gate of Sacrifice,*' Augusta said. '*There is a servitor's entranceway, located in the base of the nearest statue. It will be large enough to accommodate armour.*' The vox went silent for a moment, and Alcina guessed that Augusta was discussing the tactic with the commander, or looking over a map. After a moment, she said, '*The sappers are moving into place. The Blades will cordon off the streets. Position yourselves, my Sisters, and our assault will commence at the mid-morning bells.*' There was a distinct edge in her voice. '*We have played with words long enough. It is time for Opal to open fire.*'

XII

THE LAST TRUE HOLY MAN ON OPAL

In the Outskirt, Sister Melia prayed.

Like her Sisters, she had refused to rest, or sleep. She had stimms in her medical case, but did not like their usage – she had her faith to sustain her, and it was fire enough.

Around her, the old chapter house was still, chilly enough for her breath to curl white in the air. The lines of broken-statue alcoves were glittering grey, and the bosses on the ceiling vaults offered faces of grotesques, leering and gleefully ugly. In the closest bed, Akemi drifted peacefully, her armour removed and stored in its sacred case. On Melia's other side, Arkas still clung to life, though his skin was pale as wax, and his closed eyes sunken to pits. Like the skulls that hung along Opal's roads, his light had almost gone out.

On Arkas' other side lay the cadet, curled up under her coat like a small child. She had refused to leave him, and she snored through her broken nose, the noise impressive.

With litanies taught to her by the Order of Serenity, Melia

prayed for them all. *Bless us, O Emperor, who brings both light and mercy, and healing to those that hurt…*

It was late – or possibly early. The Sister Superior's shuttle had just left, and the rising sun was far away, on the opposite side of the Inner Sanctum. Yet the pale fingers of dawn already poked down through tiny, high windows. They touched the beds with blessing, with rays like ghosts of hope.

Bless us, O Emperor, who gathers the faithful unto the Throne…

A bootstep at the door and a soft, 'Sister?' It was the verger, Eszter. 'While it is quiet, I am going to get some rest. If you need anything, ask for Fabian and he will help you.'

'Thank you,' Melia said. 'I have done what I can. My charges lie in His grace, and He will call them home, or not, in His own time. I will continue to watch, and to pray for them. Ave Imperator, and rest well.'

'Ave Imperator.' The verger nodded respectfully, and ducked from the doorway. Melia heard her boots, then the bang of the door at the cloisters' corner.

Kamilla muttered and shifted, her rest uneasy.

'Hush, child,' Melia said, getting up to put a hand on her shoulder. The Sister's gauntlets, like her helm, were under Akemi's bed – it was difficult to tend to wounded in full armour. 'May He guard your sleep. Guide you and bless you, and banish the dreams of the foe.'

As if in response, Arkas said, quite clearly, 'Saint Veres comes.'

Melia started, her heart suddenly thumping. She turned to stare at him. The dying priest had not moved; his eyes were still closed, his colour still pallid. Had she imagined it? She was weary, certainly, and she had been sitting there for many hours – but such would surely be a weakness, an unpermitted loss of focus…

Guide me, my Emperor.

Kamilla twitched again, harder. Under her eyelids, her eyes were flickering, almost frantic. Akemi had not moved. But Melia could feel it: there was something there, something almost tangible. It hovered between the priest and the girl like the dawn mist on the river. Melia could see Arkas' fingers and feet fidgeting, his chest fluttering as his breathing quickened.

What xenos heresy haunted him?

'Be still, Father,' she said softly. 'May He guard your sleeping mind, as well as your waking one.'

'I can see them!' The words were soft, but they sounded like some cry of epiphany. His lips were colourless, cracking and dry; their skin flaked as they moved. 'Our saviours, they are close now – so close!' It was awed, almost childlike. 'I can *feel* the saint as he approaches!'

Her shivering increasing, Melia had a sudden memory of the Lycheate witch, Scafidis Zale, of the horrors that could be put in one's mind...

'Wake up.' She shook Kamilla's shoulder, not gently. 'Kamilla. Wake up!'

The girl mumbled, muttering. Arkas' chest was rising faster now; he was hyperventilating, and the bloodstain over his belly was growing, spreading out through the bandage.

'*Cadet!*' Melia kicked the bed, making it rattle.

The girl came awake with a jolt. 'Sir!'

'On your feet!'

Still only half-awake, Kamilla was moving, her training bringing her fully upright, her right hand grabbing for the rifle that wasn't there. It took her a moment to realise where she was, what was happening. As her awareness coalesced, she blinked at Melia, then looked down at Arkas.

'What? Why is he–'

'Watch the cloister.'

'What?' Still staring at Arkas, Kamilla started to say something, then stopped, and did as she was told. 'Yes, Sister.'

Melia, too, was watching the injured Father, still praying. Augusta had told the squad about Henrik, about how Arkas had withstood his call, his charisma and corruption, but had almost paid with his life. And Melia was not about to surrender her charge to the dreams of the incoming hive.

Placing her hand back on the man's forehead, she began to pray aloud. 'Stand with us, O Emperor. We beseech you – bring us your majesty and might, your courage and blessing.'

Her words were intoned, strong and clear, pitched so the sleeping Arkas could hear them – in his ears, in his mind, in his heart and soul. Her memories of the Lycheate witch felt close, the phantoms that he had created – the doubts and fears, the darkness. These dreams were not psyker-made, but they were just as profane. She would not relinquish this man to their growth, to their faithlessness, to the forthcoming death and devourment.

'Your strength and focus, that we may face the enemy...'

Then Akemi, too, began to twitch. 'Sss...' she said. 'Sai...'

'No!' Melia cried the word aloud. 'Sister! By the Throne, how can this be?'

Could the dreams of the incoming hive fleet truly touch the heart of an Adepta Sororitas? Or did Akemi's lack of consciousness remove her ability to withstand such things? But no – Akemi's faith was a part of her. It was manifest in her sleeping mind as much as her waking one.

By the blood of Dominica herself!

Melia would not permit this. She would not lose her Sister, or the Father, to the xenos nightmare. As she had surpassed her own sacrilegious dreaming, the touch of the witch, so she would overcome this heresy.

Her anger crystallising, she prayed louder now, determined

and strong, and the sounds of her chant filled the space with holiness and courage, spilling out into the cloister. She heard the cadet join her, though the girl occasionally tangled the words.

May He guard your soul, child, Melia thought at her. *And may He guard the souls of–*

With a jolt, Arkas sat up.

He sat up not like a man injured, but like some power-charged Mechanicus construct, blessed to machine-spirit life. His eyes were now open and staring, starlight blazing in their depths. Like an automaton, he made a jerky attempt to move, to leave the bed, but she grabbed his shoulders, intoning her prayer right into his face, *daring* the xenos within him to withstand her.

'You will leave him be!' The words were shouted, but not at Arkas himself. They were shouted at the perversion that was fighting to gain his heart. Behind her, the cloister door banged again, but she was locked in a weaponless battle, a war for this humble man's soul.

Slowly, he turned his head to one side. Like an augmetic iris shrinking, his gaze focused on her face.

'Sororitas!' he said. His voice was still his own, all hope and awe and astonishment. 'You could still join us – choose to reject Opal's greed, her power and her selfishness!' He blinked at her, his eyes still full of light. 'I was naïve. Preaching weakness, acceptance. Preaching the holiness of being a victim. But I was *wrong*. The dreams have finally made sense to me. I understand, now. Understand what must be done!'

'By the God-Emperor, you will leave him *alone!*' She was all but shouting it at him, now.

Outside, there was a sharp cry, a challenge. The shuffle and stamp of boots. A sudden flurry of fists and feet. Melia heard Kamilla cursing, words unsuitable for a girl her age; there was the slump of bodies falling against stone.

But she couldn't turn, couldn't help. Arkas was fighting her now, his strength crazed, impossible.

'My life, my work, everything I have done,' he said. 'My sanctuary, my holy cathedral, all of it! I have guarded this place with my life, and it has been for Opal. For Veres. For the future! All this time... and I did not know!' He was demented, making no sense. 'But he... he has always been here! And now, it is his time!'

Melia's prayer rose to a shout, a cry of rage and denial. She had heard legends of Saint Katherine, stories where Sisters had defeated a foe by song alone – she had no idea if such things were true, but if her faith was deep enough, if her courage and blessing was strong enough...

From the cloister, a livid, furious shriek – Kamilla. Akemi was shifting more now, her hands at her face as if to bat something away.

'Ssss... Saint...'

Akemi! Melia was still praying. *Be with her, God-Emperor; be with my Sister as she sleeps! Guard her dreams and her mind! I will not let this foe triumph!*

She had to move, to help. She cast about for her medical case, her sanguinator. If she could knock him cold...

But Arkas was singing, now, a hymn to Veres, a prayer of light and glory.

'Finally.' A voice from the doorway. 'Took your time, Arkas, but you're with us at last. Henrik would be pleased – he always knew this day would come.'

Melia turned.

There was a man in the doorway, a big man, black-haired and heavy-shouldered, his skin as pallid as Henrik's had been. He wore backstreet garb and carried a length of metal piping, already bloodstained. Behind him loomed a sizeable gaggle of others – men and women, young and old, all similarly pale. Two of them had the cadet, had picked her up by her elbows. She was spitting and snarling and kicking, fighting to the last.

Rising to her feet, Melia pulled her flamer, then realised her vox-bead was still in her helm. Caught by Arkas' plight, and by that of her Sister, she had made a significant error of judgement. Horror flooded her – penance, grief.

Resolve.

Arkas was still singing, the hymn to the saint, full of praise and courage. Akemi was twitching harder, her eyelids fluttering. She continued to mutter, 'Ssss... Saint Ver... Ver...'

Smirking, the man came into the room. 'Looks like you're outnumbered, Sister.'

She levelled the flamer at his face.

'You happy to kill us all?' he asked her.

'I will stand at the Golden Throne. I will not lose Akemi, or the Father, or the cadet, or *myself*, to your corruption. My Sisters are His arm and His weapon, and they *will* stop this.'

The man snorted, mocking. 'You arrogant, foolish women. We know why you're here. You're trying to stop us, defending Opal's arrogance and greed and cruelty and selfishness. And we won't let you. We will *ascend*.'

'You will not ascend, creature. You will perish, and do so screaming.'

'I don't think so.'

Behind the man, there were crowding more and more figures, now filling the cloister, and fanning out into the room. Boots scraped on the stone, eyes glittered in the darkness. She saw the glint of weapons and bared-teeth grins. Tightening her grip on the flamer, Melia raised the Litany of Divine Guidance – guidance not for her heart, but for her soul.

'Walk with me, O Emperor!'

She could hear Arkas moving, but she didn't turn. Kamilla spat and thrashed. In her sleep, Akemi hissed like steam.

The man grinned, still coming forwards. Zeal shone from him, eagerness, madness. They were all round her now, so close she could smell them; they were all round the bed upon which Akemi still lay.

'Go on, Sister,' the man said. 'Embrace your false Emperor. If you do, you will never know the light of the true saviour!'

Curling her lip, commending her Sister and the Father to His light, Melia put pressure on the trigger. But the mob were everywhere, and the mass of them bore her to the floor.

'This is intolerable! I will *not* permit this travesty!'

At the heights of the palace, the arch-deacon whirled on the dark, seated figure of the governor.

'We have the Emperor's own protection, and what you and Kozma are doing... it is nothing short of blasphemy! I gave orders that the festival would continue!'

The deacon was a big man, with a voice powerful enough to rouse a world to worship. But he could also crack it like a whip, with a sting of pure intimidation.

'The decision is made,' Vass Mihaly told him, leaning back in his chair. 'Both the festival and Opal's defences come under my authority, not yours.'

'The festival comes under the authority of the God-Emperor.'

'Which you are *not*, despite your pretensions to the office.'

The deacon coloured, flushing with rage. 'How *dare* you take His name as your insult, governor?' His voice was low, lethal. 'Need I remind you that, while you may acquiesce to these *whims*' – the word was a sneer – 'the festival is under my control. It has been eight hundred years in the making. And I will *not* have it stopped by these damned hysterical women!'

'It is already done,' the governor said flatly.

Outside, the Day of the Second Martyr, Martyr Nemes, should have fully begun – but there were no bells, no sermons, no pit-fights or holy markets. The Capital was still reeling, its people angry and fearful. Sobbing pilgrims offered penance, crying their woes or begging for blessings. Others packed the shrines and chapels, weeping; still more sang in the streets, or brandished fake weapons and boastfulness. The myriad traders had either packed up and retreated, or were doubling their sales in the face of the onslaught. At all times, the heretical broadcasts continued, exhorting the people to the love of the incoming saint.

The damage was done, and the festival was over. From here, they needed *real* faith and courage. And they needed to keep their heads.

'The evacuation is already being planned,' the governor said. 'The Blades are redeploying, and our adepts have been inspecting, repairing and re-blessing our orbital defences, and our mobile artillery. Many of these vehicles are now in motion, and some of the pilgrims are following them, as if they follow the saints themselves.' His expression darkened, but only briefly. 'A few have even hurled themselves beneath the tracks, but we do not have time to stop. Such martyrs' lives are with the Emperor.'

The deacon made an indelicate noise. 'And what of these road closures? They are causing mayhem, as if there isn't trouble enough.'

'They are necessary,' the governor said. 'We had to keep the crowds clear and under control, while the sewers were sealed. Those entrances that remain open are outside the Capital, past the Wall of Diligence and down among the habs and factories by the river. Our Sisters of Battle and three full swords of Blades – over a thousand soldiers – are fanning out across the upper tunnels. They will drive the cultists down, securing the reactor as they go. Once the Sisters' push meets the level of the flooding, the cultists will find a small amount of still-open exits, where a second force of Blades is deployed to eliminate them. The plan is solid.' He eyed the deacon, holding his gaze and staring him down. 'We can keep the Capital's streets clear of threats, and begin the evacuation on schedule. Shuttles will land in timed relays, taking as many as they can.'

The strategy was good, but despite Mihaly's apparent assertion, he knew it was a gamble – the coordination that an evacuation required was colossal, their comms were corrupted and the people already panicked. Even without a cultist attack, the streets and starports would be chaos. More adepts were working with the vox-arrays, and the Sisters and the Blades still had to secure the reactor and the cable-cars, all the critical points of the Capital's infrastructure.

The governor needed order. He needed control. And for that, he needed the deacon.

But the deacon paced like a caged canid, back and forth, his rich robes glittering. He had held a morning sermon, praying for courage and resilience in the face of the attacks, and promising, in His name, that precious Opal would not lose her shine. Afterwards, he had arrived at the governor's office spitting sparks. By the look of him, his mood had not improved.

'We will not be daunted by this... unholy rabble!' The deacon gestured, and his rings caught the light like those of a conjurer. 'We are the blessed Gem of the Segmentum Border, the Home of the Million Saints, and we are touched with His light! We are a world steeped in the courage of our past, upholding the names of our sacred saints and holy warriors, all across the galaxy! To see our festival ruined by this *mob*–'

'It's a little more than a mob, Your Holiness. Did you not

hear me? The hive fleet descends upon our world and we will be *devoured*.'

'This is *Opal!*' Bells rang from outside, underlining his words. 'Heresy and sacrilege! How dare they take the name of Veres for their falsehoods? How dare they presume to protest against His will?' In full vent, he could talk over anyone and everyone, bringing others to his point of view, less by his charm and more by the sheer force of his volume and personality. 'How dare they ruin my festival? Do you have any idea of the hours, the days, the weeks, the *years* that went into its preparations? How long it took to train the military that you and Kozma so blithely redeploy? Have you *seen* the state of the streets, governor? Our people, our pilgrims, blaming each other, turning on each other? Murdering their fellows and disfiguring themselves? Our soldiers are needed there, not gadding about on some paranoiac, overzealous whim!'

The governor raised an eyebrow – for the deacon to call anyone else overzealous was true irony – but the man was actually wagging a finger, his tone furious.

'Our pilgrims expect to *see* our military! To witness their games, their ceremonies, their marches, their music, their parades, their pit-fights, all dedicated to His glory, and to Opal's future. And what are you doing? You are sending them down the *sewers!*'

Mihaly asked, his tone ice, 'Are you done?'

The deacon inhaled, his face flushing even deeper. 'No, I am not *done*.' He stalked up the length of the table, massive and powerful, glaring down at where the governor sat. The guards twitched, but Mihaly raised a hand and they subsided.

Without standing, and without raising his voice, Mihaly said, 'You confess that the dissidents preach heresy, that they take Veres' name in vain. You admit that they rebel against His will. But it seems to me, Your Holiness, that we have rested on our...

reputation for far too long.' His tone was smooth now, but steel-cold. 'Sat here, smug beneath our halo, defended by our righteousness. Taking our ease, while the Rift was torn across the sky and a new crusade was launched.' He paused, let the words sink in. 'Terra *herself* came under attack! The galaxy is full of death, of horror, of invasion. Of people laying down their lives in His name, and laying down their lives *now*, not in some legendary and mythical past. How have we drifted so far? Assumed that we *alone* are under His protection? How did we come by such *arrogance*?'

The deacon stopped. Slowly, he seemed to deflate, his anger leaving him. But Mihaly wasn't finished.

'I need you to back this strategy. We can save our people, but only if we move forwards together. You are Opal's holy heart – you are His conduit and voice. You must stand fast, and uphold the faith of the pilgrims. Lead them, unite them. Fight their horror and despair, and offer them hope. The vox-arrays are under repair, and when they are ready to use again you must control the broadcasts. Tell the people to head for the starports, keep them moving. It matters little what shuttle or ship they embark upon, not now.' He searched the man's face, looked for that spark of understanding. 'Let Kozma deal with the soldiers, let the Sisters of Battle stand as they should, at the forefront of the attack. But we, my old friend – we must protect our people. They are our responsibility, and we must think clearly.'

The deacon gave one last flash of ire. 'I will still celebrate the Sermon of the Hero.'

'That is your choice, and a brave one. In the meantime...' The governor paused, letting the import of it all sink home. 'You must bring unity and hope. Stop our pilgrims turning upon each other, and help get them off-world.'

The deacon spun away, back to the window, looking out and

down at the Capital. Mihaly watched him, thinking. Kozma's forces were moving, and he prayed that they could withstand the cultist threat. But how long had it been since Opal's orbital defences had opened fire? Since her Tauroxes had rumbled into life? A few had still been mobile, but they had done little more than roll down the road at the height of some parade. Many had been rusted solid to the stone. Their machine spirits were too-long dormant, their engines and interiors in utter disrepair. Many more had blocked barrels or dysfunctional weaponry. Even those that could still fire had been kept more like the surviving orbital battery: used purely for celebration.

Turning back, the deacon said, 'In the streets, people say that He is punishing us for our conceit. That He sends these... cultists, these xenos... to teach us the error of our ways. Do you believe this to be true?'

'I would not presume,' Mihaly said. 'But if we are to pay His dues, then let it be with valour, and with honour. We must fight this – fight it with everything we have. Everything we were, everything we are, everything we still can be. Please, Janos.' He spoke not to the rank, but to the man. 'Take your place in the Saints' Cathedral. Hold a new service, a sermon of concord, of harmony. Hold it today, tomorrow. Pray loud, for as long as you can, for as long as He grants you the strength. Pray right through to the festival's end, and hold the Sermon of the Hero. Lead the people, help them face the shadow. Make them join together, one family under the Emperor's light. No more in-fighting, no more deaths on the street. Punishment or no, we have a common enemy, and we *must* stand as one.'

And it will stretch the Blades that much less.

Outside, a purity of voices raised the mid-morning hymnal. Its clarity was glorious, almost crystallising in the cold air. The governor shivered.

You must listen, Mihaly thought, half praying. *May He grant you wisdom as well as*—

'Very well,' the deacon said, cutting him short. For a moment, the man had the faintest look of petulance, and then it was gone. 'I will begin the sermon as soon as the comms are secure, and it will broadcast across the Capital entire. I will continue until I can preach no more. If unity will help us stop this madness, preserve our precious culture, then unity you shall have...' The faintest pause. 'My lord governor.'

'Thank you, my friend.' Mihaly meant it. 'May He guide us both through the darkness, and Opal back to the light.'

The deacon grunted, and the governor offered a prayer. Opal had her work ahead of her, and the deacon's talk of His punishment stung Mihaly like a barb. Their world had spent so long with her eyes turned skywards, blinded by her own ring-light, that the terrible truth had struck without warning.

And the task they faced was formidable.

THE WAR IN THE DARK

Heading downwards, always downwards, the sweep had been ruthlessly planned.

Augusta and Kozma had calculated the strategy carefully, coordinating the advance from its commencement at the Wall of Glory, spreading outwards and downwards to the Wall of Diligence, and then to the riverside. Thanks to the tiny projector on her vambrace, the Sister Superior could follow the same hololith map as had been on Kozma's wall, and could see the flashes where the cultists had been massing. Vox-communications were difficult through the stone, but she had synched chronos with her Sisters, and the four of them were now spread out across the Blades' massive, extended line – herself and Caia in the centre, Alcina to the right and Viola to the left, each following one of the sewers' three main arteries. As the line encountered each blocked entrance and dead end, it would halt, letting the streetrunners skirmish, and ensuring that no pockets of resistance remained.

The tactic, in theory, was sound.

While I may walk worlds of darkness and terror, there you shall walk with me. I shall know no doubts, no fears, in your name.

The upper tunnels were elaborate, narrow and comparatively clear. The advance moved swiftly, encountering the highest of the blocked entranceways. These were still clear, each marked by the tiny hololith and by a trickle of rubble and dust. As they moved lower, the tunnels began to broaden and to carry more effluent. In places, the scouting streetrunners reported desperate, isolated figures, some injured and clinging to life, others lost or mind-broken, or trying to claw their way along the stone with their fingernails ripped and broken. They told of pilgrims, shredded and dying, or clustered together in terror, and Augusta prayed for their souls.

Walk with them, O Emperor. Lead them to the light.

In the gurgling darkness, the Sister Superior moved with the hololith lighting her way, her bolter in her other hand. Behind her, Caia's auspex glowed green. Despite the stream of flowing muck underfoot, the sewers were as decorous and beautiful as the Capital's streets; purpose built, carved with vaults and bosses, prayers and emblems, grotesques that leered like tiny monsters. In places, there were stylised lines of Opal soldiers, their flak-armoured shapes engraved in the stone, or sequences of memorial plaques, the places where the exhausted workers building the sewers had simply lain down and died. These were sometimes surrounded by bones, or by mementos, each piece hammered into the wall. The fallen had been remembered by their comrades, who had gone onwards to their own deaths, and been remembered in their turn.

Blessed be their memories.

Truly, Augusta thought, as the Capital's shining streets slid over her sewers, Opal's genuine heroes lurked unseen, forgotten by the planet's pomp.

She missed Akemi, the youngest Sister's learning and wisdom. She prayed for her, and for Melia and the cadet, for Arkas, for Alcina and Viola. Viola was difficult, headstrong, and sometimes Augusta wondered how she had come through the schola at all, and had not been terminated before taking her Oath. But her strength... Augusta remembered their first mission to Lautis, the orks' assault upon the ruined cathedral, the same mission that had slain Sister Kimura. The warboss had picked up Augusta by the gorget, and Viola, barely blooded but utterly fearless, had shot the beast. She had carried the heavy bolter ever since.

Shine your light at their feet, O Emperor, that they may never lose their way...

Streams of filth ran constantly under her boots. The Capital was still packed and the refuse was plentiful – prayers discarded and mementos forgotten. The going was slippery, suffocating and treacherous. The Sisters were defended by their helms, but the Blades had covered or blocked their noses and they breathed noisily, trying not to gag.

Wherever possible, the advance stuck to the raised ferrocrete walkways that flanked the flow itself, each defended by a chain-link fence. The soldiers grumbled, but Tamas, their commander, let them be.

Walk with Opal and her defenders, Augusta prayed. *Bless this sweep and this undertaking. Guide us to the enemy that we may wreak your wrath...*

Her fear of failure had not left her. It lurked in the dark like shame.

Slowly, the tunnels expanded, sloping down towards the river. On the surface, Augusta could traverse this distance in perhaps two Solar hours; down here, it would take them ten times that, though their breaks were few. They found steps, sometimes ladders, to raised servitor-platforms with rusting prayers or diagnostics. They found glimmering screens that winked with numbers, or chinks of light that filtered from the smaller storm-drains above. In other places, they found narrow, rusting grilles, with the sewage roaring through them as it streamed to unknown depths. These caught debris: sodden prayer ribbons, shoes, relics, lost bags. One had a Path of the Thousand Humble silver chain, knotted about the bars and rattling in the water.

Pilgrims' holy treasures, never to be recovered.

Stand with this, your most holy shrine world. Stand with her people, as we seek to carry them clear...

The Blades became weary. They moved in individual swords, then individual spears, spread out across the network, and doing their best to stay in a single, extended line. Vox-beads still worked across a short range, and orders and reports flowed out and back in relays, keeping the formation.

Still they encountered nothing. Augusta's skin began to crawl.

Guard us, O Emperor. Guide us, stand beside us. Bless the paths we choose...

The Sister Superior prayed for the Blades, their attentiveness, their energy. She prayed for herself, too, for the rightness and clarity of her decision. Augusta and her squad had already been two days without sleep – but such was of little consequence, they had their faith to sustain them. But three hours had not passed before the soldiers began to stumble, to lose their concentration and to make mistakes. She sang for them, for herself, for Him, her voice poignant in the echoing stone. So much was now dependent upon their focus, upon them keeping the line, upon the numbers they really faced, and upon how thorough this sweep could be...

Bless my choices, and the orders I have given.

Beside her, the auspex blipped. Simultaneously, Tamas held up one closed fist and gave the order to hold. He was younger than

Mezei had been, his hair blond, his pale skin already greenish in Augusta's suit-light, but he had not faltered. The Blades with him, seven of them immediately close, halted and the command rolled out across the network.

Augusta stopped, listened.

And there it was: the first real change in the noise. Over the chuckle and grumble of the waste, there were rustles and whispers, feet and movement. The sounds were still a distance below them, but the enemy were definitely here...

'Caia?'

'Hundreds,' Caia replied softly. 'More.'

A flash of adrenaline, like His blessing.

'Walk with vigilance,' Augusta said across the vox, steadying the nervous Blades. 'We have higher ground, and better weapons. They can only come at us from below, the flow of the water is against them, and the tunnels are narrow enough to dismiss their advantage of numbers. Hold to your world, your saints, your faith. He is with us, and with His blessing, we can exterminate this assault before it even begins.'

'Understood.' Tamas might be young, but he was steady. At his order, the force eased onwards. The tunnels were growing wider and more numerous, making the Blades spread out further. By Augusta's map, they had systematically navigated down through almost two-thirds of the network, and were closing on the Wall of Diligence.

'This is better,' Tamas commented. 'We're less bunched. Everything behind us clear?' The query went out, and it took a moment for the streetrunners' answer to ripple back...

'Yes, sir. Far as we can tell.'

'Good job.'

Silently, Augusta prayed for their thoroughness.

'There,' she said. The hololith on her vambrace gleamed. 'Halt.'

Both the map and the surround showed the same thing: they had come to the end of the tunnel and to a major nexus-junction.

'They are waiting for us,' Caia said.

'Good.' Augusta's response was all sternly supressed violence. 'Tamas, let us see what we face.'

Carefully Tamas shone his light. The pale beam searched ahead, picking out a circular chamber with a rising ceiling dome. About its walls, it was carved with the same soldiers, a ring of them with their shoulders at exactly the angle of the roof. They had no heads. Instead, the dome's apex was a single stone boss, shaped like a gaping mouth. It made them look like they shared some eerie, unified scream.

On the chamber's far side, the nexus branched into three smaller capillaries, all heading down towards the river. In the centre of the floor, a massive whirlpool curled about a smaller, central drain.

If Augusta's plan had been properly timed, then her Sisters would have found two more sites identical to this one, one to each side.

Tamas said, 'Sound off.'

'Vigilance,' she repeated. 'We–'

''Ware!' The cry was Caia's.

But the detonation took them all by surprise.

Whether it was a warning, or whether some young cultist had been just too eager, Augusta did not know. But the single krak grenade sailed across the space, impacting right over Augusta's head and detonating in a mass of dust and fragments. Dust and rubble hissed to a pile at her feet.

Beside her, Tamas was already shouting, but she was louder, her order going out across the vox.

'Take cover! Pull twenty paces back and into the tunnels.

Guard your positions – if they advance, do not let any of them past you. Tamas, keep your forces in defensive position. We will deal with this. *For the Emperor!*'

'Sister!'

The young commander was good, but he carried the inexperience of his world. She had no wish for the Blades to celebrate their Opaline ancestry by charging out across the space, getting themselves blown to pieces, and leaving the tunnels unwatched.

'Viola, Alcina, report your locations!'

The vox crackled and spat, but Viola replied, *'We have… xus. Cult… ighted. Attack…'*

Alcina, to her other side, said, *'Enemy… ontact. …ders?'*

'Take point,' she told them both. 'Let these heretics *feel* the wrath of the Rose!'

Augusta could almost feel Viola's burning grin; she felt a need to replicate it. That part of her warrior soul, trapped by politics and social manners, was free, rising to His light and glory.

But in the tunnel-mouth on the nexus' opposite side, the cultists lingered in their own shadows, and did not advance. She had expected them to come howling, mob-handed, to charge across the space and to throw themselves upon the Blades, but they seemed hesitant, coiled like a waiting snake. Why had they paused?

Briefly, she reviewed her schola knowledge – and missed Akemi, again. If there were hybrids amidst the throng, they would have a full hive mind and think as one. But – and she squinted to see – these did not look like hybrids, they just looked like more of the Outskirt's poor, those infected and heretical locals that had succumbed to the xenos' lie.

'Caia,' she said. 'Numbers.'

'The spirit of my auspex is struggling,' Caia said. 'It does not like the stone. But hundreds, still. Maybe thousands.'

Behind Augusta, Tamas said, 'Scouts report that there is something else down there, something bigger. The enemy move before it, as if driven.'

'I concur,' Caia said. 'Whatever it is, they're more afraid of it than they are of us.' Her voice filled with wonder as she said, 'I believe He has blessed us, Sister, guided us to a leader of the cult.'

Again, that faint thrill in Augusta's nerves – He was with them, watching them. This advance had been a risk, a risk in His name, but Caia was right, it had His blessing.

With a prayer like an unfurling banner in her heart, she said, 'Then we shall *eliminate* these xenos.' There was a thrum to her voice now. She could hear the auspex blipping, see the green wash of the screen as it glimmered from the walls, feel the tension of the surrounding soldiers. This was the first true battle the Blades had ever been in. Would their hearts and courage hold?

The same flash-memory – the same glassaic cathedral, all those years before. Sister Pia the Martyr, she who had given her life to enable their victory against the beast. It had been the very first time that Augusta had seen a Sister die, and the memory of her Sister Superior's order – *Leona, fire!* – was almost vision-strong, as powerful as a key in a lock, as the clunk of a round in the chamber. Augusta raised her voice, the brass call of a trumpet.

'We are the Rose! And we say, in His name – *no foe will stand here!*'

Caia echoed her, Viola and Alcina. Voices called across the tunnels, across the vox. The soldiers, tense and wary, steadied, their hands gripping their rifles.

There!

In the entrances opposite, the cultists were visible now. They were massing up, gluts of them, like some eager darkness. It was hard to pick out their individual features; Tamas' light caught dirty faces, spreading grins, hands that gripped mostly mêlée weapons. There were rifles, here and there, a few with grenades at their belts – they still looked only like the Outskirt's poor.

But…

'Saint and Emperor!' Tamas said.

His light was catching other things: misshapen features, too many arms, fragments of glittering chitin. Goggles and grins. Claws, clacking with zeal.

'What are *those?*' The question hissed among the Blades. Many made the ring-sign of Opal, and she felt them waver.

'The enemy,' she said grimly. 'You who stand in the shadows of saints, now you show your real mettle.'

And, somewhere at the back of her thoughts, the presence of the creatures was making sense – this nest must be older. It must have already been here, waiting for the order to rise. And it – and probably others – were the locations where the Outskirt's displaced cultists had now taken refuge.

How long had the xenos really been here?

She did not know, and it did not matter. What mattered now were their deaths.

'For the saint!'

The cultists came on with fervour, frothing and bellowing, boiling from the tunnel-mouths like termites. They drowned out the ring of the Sisters' hymn and Augusta raised it louder, her bolter with it.

Drawing gasps from the Blades, muzzle flashes reflected from the carved stone, both she and Caia loosed the full wrath of their weapons.

'From the lightning and the tempest!'

The first three ranks of attackers disappeared. Bodies broke and flew and crumpled, sudden gore misted the air. In the flares of pinlights, it was a red cloud, seeming to hang in shock for a moment before falling and gurgling around and down the drain. Cultists and hybrids fell, clogging the flow. Augusta's voice carried a savage, vindictive edge, as she loosed her frustration every bit as much as her ammo.

Beside them, Tamas took sharp, single shots, red flashes aiming for the obvious hybrids. Caia raised her own voice, livid and furious. Someone gave a low, awed curse; someone else breathed a prayer.

Belatedly, Tamas growled, 'Steady.'

But the attackers did not care. Despite the destruction, the injured continued to crawl, dragging themselves on through the filth. Shuddering, some of the Blades retched, but Augusta changed her tactics, blowing the heads of the crawlers clean off.

Still, they continued to sing. *'Our Emperor, deliver us!'*

The second wave surged forth, was cut to pieces in turn. They had so sense, no fear, and the human ones howled Veres' name. The Sisters roared the litany, bolters snarled and barked. Flashes flared in the half-light, lighting the dome to a scarlet glare like bloodshed. They scythed down the faithless like they were nothing–

Without warning, the assault stopped. The cultists had drawn back, returning to the tunnels. It was not a retreat, it was regrouping – perhaps a pause to reconsider their tactics.

''Ware,' said Augusta over the vox. 'Tamas, tell your troops – the enemy may attempt to outflank us.'

'Understood.'

Then a belt-full of frag grenades splashed down at her feet.

By the Throne!

Another shock-memory, back to Sister Kimura in the Lautis cathedral. The orks' assault, the belt of grenades that had landed at the Sister's feet, and the detonation that had followed...

Going over and taking Caia with her, she cried, 'DOWN!'

With a massive, rippling detonation, the belt went off. Sewage and flesh exploded with shrapnel, coating the walls with refuse. Defended by her armour, the Sister Superior still covered her visor with one arm, prayed the soldiers were far enough back. With His blessing, the tunnels would offer them cover.

Tamas was swearing, vicious and angry. Augusta heard him barking for his troops to sound off: they were fine, just filthy. But they had another problem. The nexus' drainage hole was now blocked with an oozing sludge of flesh. The level of sewage was rising, and once it rose above the lip of the opposite tunnels, it would sweep the cultists downwards – but would make going after them absolutely treacherous.

For a moment, she wondered at their tactics – had this been a part of their attack plan? But the cultists, apparently oblivious, were still singing Veres' name. The sewage levels rose swiftly to their ankles, rancid, now-bloodied clothing floating on the top of the tide. The Sisters opened fire for the second time, and the litany rang from the roof.

The soldiers were standing back up, now, their Opal-pale camo stained with filth and darkness. Neither it – nor they – would ever be clean again. The days of the Blades' shining, marching ceremonies were over.

'We advance,' Augusta said. 'Sisters, are your locations secure?'

'...ster,' Viola replied. 'We... ecure.'

'Alcina?'

'...etreating. Do we... rsue?'

Do we pursue?

Augusta wanted only to draw her chainsword, cry His name and carve her way through the faithless and into the xenos beyond, but with an effort she held her place. With the litany clenched between her teeth like shards of glass, she kept up a continuous fire, making them retreat, forcing them to keep their heads down. The last one, a hybrid, judging by its claws, leapt from the tunnel and ran at her, impossibly fast. She raised the bolter's muzzle and splashed the beast against the ceiling.

Tamas said, quite calm, 'Concentrate on keeping your footing. Streetrunners, stay mobile. If they get round us, we're finished. Your orders, Sister?'

'Advance with caution.' Something in her heart wanted to charge, raging with righteous fury, but she had already nearly lost Akemi, and she had responsibility for Tamas and his Blades...

She could not make the same mistake.

Guard her, O Emperor. Guard my fallen Sister. Guard my choices as we advance.

They eased on forwards, wading through the flood. Blades retched, gagged, prayed, choked.

'Their withdrawal is orderly,' Caia said, after a moment. 'It is my belief... that this was only to try us, or to attract our attention. Just like the hits in the Outskirt, they press us, test our valour. Learn.' She paused, thinking, then said, 'Whatever lies down there...'

'I hear you,' Augusta said. A fierce joy was filling her heart. *Thank you, my Emperor! We will not fail!* She could feel her battle-rage, her eagerness for the foe – but still, she prayed for clarity, maintaining her self-discipline and trying to understand. Had the Outskirt cultists' lives been spent just to make this flood happen, to pull the Sisters into unsteady footing and a heavier confrontation? What kind of *numbers* were they really dealing with, that so many deaths could be thrown aside, just to assay the Sisters' plans?

Behind Augusta, one of the Blades went on his arse, swearing. His comrades picked him up, but the message was as clear as His word: with the nexus overflowing, both cultists and Blades alike would struggle to stay upright. From here, the going would be absolutely deadly, and the advance had a far greater chance of being surprised, of missing dead ends, or of being swept down to…

Down to what?

From Kozma's map, they were closing on the fusion reactor, the single largest open space in the entire system.

Leona, fire!

And something down there was waiting for them.

THE FORGE OF SIN

With the festival's filth streaming downwards past their boots, the Sisters' advance continued. Sealed in power armour, they were protected from the waste and the stench, but the Blades were not so fortunate. Many were already struggling, green in the face. Several had fallen, getting sewage in their ears and noses. Tamas, the commander, was staying strong, though his skin was ash-pale in the gleam of Augusta's suit-light.

'We will continue,' he assured her, as she glanced back. 'We carry Opal's pride with us, and we will not slow you down.'

She gave him a curt, faceless nod, and they went on. Prayers and grumbles spread out across the vox.

Past the nexus, the tunnels began to sprawl, and the line spread back to its extended formation. Echoing laughter began to follow them, vox-cast from who knew where. Expecting the ambush at any moment, Augusta kept tense hands on her bolter, her eyes on the gleam of the hololith, still gliding over the walls.

'Movement! Tamas, to your right!' said Caia.

She was a moment too late. Two perfectly timed attacks hit the skirmishing streetrunners. Augusta did not see them, but she heard the sounds. They were ranged more loosely, checking the sealed dead ends, and they came on in echoes, in cries and shouts and las-fire. Unable to reach the ambushed soldiers, Augusta and Tamas held their position. The commander barked orders to relay along the lines. He was surprisingly able to think on his feet, and she raised the sacred hymnal, echoing out through the stone.

But still, the damage was being done. Voices cursed and shouted and cried. Soldiers sobbed in pain or horror. Those around Augusta tensed, Tamas included. She understood their frustration at their own helplessness, and prayed for their nerve to hold.

They heard screams, splashes, struggles, cries. Barks of half-panicked orders.

'By the saint,' one voice muttered, just behind her.

'Steady,' Tamas said. 'Hold your place.'

'But, sir–'

'You are in His light, and you perform His duty.' Augusta's voice was flat. 'Stay where you are.'

In the dark, rank tunnel, they could only listen.

The Sister Superior heard the rallying cries, heard the soldiers gather their courage and fight back. In the vox, they raised His name, cried prayers to the Thousand Humble, to Saint Zalan, to Veres and the Three Martyrs. They fought for their world with genuine, fierce courage. There was no way to treat or retrieve their injured, and the instant infection would be gruesome, Augusta knew – yet still, they did not falter.

At last, Tamas said, 'In His name, the streetrunners are victorious.' He was panting, though whether from exhaustion or stress, Augusta did not know. 'We will continue.' His every word ached with what had just happened. 'What of our injured?'

'If they can walk, they may retreat back to the entry point,' Augusta said. 'But if they cannot, do not spare uninjured warriors to carry them. Grant them His final blessing and we will celebrate their martyrdom at the proper time. For now, we will hold the line and advance.'

No one dared object, but soon, a more severe harrying started. The unseen laughter grew, swelling and sinister, and *things* came at them –strange things, xenos things, things rearing from the dark. They were clicking things, hunched things, seething things, things with goggles over their eyes, things with flickering tongues, with claws, with too many arms. Among these, there were other, more familiar figures – some of them still in the garb of pilgrims, or in Opal's now fouled grey camo. These were more visible and more than once, the soldiers by Augusta recognised a friend, and flinched or drew back.

'They seek to bring down our numbers,' Caia said. 'To harass and unsettle us.'

'Which means we have worried them,' Augusta answered her. 'He is yet with us.'

Tamas made no reply.

More attacks came. They lurked at every junction, small in number, but swift as nightmare. They did not linger, they lunged in and were gone, hit-and-run tactics, spreading fear and breaking the spirit of the advancing line. Many of the humans still shouted Veres' name, cries that rang throughout the tunnels like a cathedral's bell-tolled summoning.

More and more of the Blades died, and not just the street-runners. They were spread too thinly; not fast enough, not experienced enough. Seeing death surrounding them, seeing their fallen friends corrupted, made them falter. Augusta saw one drop his rifle, his hands shaking. He leaned down, groping through the muck, but he did not find it and they could not wait for his search to be successful. Another cried aloud, the names of his family, perhaps, and a third sobbed constantly, tears streaking her face.

'Help us,' she said, between gulps and sniffles. 'Help us, saint and Emperor!'

Steadfast, Tamas barked orders and Augusta recited the Solidarities, her voice aloud and over the vox.

'Wherever He walks, there can be no failure.' She heard her Sisters intone them with her. 'Wherever forces are gathered in His name, there He shall be.'

Beneath the words, however, her doubts were back, gnawing at her like too many teeth. Had she made the right call? Given the right order? Akemi's sleeping form haunted her like judgement. The hours were passing, and she had no idea what was happening in the Capital, how the defences were going, whether Kozma had followed the plan, how close the hive fleet really was...

Silencing them, she prayed for clarity. *Guide me, my Emperor.* She had made her choices, given her orders. There was no place for guilt or penance, not here. Here, there was only duty. Whether she succeeded or failed, this was her sacred calling and it was absolute. She would defeat the xenos, save the people, or she would perish.

But – what of Opal herself...?

More vox-voices, exhorted cries of Veres' name, of ascendance and light and glory.

In Augusta's own vox-bead, a different communication: death tolls, tales of Blades injured and tumbling to the floor, of wounds being exposed to the sewage. Some had turned on their fellows, crying the name of the saint like some sudden epiphany; others were shot by their own side, in acts of both mercy and fear. Still more had fled, unable to face their terror.

Yet the majority held, advanced, kept shooting. They carried Opal's ancient courage, and to their hearts' depths. They rallied, and they banished their dismay. These new, all-but-unblooded warriors, they stood in the light of their forefathers and fore-mothers, of the true Saint Veres, of the God-Emperor Himself and of the lessons that they had learned as cadets. And she prayed aloud for them, prayed for their new-found strength and the courage with which they walked.

'That He walks with every Sister as she carries His name unto the void, that He hears the words of every hymn, the thunder of every weapon, the battle cry of every warrior.'

But still, the attacks kept coming. It was a war of attrition that Augusta knew she could not win – every life in her force meant so much more than every life that was thrown at her. Yet she drove on forwards, and she held to her plan nonetheless.

Guide me, she prayed, in the silence of her heart. *Tell me that this choice is the right one, that I have not left Opal to face her fate unguarded. Tell me that my Order is on the way–*

'Sister,' Tamas said. The word was aloud, and she turned.

His skin was still pale, tinged to blue round his lips. He did not look well, but his gaze was determined.

'The carvings, Sister, they have changed.'

He was right: the decorous nature of the walls had subtly shifted – no longer images of bright and martial pride, but images of chastisement, of great and burning pits and of figures tumbling to their deaths.

'Listen,' Tamas said, one finger to his ear.

She listened. And there, at the very edges of her hearing, just audible over the gurgling of the sewage, she could make out another noise, a deeper, stronger noise. It was a noise like every waterfall thundering as one, a noise like... a noise like His voice in the darkness.

Like her prayer had been answered, and she had not chosen amiss.

'He has blessed us, truly,' she said. 'We are here, and our line is still complete.' Anticipation surged through her nerves. 'We have reached the fusion reactor, and it is the farthest place to which the cultists can retreat. Below here, the tunnels will be flooded and the only place to which they can fall back is upwards and onto the streets, where more Blades await them.' She gripped his shoulder, felt him shaking. 'You have shown great courage, Tamas, and we have achieved our objective. Now, we pray to His name and glory that we can end this.'

If this leader was the patriarch, as she prayed that it may be... If they still had time...

In your name, if we have not gone amiss...

Tamas swallowed, said, 'Do you know the legend, Sister, about Opal's central reactor? They say it's older than the Capital's rebuild. They say that after the detonation, when the workers built the Capital's streets and sewers, that some of them tried to rebel, refusing to be worked to their deaths. They were declaimed as heretics, taken to this reactor, and cast into the fire.' He indicated the walls. 'Our legends call it the Forge of Sin.' There was a tension to him, a sheen of sweat to his forehead. He licked his lips, nervous and restless.

This must be what Kozma had meant. 'The place is not cursed, Tamas. The Emperor stands here as He stands in all places.'

'I know that, Sister,' he said. 'But some say that Opal's sinners... are still punished here. Some say that to come here is to die. To even speak of it... is to die.' He swallowed again, his breathing catching. 'And to die *damned*.'

'I will have none of this foolishness,' she said. 'We are here at the God-Emperor's command.' She watched him, forcing him to heed her, and said, 'You will relay this, out across the vox.

We do His holy work. We are here with His mandate. With His blessing, we will save Opal.' Her words had also gone out to her Sisters. 'Tell them, Tamas. Tell them now.'

The commander told them. In the face of Augusta's uncompromising belief, he seemed to stand taller, to breathe more easily.

'Good,' she told him. 'And also, commander, think. If to come here is to die, how do the stories of the curse get passed on? It seems to me that this legend has been spun–'

'Spun to keep people away,' Caia finished for her.

'He is with us, Sister,' Augusta said. 'He has blessed the spirit of your auspex. There *is* something down here, something with strategy. And He tells me that it has been here for a very long time.' Anticipation flooded her. 'Your tale is a key, Tamas, unlocking truths as yet unseen. We *will* find answers here.' There was an eagerness in her voice, a need for combat, for fire and resolution.

Tamas was still studying her; her faceless Sabbat helm. She answered his unspoken question.

'We have been brought here, commander. By the enemy and by the God-Emperor both. Let us spring this waiting trap.'

The space was not another nexus.

It was far, far bigger, a vast and underground basilica, lit by a central hellmouth of fire. The heat was oppressive, making the air shimmer with convection; a mighty, vaulted roof offered ancient paintings, flaking and long since faded to blurs. A ring of stone statues stood about the central pit, all facing outwards and with expressions of grim certainty. Lit from behind, they wore the same stylised armour as Saint Veres and the martyrs, but there were no inscriptions to tell whom they might have been. Similar figures were carved about the walls, all glowing in the harsh, red light.

From somewhere, there came broadcast singing, a hollow mockery of Veres' holy hymn.

'*Praise the saint and praise the martyrs!*'

But the words were hard to make out, because past Augusta's feet, over the lip of the tunnel, cascading free and in a semicircle about the room's centre, there poured colossal waterfalls of waste. Not into the fire, but into the floor about it, where a great encircling grille of filigree steel caught the last of the cast-off trash. Upon this grille, a scurry of silent servitors laboured, shovelling up the garbage and the blockages and tipping them into the fire.

'*Praise our new-found hope and light!*'

Some of these still had human faces, burned and aged and soaked in sweat. Seeing them, Tamas visibly flinched. When Augusta glanced at him, he said only, 'The sinners. They're still here.' He made the ring-sign on his chest, the warding symbol of Opal.

She had no idea if his identification was accurate or allegorical. Again, she needed Akemi and her learning... Her Sisters' absence, Akemi and Melia both, was more than unsettling. They were a hole in the hymnal, voices missing.

Guard them, O Emperor. Keep them safe in your blessing.

'Sisters,' she said. 'There is fear in this place. Let us raise His name, and banish it.'

The echoing hymn continued.

'*Praise the gods of stars incoming!*'

'*Praise our world, her new-found might!*'

Over the vox, Augusta said, 'Let us drown out this heresy.'

From another tunnel, there came a flash of a suit-light. And then, there were voices, both aloud and in the vox, raising that familiar harmony that lifted her hackles every time. Two of her Sisters' voices may be absent, but still the song was warm, like fire and courage and blessing.

'*A spiritu dominatus...*'

Rallying, Tamas issued the command, his voice carrying across the open space: 'Advance, single file, but with care!'

'Stay behind me,' Augusta said. 'Sisters, we will take point.'

The streams of sewage were carried clear from the tunnel-mouths by long, protruding gutters, like extended hands. To the sides of these, slippery and treacherous, there were curves of steps, hugging the wall and with no banister or rail. Worn dips in their stonework indicated their age, but neither Augusta nor Tamas had any knowledge of why such a pathway would be needed.

It did not matter. He had brought them here, He had shown them the way, and that was enough. Carefully, they headed down.

'Sister Caia,' Augusta said. 'Locations.'

'The auspex is confused, Sister,' Caia said. 'It does not like the waterfall's motion.'

'Then listen to His voice, Sister. Machine spirits can be fooled, but the soul cannot. Sister Viola, Sister Alcina.'

Alcina, on the far flank, now spoke clearly across the empty space. 'My force is decimated, Sister Superior, but we have held the line. I would be foolish if I claimed that we have driven every last cultist before us. Their numbers were high and our losses have been heavy. But, by His grace and blessing, we are here.'

'We also,' Viola said, from the other side. There was a whetted savagery to her voice. 'We have slain as many as we could. Hundreds. More.'

'Follow the Sister Superior,' Tamas said to the soldiers. 'Down the steps, swift but safe. We don't want to be caught halfway up the saint-cursed wall.'

Grumbles and prayers followed, and many more flickings of the Opal ward-sign. The phrase 'the Forge of Sin' came from more than one throat. It hung in the air like a warning.

Aware of their superstition, Augusta raised her hymn.

'Domine, libra nos!'

The steps were slime-covered and foul. The noise of the falls was a ringing constant, drowning out the Sisters' song. The nervousness of the soldiers was readily apparent – like Tamas, they did not want to be here.

More mutters came from the firelit murk. In their sheltered, performative lives, the Blades had never encountered anything like this, and fear rose like the reek of burning refuse. Augusta sang louder still, the litany challenging the falls' racket.

Whatever was down here, whatever was waiting for them, they were ready.

What sprang at them, Augusta saw, were not the scruffy figures of the Outskirt.

Perhaps the Outskirters had been expendable, used to harry and confuse; these things were true hybrids, older and more twisted, dark and clawed and terrible. Almost impossible to see in the poor light, they were hunkered down upon the grille, they were crouched upon the statues, they were hung upon the walls.

And they were *fast*.

The Sister Superior heard Caia's warning, but the creatures were everywhere, manifesting from the darkness, uncoiling on the walls. They were underfoot, they were overhead; the whole place was alive with motion. She heard Viola, the first down the steps, shout a prayer; heard the thrice-blessed heavy bolter hammer in full suppression. The noise was incredible. Around the central hellpit, monsters and servitors both were cut to pieces.

But Viola, for all her strength, was only one Sister.

Somewhere behind Augusta, a Blade screamed as a creature landed on her, knocking her from the steps. In her panic, she took her companion down with her and they crashed to the grille in a tangle, the creature on top of them both. It slavered at them as they tried to bring rifles to bear. The woman's scream was silenced as the thing tore off her face. The other Blade, a lad of barely twenty, dropped his rifle completely and scrambled away on his backside, his hands slipping on the hot metal. The thing turned its head and hissed at him.

It all happened so *fast*.

Augusta shot one, two, three of the creatures, calling the litany aloud. Shamed, the fallen Blade retrieved his weapon. She cut down more – four, five – rising directly in front of her. She saw Tamas and the soldiers slash las-fire, scarlet streaks bright across the horror.

But they were not enough, not nearly enough.

To Augusta's left, the spear creeping down the steps was caught, stuck, as creatures clambered up the walls, down the walls, across and all over, their claws digging at the stone. The soldiers clustered together, defended each other as best they could, but their situation was helpless. Tamas' command took shots at the beasts, but there were too many of the things, and they were too close to their comrades. In moments, it was carnage, a shock of crystal screams.

Several soldiers jumped, hoping for the best. Torn fragments of Opal-pale camo rose fluttering, dancing in the hellpit's heat. Dying and injured soldiers toppled from the steps, hitting the circular floor-grille with a metallic thump. Whether they were moving or not, the servitors collected them, and tried to tip them over the edge of the hole. More than one struggled, then screamed as they burned, and more steam filled the air.

Reaching the floor, Augusta saw more creatures, closing round herself and Tamas. One bared its teeth, its tongue flickering. Startled, the flag commander brought up his rifle and blew the thing away.

'For the glory of Opal! For our world and His blessing!' He called his own prayer, steadying himself.

As solid as a scarlet rock, Viola was still shooting, the heavy bolter chewing chunks from stone and flesh and beast and servitor. For just a moment, Augusta thought that the Sister would have the upper hand. But the hybrids kept coming, and kept coming. Claws slashed from the darkness, and another soldier fell, and another, and another; every staircase was boiling with enemy motion. The corrupted hymnal was still sounding, though it was being lost now beneath the rest of the noise.

A beast leapt at the Sister Superior, and she shot it in the face. Its head gone, its weight still hit her. She staggered, almost losing her footing. The body skidded from her armour and slumped, still. She kicked it away and the servitors, dutifully, shovelled it up for fuel. Their human eyes swivelled to look at her, but they showed no recognition.

Then, behind her, Tamas went down.

He went over fighting, trying to drive the thing off his chest. Her attention still on the seething circle of the grille, she caught the motion from the corner of her eye, turned to shoot – either him or the beast – but there was another creature already there. And another. And more. They buried him, and he screamed and kicked and was gone. Shredded like so much waste.

The Blades were being torn to pieces.

By the Throne!

She did not want to fall back, she wanted to push forwards, through the darkness and the fire, and find whatever leader–

'Sister!' Caia's shout warned her.

The hybrids had only been the first wave.

There were four things incoming, and they were huge. Massive and misshapen, clawed and hunched and with too many arms, they were hulking monstrosities half-hidden by darkness and steam. The Blades were crying and stumbling back, falling over servitors and each other. Their voices called for blessings from saints and martyrs, and somewhere, someone threw up.

'Aberrants,' said Augusta, over the Sisters' vox. The word was grim with triumph. 'They will be guarding something.'

'They will not guard it long.' With a prayer that was more bellow than hymn, Viola aimed the heavy bolter at the closest creature. Wounds exploded across its chest and belly, but it lumbered forwards and past the central pit, slamming out an arm and knocking her to the floor. She skidded on the grille's metal, kicked a too-curious servitor in the face.

Behind her, Caia was shouting. 'There is another one, further back. It is... Dominica's blessings! It is even *bigger*.'

'They are a sign,' Augusta said. 'Whatever they are guarding, we will reach it.'

Across the vox, Alcina still raised the hymnal, the words edged in rage. There was no harmony to her singing now, just a pure and focused violence. Viola came back to her feet, kicked the determined servitor a second time, aimed her bolter back at the beast.

But the beast had a workers' pickaxe, ancient and inscribed with Opaline symbols. With an almighty, ringing blow, it brought the thing down at the Sister. Viola jumped, still shooting. Metal clashed against metal and the whole grille shook.

Blades shouted warnings. Unnerved by the site, by the blasphemous hymn and by Tamas' death and the appearance of the creatures, the soldiers were reaching the end of their tolerance, their last courage evaporating like so much superheated water. This was beyond them – not only the superstition of being here, in this Forge of Sin, but these monsters they were seeing. None of them had ever dreamed – ever imagined! – that anything like this could attack their precious Opal.

'Domine, libra nos!'

Augusta took up the litany, aimed her bolter at another beast. A five-round burst; a second. She hit it clean, blinding it, but it did not seem to care. Still moving, it slashed huge claws across the grille-top, sending servitors in all directions. It seemed to be shouting something, though the words made no sense. Under it, the grille shook again.

And then, on the far side of the forge, the last one came into sight.

It was bigger than the other four, lashing a long, muscular tail tipped with a glittering-sharp barb. The Sister Superior knew what it was, what it meant – it was an aberrant mutation, a hypermorph, and it meant that the hive fleet was almost upon them.

That they were almost out of time.

It will not matter, she told the cult's unseen leaders, in the savage sanctity of her thoughts. *You will not see your 'saviour'. I will rend you limb from limb, claw from claw. I will break your control and halt your infestation. I am Augusta Santorus and I say: You will not stand before His wrath!*

Her orders – her gamble – had been so huge, aiming to drive the cult out into the open. And if the cult's leaders were down here, then, with His blessing, they had struck a huge blow against the xenos, helping to secure the Capital. Opal's people could still be saved.

'That thou shouldst spare none!'

Crying the hymnal, she shot the blinded one, taking out its throat, and making it fall into its fellow. The second one lurched and tripped, far too close to the forge. Even as it tried to right itself, Viola switched targets and hit its lower leg, her shot removing its kneecap. With a bawl and scrabble, it went over the edge.

Flames guttered and roared, and the air was filled with a thick and greasy smoke. Viola's hymnal reached a crashing crescendo, savage and gleeful. Alcina echoed her. Caia was still shooting, still watching her auspex. Even as Augusta glanced at her squad, Caia put the device back on her belt and put both hands on her bolter, shooting another of the creatures, as Augusta had done, straight in the face. It lumbered, unseeing, crushing servitors underfoot.

Around the Sisters, the soldiers were starting to rally. With no Tamas, the senior officer had taken charge and her orders rang across the half-light. Other soldiers were still caught on the wall and the curving stairways, many of them stopping in horror, holding up those behind. Above them, creatures still hung, harassing and attacking them.

'That thou shouldst pardon none!'

A third beast, the one already battered by Viola's bolter, staggered and stumbled and fell. It raised its head, trying to snarl at the Sisters, but fell back again. Some of the soldiers cheered. Servitors bustled about it, but it was too heavy for them to lift.

'You will hold!' Over the noise, Augusta roared her order. 'You are soldiers of Opal! Saints in the making! You will hold, in His name!'

The closest ones heeded her, steadying. They shot at the heaving walls, the staggering aberrants. But many others were already broken, retreating back to the walls. They had no way to leave; the stairwells were filled with Blades, some trying to retreat, some trying to advance, some fighting off the creatures that still leapt at them and bore them to the ground.

'We beseech thee, destroy them!'

Over the vox, Alcina said, 'Sister Superior, we...'

Rage roaring in her ears, Augusta didn't hear the rest of her second's comment. If they were going to die, then they would take down these defenders. With a bellow, she leapt at the biggest of the beasts.

And it came to meet her.

Whether its hive mind knew what she was, identified her, she did not know, and did not have time to worry. She shouted orders: 'Concentrate your fire! Take that last one down. We must break through!' She closed with the thing, watching its claws, its eyes, its lethally glinting tail.

Alcina picked up her order, echoed it. Bolters rattled and lasrifles sang; Augusta was aware of the fourth aberrant screaming as they cut it to pieces. But she was closing with the biggest of them, now, the ultimate mutant. She did not know how many soldiers had perished, only that their souls were with the Throne; she did not know what lay here, what this beast was guarding, only that it must be slain.

Ducking the tail whip, she sprang forwards, slashing at it as it withdrew.

But the beast was quick. She missed, and chainsword teeth screamed against the metal grille. The monster came forwards, three arms reaching, huge claws gleaming in the firelight. She ducked inside its slash, raised the chainsword hard in an uppercut, carved deep into its belly.

Intestines spilled, pale and shining. The thing squalled, but it did not stop. One massive claw rent a tear in her chest-armour, ripping it like cloth; another came down on her head with enough force to make her see stars. She hung onto the blade, driving it upwards, into the thing's chest, into its ribs and heart and lungs. It hammered at her again, battering her helm, denting the ceramite. But she hung on, and hung on, and hung on. In His name, she would kill this xenos beast.

Shouts surrounded her. Repeated impacts on her head were making her knees buckle. She found the words of the litany and roared them back at the monsters as if to say, 'By the Throne, you will *die!*'

The hammering stopped.

Stumbling, she shook her head; regretted it. Her whole skull was one great pound of pain, and the rip in her chest had not only gone through her armour, but through her padding and into her flesh. It was not deep, but it hurt like fire.

Still squalling, the thing staggered backwards, back towards the forge. Reacting instantly, Alcina bellowed, 'Alpha strike!' Almost without thinking, Augusta raised her bolter.

All four Sisters opened fire at the beast. It staggered further backwards, trailing guts. It caught its knees on the edge of the forge, pinwheeled its arms. But still it did not fall.

'By the Throne!' Augusta roared at it. 'That is *enough!*'

She would have moved, but Viola was already there. At point-blank range, the Sister emptied the last of the heavy bolter's ammunition into the thing's chest.

It sat down, suddenly, then tipped over backwards and was gone. But not before it had cracked one claw at Viola, caught her, and sent her spiralling to the floor.

Augusta barely heard her own prayers. Alcina and Caia with her, the last of the soldiers at her back, she pushed through the darkness to see what lay on the forge's far side: a small chamber, its walls lined with standards.

But it was not the patriarch itself, not some massive and looming monster, lurking in Opal's forgotten belly. No; it was a single, far smaller figure, bald-headed and carrying some tall and elaborate vox-array, a device almost like a staff.

Sudden, sickening fear hammered against Augusta's heart – she had been so *sure*…

By your name and blessing! Where do we look now? How do we stop them?

But still, she raised her bolter and blew the clamavus away.

Part Three

Gods and Monsters

XV

THE BEAST IN THE CRYPT

For decades uncounted, the thing had dwelled in the Outskirt's silent and forgotten belly, unseen and unremembered. It had no memory of how it had come here – and it did not matter. Its past was unimportant; there was only its present, its future, and itself.

Everything that it had become.

Steadily, it expanded. It was discovering, exploring. It was watching this ripe world through ever-increasing numbers of eyes, their gazes multiplying. In every corner, in every street and shrine, there now lurked a myriad reflections of its thoughts. All prisms and angles, layered one atop another.

And making *one*.

Anticipation and hunger thrilled its cold nerves, and it spread further. About its movement, there rose scuttling servants, but it paid them no heed. As it began to stretch, it reached out more and more and *more*, to the Outskirt, to the city, to where its minions were multiplying. And it touched them with one word.

Soon.

The thing was hungry. It had waited long and its appetite was already bigger than this foolish world, than the tiny life forms that crawled around upon it. But they would do – they would keep it sated.

Until the next time.

Sundown, and the Mass of the Second Martyr, Martyr Nemes. Bells were clamouring, white sleet drifting like ash across the breeze.

The deacon, true to his word, was still praying. With the Capital's comms now fully operational, he had spent the whole day preaching from the Saints' Cathedral, controlling the panicking people. His hololith stood fully eighty feet tall, a towering titan at the apex of the city, and his voice rang out through the streets. Janos was no soldier, but he did his best to bring unity to Opal's faithful.

As if called by his holiness, the orbital batteries clanked and graunched, their rust scraping as their domes began to turn. The newly re-blessed Tauroxes and Chimeras rumbled in sacred processions down the roadways, the skulls' eyes lighting them as they passed. Hymns rang from the vehicles' voxmitters, and their adepts walked with them, red robes flapping. Spears of Blades ran beside them, shouting orders, playing their pipes and drums. Swinging cable-cars rattled slowly over the streets, carrying people and spraying holy water, blaring both orders and benediction.

Blessed pilgrims of Holy Opal, they said. *Proceed to your nearest cable-car station. Do not wait for family. Do not collect belongings. Walk with Him, and with penitence. Walk calmly and with swiftness. Blessed pilgrims of Holy Opal. Proceed to your nearest...*

Out past the Wall of Diligence, driven forth by the Sisters' advance, the cultists surged up in a foul and blackened tide. Madness drove them; fear rolled before them, hot and sick. Under Kozma's steady command, a force of Blades was mustered about the last still-open sewer mouths, their positions banked and defended, their weapons ready to fire. Their nerves might have been frayed, but they kissed their pendants and their icons and, lambasted by the deacon's sermon and the bells of the mass, they prayed for strength.

Saint Veres, be with us, they said, unaware of the irony. *God-Emperor, be with us. We fight in your name. We fight for Opal.*

But nothing could have prepared them for the sheer scale of the attack.

Emerging from the sewers, turned to shadowed horrors by the dusk and the ring-light, the cultists had no need for cover, or for sense. Howling Veres' name, corrupted canticles and accusations of heresy, they hurled themselves into the Blades' lines of fire. Spitting scarlet, lascannons moved back and forth in arcs, cutting through the attackers in swathes. Cultists shrieked, squealed, sprayed blood and fell in their hundreds, but there were more, more, always more. Uncaring of their own dead and dying, the next wave poured upwards and outwards. And the next. And the next. They cried the names of Veres and the martyrs, and their vengeance upon Opal's greed.

And the Blades quailed at the onslaught. These first attackers were their friends, their fellows. People they knew. They were fallen pilgrims, deserting soldiers; they were the denizens of the lost Outskirt, desperate for food and clean water. Yet that was not all, for after them, there came something else completely, creatures hunched and twisted, darker and somehow older. Beasts with eyes like pits and terrible claws, and arms in the wrong places, and eager, horrific grins. Some of them howled, slobbering and singing in a ghastly mockery of the hymns of the Capital itself.

Saint Veres comes!

The lascannons roared, the rifles sizzled and sang. The night air rippled with rising heat and broken fragments of prayer, with shrine-bells ringing rounds of defiance and courage. But for every enemy that fell, ten more took its place; for every ten, a hundred. Taking strength from the arch-deacon's preaching and from their own furious officers, the Blades did their best.

Saint and Emperor, they cried, as they gunned the creatures down. *For Opal! For the fleeing pilgrims of our most holy world!*

Still, it was not enough. Drowning in screams, they were swiftly overwhelmed, their carefully placed positions torn apart in moments. Hundreds of them died, then thousands. Thousands more were left squalling, helpless, in pools of their own steaming blood.

Why? they pleaded, sobbing as they died. *Why have you abandoned us? Why have you left your holy world, your Opal, your gemstone, to die?*

But the Emperor did not answer.

Some of them held, defying their own fear and living up to their ancient saints. Others broke and fled, weeping. More than one, faced by their god's desertion and by the crumbling of their own faith, put their rifle beneath their chin and pulled the trigger.

The creatures did not notice. They were in among the soldiers, clawing their way up the walls, slashing to left and right, tearing the face from one and the weapon from another. They broke out of the defences, and surged onto the roadways, massing in huge, seething numbers – and yet they seemed canny, somehow. Aware. As if they knew of the autocannons awaiting them, the stationary engine-rumble of the Tauroxes and Chimeras that now blocked the roads, for they did not assault the Capital or the progressing evacuation, nor race for the Inner Sanctum or the Saints' Cathedral. Instead, they vanished out among the tangled habs and manufactories like a hundred thousand salivating ghosts.

And the buildings were perfect cover – mazes of cubicles and dormitories, of basements and corridors, of warehouses and of unnamed depths where piles of newly made relics still waited. Now, the creatures claimed these as their own, breaking down doors and scrambling through windows, climbing like spiders and vanishing like denizens of the dark. Chased from their sewer hideouts, they simply shifted to new sanctuaries, killing everything they found.

And here, the soldiers could not follow. The heavy weapons had no advantage or field of fire, the Tauroxes no lines of sight nor ground to advance. Smarter commanders called for adepts and sappers, for the swiftness and stealth of the streetrunners... But the scouts had been in the sewers, and their numbers were severely depleted.

Even as the night progressed, even as the ring-light blurred with relays of shuttles as the people began to leave, even as the tireless arch-deacon called for faith, for valour, for honour, for courage...

As dawn rose on the Day of the Third Martyr, Martyr Kis, so did the Blades of Opal fail. They had not numbers enough, nor training enough, and they could not halt the horror.

Kamilla woke up with a headache.

No, not just a headache, her whole damned *face* hurt – her eyes, her nose, her teeth, her skull. She was aching in muscle and bone, and her ears were singing with a high-pitched, tinnitus buzz. Reflexively, she went to turn over, to check her chrono and see how early it was, and whether she could sleep any more. But her hand found only stone, cold and flat.

Groggy with pain and incomprehension, she sat up.

Her dreams floated, broken, like ice in water – the bridges over the Varadi, the Martello towers that lined the far bank, all bristling with cruel, flint-faced soldiers, vicious and aggressively disciplined. Slashes of las-fire flashed at the poor, the needy, the hungry, the desperate. There were screams, deaths, bodies in the water. But the people had courage. They flew banners, and they kept coming, and kept coming, and kept coming. They sang like hope and benediction, sang like deliverance, sang as they were unified into one massive, eager family, blessed and whole again...

Saint Veres comes!

Confused, she blinked, tears streaming from her eyes. The funny thing about pain in the face, she thought, with loopy clarity – it was so hard to dismiss. If pain was anywhere else, you could ignore it, shut it out, but not when it was that close, that personal. Not when it filled your world.

She sank her head into her hands, groaned, rubbed at her puffed-up eyes – then remembered why she shouldn't. With an effort that felt like it would split her head wide open, she opened her eyes and forced her vision to focus.

Darkness. *What?*

Holding down a flutter of panic, closing her eyes once more, she pressed her fingertips gently against them. Saw the little spots in her vision. Okay, so she wasn't blind. But she was...

She had no idea where she was.

Dreams still dangled, fluttering like the echoes of screams. Something huge, in the darkness, coiled and writhed and stretched. It had that familiar touch, wonderful and paternal, vast and gentle. And yet... She grappled at the image, trying to make it make sense. There were things she should remember, things...

Whatever they were they did not matter. The dreams were

wrapped around her, now, with some glorious sense of awakening, an awareness beyond her comprehension. The irresistible cloud-vortex was pulling at her, like an event horizon. Some gateway to another galaxy, to something more wonderful than she had ever imagined–

A chink of light.

It was tiny, two right-angled streaks, the corners of a door. They swelled, suddenly, making a fan of yellow brightness stream down stone steps and spread wide across the floor. It was warm, the familiar hue of electro-candles. And the floor itself...

Saint and Emperor!

Shaking herself, she scrambled fully upright, half to face whatever was incoming, and half to look around her properly. The floor was all embedded gravestones, lines and lines and *lines* of them, irregular and ancient beyond measure, some of them fouled with moss. They had names, icons, emblems, but were blurred with countless centuries. She could not make them out.

The light swelled wider, reaching the far wall. It caught propped lines of flags and banners, standards and effigies, none of them familiar. They rested against recessed shelving, dug out of the heavy stone. These alcoves glittered with bottles, with brass and crystal and pottery, large and small. Some of them bore the fine marks and colours of the Capital, others were far older, and so filthy she had no idea what they could have been. There were leather bags and sealed boxes, glitters of instruments–

'Kamilla.'

A figure, silhouetted at the top of the steps. She could not see his face, but she knew who it was. Knew that voice, that shape, that long, dark robe.

'Father!'

Flooded with relief, she ran. Ran to him like she was a little girl, needing safety and reassurance, needing to be swept up in his embrace. He opened his arms and greeted her, holding her safe in the smells of incense and shelter.

She found herself babbling. 'What happened... what *happened?* Where am I?'

'Home.' He let her go, took hold of her shoulders and pushed her back so he could look at her, though his face was almost unseen in the darkness. 'You've found your family, Kam. At last.'

'But...'

'I had a vision,' he told her, his voice alight with wonder. 'A realisation of the sacred truth. As I drifted close to death, I saw the dreams, the ones we've all shared... And in them, I found *hope.*' His grip and gaze were intense. 'Henrik was right all along – I've been so foolish! I've been cowering, preaching my doctrine of weakness, of cravenness, and now I am shamed! We must *fight,* Kam! The faithless, greedy powers of Opal must be cast down! Veres will come! He will bring us food, family, acceptance. Health, and future. He will bring us the end of poverty, of sickness, of desperation. All my life, Kamilla, *this* is what I've worked towards, what Jakob and I did together. We followed the blind Imperial dogma because we knew no better, but now, I *see.* He is here, and he is with us, and I see clearly.' The glitter in his eyes was like stars, like that of Opal's own stonework. 'I understand now. I must bring my poor, suffering people to the *truth.*'

The call of his belief was powerful, and she struggled to throw it back. Dream images harried her, battering like wings.

'What are you talking about? Who's here?'

'The raid on the bridges, Kam, the one that Henrik wanted. It's still going to happen, and it'll clear the way to the Capital, to the festival's summit. Saint Veres comes. And the Father – he's with us! He will lead us, lead us to meet the saint's arrival!'

She stared at him, caught by the star-gleam in his eyes. And something in her thoughts, her heart, understood him – she could feel something uncoiling, starting to move. It felt like need, like a soaring surge of pure optimism, more than the Outskirt had felt in generations. Something that was more than just the dreams, something that was almost a physical resonance in her head, a new and growing awareness, a feeling of belonging, of family, of a warmth and acceptance that she had never known…

He will lead us, lead us to meet the saint's very arrival!

'You can feel his touch, can't you?' Arkas cupped her jaw in his hand, a gesture of filial affection that he hadn't used in years. 'All your questions, Kamilla. Did not Jakob tell you that questions lead to the truth, in the end? That they are the markers that show us the way?' That chuckle again. 'In this, he was right. More right than he ever knew.'

She moved her jaw, tasted drying blood. Struggled to remember anything that wasn't the dream. 'But…' Her voice sounded thin, like it came from far away. 'Jakob. He used to call you the last true holy man on–'

'Holy.' The word was a spike, painful with bitterness. 'I was never holy. Suffocating on my own piousness. Counselling the people to accept their rejection, their pain and suffering, their disease and starvation – because it would take them to some unseen glory. So much spinelessness, sulking in my little haven, thinking I could bring them… what? A good death? Now, I have a different sermon – one of faith, *real* faith. One of enlightenment. It is almost time! We will cross the bridges! We will be there to welcome the saint when he returns! And Veres will heal us all!'

She stared at him, caught – because he was Arkas, and because his words vibrated down through everything she had learned, everything he and Jakob had taught her.

She repeated, 'Saint Veres comes.'

'Yes!' Arkas told her, livid with unhallowed joy. 'Kam, *think! Think* what he will bring us! Think how Opal – how everything – will change! Think what we can do with the freedom! This world can be whole again, not riven in half. Our people will know an end to their suffering! And it is Veres, not the dead and rotting Emperor, that will lead us to our future! Behold!'

Letting her go, he switched on a pinlight, and lifted it high. Kamilla backed up, looked around her.

The room was as before, banners resting upon stone shelves. But she could see more now – ammo boxes, racks of weapons, stubbers and rifles and cannons. They stretched backwards into darkness, into a vast warehouse-style space, long walls lined with jars of ointments and potions, or with powdered foodstuffs that had no explanation. Something in her understood that she was beneath the cathedral, in what must have been its crypts or reliquary, but she had never seen this before.

Yet that sense of belonging was so, so strong.

She turned back to Arkas, her face one single question. He smiled, just like he always had, gentle and filled with wonder.

'This is my storehouse,' he said. 'Cool and safe, and good for keeping foods and medicines. For *helping* people. And now, my people bring me weapons, as Henrik had always intended. Weapons of *hope*.'

She stared at him. Somewhere in her, there was a tiny, struggling mote, still striving to get free.

'You...'

But she could not articulate the thought. Any memories of her previous life, of the Sisters, of even Arkas as he had been, were gone.

Because deep in the crypt's darkness, something moved.

Something *huge*.

* * *

Tamara Kozma, against the wishes of her aides and advisors, had departed the security of her military command centre. Hearing her Blades over the vox, she took a personal guard and a second wrist-mounted holo-projector, and she ascended to the skies in her personal, camo-painted Aquila.

But there was nothing she could do – her searchlights scanned the habs and manufactories, but she could only watch. There were no tell-tale flashes of red armour – the Sisters of Battle must still be in the sewers – but it was clear that the numbers were just too badly unbalanced. Kozma had estimated the insurrectionist rabble at fifty thousand, maybe a hundred. She had assumed that they were just the underarmed faithless of the Outskirt, no match for her trained Blades. But they were far more than that, driven and fanatical. They seemed like some frenzied horde, thronging with monsters. Beneath her eye-in-the sky, they teemed like a vast spread of termites; they rippled outwards and then vanished into the dark, and the buildings' cover. She saw her Tauroxes and Chimeras boom in manifest rage, blowing craters in roads and walls. Some of them were torn down; angry creatures by the dozen swarmed over the vehicles, ripping off periscopes and antennae, trying to claw open the hatches.

And Kozma could only stare, her heart like cold lead in her chest, her error towering over her like His judgement. The *numbers!* Even if she'd focused her entire force in one place, it would not have been enough. Did she even have the weapons, the power packs, the *ammunition*, to face this impossible tide?

And then, with the dawn of the third day, the ripple of enemy was gone. A few last specks, still dissipating, and that was all. They'd left her Blades dying, her defences in pieces, and they'd gone to ground, again. Pushed out of one place, they'd simply taken another.

As if they were *waiting* for something.

God-Emperor, bless my weapon. God-Emperor, bless my armour…

Kozma's prayers were regulation, just like everything else – but this, this was too much. This was Opal, Gem of the Segmentum Border, Home of the Million Saints, saviour of the worlds about them, their role gifted by the God-Emperor Himself… How could such a thing have happened to *them?*

Some part of her soul was twisting, vicious and angry and grieving. In the harsh light of her full understanding, the final comprehension of her naïveté and the naïveté of her world, she wanted to lash out, to accuse, to find something to blame, to punish someone for the plans that had not worked. Augusta had failed to keep the cult in the Outskirt. She had ordered the sweep, had driven the creatures from the underside of the city, had forced them out into the open. But, in her arrogance and foolishness, she had failed *again*. She had sentenced Opal's Blades – Opal herself! – to death.

Still hovering over the streets, the commander felt her judgement curling high, rearing upwards to lift her laden heart and to fill her whole chest. But she would not despair – she was Tamara Kozma, and this world was hers to defend.

Because Sister Augusta could not.

In the Outskirt, they came. The homeless and the desperate, the hungry and the sick. With the awakening touch now in their minds, the old cathedral called to them, and Father Arkas stood at its heart – their friend, their mentor, their guardian. They trusted him, as they always had. They brought their families, their children, their elderly, trembling parents. They brought their dreams, brought everything they loved. And they brought *hope*.

Saint Veres comes!

Many had made banners, and more of these now lined the cathedral walls. Kamilla's head was full, dreams and glory, hope and wonder – she was caught by them, fascinated and compelled by their strange, curling-dark worms, the symbols of the returning saint. Forgotten were the barracks, her friends and her fellows, her old life. Forgotten too were the Sisters – whatever had happened to Akemi, or to Melia, or even to Augusta herself, she did not know, and did not care.

For now, she *understood!*

Blinded by starlight, she walked with Arkas on his medical rounds. He carried the bottles and sanguinators from the crypt, and he was as sincere, and as gentle, as he had ever been.

'This will heal you,' he told one middle-aged man, his face webbed with broken veins.

'This will help you sleep.' To a young woman, sobbing with weariness.

'Trust me,' he said to a child cradling a fractured arm. 'Let me take away the pain.'

And they did. They leaned on him, needed him. They begged him for his help. They let him treat their every injury, let him hand out broth, and gruel, and blankets. They fell to their knees and they thanked him, sobbing in gratitude and casting their eyes to the saint.

And Veres stood above them, proud and stern and protective, brother and father and martyr and saviour, as he had always been.

'Soon,' Arkas told them, smiling, and offering more soup. 'Soon, this will all be over. Soon, this world will be whole again.'

And still, with the saint in their eyes like reflected starlight, still they came.

And they too said, *Soon.*

XVI

THE BLOODY ROSE

Emerging from the sewers' filth, ragged from almost a day and a night, Augusta saw the miracle. Round, dark spots against the pale Opal morning. Six, eight, ten of them, every one flaming wrathful about its edges, and searing its way down through the planet's upper atmosphere.

Thank the Emperor!

She was dizzy and wobble-legged, but she would not falter. Around her, the last of the tail-end Blades were welcoming the air and the light, many of them falling to their knees to retch or to offer thanks.

'By the Throne,' Viola said, gazing upwards.

'It is quite a sight, is it not?' Augusta said, her voice rich with feeling. Her head was pounding and the cut in her chest burned, but she had forgotten the pain, utterly compelled by what she was seeing. 'One I have witnessed perhaps five times in my life, certainly from the ground. It seems the God-Emperor has forgiven Opal, after all.' Almost overcome, she caught her breath and began to sing the Hymn of the Dawn.

'*O Emperor, the Sun of Justice...*

'*Emperor, hear us as we declare your praise!*'

Called across the void, the Rose had come.

In the street, the last of the battered soldiers were sinking to the stonework, exhausted. They had clustered in weary groups, shocked and grieving. Some gazed skywards in disbelief; others supported green-tinged comrades, or treated minor injuries, or turned and vomited in the gutters. The fighting – and the pollution – had taken a terrible toll, and only now was Augusta realising the full truth of her choice, and what it had cost.

All those souls that now knelt at His feet. All those here, who had not been able to withstand the assault. All those down there, still dying. But better to perish in His service than be devoured by the incoming monstrosity.

'*O Emperor, Thou who blesses each new day!*'

'Get up!' She was already barking orders. 'Defensive perimeter! The cultists are not defeated and they must be slain before they can assault the Capital! The hive fleet is not far away, and do *not* think you can rest!'

The Blades grumbled, but obeyed. In moments, they had formed their perimeter, lining the street forward and back, though many of them still had an eye on the sky. And Augusta could see, at the roadway's far end, the blocky, camo-painted shapes of a pair of Tauroxes, their autocannons covering the area.

Kozma, it seemed, had been as good as her word.

'Report,' she said to the nearest officer.

'The surviving streetrunners will scout the buildings,' the man responded. 'We should anticipate an ambush.'

Augusta eyed the myriad windows that overlooked the road, but Alcina snorted and nodded upwards.

'Praise the Emperor, the Order is in time. We will yet save the people of Opal, perhaps even Opal herself.'

The burning spots were descending like meteors, now, growing bigger by the moment. Behind them, the torn-open clouds made blazing, livid trails, and endless flotillas of shuttles all sparkled like hope in the early morning light. The morning air was alive with an ever-increasing roar.

'Once the accursed have been silenced,

'Sentenced to acrid flames,

'Call me thus with the blessed!'

Augusta snapped a command, and the battered squad stood tall, their armour damaged and streaked. Officers gave orders, directing the Blades' deployment, but Augusta's attention was all skywards, her prayer aloft in her heart.

By the Light! That we yet live to see this moment!

'We have been blessed indeed,' Alcina commented, over their vox-channel. 'But there is much work yet to do.'

'Our assault has accounted for maybe five thousand cultists,' Caia told them. She was watching her auspex, blinking at significant surrounding blips. 'More than five times that number have moved into the buildings, though they do not attack the Wall of Diligence, thank the Emperor. They seem more concerned with slaying the remaining workers.' She snorted. 'They are hiding, I think. They must understand what our Sisters' arrival means.'

'They can hide all they wish,' Viola growled, exultant. 'It will not matter.'

The blazing spots grew closer still, becoming discs, then growing into familiar, five-sided shapes, all of them limned in fire. Many of the soldiers were still staring, mouths agape – like Viola, they had never seen anything like this. This was the stuff of Opal's legends, their own rhetoric and celebration, now brought to noisy, burning, incoming life. As the pods scorched closer, Augusta began to see their cathedral-like exteriors – their flying buttresses, their crouched gargoyles, teeth bared and ready to spray holy water, their prayers and seals. And every one of them bore the mark of the Bloody Rose upon its base – the symbol of Saint Mina, now returned to this world that had, in its own way, faced the Heretic himself.

Even as Augusta watched, their vox-casters kicked in and the full glory of the 'Day of Wrath' hymnal raged across the sky.

'That day shall dissolve the world in ashes!'

'Truly, the cult cower,' Caia said, rich with feeling. 'They will not face the Rose, nor the fury of the Emperor that it brings.'

'They will face His fury,' Augusta said grimly. 'One way or another.' Her pulse sledgehammered, hope and faith and trepidation. She took up the prayer almost unconsciously, heard her Sisters join her, their crystal-pure harmonies instinctual.

'Call us thus with the blessed!'

And with the hymn, like the rise of a cathedral organ, there came the huge, roaring gale of air and wind, the wash of heat, the scream of red-hot metal...

The closest pod was heading right for them.

'Down!' Alcina bellowed at the soldiers, but the officers were already shouting. Men and women pulled themselves back to their feet, running for the towering, bar-windowed cliff faces that were the habs and the souvenir production-factories.

The Sisters, all four of them, did not move.

The other pods were scattered about them, descending like pure rage to the nearby streets. The one above them grew rapidly larger, blotting out the very sky. The racket was immense, and the hymn became deafening, reverberating between the walls. The Sisters did not move. The singer was unmistakably Elvorix Ianthe, the canoness herself, her pure, furious zeal accompanying the thunder of the incoming pod.

'Day of anger! Day of terror!'

With an immense, percussive *boom*, the pod struck stone.

Despite herself, Augusta staggered. A blast of heat and impact tore at the air; roads and walls rippled and cracked, windows shattering in sequence like some huge, resounding crescendo. From other streets, the same noises came, one after another, the crashing reports of some titanic, Emperor-given weapon. The ground seemed to heave with every strike.

'The Day of Wrath is come!'

The hymn still sounded, now echoing from the gargoyles' mouths. Even as the Sisters watched, five rampways crashed down from the pod ahead of them, and five red-armoured figures ran out in perfect sequence, bolters in hands, to secure the immediate area.

And there she was, standing at the top of the ramp with a commander's clear authority. Her helm was off, her skin lined, her ice-white hair as cold as Opal's winter. The fleur-de-lys on her cheek was blue and blurred with her age, but Elvorix Ianthe was the ultimate warrior, and her face was cast in stone. With her came an elderly figure, in full white armour but trimmed in scarlet, a wimple upon her head – Rhene, the Hospitaller. With them was a younger Sister, her skin dark, her black curls cropped short, and a data-slate in her gauntleted hand – the canoness' adjutant, Sister Aitamah. And over the three of them there hovered an insensor cherub, with its plump body and grinning skull-face. Smoke and rose petals billowed in the heat currents, and drifted out to the sky.

The canoness met Augusta's gaze.

And the tension kicked at the back of the Sister Superior's throat. *I have failed. Akemi is fallen, Melia abandoned. I did not find the cult's true leaders and now Opal's Blades lie dying. I...*

No, in your name, I will not falter.

Her foreboding was unseemly and she would face the canoness' judgement with her chin up, as she had done before. She knew she had to explain – her choices, her tactics. Her inability to get the rulers of Opal to heed her military experience and cancel the festival in good time. Surrounded by death and ruination, by her own errors, she snapped to attention, her chin lifted and her hands by her sides.

Loud as metal drums, the canoness' boots hit the rampway.

'Sister. Superior. Augusta.' Reaching the cratered road, she stopped, her gaze noting the claw-rend in Augusta's armour, the dents in her helm. The air was still hot and the ends of the canoness' hair floated free, halo-like and oddly sinister. 'Where is the rest of your squad?'

'Milady.' Her knees still shaking, Augusta kept her chin lifted, her eyes straight ahead, though she could feel the thousand gazes that were the soldiers, now packing the broken windows of the building. 'Sister Akemi Hirari lies critically injured. Sister Melia Kaliyan is caring for her, and is securing the Outskirt against the enemy.'

Rhene cackled. 'Quite the mess you've got here, Sisters. How has such a simple mission gone so far awry? Cultists lurking where they shouldn't, what is this shrine world coming to? And Sister Caia.' She winked, almost impertinent. 'First time I have seen you since Lycheate, and glad to see you still with us. Not destined to be Famulous, after all.'

'Yes, Sister,' Caia said. 'My fears were groundless, and He has blessed me to remain Militant.'

'Fears often are,' Rhene answered. 'Do not allow them to rule you.'

The canoness shot the Hospitaller a look and she quietened, holding onto her flapping wimple with one thin, age-spotted hand.

'Our astropathic communications failed, even as we came out of warp,' the canoness said. 'By His grace, we have arrived in time – but only just.' Her tone was grim, as severe as her expression. Raising her voice, she went on, 'Make no mistake, my Sisters, the cultists' beacon has been sent, and the hive fleet has heard its call. The failure of my comms means that they are in the system, that their shadow has begun to fall. Even now, the people of Opal will be feeling its touch. They will lose their faith, their sanity. They will lose their hearts, their minds, to the incoming xenos. And the cult will *rise*.' She paused, looking from face to face. 'Which means we face a war not on one front, but on two. A war from the sky, and a war on the ground. Yet He is with us, and we will prevail.' Her gaze stopped at Augusta. 'Your progress on the infestation?'

'We have driven the cultists forth from their lairs and nests, milady, forced them onto the surface in the hope of slaying them all. The survivors have taken refuge in the factories–'

'Understood. You will give me your full report, Augusta, but not here.' The canoness shot the adjutant a look. 'Execute plan delta. I want this area completely cleared, every last cultist exterminated. Once the bulk landers make planetfall along the riverside, tell the Exorcists to form up and advance between these buildings. Tell Sister Jolantra to shell this entire section of the city. The Penitent Engines will walk the rubble, and exterminate everything that moves. With this area secure, all forces will move into the Capital, and defend the evacuation. Tell the *Pride of Faith* she must safeguard the transports, allowing them to move towards the Mandeville point.'

Aitamah turned away, one finger on her vox-bead, issuing a firm stream of instructions. Bureaucracy, deployment, politics, social status – while Elvorix Ianthe was a warrior without peer, Aitamah was her eyes, ears, mouth and right arm. Listening,

Augusta wondered just how large the Order's force was – bigger than the mobile artillery assault upon the hereteks at Lycheate, certainly.

After a moment, the adjutant said, 'A message from the arch-deacon, milady. He... requests your attendance in the gover-nor's briefing room.'

The canoness snorted. 'He can wait,' she said. 'We are here at the Emperor's bidding, and this is a matter of war. The time for his Ecclesiarchal posturing is over.'

Augusta wanted to say something, wanted to explain the ongoing diplomatic tensions, but she held her place – she had not yet been given permission to speak. Rhene's attention, how-ever, had wandered to the surrounding buildings, and to the Blades that still lingered at the windows.

'You have injured?'

'Go,' the canoness said, before Augusta could reply. 'Offer them care. And secure all the information they have. Sister Caia, you will accompany the Hospitaller. No harm is to come to her.'

'Yes, milady.'

Surprisingly spry in her armour, its whiteness shining against the backdrop of pain and bloodshed, Rhene moved to help the soldiers. Caia, struggling with a pronounced limp, went with her.

But the canoness was still speaking.

'Sister Mikaela,' she said to one of the Sisters in the squad that still surrounded the pod. 'I want a secure location, building to my left. Sister Alcina, you and Sister Viola will assist in holding the road. And you...' She measured Augusta with a long, unreadable look. 'You will come with me. Whatever has happened here, I will know every last detail.'

The report took half an hour.

Her head still throbbing, standing at parade-ground ease

in a sombre hab-chapel, verses of care and industry inscribed upon every wall around her, Augusta went through each detail, holding nothing back. The squad's arrival, the governor's reluctance to give up the relic, the encounter with Father Arkas and his half-ruined cathedral, the cadet and Henrik, the kelermorph, her own conversations with the governor, the deacon and the commander. She made no secret of her frustration at the stubborn, ongoing bureaucracy, offered a full tactical assessment of the cult's apparent move from the Outskirt, and of her decision to drive them up from the sewers, despite the unbalanced numbers.

'In His grace and wisdom,' Augusta said, 'He guided us to the cult's presence, and before it was fully ready to rise. In this, we have been blessed. The Outskirt remains clear, and I have left Sister Melia and Sword Mezei to hold the area.' The electro-candlelight in the small space was poor, and she could not see the canoness' expression. 'Once discovered, however, the cult became more overt and aggressive, attacking the festival.' The words were acid. 'For this reason, I chose to deny them the time to regroup and attack again, instead driving them upwards from their sewer concealment and out into the open where they could be faced and defeated, in His name. This has given Commander Kozma the time to fully mobilise her artillery, and to begin the evacuation.'

'That was not an easy decision.' The canoness was pacing, reading the building's ancient prayers. 'Sister Akemi lies injured, your squad's strength is divided, and the Blades' losses have been heavy, though their souls rest with the Emperor. They have fulfilled their most ancient duty and become saints in their turn. Their names will be remembered by their world. And the cult... This must be the Pauper Princes – ever have they thrived in areas of poverty and neglect.'

The little sanctum had no windows and she paused before the open wings of the lectern, though it no longer held a sacred text.

'The Princes have used such tactics before, letting the appeal of a social rebellion attract new, non-hybrid members, and using it to mass up their numbers. Such has occurred at the Sediment Banks mining world and out on Sorrowreach.' She turned back, her eyes in shadow. 'And what of the cult leader you encountered? You say it was the clamavus?'

'I believe so, your eminence. I had prayed – hoped – we would encounter the patriarch, but such was not His will. With his aberrant guards dead, the clamavus was easily slain. We are blessed, as we have now denied the cult its access to the vox-casters of the Capital.'

The canoness snorted, thoughtful. 'What of Mihaly, Kozma, the deacon? Do you detect any xenos taint in Opal's rulers?'

'No, milady. Mihaly is a good man, both honest and honourable. Kozma is... exasperating in her inexperience, but she has genuine courage and her command of her forces is absolute. The deacon...' She stopped herself rolling her eyes. 'He is–'

'A windbag,' the canoness finished for her. 'He is very proud of his world, and his saint, is he not?'

Augusta refused to let herself react. 'Yes, milady.'

The adjutant had shot her mistress a look, but said nothing. Augusta noticed, however, that her scribbling had paused for an instant as she omitted the canoness' comment.

'And what of this Outskirt cathedral? You say the cult tried to take the location?'

'The cathedral is by the bridge, and in a strong position,' Augusta said. 'I believe the cult had intended to use it as their muster point, the base from which to launch their assault. Sisters Akemi and Melia are still there.'

'Your Sisters' lives rest with Him. As do those of us all.' She glanced at Aitamah, who was still scribbling. The cherub hovered close overhead, flashes of data in the depths of its eye sockets, its wings stirring the dust. At the chapel's doorway, Sister Mikaela stood silent guard, her helm on and her back to the room. Familiar from Lycheate and weapon-in-hand, she looked indomitable. 'Yet still, your description of this Outskirt cathedral bothers me. He tells me all is not as it seems. Why would the kelermorph reveal itself at that exact location?'

Aitamah said, 'Permission to speak?'

'Granted.'

'Plan delta is in place. Sisters Superior Eleni and Roku have deployed their squads to sweep the still-open sewer entrances along the riverside, and to ensure that the cult has not attempted to retreat back under the water. The bulk landers have achieved planetfall and Sister Jolantra has commanded the Exorcists to shell the habs and factories, as ordered. The Penitent Engines will walk the rubble. And Mistress Susanti awaits your command, milady – she wishes to take her charges to where the fighting is heaviest.'

Augusta almost reacted, but controlled herself. As shock troops, the Sisters Repentia would be unmatched. But the shiver that came with their presence...

Before the Emperor, I have sinned...

After the death of the fallen Inquisitor Istrix, Augusta had come far too close to wielding that eviscerator blade for herself. Had He decreed it, she would be here, under Mistress Susanti's command, spearheading every attack until her life was spent, and her redemption attained. The Repentia served a purpose, and one most holy. Yet still, even other Sisters would occasionally shudder at their passing.

Though if she made any further errors of judgement...

Bless me, O Emperor. Bless my defence of this doomed world.

If Elvorix Ianthe perceived Augusta's tension she made no comment. Instead, she said, 'Very well. Tell the commander – Kozma – to pull her artillery back to the Wall of Diligence. They are to set up a full perimeter and defend the Capital, the evacuation and the orbital batteries. She is to relocate her infantry behind their line, to defend the starports and the cable-cars, and to keep control of the people. And I will attend this... meeting with His Holiness the arch-deacon.'

Did Augusta imagine the flex of cynicism to her voice? Surely, such a thing would be unseemly.

'We are the Rose, and we shall enact our battle-plan, in the Emperor's name.'

No ceremony greeted the Order. The Day of the Third Martyr, Martyr Kis, should have seen the festivities heighten, the services reach an almost feverish crescendo, and the first of the full-on death matches in the Inner Sanctum's combat-pits. But a great and silent shadow had fallen across bright Opal, and now, her streets were soaked in dread. Terrified pilgrims fled from their ordered queues, gathering in hysterical huddles in temples and sanctuaries. Wailing prayers of abandonment, they threw themselves from cable-car and balcony, or attacked each other, or the already faltering Blades. Some took their own lives, offering themselves to the saint and the Emperor. Others preached Veres' return, their eyes alight with heresy and madness. Lost prayer-scarves blew across the drifting sleet and the boiler-plate vox-cast command still blared, clear, across the chaos of the Capital:

'Blessed pilgrims of Holy Opal. Proceed to your nearest cable-car station. Do not wait for family. Do not collect belongings. Walk with Him, and with penitence. Walk calmly and with swiftness. Blessed pilgrims of Holy Opal. Proceed to your nearest cable-car station...'

Joining the Capital's efforts at control, the deacon had preached for almost twenty-four hours, but now, he finally stepped down. Even the bells had gone quiet, leaving only that endless demand, repeated over and over and over.

'Blessed pilgrims of Holy Opal...'

In the cupola of her Immolator, the canoness stood as she had done during the Order's assault on the rusting Mechanicus world of Lycheate. Then, Augusta had been in the belly of another vehicle, chafing with restlessness. Now, buffeted by the great Rose battle-banner at her back, she stood at the woman's shoulder, watching the unmindful servitors still scurrying about the trash-strewn roads of the Capital below.

The festival was in ruins. Here and there, sobbing pilgrims still queued at the cable-car stations, their heads down, their costumes bloodstained and filthy. Others had formed gangs, and bristled with collections of simulacra weapons. Still more hid in doorways, waving knives to keep people at bay, or fighting amongst themselves, shouting blame and retribution and decrying each other as heretics. Penitents thrashed their flesh, begging for His blessing. On a few corners, there were still stationary Tauroxes, the ones too rusted to move. Adepts yet bustled about these, blessing their spirits to life. A single voice rose, a hymn that was more like a sob, and then it was gone.

'Blessed pilgrims of Holy Opal. Proceed to your nearest cable-car station...'

In her vox-bead, Augusta had tried to raise Melia, and failed; tried to raise the cadet, and had not found her either. With the canoness' remarks about the Outskirt cathedral, a new shard of worry had entered her heart, but she could do nothing – only pray that her Sisters were safe.

'Opal is almost out of time,' the canoness said, her breath frosting on the wind. 'From everything you have reported, the

cultists have been throwing their recruits' lives awa
to harry and to cull the Blades' numbers, and to
Kozma's defences. You have eliminated the kelerm
clavamus, and this is well done. But you have no
the cult's critical leaders – the patriarch, the pri
magus. This makes me believe they yet hold their
back.' She might as well have said *the worst is still*
Aitamah. Progress?'

In the vehicle's belly, the adjutant had a street m
the metal walls – an exact duplicate of Kozma's
scarlet markers tracked the Order as it dispersed.

'Eleni and Roku are following the line of the
open sewer ports. Sister Roku confirms that mo
fled the riverside area, moving into the buildin
everything they find. Some have tried to retreat, b
the tunnels to the Outskirt, but they are few, and
shown justice.'

'What of the Blades at the sewer entrances?'

'There is little more they can achieve. As orderee
Kozma is relocating her forces behind the Wal
They will guard the starports, and endeavour to
the Capital's streets.' Aitamah paused briefly; see
her strength before she continued, 'The shadow
upon the people, milady, and the roads are filli

'Tell Kozma, if they don't move, shoot them.'

'Milady, the deacon–'

'I will deal with His Holiness. Complete your

Briefly, Aitamah described the situation in the
of shuttles were still ferrying hundreds of thousa
ing transports, but fighting at the landing pad
to critical levels. People were overloading the ve
at them as they tried to land, or leave. Wealth i

Joining the Capital's efforts at control, the deacon had preached for almost twenty-four hours, but now, he finally stepped down. Even the bells had gone quiet, leaving only that endless demand, repeated over and over and over.

'Blessed pilgrims of Holy Opal...'

In the cupola of her Immolator, the canoness stood as she had done during the Order's assault on the rusting Mechanicus world of Lycheate. Then, Augusta had been in the belly of another vehicle, chafing with restlessness. Now, buffeted by the great Rose battle-banner at her back, she stood at the woman's shoulder, watching the unmindful servitors still scurrying about the trash-strewn roads of the Capital below.

The festival was in ruins. Here and there, sobbing pilgrims still queued at the cable-car stations, their heads down, their costumes bloodstained and filthy. Others had formed gangs, and bristled with collections of simulacra weapons. Still more hid in doorways, waving knives to keep people at bay, or fighting amongst themselves, shouting blame and retribution and decrying each other as heretics. Penitents thrashed their flesh, begging for His blessing. On a few corners, there were still stationary Tauroxes, the ones too rusted to move. Adepts yet bustled about these, blessing their spirits to life. A single voice rose, a hymn that was more like a sob, and then it was gone.

'Blessed pilgrims of Holy Opal. Proceed to your nearest cable-car station...'

In her vox-bead, Augusta had tried to raise Melia, and failed; tried to raise the cadet, and had not found her either. With the canoness' remarks about the Outskirt cathedral, a new shard of worry had entered her heart, but she could do nothing – only pray that her Sisters were safe.

'Opal is almost out of time,' the canoness said, her breath frosting on the wind. 'From everything you have reported, the cultists have been throwing their recruits' lives away, using them to harry and to cull the Blades' numbers, and to wear down Kozma's defences. You have eliminated the kelermorph, and the clavamus, and this is well done. But you have not yet located the cult's critical leaders – the patriarch, the primus and the magus. This makes me believe they yet hold their full strength back.' She might as well have said *the worst is still to come.* 'Sister Aitamah. Progress?'

In the vehicle's belly, the adjutant had a street map shining on the metal walls – an exact duplicate of Kozma's hololith. Tiny scarlet markers tracked the Order as it dispersed.

'Eleni and Roku are following the line of the river, and the open sewer ports. Sister Roku confirms that most cultists have fled the riverside area, moving into the buildings and killing everything they find. Some have tried to retreat, back and down the tunnels to the Outskirt, but they are few, and they have been shown justice.'

'What of the Blades at the sewer entrances?'

'There is little more they can achieve. As ordered, Commander Kozma is relocating her forces behind the Wall of Diligence. They will guard the starports, and endeavour to keep order in the Capital's streets.' Aitamah paused briefly; seemed to summon her strength before she continued, 'The shadow in the warp is upon the people, milady, and the roads are filling with fear.'

'Tell Kozma, if they don't move, shoot them.'

'Milady, the deacon–'

'I will deal with His Holiness. Complete your report.'

Briefly, Aitamah described the situation in the Capital. Relays of shuttles were still ferrying hundreds of thousands to the wait-ing transports, but fighting at the landing pads was escalating to critical levels. People were overloading the vehicles, jumping at them as they tried to land, or leave. Wealthier pilgrims were commanding personal shuttles to land in the roadways, then being attacked by gangs as they attempted to board.

Casualties were high and the Blades were struggling.

'Sororitas!'

There was a sudden cry, swiftly taken up by more voices. Around them had gathered a group of pilgrims, all clad in the battered remnants of market-stall, quasi-military uniforms. With them was a priest, one of the figures from the Path of the Thousand Humble, a broken skull embroidered on his chasuble. All were holding their hands up to the vehicle, sobbing in terror and incomprehension, pleading with the Sisters for absolution, for an explanation as to what had befallen their world.

'Help us!' the priest was begging, tears pouring down his face. 'Teach us! What did we do to deserve the Emperor's fury?'

Augusta almost expected Elvorix Ianthe to pull her plasma pistol and execute the man on the spot, but she gave a command over the vox and the vehicle paused. The pilgrims clustered about the Rhino, touching the metal and exclaiming in wonder and awe.

'You are Sisters of Battle!' The priest wrung his hands – he was barely more than a lad, perhaps nineteen. 'You are His daughters, you know His will, His thoughts. What did we do?'

The canoness glared down at him, like he was the voice of suffering Opal herself. 'I do not presume to know the will of the God-Emperor,' she returned, her tone grim. 'But I say to you this – did you not deny the outskirts of your own city? Did you not ignore and dismiss your own people? Refuse them not only food and water and medicine, but their very faith? His blessing, and His holy light? In such darkness does the rot of heresy spread.'

The pilgrims stared at her. The young priest twisted his hands further; his mouth jumped as he fought his tears.

'We did not know,' he said. 'We did not know...'

That made the canoness angry. 'Of course you knew – all of you! But you chose to ignore it. To brush it aside, to leave it on the far bank of the river, to let it fester, not only in poverty, but in sacrilege and faithlessness. The mortal body may suffer, but always, there is redemption in His grace. I do not presume to know the will of the God-Emperor, but I know sin where I see it. You are a planet of fools!'

The lad had crumpled to his knees now, hunched over his own pain. 'Forgive us,' he said. 'Forgive us...'

Around the tank, the others took up the refrain. 'Forgive us, you who are holy! Forgive...'

Aitamah had paused, and was looking up. Augusta watched the road. Outside the wall, the plumes of smoke that marked the Exorcists' advance were almost continuous and a thick, grey pall now hung over the collapsing habs. She had no idea how many workers had still been inside them.

'Your eminence,' the adjutant said, slightly cautiously. 'The deacon... ah... he demands... that you–'

'Damn the bloody deacon!'

Augusta had never heard the canoness raise her voice, and she started. The woman's battle-rage was towering, but this... this was unusual. And unnerving.

'You.' The canoness pointed at the priest. 'Get up.' The lad scrabbled to obey. 'You will take these people to the nearest starport, and you will ensure that they leave. And you will pray as if your very soul depended upon it. You will tell all that you meet the following – Opal's punishment is upon her. We are the Adepta Sororitas and we will save you if it lies within His will, and within our faith and might. But if we fail, if we all perish as the Devourer comes, then know that your heresy, and your hypocrisy, and your *blindness*, have been your world's undoing.

If you wish to save your soul, child, then you had better teach this prayer to everyone you encounter. Because if you do not, then only the void awaits.'

The lad was gazing at her, ash-faced and wide-eyed.

'Go!' She gestured at the road and he recovered his wits, rounding up the pilgrims and ushering them along.

'Blessed pilgrims of Holy Opal. Proceed to your nearest cable-car station...'

The canoness watched them cluster, wailing as they went. Then she turned to Augusta.

'This world has a great deal to answer for. Let us deal with this deacon.'

And Augusta could only answer, 'Yes, milady.'

XVII

THE PUNISHMENT OF OPAL

Along with Sister Alcina, the Repentia and the Penitent Engines, Sister Viola moved ahead of the Exorcists, but behind the line of their shelling. Before them, building after building came down in a roar of smoke and dust and rubble...

And the death toll steadily mounted.

This second sweep aimed to eliminate the cult completely, trapping it between the advancing Order and Kozma's mobile artillery, now defending the Wall of Diligence. With the sewer exits sealed or being watched by Eleni and Roku, the cultists were forced to remain on the surface, and they fled from building to building, trying to keep in cover as the spread of their obliteration grew.

Moving at a steady half-speed, the advancing Order did not have the numbers – or the intention – to explore these buildings room by room and corridor by corridor. Instead the Exorcists, with their long-range organ-pipe missile launchers, were simply bringing them down, shelling huge craters in their ferrocrete. The air was filled with destruction, with drifts of thick smoke and sparkling grey dust, with the continuous, thundering rumbles of falling masonry, like storms of annihilation. And, as the shelling cleared the area ahead, so the Penitent Engines walked the wreckage, their servos whirring. They clambered over the debris, smashing their way through anything standing, and demolishing all in their path.

Recalling a recent mission to the Skull Forge, where the Penitent Engines were created and blessed with life, Viola watched these with a new interest – massive, bipedal walkers, controlled by a heretic neurally wired to the machine's spirit. They were fearsome, terrifying, their pilots those who sought absolution for their sins against the God-Emperor and strove to attain redemption. The young Sister found herself staring at the closest one, fascinated by the still, robed figure at its heart, his hood cast over his face.

As she watched, the machine lumbered over to a smoking pile, its huge feet kicking as it went. A scatter of tiny figures tried to flee the thing, but there was the high-pitched scream of a running power saw, the cough and roar of flamers.

'By the Throne,' she said, awed.

Missiles streaked overhead, and the buildings crashed down.

'There!' Alcina indicated a cluster of shapes, fleeing through the billowing dust. There were five or six of them, every one oddly hunched, their arms curled into their bodies. They were parallel to Viola's position, behind the engines' advance, though still ahead of the Exorcists themselves.

Viola, a prayer on her lips, moved the heavy bolter to open fire.

As she did so, a lone figure ran forwards, right across her line of sight. It was close, and despite the dust, she could see it – her – quite clearly. Her head was shaven, her limbs bare and carved with bloody prayers. She wore only a short tunic, and there was a bandage about her face – over her eyes, Viola thought.

But the sword...

The Sister Repentia's eviscerator blade was terrifying, snarling like pure fury. Viola shivered, remembering the death of the fallen inquisitor upon Lycheate and how close they had all come to taking up those blades for themselves. Remembering her own relief, her exact thoughts, when the canoness had given the squad its reprieve.

Seeing the lone Sister, the six hunching creatures stopped. They spread out, moving to surround her, their teeth bared in glistening grins. The Repentia paused, that huge sword shining with teeth of its own.

Before the Emperor I have sinned. Beyond forgiveness. Beyond forbearance. Beyond mercy...

Viola heard the prayer in her thoughts, watched as if caught on a hook. The creatures, all of one mind, circled steadily then all leapt together. The eviscerator carved one clean in half, cut deeply into the second. The Sister dived and rolled, came up to take out a third. Viola was aware of three more Repentia, of the Mistress' voice calling orders like whipcracks, but the one fighting – who was she, what had she done? – was still moving, with three of the beasts still about her.

Again, they leapt together. The Repentia threw herself forwards, between two of them, took one down on the way past, spun back to face the other two. She fought like a thing demented, swift and fierce. Wary now, they crouched lower, their claws extended and eager.

Across the rubble, Viola heard the Sister singing. She whispered the words, echoing them reflexively: *'That thou shouldst spare none.'*

Alcina said nothing.

It occurred to Viola to wonder if Alcina was making some sort of point, but the squad's second did not speak. The Repentia slashed at another creature, but her ankle turned on the steaming rubble and she lurched sideways and missed it. It snarled, leapt forwards. She met it with the blade, carved a great gouge in its skull...

But she'd left her back unguarded. Even as Viola watched, absolutely mesmerised, the final creature landed on her shoulders. She went over forwards, not releasing the sword. Despite herself, Viola stepped up, craned to see what was happening. She wondered if the Repentia Mistress would help the fallen Sister, do anything, but she had directed the other three to spread out, to keep scouring the rubble for more threats. They offered their dying Sister no aid, and Viola instinctively understood – knew – that the Sister would not have welcomed it.

Death was what she sought.

By the Light!

Viola saw the blade rise, blood-covered, saw the surviving creature's clawed arms slash – it seemed to have more than one set. There was a cry like a plea, a final prayer, and then the beast reared back up, its face all covered in still-warm gore.

Grimly, the Mistress raised her pistol and shot it through the head.

Shuddering, Viola said, 'Blessed be her memory.'

This time, Alcina echoed her. 'She has Repented,' the older Sister said. 'She may kneel at the Throne in honour, her trials over. Let us pray that her Sisters may do the same.' She paused, turned her visor to Viola like a warning. 'We must move. The xenos must be exterminated completely, and we have duties of our own.'

'Our Emperor, deliver us!'

Advancing over the ruins, Viola aimed short, five-round bursts, conserving her ammunition. It mattered not if the rising shape was a cultist, or a worker, or a lost Opal pilgrim, not now – all would offer their lives to His grace.

In the rubble, an injured man cried out, holding up a hand for help. He was half-crushed, his legs broken. Alcina's single shot struck him between the eyes, took out the back of his skull.

'Do not trust them,' she said. 'There may still be saboteurs, waiting with explosives or worse.'

As they moved through the flattened buildings, so their lines of sight became clearer. Far behind them, Viola could see the lead Exorcist, its paintwork glaring red, its holy pipes shining in gold and bronze. Each pipe coughed in turn and more missiles streaked overhead, every one a promise of His wrath.

In places, gangs of cultists lurked waiting – the Sisters saw a swarm of scurrying figures assault one of the Penitent Engines, throwing themselves at it bodily, climbing its limbs. Viola raised the heavy bolter, but Alcina made a gesture to stop her.

'Do not. We are too far away and you may hit the pilot.'

Crying Veres' name, the cultists planted krak grenades in its joints, and around the pilot's exposed body. Saws and flamers took down dozens of them, but there were more, there were always more. Viola saw the explosion, saw the red splash that was the pilot's life, saw the machine totter, stumble and fall.

As it hit the ground, she opened fire, grim and merciless. The distance was considerable, but the retreating cultists had little cover, and they were gone in a shower of scarlet.

'What happens to it?' Viola asked. 'Does it go back to the Skull Forge?'

'It will stay. We have neither the time nor the hands to retrieve it.' Alcina gave Viola a steady look. 'We must increase our vigilance, and make up for its loss.'

'Yes, Sister.'

The closeness of Repentia and Penitent Engines both was bothering her, and she was not quite sure why – perhaps it was just her memories of the machines' construction.

In the rubble, more figures loitered, and the Sisters kept shooting. The Exorcists' shelling was constant and indiscriminate, accompanied by broadcast hymnals of vengeance and purging and death. Many of the buildings still had walls and corners, places where workers cowered or where cultist groups could hide. Several times, lingering gangs waited and then assailed the Exorcists themselves, endeavouring to scramble upon them, and to tear the pipes free, or to drop grenades down their lengths. The drivers ran hundreds of them over, uncaring, crushing a multitude of frail bodies beneath the vehicles' tracks.

'The Exorcists have long range,' Alcina said. There was a note of victory in her voice, a tangible paean of savage glee as the vehicles boomed forth another volley. 'They clear the ground, removing the cult and securing the area. They bring His wrath to the streets of this world, just as they did to the hereteks of Lycheate. Opal may yet perish, Sister, but we *will* exterminate the faithless.'

All at once, the line of Exorcists paused, engines thumping but pipes still.

There, ahead of them, the Gate of Nemes and the rising might of the Wall of Diligence, the barrier between the demolished hab-blocks and the holy Capital itself. Squat, dome-topped towers stood tall against the sky, each one carved with an aquila, the globe-in-hand symbol of Opal, and a thousand warrior prayers. As Viola looked, the head of the closest tower turned through ninety degrees, and a huge cannon muzzle hove into view. Beneath it, at the wall's foot, the pale-camo shapes of the Tauroxes and Chimeras seemed tiny by comparison.

'Orbital batteries,' Alcina said, nodding at the towers. 'They will not be enough, but they will bring us more time. Pray with me, my Sister. *With your grace, we shall know only courage…'*

The Penitent Engines, four of them remaining, were still stamping through the ruins. Flares of flame accompanied them as they exterminated any pockets of resistance. They brought their saws down, smashing through any still-stable floors; they wrenched and kicked at any stubborn steel uprights. Every one was a death machine, and little escaped their wrath.

'*With your grace, we shall stand strong in the face of the enemy…'*

Joining the prayer, Viola watched, taking neat shots at running cultists.

'He is with us, truly,' Alcina continued, still with that ripple of savagery. 'We will cleanse this place, Sister, before we stand at the Throne.'

At the governor's palace, Augusta stood at the canoness' shoulder, her helm on, her face concealed. She bore bolter and chainsword both at her hips, but had drawn neither, and she stood at parade-ground ease, her chin lifted, her feet apart, both hands behind her back. Her armour and cloak were still ruined and filthy, but every stain was a mark of her conflict, how hard she had fought for this world.

Elvorix Ianthe, by contrast, was clean, bright scarlet and helm still off. Her black-and-white robe fluttered, her white hair shone like frost, and her attitude was dangerous. With her were Aitamah, slate in hand, and the ever-present cherub, its skull-sockets watching.

'Your eminence,' the governor said. He had risen to his feet, his tone respectful. 'You do Opal great honour.'

At Augusta's initial audience, the governor's retinue had been minor. This time, the man was in his full robes of office, layered and embroidered with gold, complete with hand-stitched prayer-chasuble and Opal's globe-in-hand medallion around his neck. A full squad of dress-uniform guards accompanied him, two at his shoulders, and seven along the back wall, neat and expressionless. Each of these bore a flag – of Opal, of the governor's household, and of the Blades themselves – with its pole rested in a belt loop.

Kozma was also there, her uniform unchanged, her face unreadable. She flicked her gaze from Augusta to the canoness and back, though she said nothing. She had both aide and vox-operator, and a third, dress-uniformed figure that was presumably Opal's equivalent of a commissar.

It was the deacon, however, who held Augusta's attention. While he stood to one side, he still filled the room, all shoulders and rage. He still wore his sermon-robe, and he was flushed and bright-eyed, a shine of work-sweat across his forehead. His vox-cast rallying cry had been booming out across the Capital for a day and a night, almost without relent. It had been steadying the people and bringing them hope and faith. He looked like he resented this distraction.

From outside, the vox-casters still issued their final command. *'Blessed pilgrims of Holy Opal…'*

'An honour indeed,' the deacon said, loudly taking up the governor's greeting. 'He has brought you to Opal at the time of our greatest need. There are no Sisters more warlike, no warriors more zealous, than the Order of the Bloody Rose. Is that not so?' It carried the faintest flex of sarcasm and he did not wait for an answer. 'I fear, milady canoness, that you do not catch precious Opal at her best. My streets are in chaos, my infrastructure overloaded. My factories are in ruins, my workers dead, my buildings collapsing, my sewers blocked and my festival destroyed. My pilgrims are fleeing in terror, or fighting amongst themselves. Eight hundred *years* of holy preparation, all of Opal's past, her saints and her glories, and her praises to Him – and it lies now in rubble. Truly, this is a time of tragedy.' There was an edge to his voice, less a lament and more an accusation.

The canoness didn't care. 'It is a great deal more than that, arch-deacon,' she said. 'The hive fleet has entered the system. With no communications, Opal is now alone, undefended but for my Sisters and your own Blades. We have secured the Outskirt, and moved upwards through the habs and factories. Now, we advance across the Capital itself. We will scour the cult from every last hiding place, that the evacuation may continue.'

Mihaly blinked. 'Then… you cannot save my world.'

'It is too late.' The canoness' words were a knell, and Augusta saw the shudder that went through the governor's frame. 'The xenos close upon us, and we can only fight to buy time. We will save your people, Mihaly, as many as we can.'

'Saint and Emperor.' He dropped his gaze, supporting his forehead in one hand.

But the deacon came forwards, his forehead gleaming. The windows, again, were open and the air was chill enough for them all to breathe steam, yet patches of darkness still showed at the man's armpits.

'This is Opal, canoness. We will not simply abandon her.'

'You will do as I command.' Elvorix Ianthe laid her gauntlet on her plasma pistol. 'The hive fleet will be upon you in hours. You have very few combatant ships, and little surface-to-orbit capability. When the spores start to sear through the atmosphere, Opal's death will be upon her. Everything will be dissolved in acid and eaten.'

'Then you will have failed.' The deacon's words were mild, but their impact was like a shock.

Elvorix Ianthe all but rocked on her heels. Her voice soft and lethal, she said, 'You do not *dare* speak to me in such tones, and you will defend your people.'

'What do you think I've been doing?' He gestured at his own

sweated robes as if they were the bloodstained garb of the soldiers.

'I think you have been blind. I think you have been stubborn and filled with your own pride.'

Stung, the man inhaled. 'Milady canoness–'

'Your eminences, please.'

The governor had looked back up, his face etched in pain. He gestured, and a guard moved, standing by the deacon with a stance that was both insistence and threat.

'My gem, my sacred Opal – you say she cannot survive.'

The deacon had stopped, his face puce. The canoness flexed on her toes, her armour creaking. Augusta could not see her expression, but could guess at it. Outside, bells chimed, their sounds funereal. Occasional voices called hymns, or screams like pleas. As Mihaly paused to gather his thoughts, the Capital's dread and horror were tangible. The cherub hovered. Aitamah scribbled on her slate. Outside, the order to evacuate continued.

'*Blessed pilgrims of Holy Opal…*'

'Milady canoness,' the governor said. His voice was almost breaking. 'Please understand – this world is precious to me. To us. To Him. All down the millennia, Opal has offered her most accomplished sons and daughters to the defence of the Imperium – and now, you tell us she will perish, and that there is little you can do. My people cry in the streets, milady. They riot, and they tear each other down. Perhaps you can explain why He has brought this fate upon us?'

'Opal has her sins, governor,' the canoness replied.

In the distance, there were the rumbling booms of falling buildings – the Exorcists were doing their work. A great cloud of shuttles still circled in the air. The deacon narrowed his eyes, then turned away. Kozma stayed watching Mihaly.

'My adjutant, Sister Aitamah, has made a full study of your

history.' Elvorix Ianthe threw words like spears, every one striking its target. 'You, with all of your drums and your noise – your Imperial tithes are but the barest minimum. You boast of your holiness, yet you have skirted this, your most basic and sacred duty. All these great saints that you tout so highly – they are not recent. They are lost to the mists of the past. Empty legends. Hot air. You are hypocrites and liars, all three of you. Trading on nothing. Opal's failures and insincerities go back *generations*.'

Mihaly did not move; his face was a mask of guilt and sorrow. He said, 'Then it is true. He is punishing us.'

Kozma still stared at him; the deacon was scowling at some internal thought. Glowering, he said, 'We are *Opal*. We are Chosen.'

'You are nothing of the sort.' Still, the canoness did not raise her voice. She walked the length of the table, past the paintings of the long-lost saints, and stopped, almost in the deacon's face. 'Before this is over, you will give Sister Superior Augusta the skull of Saint Veres. She will take it safely to Ophelia VII, where it will be held in both safety and veneration.'

The deacon curled his lip. 'I still intend to celebrate the Sermon of the Hero–'

'Then let us hope that the hive fleet gives you time.' The canoness' sarcasm was biting.

The deacon glowered for a moment longer, then stepped back.

'Tamara Kozma,' the canoness said.

'Milady.'

'Your infantry – your Blades of the Holy Interior – they will continue to secure the Capital, and control the evacuation. Your Blades of the Holy Exterior will remain at the Varadi. Your mobile artillery will defend the Wall of Diligence, and the orbital cannons, right up to the last. Once your adepts have completed their blessings and repairs, they are to proceed down the sewers.'

Kozma's expression was unchanged. 'Milady?'

'They will commence laying charges. If necessary, we will destroy the Capital entire.'

The commander swayed where she stood. 'But my people, your eminence – we cannot possibly evacuate them all, not in the time we have. And my Blades...'

'Your Blades will remain at their posts. It is a better death than being left for the xenos.'

Kozma visibly paled. 'In His name.'

'Good.' The canoness gave her a single, stern nod. 'Now,' she said. 'My Order will commence its securing of the Capital. And with His grace, we will exterminate every last trace of this cult.'

xviii

THE SISTER'S COURAGE

Still at Arkas' side, Kamilla was lost in wonder. Her head was full of imagery, of glory and exultation. At the cathedral of her dreams, the figure cried aloud, a hymn of splendour and welcome that made her blood race and her pulse thump and her face redden with a fervour she had never known. Above the man's upraised arms spun the vortex, dark with secrets. It was herald and prophet, hope and phenomenon. And even as she watched, Saint Veres was manifest, in starlight and in wonder. And he would descend unto Opal, and he would walk amongst her people, and they would touch his outstretched hands. He would raise his own sacred, golden skull, and it would flash in the light of the incoming ships, show the arrival of Opal's true saviours.

And her people would *ascend!*

Even in her dream-state, Kamilla remembered: she had wanted – still wanted – to be blessed enough to attend the Sermon of the Hero, to see the saint's skull for herself. But another thought was creeping in now, an understanding that she had not before realised...

That image in her dream was not just one cathedral.

It was two. Siblings, one reflecting the other.

In the dream, it made complete sense – one cathedral was the peak of the Inner Sanctum's mountain, it was glassaic and holiness, it was the Sacred Scope and the sight of Terra itself. Its coloured roof shone with glory, and light-motes danced in the aisle. Truly, it was the centre of Opal's wealth and wonder.

But this was the other, and its shadow. It was mirrored, like the Outskirt in the Varadi, as if it was the Saints' Cathedral's forgotten, quieter self. A humble place, a place of kindness, a place that had been offering food and water and care and medicines for many, many years. Its people – *Kamilla's* people – had been dying, bereft, rejected and abandoned. They had been starving and suffering, empty of hope. But the saint had been a poor man, and he was come to save them, too. He would give them reason to live, to laugh, to hope again. Reason to give up the lho and kyxa, to throw aside their despair and to find new energy, to take pride in themselves and their world and to stand up straight once more...

And they would *sing!*

Walking the transepts, the dream filled and lifted her. She could see the saint's arrival in her mind's eye, see his beneficence and generosity, see the help and gifts he bore. She could see the Three Martyrs and the ring-light that bathed them in holiness, see them walking the streets and giving out food, and water, and help. She could see Opal reborn, her two sides truly and finally united under Veres' banner. The world was shining with her gemstone brightness, with the perfect shimmer of her stonework. Overjoyed, Kamilla shared her visions with those she helped, and they welled up with tears, with thanks and wonder, with empathy and deliverance. And she *understood* now; she understood what had happened to Arkas, his change of heart and the epiphany that had struck him – all his life, he had struggled to help these people, and now he could fulfil his every promise. The true Father was with them and the visions had such power, such *potential*... A rising, bubbling jubilation was manifest in every dream-image, an anticipation of the miracles to come, and it was almost too much to be borne.

What nudged her to tumble from her ecstasy, she did not quite realise at first.

Perhaps it was the sensation of passing time, of daylight on the statues' faces. Perhaps it was the deacon's distant sermon, as it stopped and then restarted. Perhaps it was the sheer *number* of banner-carrying, weapon-hoarding, starry-eyed hopefuls that now packed the aisles, the transepts, the grounds, the cloisters, the quadrangles, the listing, weed-filled graveyard. Perhaps it was just the spark of her own, true faith, still alight in the core of her heart...

Or perhaps it was the gleam of red in the corner of her vision, something strong and curved and shining. The flutter of black and white, and the throaty, contralto voice that said, 'This is a place of *treachery*.'

The anger in it was contained, but powerful. It made Kamilla shiver, made her push through the crowds to see what it was. Muttering in surprise, the people were falling back, glancing at one another for understanding, or for reassurance. And through them, she could see...

By the saint!

She could see a woman, alone and unarmed, now standing by the lectern. Her head was bare, and one side of her short, dark hair was stuck to her skull with dried blood. Her face was dusky-skinned, a mass of contusions. One of her eyes was blackened and swollen shut, and she seemed to sway where she stood. But still, her chin was lifted and her *armour* – it was perfect, beautiful. Red and shining ceramite, a scarlet glow of pure and holy strength.

A Sister of Battle.

For the first time since the crypt, a sliver of Kamilla's cognisance returned. As if the Sister's very presence were a flame, forcing back the darkness, the imagery of the dreams was starting to char, smouldering to ash around the edges. Kamilla stopped, staring at the newcomer. She *knew* this woman, this Sister, she had seen her before.

But...

Her thoughts were confused, full of fog. She shook her head, and remembered something else: *pain*. It clanged back and forth like bells.

'Father Arkas.' Walking forwards, the Sister growled his name. Her hands were bare, bereft of gauntlets, yet her presence and authority were tangible. 'You are a heretic and traitor.' Though her steps were unsteady, she looked fully capable of bringing the whole cathedral down round their ears.

'I have only seen the truth,' Arkas told her. 'The way to help my people.'

The Sister stopped in front of him, ire blazing from her gaze, her stance, her pauldrons. Around her, the crowd seemed held in place, watching her with eyes like starlight. Kamilla stared too, mesmerised.

'I should slay you where you stand,' the Sister said. 'Yet I hear His voice in my heart, and it speaks to me of serenity, of my long training as a healer. Arkas, hear me – you do not have to lose your soul. You are a good man, a holy man, and the God-Emperor has not forgotten you. Always, He is your hope, your future. Will you not come back to His side, bring your people with you, back to the light?' Her gaze searched his face. 'That way, you can truly save them.'

Something in her – the sheer, powerful emotion of the appeal she voiced – cut at Kamilla like a blade. It split her thoughts up the middle, slicing a line between Arkas on one side, his expression alight, and the Sister herself on the other, her courage and resolution. Her armour, her compassion.

My training as a healer.

Welcoming the pain, needing it, Kamilla shook her head a second time. More memories were coming back to her now: the fight in the street, her broken face. Arkas, and the blade in his gut...

Arkas! There was no sign of his injury now. His robes were new and clean. What had happened to him?

What had happened to *her*?

But he was still speaking. He said, soft and insistent, 'You can join us, Sister Melia. We will know joy. We will know hope. We will know wonder!'

'You will know *death*.'

More images, beating like wings. Kamilla was a little one, scribbling on a torn piece of her uncle's vellum. Laughing, Arkas grabbed her, picking her up and making her giggle. 'Kamilla! Where did you get that? Don't let Jakob see it!' He was like that gentle, paternal presence, that thing still in her head. Safety, family, belonging. She trusted him with her life.

But the Sister...

Gritting her teeth, Kamilla shook her head a third time, needing the banging agony, trying to sort out her thoughts: what was dream, what was reality. Her mind was hurting, spinning, grappling for anything that made sense. She felt sick.

The Sister closed her hand in the front of Arkas' robes, stared into his face.

'Pray with me,' she said to him, her tone almost a rasp. 'Arkas, you can still save your soul, save your people. Help save your world. Sing with me the litany. *A spiritu dominatus...*'

Those words! They were a shock, a clarion, a paean of faith like an organ's opening notes. They brought a rush of realisation, a sudden, holy blaze of light. There were more images, so many images, now tumbling like rose petals. Red-armoured figures, six of them, moving in a flawless combat-harmony. One was a Sister with a heavy weapon, another had an auspex. An older Sister, grey-haired and severe, and completely in command. Kamilla could hear the crystal perfection of their battle-hymn, even as Sister Melia sang the words aloud:

'*Domine, libra nos!*'

But Arkas said only, 'Please, Sister.' He'd made no move to defend himself, and his eyes were full of starlight. 'We've taken your weapon, your helmet, your vox. What can you do? Saint Veres comes!'

The people echoed him, muttering, 'Saint Veres comes, Saint Veres comes.' They sounded oddly, eerily mindless, and Kamilla shuddered.

The Sister glanced at them, but she did not let Arkas go. 'Had I my weapon, you would be paying the price of your heresy. But in taking it, you have gifted me His message. He has guided my hand, my choices. And He tells me – you can still repent.' She raised her voice. 'All of you! You can still repent! You can be truly saved!'

She was trying to *help* him, Kamilla suddenly realised. Trying to save him. Trying to save all of them.

But from what?

'I have no fear for my soul,' Arkas replied, smiling. 'For my people, or for my world. We–'

'You will be *devoured!*' With a sudden cry, Melia shook him like a rat. 'All of you!' She looked around. 'Is this truth? Is this hope?' She turned back to Arkas. 'Is this the culmination of your life's work? The presence in this building is not the saint. It is not your glory, your blessing, your future. It is a hunger both ancient and terrible, and it will devour every last one of you. You will perish, you will perish screaming, and you will perish *cursed!* Will you do this to your people, Arkas? Will you bear the responsibility for their deaths, for the deaths of those who follow you? Who love you? It is a beast of darkness!'

Darkness.

A final shock of memory, and comprehension like ice-cold water. Somehow, Kamilla had thought that the *thing* had been a part of the dream... But it had not been in her head, it was here. Physically, tangibly *real*. The understanding made her shudder, like a touch of acid on her skin. *Darkness.* She hadn't even seen it clearly, but it had been down there, seething, swelling at the edges of the light like a gnawing of maggots, eating away at her thoughts. Like a sound in her head, the screaming of a million worlds. And a *smell*... A musty, chitinous smell of age and time and appetite, of limitless ambition and savage, eager cruelty.

You will be devoured!

And another thought, as real as the monster. Not exultation, not blessing and wonder, not that gentle, paternal touch, and not the arrival of the saint, but the truth that really lay beneath it: other things, scuttling in the darkness, smaller and more numerous. Things crawling and writhing and eating and eating and *eating*. The touch of the acid was all around her and it was dissolving everything – the buildings, the people, the bridges, the markets. The hope, the trust of the saint. It mattered not whether they were faithful or Outskirter, or what path or banner they followed. They were all the same, they were just...

Food.

The flash of absolute terror was stark as white ice. It tore her from the very last of the dream and landed her, coughing, on her knees on the cold stone floor. Shudders wracked her, she almost threw up. As if etched into her mind, she understood at last.

Arkas! What have you done?

As if the stars had finally fallen from her own eyes, her vision cleared properly and she could see stains, drying puddles of blood poorly washed from the cathedral's flags. And where were the vergers – Eszter, Fabian? Those gentle grey ghosts that had always guarded Arkas' flanks?

He couldn't have…

But she knew, in her heart: they were gone. Perhaps they had tried to stop him, she didn't know. Perhaps he had taken them down to the crypt, as he had taken her. Her belly churning, she lurched back to her feet, staggered forwards. She could see only death, death everywhere… These poor people, gunned down on the bridges. Or betrayed and crying in pain, dissolved in stench and corrosion while the monsters feasted…

Yet Sister Melia was trying to *help*, trying to save Arkas, save the people. She was an icon of faith and courage, true to her holy calling. Weaponless and injured, yet still filled with such pure, powerful belief…

All this spun through and past Kamilla in a fraction of a second. Enough time for Melia to turn to stare at her, her expression stunned.

'Cadet?' Her tone carried pure amazement, a note of genuine, holy awe. 'Do you yet stand in His grace? By the Throne! By His very strength and light!'

'Sister!' Stumbling forwards, Kamilla was sobbing, reeling with the enormity of what she had seen, understood. 'Help me! What *is* that thing? What is it?'

'Dominica's eyes! Truly, He has blessed you, child, blessed us.'

Flashing a look at the gathered, chanting people, she came to grip Kamilla's elbow, hold her steady. 'Listen to me.' Her voice was low, urgent. 'You must speak to the Sister Superior. You must retrieve your vox – it is still in the pocket of your coat. In the hospice. Look at me, Kamilla! Arkas' life, his soul, depends upon this. *Your* life depends upon this! You must pray for him, pray for yourself. And you *must* tell the Sister–'

The pistol shot was deafening.

It was ballistic and sudden, echoing through the building like a thunderclap. Jolting with the impact, Melia staggered two steps sideways, one hand pressed to the side of her neck. A split second too late, Kamilla screamed.

'*Meliaaaaa!*'

With a crash of ceramite, the Sister went over. The people were surging forwards now, their voices chiming as one, 'Saint Veres comes! Saint Veres comes!'

But Melia was getting up. She was getting *up*. Thick gore oozed through her tightly clamped hand, enough to soak her armour, her robe. Her legs were visibly shaking, but her face was carved in stone.

'Go!' she snapped at Kamilla. 'You are a message of hope, child, and from the God-Emperor Himself! You *must* tell the Sister Superior!'

'I can't leave him! I can't leave *you!*'

'That was an order, cadet! Do not look back! The hospice. *Move!*'

'But, Sister–!'

'*Now!*'

It was a bellow, a rage of pure authority. All but in tears, Kamilla erupted into motion, shoving her way forwards, pushing through the people to reach the cloister door. Yanking it open, she ran down the cloister. She heard it bang shut, bang open again. Heard shouts and curses as Arkas himself came after her.

Heard other noises, the crash of metal on ceramite. The cry of the sacred hymnal.

'From the lightning and the tempest!'

Melia!

But Kamilla had orders. She had to save Arkas. She had to speak to the Sisters, tell them what had happened. What she had *seen*. All the time that they had spent, searching the Outskirt for the enemy...

And the enemy was *here*.

The hospice was quiet, the only sound the beeping of Akemi's support machinery. Kamilla barely had time to register that the young Sister was still there, still sleeping.

Because Arkas had come straight down the cloister after her.

'What have you *done?*' She rounded on him, furious, horrified. Betrayed. 'What have you *become?*'

'Kam,' he said, still radiant with sincerity. 'You must trust me. The Sisters are not your friends. Not allies of Opal. They preach only intolerance, only brutality and punishment and death. They came here to stop us, to *stop* our people getting the help they need. The lives they deserve. To stop them from greeting the saint.'

There is no saint! She wanted to cry it at him, but his voice still pulled at her heart – she had seen the Sisters' pitilessness for herself. And Arkas was family, the only family she had left. He'd been there for her since she'd been a child, and his every stance and motion was familiar.

Which side are you on, Kamilla? Which side of the river?

'But they will see the truth, Kam, in the end. They'll have no choice. They will be brought to glory.'

'What does that even mean?' Staring at him, at the cold stars in his eyes, she backed up until she had a bed on either side of her. Akemi lay in one; there was an indent in the other where Arkas himself had been. Her coat was on a third.

'Our peace has been our enemy,' Arkas said, avoiding the question. 'Our undoing. *That's* what Henrik was trying to tell me, and fool that I was, I didn't listen. Why should the Outskirt suffer, when Opal has so much? Why should we starve, when her food is thrown away? Thirst, when water flows down her streets? You know the truth of this, child, you *know* the suffering! You told me yourself – you've had the visions. The visions of our saviours!'

'They're not saviours!' The words were out of her before she could help herself. Shudders of horror still wracked her body. 'They'll kill everything, eat everything! That thing in the crypt – how long has it been there? Did you even *know?*'

She wanted to pray – for him, for Melia, for Akemi, for herself – but her mind was clamouring. *Arkas! How could you do this? How could you betray everything, everything you've been?*

All at once, she was angry. Grief-stricken and overwhelmed, furious and heartbroken, outraged with the unfairness of it all. She wanted to understand *why*, why all this had happened – to Opal, to Arkas, to the Sisters, and to her. Why the dreams had taken him, but freed her. Why Melia... Kamilla had not known that a Sororitas warrior could be compassionate, but Melia had been trying to *save* him!

Without warning, she was shaking, weeping, her tears hot on her skin. She couldn't just leave him, leave Melia, leave Akemi. Where was He, when His daughters needed Him? When Opal needed Him? Why had He abandoned Father Arkas, a man of gentleness, a man who'd done nothing but help people? Why had He done this to Opal, and to Kamilla herself? And still, she *hated* herself for her doubts, her weakness, her endless questions – because, ever at the edges of her thoughts, her dreams were still calling, calling, calling her...

The Sisters bring only death, they said. *But the saint is coming, and he will make you well again. He will make Opal well again. He brings blessing, and holiness, and there will be no room for doubts.*

Which side are you on, Kamilla? Which side of the river?

She realised she was shouting, at herself, at Arkas, at everything.

'*Why?* Why would you do this? When you dedicated your life to Him? When you brought His light to the people who needed it most? Even after Jakob died, you never lost your faith, your love for Him. You taught me that He could be kind, even to the poorest. So why? *Why* would you, would *He*, let this happen?' She was sobbing, new rushes of tears pouring down her cheeks. 'What do I do? What do I do from here?'

She knew that she was being foolish, that Spear Takacs would have belted her for such weakness, but she couldn't help it. Suddenly, she missed the structure of her cadet life, of its regimented hours, of always knowing what orders came next.

'*Tell me what I should do!*'

Arkas was staring at her, something shifting in the very back of his gaze. Memory? Faith?

She held out a hand to him. 'Arkas...'

But then he said, his tone saddened, 'Kam, you should trust me. The Father... It's been waiting for this, for a very long time, but it's nearly ready now. And when we cross the bridges, it will be at our head. It – and its servitors – they will pass the Blades for us. They will help us reach the saint!'

'You're mad. It's eaten your brain.' Staring at him, as if still hoping for some last glimpse of the man he had been, Kamilla then took up a fighting stance, one foot forward, one back. She raised her fists. She would not succumb to the dreams again, nor follow the monster. She had to fight.

In her head, she heard the hymn. Heard Sister Melia.

'That was an order, cadet.'

It brought her structure, decisiveness. Clarity and courage. She had no wish to leave – it was desertion, cowardice of the worst kind. But what else could she do? She couldn't fight the whole gang; there must be hundreds of them. More. And she had to speak to the Sister Superior, had to let her know about the beast.

Arkas was coming towards her, his hand extended. 'Kamilla, please. You must trust me.'

'Trust this.' She punched him, a swift uppercut to the belly. Not with her full strength but enough to knock the wind out of him, to make him fall back with a grunt.

And then she was grabbing her coat, and ducking past him.

Which side of the river?

Running away from the place she'd called home.

XIX

THE MATTER OF MARTYRDOM

Across the squad's vox-channel, Augusta said, 'Sister Alcina.'

The Day of the Third Martyr was drawing to a close. Augusta and the canoness, along with Aitamah and the cherub, had joined Kozma at the Blades' command centre. The hololith city map was shining upon its wall, and Kozma and Aitamah both were marking the lights across the Capital – the deployment of the Blades, the adepts and the Order.

Marked also were the starports, the cable-car stations, the orbital batteries, and the cleared, outlying area that had been the habs and manufactories, now a killing ground for the last of the surviving cult. Two lines of defences were in place – the Blades of the Holy Exterior, securing the bridges and the Outskirt, and Kozma's mobile artillery, standing at the Wall of Diligence.

Though against the hive fleet, Augusta knew, they would do next to nothing.

Elvorix Ianthe contemplated the map, her hands behind her

back. Kozma, visibly tense, barked an ongoing stream of orders, moving her forces to the critical locations.

Through the vox, the squad's second replied, *'Sister Jolantra has fulfilled her orders and the streets behind us are in ruins. The remaining Penitent Engines still stalk the rubble, hunting the last survivors. The machines are unwieldy, and pockets of resistance do escape their notice, though Mistress Susanti sends her Repentia to eliminate anything they miss. Sisters Caia and Rhene have now joined us. Sister Caia scans, but the area is almost clear. We will be moving into the Capital as soon as we have orders.'*

The Sisters had been seventy-two hours without sleep, and the weariness in Alcina's voice was tangible, though she made no comment.

'The canoness plans the Order's deployment, even as we speak. For now, you will ensure that the location is completely secure,' Augusta said. 'Sister Viola?'

'I have but two belts of ammunition remaining, Sister.' There was a twinge of regret in Viola's voice. *'But we will walk the ruins, as ordered.'*

'He will walk with you,' Augusta said. 'What of the Blades' vehicles?'

'All are now in place, defending the batteries. The batteries themselves are now reconsecrated and fully operational. They scan the skies. Adept Kende leads his faithful to the sewers. They will lay charges, as ordered.'

'Good. Has Sister Melia been in contact? I have not heard from the Outskirt cathedral, and we must know their situation, and of the health of Sister Akemi.'

'I have heard nothing, Sister. They are in my prayers.'

'Mine also.' She felt a twinge of fear, of her ongoing concern for her silent Sisters, for her own commands – but she could not afford such things. Over the vox, she said only, 'Very well. Listen for more orders, Sisters. We will finish this, in His name.'

'In His name, Sister.'

At the map, the canoness said, 'Sister Superior.'

'Milady.' Augusta took her attention from the vox and followed where the canoness' scarlet gauntlet pointed.

'Sisters Eleni and Roku have cleared the riverside,' she said. 'They will muster at this location, as we will need them in the Capital.' She paused, still examining the map, its streets and nodes and markets. 'The Blades falter. The shadow falls upon them also, and the rioting worsens. The people tear each other apart, each striving for their own escape–'

'Sisters? Sister Superior?' In Augusta's vox-bead, the faint, distant sound of a voice.

It was not her Sisters, who had just reported in. Nor was it Sister Melia; it was too small and too hesitant. Still listening to the canoness discuss the Capital's situation, Augusta turned the other ear to the peculiar sound. There were rustles and shiftings, faint noises of outdoor movements. She was about to order the squad to shift channel when the words came again.

'Sister Superior Augusta? It's... it's Kamilla.' The girl sounded almost in tears. *'Please... Can you hear me?'*

'Cadet!' She barked the word, surprised. The child should still be at Arkas' cathedral. 'Report! What is your situation? What of my Sisters?'

The canoness shot Augusta a look, her face intense.

Quietly, Augusta said, 'Forgive me, milady, this report is from the Outskirt, and necessary.'

Aitamah and Kozma had both looked up. The room was still, but for the flashing lights on the map. From the Saints' Cathedral, the deacon was again praying, his boom rolling out through the streets.

Elvorix Ianthe gave a brief, curt nod. Augusta knew she would have changed channel to listen herself, her and Aitamah both, though neither of them spoke.

In the vox, the girl's voice was cold and thin; Augusta could hear her shiver. But there was something else to her now, a core of resolve.

'Cadet,' Augusta repeated.

The girl drew a breath, then everything spilled out at once. Melia, Arkas, Akemi, the thing in the crypt, the arming of the people, the coming assault on the bridges. And as she described the massive mental presence of the beast, Augusta saw the canoness' gaze sharpen, saw the rise of savagery in her expression. Felt it in her own heart.

Softly, away from the vox, Elvorix Ianthe said, 'The child is blessed indeed, if she has located the patriarch, and her mind is yet her own.' One white eyebrow was almost in her hairline. 'You will tell me of this cadet, Sister.'

'Yes, milady–'

'But that briefing will wait. If the patriarch is moving, then our time is almost up. Sister Jolantra, four of your Exorcists will shell the building. Leave nothing standing. When the cathedral is down, you will advance on foot and destroy the xenos.'

Augusta caught her breath. 'My Sisters, milady.' She said the words, braced herself for the reprimand. 'They are wounded. I must know what has happened to them–'

The canoness shot her a look that should have frozen the blood in her veins. 'Sentiment, Augusta? From you? What has occurred upon this world that you think such a request is even appropriate? Their lives rest in His hands, as do we all.'

Gathering her courage, Augusta said, 'Yes, milady. But Akemi is badly injured, and Melia–'

'Enough.' The word was a snap, unimpressed. 'This is unworthy of a Sister of Battle, and you still have a mission to fulfil.'

'Your eminence.' Her words almost shook, both realisation and confession. 'The monster – it must have been lying beneath our boots! We have walked upon its lair, oblivious. It has amassed another entire assault, and we did not *know*, we did not even detect it. I *left* my Sisters…'

She paused, pain in her tone, her jaw jumping. Her heart felt filled with grief – had she done nothing but fail, ever since she had arrived?

'I beg you, permit me to pay my penance, to accept this blessing that He has given and to cleanse my heart and soul, before the fleet falls upon us. Permit me to face the monster myself, to stop its attack, before I retrieve the skull.'

The canoness' look did not change. 'And what if you fail? You would sacrifice your objective, sacrifice Opal for your own gain?'

Augusta lifted her chin, met that ice-blue gaze. 'No, milady, I would not. And thus has my every choice been guided. It would have been simple to have thrown my life aside, martyred myself, but I did not – because Opal depended upon me, and because she belongs to Him. I have seen this world, in her wealth and in her poverty, and all of it should stand in His light, united. Thus I have survived, that this world may survive with me. For sometimes martyrdom in itself can be an act of both cowardice and self-interest.'

The canoness still held her gaze, eyes narrow. Augusta did not flinch, and slowly, the older woman nodded. She said, 'That is a complex question, Sister Superior. One that I have prayed upon, many times.'

Augusta said nothing, though her jaw still jumped with tension.

After a moment, the canoness said, 'Very well. You will take your squad to the Outskirt cathedral – but you will not go alone. You will also take Mistress Susanti and the Repentia, and two of the Penitent Engines. You will stop this Outskirt muster in its entirety, is that clear?' The canoness didn't wait for an answer. 'Sister Jolantra,' she said, over the vox-channel.

'You will command your four Exorcists to muster at the riverside. They will be ready to level the cathedral, but only on my command. The remainder will come with me.'

Jolantra's voice came back. *'Yes, milady.'*

The warning in the canoness' tone was strong. She did not speak the words aloud, but Augusta heard them anyway: *Do not fail in this. Because if you do, I will shell not only the cathedral and the Outskirt uprising, but you and your entire squad. And let that be your penance.*

'We must also secure the Capital.' The canoness eyed the map, the faces of the others. 'We may slay the patriarch and stop its invasion, but it is only a single battlefront. And we already have too many.'

Aitamah was looking from canoness to Sister Superior, awaiting a decision or a change in orders. Kozma was staring at the map, her face contorting in a frown.

Into the vox, Augusta said, 'Cadet. Where is the beast now?'

'Still in the cathedral, still in the crypt,' Kamilla said, like an admission. *'It was the thing that Henrik came to find. I think the cult was waiting for it, waiting for it to move.'*

'So it could lead the assault upon the bridges,' Augusta concluded.

'Then you will stop it,' the canoness said. 'No more pleas, Augusta. You will remember what it means to be Sororitas. You will slay the xenos, halt the invasion, or you will perish.'

Augusta stood taller, as if some great, oddly nebulous weight had passed from her shoulders. But she said only, 'Yes, milady.'

Sister Viola rounded on the squad's second, her voice almost shaking with rage.

'Sister Alcina,' she said. 'We will not abandon our Sisters. Akemi was unconscious, Melia hurt and outnumbered. Our squad is under-strength. Surely, our priority–'

'We are Adepta Sororitas, and our orders come from the canoness,' Alcina told her flatly.

The Sisters had regrouped with Caia and Rhene at the Gate of Nemes, and were awaiting Augusta's shuttle. Below them lay the flattened, ruined expanse of habs and manufactories, the engines lumbering across its breadth and bringing down the last of the stubbornly standing corners. Mistress Susanti and her two surviving Repentia moved with them, still seeking absolution.

Of the sixteen Exorcist tanks, four were in motion, heading for the riverside. The other twelve were heading for the Capital. Behind the Sisters, arranged along the Wall of Diligence were the Tauroxes and Chimeras of the Blades, some of them battered from being overrun. They still had autocannons, however, and they waited, silent, for any assault. Above them, the orbital defences were now fully deployed, scanning the skies for threats.

Behind all of this, the Capital itself was oddly still. The people on the streets had gone silent, overcome by dread and terror. There were not even bells, any more, only the arch-deacon's booming, ever-constant sermon. The man's relentlessness was impressive.

'They are our *Sisters*,' Viola said, her voice low. She was next to Akemi in age and the two of them had been close, ever since Lautis. 'We should assault the Outskirt cathedral *now*–'

'They were wounded, and in hostile territory.' Alcina's tone was ice-cold. 'They may well now kneel at the Throne. We will follow our orders, and bring down the patriarch. As He commands.'

The air was darkening and the swarms of shuttles grew denser, all circling the starports. The clouds had cleared and Opal's halo shone brightly, but whether it was reminding her people of their blessing or of their imminent death, the Sisters did not know.

'We should locate and retrieve them first,' Viola said stubbornly.

'Akemi is our scholar, Melia our medicae.' She shot the second a vicious, hard look. 'We must not repeat our error, Sister. We have already left them behind once–'

'Our Sisters' lives rest with Him.' Caia's words were brutal, edged in pain, but they brooked no disagreement.

Shooting her the look of one betrayed, Viola glared from one Sister to the other. 'We must–'

'You *will* be silent.' Alcina took a step forward. She was taller than Viola, more heavily built, and her visor flashed in the sunset. 'And I will not tell you again. The Sister Superior has already warned you–'

'They are our *Sisters*.' Viola lifted her chin, glaring back. 'We will need–'

'If they have faced torment and death, then they have done so with honour. You know this, Sister, and to deny it is an act of heresy.' A pause, making the point. 'Are you a heretic, Sister Viola? Because if you are, there is another place in this battle that requires your *strength*.'

The threat in her voice brought Viola to a sudden halt.

Before the Emperor I have sinned.

Almost despite herself, she looked back at the rubble where the surviving Repentia still sought their redemption. They were small figures, toiling over the mounds of broken flexsteel and ferrocrete, but their agony was loud as a shout, even from here. With them, one of the Penitent Engines lumbered and creaked, coughing flame at something Viola did not see.

She watched them, feeling that same flash of fear that she'd felt upon Lycheate, when the squad hung under threat of Repentance... It was too much. Viola had defied her orders once before, facing the Lautis daemon, and it seemed that Alcina was well aware of the younger Sister's history, of the warning that Augusta had already given her.

More gently, Sister Caia said, 'I understand your loyalty, Viola. But you think only of us, of our squad, and this is not appropriate. We face a far greater terror, and one that must be stopped, lest it infect the entire segmentum. You know this, in your heart, do you not? Does He not tell you what you must do?'

Alcina levelled a faceless glare at Caia, but Rhene suddenly gave a characteristic cackle.

'There you go again, Sister Famulous.'

Caia shot the old woman a look that was somewhere between exasperation and fondness. The old Hospitaller, however, had come to take Viola's red shoulders in her white ceramite-clad hands. Under her wimple, her lined face was gentle, her eyes warm.

'Your love for your Sisters does you credit, young one,' she said. 'But our love for Him is greater. Trust Him, and let Him guard your squad.'

Viola stopped. Unable to look the old Hospitaller in the face, she lowered her head, shamed.

'You are very wise, Sister Rhene,' Alcina commented.

'I have served Him long,' Rhene said. The cackle had gone from her voice, and she sounded very tired, and very sad. 'And I will serve Him longer still. I have seen Sisters rise, and fight, and fall, and fail, and die. I have seen Sisters embrace their martyrdom, and refuse my medical care. I have seen Sisters I could not save, who died under my hands. I have seen dying Sisters live and fight on, blessed by His grace. And I have prayed for them all. And now, I pray for you, all of you. You have refused your own martyrdom in order to save a world – and that is well, in my humble, healer's eyes. It is selflessness and true courage. Our shuttle comes. May He bless us and walk with us, into the dark. And may He gather this world back to His grace... even if it is in death.'

* * *

As the shadow swelled, so the rioting at the starports grew worse.

It had been inevitable, Kozma knew – the Blades of the Holy Interior were as touched by the incoming horror as the terrified pilgrims. Some panicked, some fled, some cowered in terror. But, just as they had in the sewers, some found their true Opal courage, and stood tall. Their numbers may be diminished, but this was a task that they comprehended and one that could re-inspire their faith and morale.

As the fourth and final day, the Day of the Blessed Saint, finally dawned, the sky cleared of sleet and turned a brilliant cobalt blue, like hope. The air was crisp, and cold, and sharp, and it seemed like He cupped His hands over them, guarding them at the last. The vox-cast evacuation order still broadcast – *'Blessed pilgrims of Holy Opal!'* – and prayers rose like cries, forlorn.

Under the ever-visible ring-light, swarms of shuttles bustled back and forth, like clouds of glittering flies. Queues of pilgrims watched them, and wept and wailed and tore at their garments. They begged for rescue and they assailed the faltering soldiers repeatedly.

Kozma did her best, and she prayed for her forces.

But in her heart, she still needed someone to blame.

Governor Vass Mihaly paced a furrow in the carpets of his bedchamber. He had no family. His wife had perished in childbirth, along with his infant son, and he had dedicated himself only to the rulership of his beloved Opal. His windows were open, as ever, and he could still hear the deacon's tireless sermon, see the man's glittering hololith as it towered above the streets.

The last day had broken upon them. The holiest day of their sacred calendar, the day that should have been the festival's very height. At its sunset, they should have been standing in the Saints' Cathedral, holding the Sermon of the Hero and raising

Veres' golden skull to the sacred conjunction, celebrating the life of their world.

Now, they might well celebrate its death.

Mihaly now knew what would happen. He understood the death that the xenos would bring, understood how even their most dedicated followers would be devoured, and how Opal would follow them, dissolved in acid and digested.

But the governor had explored his humble spirit, and found the true core of his faith. Whatever it took, he would remain with his world, as a captain with their ship. This was his penance, and he would pay it willingly.

With more humility than he'd had in many years, he knelt at his private altar and began to pray.

In the Saints' Cathedral, the deacon stood in his wondrous glassaic pulpit. He was no soldier, but he had taken almost no rest and his voice was both banner and trumpet, the rallying cry of his people. It was their courage and their faith, their love for Saint Veres and for the festival of his triumph and sacrifice. The deacon had spearheaded Opal's pride, it was true, but he also had a duty to perform and he would not fail. Even though the festival itself had ended, he would stand at its heart nonetheless. Whatever else happened, he would celebrate the Sermon of the Hero, he would raise that most holy skull, he would greet that most sacred conjunction. If no one else upon his entire world sang the hymns of Veres' memorial, it did not matter. He would sing them alone, if that was what it took.

But he was not alone. His voice, Opal's voice, the faith of its people and pilgrims – they were strong. Even as thousands of pilgrims still converged on the starports, desperate to escape, so more thousands crept forth from their hiding places, heeding the deacon's call. Slowly, the cowering and fearful were offered new hope. Emerging from their shrines and basilicae, they stood blinking in the Capital's roads. Stepping over the scurrying servitors, they formed small groups, hugging each other and sobbing. And the small groups moved inwards, coalescing to larger ones, and then to full crowds.

In numbers, they found reassurance, an end to their dread. They found belief and joy and wonder. Disdaining any remaining authority, they headed for the Saints' Cathedral, gathering yet more numbers as they went. Some found banners, retrieved from gutters, others raised the prayer-scarves they had worn upon their hair. Still more were in their mock-camo, or jangled the Path of the Thousand Humble, the silver chains yet looped about their necks. And among them, here and there, were deserting Blades – the soldiers who had been through enough.

Pulled by the deacon's call, their rivalries were forgotten, and they sang as one, unified.

Steadily, the crowd became a horde.

Steadily, the horde took up the name of Saint Veres.

And steadily, on the Varadi's far side, did the building's shadow-sibling do the same.

THE FATHER

Ducking through the Outskirt's backstreets and watching the dawn rise, Kamilla saw shuttles. Three of them, flying low and without lumens. They were cut-outs against the rose-tinged sky, against the planet's arcing halo, motes of a deeper dark. And they were…

She blinked. She was beyond tired, muscles leaden with weariness. Was she seeing things? She had wrapped her coat tightly round herself, and in its pockets were her compass and the stimm-pack that the medicae had given her.

How had that only been three days before? It felt like a lifetime.

Wondering if she should take the stimm, she studied the incoming vehicles. One seemed normal, but the other two had an odd, hanging shape, like they were airlifting something. No, she wasn't imagining it – they had large, bipedal shadows suspended from their bellies. Whatever those hanging things were, they were bigger than human and they glinted like they were mechanical. Fascinated, she stirred herself and started to jog.

Augusta had told her to wait at the corner of Kelemen Street, not far from Arkas' cathedral, told her that Sword Mezei and his surviving troops would be mustering at the same location. As her movement warmed her blood, she found herself increasingly anxious, suspended like the shapes over something that was both fear and adrenaline. The Sisters' wrath was coming, she could feel it. What would become of the cathedral and its people?

What had happened to the Sisters, to Father Arkas?

She felt a twinge of pain, of guilt. Melia had tried to save him, may even have given her life so that Arkas could keep his soul. And Kamilla had fled, left both Sisters to the wrath of the beast. Orders or no orders, shame burned in her cheeks.

As she reached Kelemen Street, she stopped. There was a broken plaza ahead of her, and Mezei's three spears, weary and dirty, were forming up in ranks. At his order, they came to parade-ground ease, upright, their feet apart, their rifle butts resting by their boots. Of the three hundred, less than a hundred remained – she had to count them twice. She wondered what had happened to them, where they had been.

Like her, they were watching the trio of shuttles. Two of them, the two squarish ones that were carrying the shapes, were dropping below the level of the buildings, but they did not land. She could still hear their engines. The third one was coming down where they stood. There was a reek of promethium, and the hot blast of convection seemed to scour Kamilla's skin from her face.

Mezei barked orders. 'Listen up! Atten-*tion!*'

As one, the Blex responded. Their boots came down in a single, echoing stamp; they raised their rifles to their shoulders, their movements unified and flawlessly timed. *One-two-three, one.* The motion was as familiar as childhood, and oddly comforting.

In the midst of the madness, some things still made sense. Kamilla crept forwards; saw the ring-light catch briefly on the lone shuttle's Rose emblem…

Saint Veres comes!

Coiling in the back of her mind, the dream still caught at her. She had seen the monster, felt its closeness, its hope, its lies, its ravenousness. But Sister Melia, her courage and her strength, the way she'd still had hope…

Kamilla sniffled, the memory almost too much. Did the Sister still live? Tears pricked at the back of her eyes. She was over-tired, and getting overwhelmed. Maybe she should take that stimm, after all. But the shuttle ramp was down now, and four sets of scarlet boots were stamping to meet the Blex. Four sets of scarlet, and one white.

'In His name, Sword Mezei,' Augusta said. 'We greet you once more. We are the Rose, and we are here to slay the xenos.'

He saluted, hand to rifle.

Gravely, Augusta gave him the aquila in return, spread gauntleted fingers over her chest. 'The enemy converge on the cathedral. They have seen our shuttles incoming and they rally to defend the building. But we will press our attack, and trust in His grace. We are all warriors of Opal, and we will not fail.'

'Sister. Ave Imperator.'

'Report. What have you found?'

'Evidence of the cult's presence, and going back many years,' the Sword said. 'With the aid of the shuttles from the *Star*, we were able to explore a great deal of the Outskirt. We found hundreds of nests, lairs, places where they had been hiding for generations. Some of the sites were still occupied, and many revealed caches of weapons, or were wired with charges. It is my belief that, since the flooding of the sewers, the cult has been steadily converging upon its muster locations.'

'The hive fleet is closing by the hour,' Augusta said. 'If the patriarch is moving, they must be almost upon us. Where are these muster points?'

'By the two intact bridges, Sister. Here, at the old cathedral, and in the warehouses at the Bridge of Souls. We...' He paused, almost flinching. 'I had been concentrating our reconnaissance at the dockyards, in the old industrial ruins, as I judged that–'

'That was where they would still be hiding,' Augusta said. There was a flex of tension to her words, something that might even have been shame. 'Now, we redeem our errors.'

'Yes, Sister.' There was shame in him too, as visible as the scar on his face.

'This battle cannot save Opal,' said Augusta, 'but it can help her people. We will fight, until we cannot. All of us. Do you understand?'

He repeated, 'Yes, Sister.'

She had pronounced them a death sentence, but Mezei seemed almost to welcome it. Whether it was to cleanse his soul, or because he was an Opal warrior – or both – Kamilla did not know, and did not ask.

Feeling very small against the courage arrayed round her, she wondered if she should say something, but had no idea what. Mezei glanced at her, then back at the Sister Superior.

'What of the cadet? She is a Blade and should come with us, if you deem her worthy.'

Suddenly, all eyes were upon her. She pulled her coat tighter, and felt rather like an insect, pinned to a board.

'Are you worthy, child?' Augusta asked. 'You who have been closest to the beast?' There was an unvoiced question in the Sister Superior's words, but Kamilla did not quite understand. She swallowed, trying to summon the courage.

She's a Blade, and should come with us.

'I want… I want to fight, Sister.' The words were like a choice, the declaration of where she belonged. Like a promise to the Sisters she'd left alone. 'While I may be only a cadet, my training has been thorough and I…' *Arkas!* 'I have lost family to the xenos. I have felt their presence in my heart. I wish to cleanse myself, and to strike a blow for those I love… loved. For Opal, and for the Emperor.'

For Sister Melia, and for her courage and selflessness.

Augusta gave her a long look, assessing, but it was the white-clad Sister that said, 'You are weary, little one. Injured. You should rest.'

A sudden ball of bitterness in her mouth, Kamilla answered, 'Could you?'

'Let her fight.' This was the biggest of the Sisters, a broad, strong figure in her armour. 'She is of novice age, and this is her world. It is right that she should take a stand against the xenos.'

'You shall fight, cadet,' Augusta said. 'Every weapon is welcome. You will obey the commands of Sword Mezei. And you will trust in Him.'

'Yes, Sister.' Her cold fingers closed around the rifle that Mezei handed her. She had not consciously realised how much she'd missed it, how much she'd missed the strong bonds of brotherhood and sisterhood, the strange security of being part of a fighting unit.

'Very well,' Augusta said, over the vox, so that all could hear. 'Sisters, warriors of Holy Opal, this is our penultimate battle. The xenos creature must die, whatever the cost. If we lay down our lives to secure its elimination, then such is His will, and it is something we will embrace with hymns, and gladly. Our path is clear. We will know no more fears, no more doubts.' There was something different in the Sister Superior's voice, a ring of steel and resolution. 'If it lies within His will, Sister Rhene' – she nodded at the Sister in white – 'will locate and retrieve both Akemi and Melia. But this will not interrupt our mission. We *will* destroy the xenos.'

The clarity ringing from Augusta's voice had all the power of her faith behind it, all the strength of her weapons and armour, and her absolute trust in His presence. It touched Kamilla to her heart and she felt her blood rise, as if caught in the shuttle's convection.

Lucky – and blessed.

'You will follow my orders,' Augusta said. 'You will show no mercy. Some of these people may have been your friends, your family, your comrades. But they are none of those things, not now. They have been taken by the xenos' awareness, possessed by the monster and by heresy. They are shadows, hollowed-out versions of their former selves. If you have felt the touch of the cult's dreams, the presence of the xenos in your soul – now is the time to throw it down and to deny it with every prayer you can voice. Make no mistake, the beast will be huge. It will rear in your minds with a savagery – and a puissance – that you will struggle to encompass, and to resist. But we are Sororitas, and we stand in your midst and at your side. We have forces with us that will spearhead our attack, and will break the ranks of the cult. We will follow these forces and take up His banner, the banner of the Rose.' She seemed to address each man and woman in turn, meet every gaze. 'If the creature promises you salvation, it is a lie. If it promises you family, it is a lie. If it promises you food and water and medication, it is a lie. All it offers is death. Blood, acid and devourment. Hold fast, refuse its call, and we will succeed. In His name. Ave Imperator!'

The soldiers shouted back, 'Ave Imperator!' and Kamilla felt her heart sing. She had felt the beast, and she understood – but she had no fear.

Which side of the river?

As Henrik had warned her, she had made her choice.

Like death from the skies, the two Penitent Engines crashed down in the centre of the old cathedral. Mustered and waiting, the cultist hordes scattered, tumbling away from the engines' landings like so many broken playthings.

The noise was incredible. Hitting the ground with saws and flamers running, the Penitent Engines roared into motion, their knees bending to absorb the drop, their feet stamping, crushing stone and flesh, their weapons lashing in every direction. Hundreds fell, screaming. Pillars cracked and crumbled, killing more. Flares of fire roared across the gathering heretics.

And something *shrieked.*

It echoed in Augusta's head, rang in her ears. The noise was hideous, a screeching of claws on ceramite, a crystal-sharp shriek of shock, of agonies and betrayals.

Now we have you, xenos creature! Triumph clanged like bells in her thoughts. *You will hide from Him no longer!*

Waiting in the street, the cathedral's grounds and lych-gate ahead of her, she boomed back at it, at once addressing the Sisters and the soldiers.

'We fear no heretic! We fear no witch! We fear no xenos!'

'Saint and Emperor!' Mezei stood stock-still and wide-eyed, both hands gripping his rifle.

The Penitent Engines would fall – it was inevitable – but they would take hundreds, even thousands with them, and they would bring the beast out of the crypt. Augusta heard shouting, both human and xenos; she heard the rip of saws and the rumbles of masonry. She saw the flamers as they lashed out, saw the tiny figures that burned, and stumbled, and fell.

She offered a prayer for her missing Sisters, for their lives, their souls. But her heart, finally freed from its prison of doubts and politics, sang with the pure joy of the Order's unleashed rage. *This* was why Augusta had come to this world, *this* was what she knew, what she understood. She was bringing the xenos monster forth from the cellars, to where it could be faced and slain. She was the Bloody Rose, and this was bloody vengeance.

Beside her, Mistress Susanti was descending the shuttle's ramp, exhorting her two Repentia to new heights, and lashing them with her voice and neural whip. The cadet gawked, remembered herself and looked away; many of the soldiers stared, both compelled and horrified.

Her attention on the fight, Augusta glanced at the Sisters Repentia, still finding them deeply unsettling. One was dark of skin, her scalp shaven, her eyes – or eye sockets – covered by a bandage inscribed with bloody prayers. The other was no older than Akemi, barely more than a novice. She had a long, slick burn-scar down one side of her face, gnarling her ear, twisting her skin and pulling one side of her mouth to a permanent grimace. What they had done, what heresy they had committed, Augusta did not know. But they would spearhead the Sisters' assault, and the damage they would inflict would be horrifying.

'Eyes front,' Mezei growled at his troops. 'Be ready to move out.'

At the Sister Superior's side, Viola waited impatiently, her sacred weapon reloaded and now in both hands. Caia bore her auspex, though there was little need for it here. Alcina was chin up, the ring-light shining from her big scarlet shoulders. Like the Repentia, the squad all welcomed this battle.

Rhene, her face etched in the anticipation of pain, had fallen back. While the old Hospitaller could fight – had slain xenos even as they had thought to harm her charges – such was not her holy calling. She would stay clear of the battle and, if He permitted, she would locate Akemi and Melia.

Walk with us, O Emperor…

The screech in the Sister Superior's head was growing louder, ringing and outraged, harsh and cruel. It was the sound of something massive, laughing in rich and livid mockery. In exultation at the feast to come.

You cannot stop me. Slay me in the Outskirt, and you will find me in the Capital. Slay me in the Capital, and you will find me in the Outskirt. Slay me on the surface, and you will find me in the air. You squeaking, tiny morsels – you are not enough!

Gouts of flamer fire came from the broken building, dancing in its doorways and broken windows, flashing through the shattered roof with bursts of cleansing flame. Called by the scream, the spilling throng of followers was being pulled back into the cathedral, now fighting amongst themselves, tearing each other down in the bid to reach and save their master. They howled the name of the saint, their need for the coming glory.

Waiting to time their assault, the Sisters whispered the battle prayer. With a chill, Augusta realised that the Repentia, too, were calling for His blessing, their blades rasping in savage counterpoint. They stared at their own deaths, and they welcomed them.

'Know us and know fear. We have no faces but these, and they are dedicated to your death and His glory. May He forgive us our sins…'

Kamilla, too, was whispering a prayer, her head up and a glitter in her eyes that might have been grief or anger. Augusta was beginning to understand why Kamilla was with them – why He had put the cadet in their path. The thought had not yet crystallised fully, but–

With an ear-splitting screech, the first Penitent Engine went down. Something huge had come forth, rearing up, taller than the broken walls. It had blocked the engine from view, then crashed down upon it, crushing it to the floor. Its shriek took on a new note, one of almost frenzy.

The people echoed the scream, its savagery and victory.

'Saint Veres comes!'

'They have brought the beast out from the crypts,' Augusta said, one hand raised. 'On my command...' She watched the other Penitent Engine. It stamped and slashed, this way and that, but she could already see the figures that were clamouring upon it, striving to tear out its pilot.

It teetered, and started to topple.

'Move!' The word was a bellow. 'Mezei, you will stay in line with me. Repentia, redeem yourselves and stand at the Throne!'

Her whip crackling, Susanti snarled at her charges. 'For the Emperor!'

The Mistress at their heels, the two of them broke into a run, flat out and swift, eviscerators screaming. They swiftly pulled ahead of Augusta and the squad, and ahead of the advancing Blades. The eyeless one, guided by His grace, made no misstep and they both raced through the lych-gate, howling the battle-hymn.

Even as the second Penitent Engine fell, the two charging Repentia hit the crowd in the back, carving through cultists and xenos like they were meat. Susanti stayed with them, using her whip as a weapon, shooting with her bolter. Advancing more slowly, scanning the roadway and the grounds as well as the cathedral itself, Augusta could make out the Repentia's shapes as they forced their way forwards, dragging the monster's attention to the lych-gate, and to the outside of the cathedral.

The thing was still shrieking, the noise appalling. Rising up, claws stark against the planet's halo, the bright and pale sky, it surged forwards. In the ranks of the Blex, there was horrified muttering.

'What is *that?*'

'Steady!' Mezei told them. 'Hold the line.'

Augusta advanced at their centre, her stamp implacable, like the tolling of some huge church bell. She sang, raising the litany as she had done a hundred times, a thousand times, on worlds all across the Imperium – the harmonies in her blood were as much a part of her faith as her bolter, her armour, the blade at her side, its teeth still for the moment.

'From the lightning and the tempest!'

Alcina's throaty contralto, Caia's soprano. Viola's mezzo, between the other two but more rage than hymn… Augusta missed Akemi, missed Melia, her Sisters' voices that would have made the prayer complete. As if in answer to her thought, Rhene's quavering tones joined them, carrying a passion and pain and sorrow that Augusta had never heard before. The voice of His blessing and conscience, the song of the Sister Hospitaller. A shiver went down her arms.

Past the lych-gate and now deep among the gravestones and ruined sarcophagi, the Repentia had slowed, stopped by sheer weight of numbers. The cultists' lasrifles were slashing at them, their stubbers barking. The enemy was recovering from the Penitent Engines' attack, and they had found their weapons.

'Guard their flanks,' Augusta barked, 'but watch your aim. Single shots!'

Still steadily advancing, the Blades' slashes of scarlet hit back; the Sisters' bolters hammered.

'Attain absolution!' Susanti shrieked. 'For the Emp–'

The horror's claws slashed. Augusta saw bodies, parts of bodies, fly sideways – parts of cultists, parts of Sisters. An eviscerator blade, Susanti's whip. The Repentia's hymn went suddenly silent.

No, not silent. Not quite.

The Sister Superior's prayers caught in her mouth. Still advancing, she shot a lurking three-armed xenos, then another. She saw the younger Repentia, the one with the burn, still moving. Saw her assail the monster with her still-singing blade in one hand. Her other arm was dangling uselessly, almost severed at the elbow, but she hurled herself at the thing, absolutely fearless. It reared up again, ready to bring its claws down upon her and she buried her eviscerator in its belly, right up to the hilt. Clung on as the monster thrashed, driving the running teeth even deeper.

Then the claws came down, again, and she was gone.

Blessed be her memory. Blessed be all their memories. Augusta's thought was brief, but poignant. The Repentia had accomplished their task – they had brought the beast out, right up to the lych-gate, a mass of darkness and lies and horror.

Savagely, Caia proclaimed, 'That. *That* is your Saint Veres, heretics. Look at that, and be dismayed!'

Somewhere, one of the soldiers was throwing up. Others were faltering, their cries and mutters growing louder. They made the ring-symbol of Opal, cried the names of the planet's saints.

'For Opal, and for the Emperor!' Augusta shouted. *'Alpha strike!'*

With a shout like a celebration, Sisters and Blades opened fire together.

Looming high against the pink-tinged, cobalt sky, the thing was huge. Even as Augusta loosed her full rate of fire, she knew it was the patriarch. She had seen one exactly like it once before, twenty years ago, crashing down through the roof of that far-distant glassaic cathedral. The first time she'd ever seen a Sister die in combat.

This one was even bigger, its teeth shining, its four arms outstretched. Rounds spanged from its body, las-fire flashed furiously but could not touch it. It came forwards like a juggernaut, deliberate and slow, but she knew how fast it could move if it wanted.

Snarling, it lashed at Viola, sending her skidding. The young

Sister regained her feet in a moment, bringing the heavy bolter to bear.

'Perish, xenos!' Screaming at the thing, standing fast against the massive pressure of its presence, Viola opened fire once more. The monster felt like a black cloud, like a physical weight, pressing down upon each of them. And under it, Viola was finding her anger.

The Blex cried prayers, resolute or desperate. In response, the cultists' voices rang with zeal and fury. The Sisters sang, daring the great beast to press its psychic power upon them.

Somewhere, someone sobbed, 'What is that thing? What is it?' and it seemed to be the voice of Opal herself, a cry of horror, a plea for His understanding.

Why has this happened to us?

What did we do to incur this punishment?

'Mezei,' August barked. 'Focus your fire on the smaller targets. Leave the beast to us.'

Las-fire sizzled, bringing death to the surrounding cultists.

The monster roared defiance. Bolter rounds barely cracking its chitinous armour, it reared high, tail lashing right and left. The Repentia's eviscerator was still stuck in its belly, and the injury tore as the thing moved, showing a white gleam of organs. Gravestones and sarcophagi were smashed to dust and powder; cultists tumbled, broken. The Sisters were still singing and some of the soldiers had joined them, carrying the tune the best they could.

But around the beast's feet, there lurked minions. These were not cultists, nor were they hybrids. They were small and nimble and many-limbed, and they scuttled about the thing as if it were their god.

With a snarl like pure viciousness, the beast moved. And by the *Throne*, it was quick. It was also not stupid; it had recognised Viola as the greatest threat. Its minions boiled forwards on her position, a welter of them, throwing their bodies into the line of fire and being killed in their dozens – but they completed their task. They distracted her long enough for the beast to smash a claw at her helmet.

Rounds spraying skywards, Viola went over.

'Our Emperor, deliver us!'

Beside her, Caia cried the litany, her bolter ripping down everything in front of her – but she could not hold. There were too many creatures, too many cultists; the monster itself was too big. It was right on top of them now, slashing left and right.

Caia shouted, 'We cannot–'

Her voice broke off in a cry, and she was gone.

Augusta, her heart hammering, pulled her chainsword from its mag-fastening. Akemi and Melia, missing. Viola down. Now Caia... For just an instant, her doubts returned, bigger and darker than the beast itself. They were at the precipice, threatening to fall...

'From plague, temptation and war!'

Bellowing the hymn, she silenced her uncertainties. Her task was clear: she would slay this beast, or she would perish in the attempt.

The beast was like some colossal destroyer, shattering everything around it. Yet Alcina was still there, still upright. From somewhere, Caia was still singing. Again, that memory of the glassaic cathedral, of Sister Pia the Martyr, grabbing the monster by the tongue and dragging its head down bodily. Of Sister Leona, loosing the wrath of the squad's heavy bolter...

Leona, fire!

The memory was only fleeting; there was too much happening for it to stay. And this monster was too big – Augusta could not even reach its head. She started the chainsword's mechanism. The weapon snarled like a live thing, hungry for blood.

The beast's head whipped round and it saw her, its eyes glinting like starlight.

'That got your attention,' she told it. 'Flank it, Sister Alcina! To the side!'

The manoeuvre was risky but they were Adepta Sororitas and He was with them. Their shots were at close range and they would not miss.

Alcina moved. Caia was back on her feet. Augusta could see that Caia was limping even more than before, favouring her right knee; she did not have time to worry about it.

Lunging with the chainsword, she struck.

'Our Emperor, deliver us!'

The beast was too quick. It reared high, came down heavily with all four sets of claws. Augusta went backwards, and the talons swished past her nose. She lunged, carved the rasping blade hard up into one arm and the creature shrieked, the noise enough to bring dust from the ceiling.

The arm fell free, still twitching.

Las-fire sizzled as the Blex faced the cultists. Two bolters hammered, every shot hitting its target. The beast rocked under repeated impacts, but its armour was thick, and it did not stop. Around it, its creatures were scrabbling over the fallen gravestones. The hybrids were surging forwards again, ripping the soldiers to pieces. There was the glint of fire from combat knives as the fighting became too close for ranged weapons, but it was little short of a massacre.

Again, the beast's claws flashed. Again, Augusta jumped back. She tried for another arm but it was too fast. Caia and Alcina, both singing aloud in livid, furious harmony, continued to shoot, but their magazines must be almost empty.

'From the scourge of the Kraken!'

With the blade in both hands, Augusta went in under the

chest of the monster, inside the reach of its claws. The move was dangerous – either of her Sisters could hit her – but adrenaline and prayer fuelled her like promethium. With a hymn that was almost a bellow, she dropped her bolter, grabbed the Repentia's blade with one hand, twisted it and drove it even deeper, then slashed the thing across the belly with her chainsword. Chitin split and buckled, and a great red tear opened in its gut. Organs spilled forth, pale and greasy. The thing screamed, a noise like breaking glass.

Caia's bolter thumped empty; Alcina shot it again – twice, three times, then she too was out of ammunition.

But a voice in the murk shouted, 'Drop!'

It was Viola, on her knees, bringing the thrice-blessed heavy bolter up and aiming it at the monster. Augusta gave a shout of prayer and wonder, and dived out of the way.

And Viola loosed a directed burst at the wound on the thing's front.

Its scream redoubled. The noise split Augusta's ears, made her head ring. Viola was roaring wordlessly, holding the weapon hard as it emptied its full rate of fire at the wounded beast. And then, all at once, the thing crashed over and the whole cathedral shook. It was still thrashing, tail like a whip knocking Caia once again from her feet, bringing the walls down. She fell with a cry on her already wounded leg.

But Augusta was still upright. As the heavy bolter coughed its last, she stood over the thing, met its star-filled gaze.

'Xenos creature,' she said. 'We are Adepta Sororitas and we stand sentinel here, in His name. You will not be permitted your victory.' With a sound that was almost a howl, she buried the chainsword point first in its eye, and through into its brain.

And the scream of its death rang out across Opal like the bells of the festival itself.

XXI

THE CRY OF THE DEACON

The scream was more than human, splitting the ring-lit sky like lightning.

In the palace, the governor heard it, a savage sound of both horror and death.

At the Blades' command centre, Kozma heard it, and heard the vox-message from Augusta that came with it, underpinning its cry with a steel-hard, zealous severity. With a bark, the commander ordered the Blades of the Holy Exterior into full motion, roaring across the Varadi's bridges and into the Outskirt. What was left of the cultist rebellion must be removed.

Deploying her forces out across the Capital, reinforcing the Blades and bringing His courage to the people, Elvorix Ianthe heard it, and understood. Alone of her Order, the canoness had heard this before, in her youth on Xevania. She raised a prayer of praise for the death of the patriarch, for the agonies of the cult, but still she knew: *it was not enough*.

That scream, its fury and power – it was more than just the

cult's hive-minded grief. It was the herald, the first sound of the arriving hive fleet. And it did not come from the dying monster, not completely.

It came from the Inner Sanctum.

Shattering the morning, vox-cast out across the streets, it rose from the heart of the Capital, from the site of Veres' sacrifice, from the pulpit of the Saints' Cathedral itself.

From the throat of Opal's ecclesiarch, Arch-Deacon Janos.

'In the name of the God-Emperor!'

The canoness' understanding was instant. She was His blade and right arm, His daughter, His wrath made manifest, and she had slain His foes from one end of the Imperium to the other. More than even her most experienced Sisters, she was a creature of war, of vengeance, of vehemence, of fury. She was the bearer of the Bloody Rose. She was warrior and executioner. And she would not be denied.

Now, she ordered her forces, her Sisters, to their final clearance of doomed Opal. To secure the streets. To control the people – at gunpoint if necessary. To defend the starports and the ever-cycling shuttles, and to exterminate what cultists remained.

The scream of the arch-deacon was clarion-pure, a blaze in the bright, cold morning, and staggering in its power. And it made sense, with as much clarity as His message to her heart. This was the core of the planet's political tangles. This was why the man had been so determined to celebrate the Sermon of the Hero, and why he had tried to foil the Sisters at every turn.

Even with the patriarch slain, he could still rally his followers. Still sabotage the Sisters' deployment, harry and distract them, and slay the last of Opal's faithful Blades. Still damn her star-eyed pilgrims to death and devourment, this world to dissolution in acid.

Opal, like her people, would perish screaming.

Barking orders at Aitamah and out over the Order's vox, the canoness gave a great cry of battle. If she perished in the process, if she destroyed the Capital entire, then that was His will. But she *would* eliminate these xenos, once and for all. She would retrieve the blessed relic. And she would slay the heretic.

Even as Mina had done.

In the heart of the old cathedral, Kamilla was sobbing.

She could hear the scream in her mind, feel it in her heart, feel the maggots writhe and squirm and burn. She knew that the dreams had been the xenos presence – but that noise, that *noise!* It cut into her skull like a knife, as if the shards of the shattered building were slashing at her flesh, into her ears, stabbing and hurting.

Augusta was upright, though the Emperor alone knew how. The split in her breastplate was covered in blood – her own or that of others, Kamilla did not know. Her Sisters were with her, Viola staggering, Caia limping heavily now, her auspex in hand. Alcina, by His grace, still stood untouched – though she staggered with weariness and fought not to show it.

'By the Light,' Alcina said. 'And by His grace, they are in flight.'

'Not flight, Sister,' Augusta told her grimly, 'The beast's death has tipped them into madness.'

As the scream had sounded, so the gathered cultists had gone berserk. With a livid, furious savagery, they had dropped their weapons and leapt upon the soldiers. Many had attacked with their teeth and fingernails, biting and clawing with no humanity left. Driven past reason, some had turned on each other, while others, shrieking, had massed up and run from the building, clawing their fellows down in their effort to follow the scream. In a chilling after-echo of the fights between the festival's rival factions, they had pushed and jostled and stamped and bitten and throttled, many of them screaming in their turn. Kamilla had seen Mezei batter two of them to death with his rifle butt, right there in front of her. She'd fought them herself, hammering savagely with her fists and feet, just as she'd done in the combat-pits.

Saint and Emperor!

Unlike the fights of her youth, however, these were real. They were not Endre, they were filthy, stinking xenos traitors, heretics and unbelievers, and she'd felt a savage sense of vindication at their deaths. At the *rightness* of them. Mezei's brutal howl of triumph had been almost as loud as the scream itself, and she'd howled with him, visceral and triumphant.

Someone shouted, 'They're heading for the bridge!'

'They'll be gunned down in their thousands,' Augusta told him. 'The Blades of the Holy Exterior have begun their final advance, and four of our Exorcists stand ready. The faithless cannot be permitted to assail the Capital.'

In the midst of it all, Augusta and her Sisters had still been fighting, the rush of now demented cultists shattering on their wall of armour and falling broken to the floor. The Sister Superior had *sung* as she hacked them down, her voice fierce with violent joy, her rasping, toothed blade slashing left and right.

As the wave had faltered, Augusta had shouted, 'Sister Rhene! Report!'

With a startled look round, Kamilla had realised that the whiteclad Hospitaller was nowhere to be seen – she must be seeking Akemi and Melia.

And *Arkas.*

It was then that the wave of feelings broke over her – fear, adrenaline, exhaustion, relief, victory, pain. Everything at once. As the mass of enemy began to waver, many falling, others fleeing, Kamilla had tumbled to her knees, let go her rifle, and buried her face in her hands.

Arkas! Why did this happen to us? Why?

She stopped, very suddenly, as a red-armoured boot appeared beside her.

'You must stand, cadet,' Augusta told her. 'This is not over. That noise... We yet have a mission to complete.'

'But your Sisters. And...' Kamilla's voice broke. 'And *Arkas*. We...'

Even as she spoke, however, Viola and Caia both were kicking their way to the back of the building, to the door into the cloister that Kamilla knew so well. The sight of it reignited her awareness, made her look up and around at the old, familiar cathedral, at the spars of its shattered roof, its smashed pillars and statues. The floor was covered: the fallen Penitent Engines, their pilots no more than cloaked red splashes; pieces of stonework; smashed tables; bodies of cultists and soldiers alike, some of them still struggling. Alcina had started walking among them, her bolter ending the lives of both with ruthless, single shots. The soldiers were touched with her blessing, the cultists were not.

This place – this place Kamilla had known since her childhood, this home, this haven – it was a charnel house, reeking of death and betrayal. Nausea rose in her throat again and she turned sideways, emptying her belly on the flags.

Augusta offered no compassion, and no judgement. She seemed like a scarlet wall, angry and indomitable.

'We must find Akemi and Melia,' the Sister Superior said.

'And Father Arkas.' Kamilla thought about his hospitality, his humility, the way he'd always helped. 'Melia was trying to save him, but he said something about leading her to glory. Leading all of you.'

'To *glory*?' The words were ice, and the Sister Superior gave her a long look, inscrutable beneath her helm. She looked like a warrior, like some bloodstained icon of vengeance. Half expecting some reprimand, Kamilla tried to square her shoulders, but the Sister only said, 'We will regroup, and complete this mission. You must show us the lair of the beast.'

The canoness thundered through the streets of the Capital. Upright in the cupola of her Rhino, Aitamah beside her and the great Rose banner at her back, she vox-cast the battle prayer out over the city, every bit as loud as the deacon's ongoing scream. It was a warfare of noise, a cacophony of ideology that seemed more than human, but Elvorix Ianthe had the God-Emperor in her words and in her heart, and His power rang from the very buildings.

At her command, her Order brought death. Four of Sister Jolantra's Exorcists were still at the bridges, but she had instructed the remainder to spread out through the Capital, their organ pipes loaded and ready to fire. Sisters Eleni and Roku had moved up on the double, their red boots pounding the roadways. Sister Mikaela had come with them, her squad eager for the battle they had not yet faced. With them was the last Penitent Engine, its saws and flamers running.

Kozma's mobile artillery was still at the Wall of Diligence, securing the orbital batteries.

'As the hive fleet closes,' the canoness had told the commander, 'the batteries will open fire. Spheres will fall like meteors, and you must eliminate every single one that you can. Do you understand?'

'Yes, milady.'

'I have deployed my Sisters, Eleni and Roku, to the streets. They will assist with the evacuation. The Exorcists will focus their demolition upon the starport areas, clearing the ground and then defending the ports themselves. I have also commanded the bulk landers to the ports, to assist with the removal of the populace. But' – her tone was ice and steel – 'none of this will be enough. We will defend the people until the final possible moment, and once that moment is upon us, Adept Kende will destroy the city.'

She saw Kozma shudder. 'Milady canoness–'

'Those we cannot save will rest with Him.' Still delivering her briefing, the canoness had barely paused for breath. 'In the Outskirt, the cultists assail the bridges, but I have Exorcists standing ready. With everything we still have to defend, I do not wish to be hit in the back.'

'Milady.' Facing the death of her world, Kozma had faltered. 'My Blades, at the bridges–'

'Do not test me, commander. I will do whatever He deems necessary.'

Little made Tamara Kozma blanch, but she hadn't argued.

And the canoness' force had moved. Under the Gate of Saint Nemes and up through the streets of the Capital, the hymnal broadcast before it like some huge percussion wave. It was almost noon now, the sky bright, the wind a frozen blade, edged and fierce. The Exorcists boomed, turning great and shining cathedrals to piles of smoking rubble. Squads of Sisters patrolled the streets, defending the clusters of pilgrims and commanding their obedience. The Order's banners flapped red – red as bloodshed, red as rage.

Yet the scream of the deacon, the howl that had accompanied the death of the monster – it was changing, now, crystallising into something edged with pure, cold zeal. With *need*, with hunger. Against the heat of the wrath of the Rose, so did the magus pitch his own unholy strength, and the bells of the Saints' Cathedral, all clamouring and tuneless. He was the centre of the rising vortex, the core of the cult's awareness, and his call would not be denied.

Saint Veres comes!

All across the city, more and more monsters were emerging. Not up from the sealed sewers, not across the bridges from the Outskirt, but now from vaults and cellars, from crypts and reliquaries. Just like the Outskirt cathedral, hundreds of the buildings had hidden necropoli, places secret from Opal's life and faith that had never before been opened or seen. All the monsters that Augusta's sweep had missed – had never even suspected were there – now did they reveal themselves, hunching forth, emerging onto the cold and windy streets. Now did they unfurl the full might of their worm-banners; now did they crawl through the trampled remains of the forgotten festival. As if every one of a hundred thousand Opaline shrines had concealed beasts in its basement, so did they rise to the deacon's call.

And Arch-Deacon Janos felt them, knew them, welcomed them. From the cultists of the Outskirt to the genestealer hybrids of the city, from human to aberrant and everything between, every creature, every fragment of awakened flesh, every curl and coil and writhe. He felt the monstrosities. He felt the roars of the poor and starving as they began their rebellion and assailed the bridges at last. He felt the vehemence and hunger of those who charged at Kozma's defended nodes – the starports, the water tower, the vox-arrays. He felt the rippling elation of his victory, the closeness of Opal's true saviour.

Saint Veres comes!

As the sun reached its peak and began its descent towards the river, as the wind grew ever more savage, so did he stand at his glassaic pulpit, its colours blurring upon the building's heaving pews. And he could feel these people, too: the men and women and pilgrims who had held true to their *real* faith, to Opal's legends and history and holiness, and who would see the saint arrive at last.

See Opal returned to full glory.

Janos was a champion, a herald, a summoner. The last of his line. Generation after generation, his predecessors had carried Veres' awareness, the knowledge of the festival's importance, of the saint's final return as the conjunction took place. And this world would sing! She would be free! No longer chained to the rules of the greedy Imperium, no longer enslaved by the false Emperor – the Gem of the Segmentum Border, the Home of the Million Saints, restored at last!

Unseen in the brilliant sky, the three gas giants – Kira, Ava and Sara – grew closer and closer. And, as if pulled by their very conjunction, the great vortex began to turn.

'Sister Rhene,' Augusta said, 'report.'

'The hospice is empty, Sister Superior,' Rhene said. 'There is no sign of our Sisters.'

Augusta stopped, her pulse hammering. She was yet to fulfil her mission, but she would not leave them – not if she had the chance to redeem her error.

'Mezei, watch the grounds.'

'Sister.'

The commander's hundred remaining soldiers were down to less than forty, but he was resolute – a strong man and a good one. He formed them up, and sent them to comb the grounds.

'We would be foolish,' he told them, 'if we believed this building safe.'

'The last of the cult have fled, and are attempting to cross the bridges,' Augusta said. 'You will secure the area.'

He nodded, his scarred face filthy and covered in blood. There was a ghost in his eyes – the loss of his Opal-born naïveté – but Augusta had no words of comfort for him. He was a soldier, and his life belonged to the Emperor.

'You are blessed, this day, Mezei,' she told him. 'The Throne has seen your courage.'

Under his dusky skin, he coloured. 'Yes, Sister.'

But that was all she would offer. She turned now to the girl. 'Cadet, we must scout this crypt. And swiftly.'

The cadet nodded. She was still on her feet, but her broken face was pale – she would falter, and soon. Silently, the girl guided them to the crypt's entrance, by the opposite cloister to the hospice. Down the grey stone steps to the ancient, uneven gravestones of the floor. Leaving Caia and Viola to watch the building, Augusta, Alcina and Rhene raised their suit-lights and looked round at the recessed shelves, at the last of the remaining weapons and banners, at the bottles and jars and instruments. Frowning under her wimple, Rhene picked some of these up, turning them over and inspecting their marks and labels.

'They seem genuine,' she said. 'Witchbane, tetraporfaline, sanguinators, basic stimms – simple medical tools and treatments, as one would expect.'

Augusta nodded, shining her light through the dark. The monster's presence had soaked into the walls, the floor, the stone – even Opal's quintessential glimmer was faded here, as if the beast had eaten it away.

'How did we not know?' she said, a shard of pain in her voice. 'It was under our feet, and we did not know it was here. Did He tell us, and we were too blind to see? How did we err so shamefully?'

Then Sister Alcina gave a cry, and there was the sound of an armoured figure crashing to its knees. Bolter drawn, Augusta ran to her side, Kamilla with her. Rhene had stayed by the shelves, picking things up and muttering to herself.

Augusta's light found red boots, and then her second kneeling, helm off, shoulders bowed in pain. She was praying, words a whisper under her breath. Ahead of her...

A sudden rise of nausea and fury almost robbed the Sister Superior of breath.

'Blessed be her memory,' Alcina said. 'She has attained the Throne.'

The floor's flag-tombs were blood-soaked, the stain almost black – she had lain there for some time. Whoever had placed her there had arranged her, still in her armour, like the carved effigy on the top of a coffin, her repose perfect, her hands placed in the aquila. The wound in her neck was clearly visible and it was apparent from her pallor that her body was almost bloodless.

Melia.

Appearing beside Augusta, Kamilla suddenly sobbed. She went to run forwards, but Alcina stopped her.

'Hold where you are, child. She stands before the Emperor.'

'I'm sorry.' She crumpled, shaking. 'Saint and Emperor, I'm sorry. I should have stayed–'

'Hold where you are!' Augusta's snap was louder than she'd intended. With a prayer, she fought down the grief, the spasm of horror and catastrophe that clutched at her heart.

Melia. Warrior and healer, always the gentlest of us, truly I have failed you. Blessed be your memory.

Her voice cracking, fighting down the need to sob, she said, 'Sister Alcina?'

'She bears many contusions,' Alcina said. 'Perhaps she was overwhelmed, or the beast invaded her mind, I do not know. But she was Sororitas, and guarded by Him, and it must surely have failed. Perhaps it sought her death because it could not break her faith.'

'I'm sorry,' Kamilla repeated, rocking back and forth. 'I shouldn't have left, I'm sorry...'

'You followed your orders, and you enabled us to slay the

beast.' Overcome, Augusta knelt by her fallen Sister, touched Melia's cheek. *The beast to which I left her.* Her tone shook, and then steadied as she said, 'We must still locate Akemi. I will lose no more Sisters.'

I will fail my squad, fail Opal, no more. Or I will take up that eviscerator by my own choice.

'I'm sorry...' The cadet wiped the back of her hand over her broken nose. It came away streaked with blood and snot. 'I'm sorry...'

'It is a message, I think,' Rhene said from behind them, her voice quiet. Outside, Mezei was barking orders and lasrifles hissed and crackled at unseen foes. 'Perhaps left by Arkas, or by the cult. They still intend to greet their saint, and they will not permit you to stop them.'

'Oh, we *will* stop them.' Augusta's words were a snarl, her grief crystallising to anger. 'We will eliminate every last faithless heretic, every *single* corrupted xenos.' She came back to her feet, fury in her every move. 'In His name.'

'Did the deacon not comment,' said Alcina suddenly, 'that he wished us to be present at the festival's height, at the Sermon of the Hero? That he had a particular role in mind?'

'He did.' Augusta turned to stare at her Sister. 'And he made a particular point about us all being in attendance. Refused to show Viola and I the relic.'

'Maybe that was what Arkas meant?' Kamilla sniffled. 'By glory?'

'By the Throne.' Augusta and Alcina exchanged a long look, a growing understanding as clear as His command. 'If it was Arkas that left Melia for the patriarch–'

'Then he surely took Akemi to the magus,' Alcina said. 'To the Sermon of the Hero, as the deacon intended.'

'But how did he get across the river?' Augusta asked. 'The sewers were flooded, and the Blex on the bridges–'

'There's an old servitor tunnel,' Kamilla said. 'Tiny, and separate from everything else. It's how I... how I used to come and go.'

'Perhaps they intend to lure us?' Alcina said. 'To their "saint", or to some final confrontation?'

'Then we will take that lure,' Augusta said, one hand on her bolter. 'I will inform the canoness – we will attain the Saints' Cathedral, retrieve our Sister and the relic. And when we find the deacon, I will ram this down his throat and pull the trigger.'

'In His name,' Alcina said.

'And Arkas?' Kamilla asked, her tone fearful. 'She was trying to help him.'

'He is a traitor,' Augusta said. 'He is not worth the death of my Sister, and I will show him no mercy.'

XXII

THE FINAL ADVANCE

Missiles rained upon the streets of Holy Opal. Shrines and cathedrals, statues and basilicae, streets and mosaics and their still-cowering people – everything crumpled beneath the Exorcists' assault, clearing the ground to the starports. Advancing upon the Saints' Cathedral, the canoness' Immolator rumbled forwards, her hymnal broadcast loud across the booms of demolition.

'We are the Rose, and we bring His wrath!'

In response, the bells rang rounds of disharmonic ire. The deacon's scream was continuous, inhuman, impossible, but Elvorix Ianthe knew no fear. As she had once raged forward upon the volcanic islands of Lycheate, so she did now, challenging all in her path.

And the monsters answered.

From the rubbled remains, the hidden hybrids still swarmed forth. Some had pilgrims with them, men and women who had lost their minds to the power of the xenos, taken by dread, or by both hope and falsehood. Others were already covered in the blood of the fearful and faithful, those who had been praying for the God-Emperor's salvation.

Whatever they were, it did not matter. Blazing with scarlet ire, the canoness sent death crackling from her plasma pistol, merciless golden streaks of His judgement and fury. The cherub circled her like a silent guardian, scattering ash and petals; Aitamah, her slate laid aside, shot with the same dedication as her mistress, slaying anything that came within range.

The roads were full of panic and struggle and dust, and her advance through the Capital was not swift – though the tracks of her Immolator crushed hundreds, covering the streets in more death. Mikaela and her squad defended the vehicle's flanks, the bark and boom of their bolters keeping the creatures back. In their midst, Elvorix Ianthe was a warrior of supreme strength, experienced in victory. She was a burning icon of pure and righteous rage.

And she drew the main attack upon herself.

Across the Capital, Jolantra's Exorcists rumbled and boomed, bringing rubble and destruction. Sacred churches crumbled in their dozens; market squares were pitted with ruin. No place would remain for the hiding cultists, for the landing tyranids to take cover, or to assault the evacuation. Occasionally, the missiles struck the cable-cars and brought them crashing to the ground, many still full of people – but that did not matter, not now. The greater number would still be saved and the souls of the fallen would stand at the Throne.

Moving the people, Eleni and Roku sent reports of vicious, panicked fighting, but there were still steadfast Blades in place, the few that remained, shooting anyone that fell out of line.

Soon, however, the canoness saw the first organised defence.

Tauroxes and Chimeras, in rusted Opal colours. The ones that Kozma had said were too damaged or old to move – these had now been gained by the enemy. For a moment, the canoness prayed for the commander's honesty – was Kozma, too, xenos-fallen? – but He told her truly that this was not the case, that Kozma's heart was prideful, but clear. Yet the xenos' stain had sunk deep into the denizens of Opal, be they pilgrim or local or Outskirter. Whether they had been following the cult for many years, or whether their assimilation was recent, the canoness did not know and did not care. She cared only that the enemy was finally, fully rallying, was finding its weapons and teeth.

And that His retribution would not be gainsaid.

At her command, the last Penitent Engine lumbered into a run, buzzsaws screaming, flamer ignited. Charging at full speed, it hurled itself towards the vehicles' barricade, ready to tear and stamp. Mikaela barked an order, and her squad stood ready.

The engine hit.

The canoness' Rhino had stopped, still out of range of the Taurox autocannons. Focused at the centre of the enemy's waiting line, the Penitent Engine hammered into the vehicles, stamping and smashing. Dust and smoke rose in filthy eddies, filled with grit. A second later, they hid the rampaging engine from sight. Tearing metal screamed in protest.

Mikaela said, quite calm, 'We are surrounded.'

From the side streets, the plazas and marketplaces, more and more of the creatures were stealing forth. The Sisters were tiny scarlet dots in the centre of a massive, closing ring of writhing, toothsome darkness; of curling, coiling things that clung to walls and balconies, that crept across roofs. However many of the hybrids, of the cultists, Augusta had already slain, there were more – there were always more. Endless numbers of them had seethed onto the streets, called by the deacon's cry. Among them, the tiny spots of pilgrims' colour that were the last lives of Opal herself.

The canoness said, 'Immolator. On my command!'

Twin flamers spat searing death. The creatures, screaming, burning, came on. But Mikaela and her squad were ready at the flanks, and their bolters sang with reckoning. The battle-hymn raging, the canoness shot the closest hybrid, another, a third. Aitamah was still firing, her accuracy devastating. But they were not enough, and the Rhino, Sisters and all, would be buried at any moment.

Smoke and dust spread down the roadway. The bells still rang a deafening clangour. The deacon's scream was the death-scream of Opal herself, her final burst of heresy and false hope, of loss and betrayal. Through it, the canoness could hear the enemy's mobile artillery begin to advance, emerging from under the engine's dirt-cloud, and into a range where their weapons could be used. Barking orders into the vox, she aimed her plasma pistol at the nearest beast, pulled the trigger. It squalled, and gore splashed out across the roadway. A second shot killed another, but still there were too many and the clouds were parting now, letting the cultists' Tauroxes into full view.

Mikaela shouted orders, shot and shot again. At their full rate of fire, the bolters blew the beasts to bits, blood and gore exploding from the flying corpses. But for every one that died, ten took its place, and for every ten there were a hundred, a thousand. One of the squad went down, covered in a swarm of crazed cultists. Claws slashed at her armour, carving it open. She screamed the battle-hymn, livid and furious. Then she was silenced, her body broken.

'Driver! Advance!' the canoness ordered. The Tauroxes were in range now.

But so was she.

One savage yellow streak stopped the leading vehicle in its tracks, black smoke pouring from its shattered engine. There were more figures surrounding it and surging forwards – but not the creatures, this time. These were the people of Opal, their finery tattered, their mock-uniforms torn and covered in soot, their screaming demented. Their old rivalries were forgotten now – from the followers of the saints to the Path of the Thousand Humble, from the preachers of the shrines to the humblest, brown-robed faithful, all were the same in the eyes of the incoming hive.

Uncaring of the autocannons, the cultists came on in a frenzy, shrieking Veres' name. Behind them, oblivious to their own side, the Tauroxes opened fire. Hundreds fell, dead and injured and screaming. Mikaela and her squad still fought, and the canoness stood in her cupola like she could repel the assault by the force of her presence alone.

Then a voice in the vox said, *'Orders, milady? Two of my Exorcists have range on your position.'*

Sister Jolantra. The canoness bellowed her response.

'FIRE!'

The arc of missiles was audible: a whine of darkness that peaked above the canoness' head, then fell upon the standing Tauroxes like a cluster of descending predators. The roadway exploded, toppling shrines and saints, obliterating the waiting line of artillery. Around the Immolator, the monsters still curled and swarmed, burned and died. Mikaela had drawn her chainsword and was carving through limbs and heads. Aitamah shot one as it clambered up the very side of the vehicle. The canoness, her song a peal of death, punched another in the face.

At a sharp command, the driver moved forwards once more, tracks rumbling over the rubble.

But Mikaela said, breathless with horror, 'Milady, the sky. By the Golden Throne!'

And there, high above them, above the circling flotillas of

shuttles and the great, hovering shadows of the waiting bulk landers, tiny sparks of fireworks were just becoming visible. A dozen of them. A hundred.

More.

'Opal's time is upon her,' the canoness said, her voice laden with feeling. 'Blessed be her memory.' The tank lurched and rumbled. 'We must attain the Saints' Cathedral swiftly, my Sisters. Our mission must still be fulfilled. And we must support Augusta as she faces the traitor.

'The hive fleet is come.'

With her Aquila now speeding over the Capital's streets, Augusta could see the clouds of devastation that marked the canoness' progress, could see the red of the Exorcists as they moved upon the landing pads, destroying everything as they went. She could see her Sisters, Eleni and Roku and their squads, and the heaving swarms of creatures that seethed about the fighting, attacking not only the Sisters but the remaining Blades too. She could see the lines and clusters of the still-fleeing pilgrims, and the clamouring hordes still stuck at cable-car stations and at starports.

Her heart recoiled, her mouth filled with bile. How could she have missed so many? How could there *be* so many? How could she have missed the presence of the patriarch, lost not one but two of her squad?

You failed to halt the invasion, you failed to stop the cult. You left your Sisters to the xenos. For a moment, her Repentance loomed large, but this was no time for faintheartedness or guilt. She would face the betrayer, and fulfil her mission.

Viola cursed, and Alcina did not correct her. Caia had not spoken; her body was taut with grief, rage, tension. Her need for holy vengeance. Kamilla was staring from the Aquila's windows with a look of absolute horror on her face.

'Where did they all come from?' It was a whisper.

'They must have been there all along,' Augusta told her, only really starting to understand this herself. 'Like the monster. They...' Her voice threatened to shake and she controlled herself with both iron and fury. 'They have been waiting in your basements, your crypts, your reliquaries, your storage holds. The Emperor only knows for how long.'

Years, she thought. *Decades. The ones we slew were not even the beginning.*

Surrounded by an ever-rising spiral of cloud, she could see the Saints' Cathedral, the last glimmer of its glassaic roof. It was His heart upon this broken world, now fallen to the gene-stealer magus.

Over the vox, she reported their position to the canoness. In return, she got a brief crackle, as if Elvorix Ianthe was considering her next words carefully.

Then the canoness said, *'We are out of time. The orbital batteries are opening fire.'*

The orbital batteries are opening fire. The Sister Superior caught her breath on a desperate prayer, felt a sudden rush of nausea.

As if she had heard, the canoness said, *'I am incoming on the cathedral. If He wills it, I will support your assault upon the deacon. Sisters Jolantra, Eleni and Roku now muster at the starports. They will be the last to board the bulk landers. Once our objectives are achieved, and we are all clear of the Capital, Adept Kende will destroy the city. Ave Imperator, Sister Superior. May you walk with Him.'*

The vox shut off, its emptiness suddenly terrifying. At some point, the vox-cast evacuation command had fallen from the air and Augusta had not even noticed. Now, she was abruptly aware of the outside silence, and of the roar of the Aquila's engines.

The four standing Sisters, three of them injured, shared a moment of prayer and clarity. The cadet, pale-faced and broken-nosed, stood quiet, her eyes wide. Despite Augusta's feelings of remorse, of guilt, of horror; despite her failure to save her Sisters, to not estimate the sheer scale of the assault, the numbers of monsters, or the overpowering presence of the deacon himself…

May you walk with Him.

I will complete my mission, she thought. I will find my Sister, and execute the heretic. And may I exonerate myself enough to stand before the Throne.

At the command centre, Kozma was bombarded by reports. The servo-skull at her desk, its jaws holding the vox-caster, spat numbers and locations, orders and bridges and movements and deaths. Most of the Order had now converged upon the starports and were holding them against the cult. And the Blades of the Holy Exterior were successfully taking the bridges – the invaders were suffering heavy losses, and being thrown back.

But the enemy had started swimming the river.

The Varadi was wide and still, and very cold. Hundreds of them were drowning, but hundreds more were succeeding, reaching the far side. The Blades at the Martello towers shot them as they came ashore, but more were always coming. In ones and twos, then in fives and tens, the cultists that had gathered at Arkas' cathedral, and at the Bridge of Souls, were making it to the far bank, and to the fallen wreckage of the habs and manufactories. Called by their false hopes, and by the deacon's power, many ran straight for the Wall of Diligence, aiming to assail the Tauroxes and the orbital batteries. But others were circling around, heading back over the bridges to attack the defenders from the rear.

Listening to her forces fight, and panic, and despair, and die, the commander's rage was growing. What had these so-called Sisters done? Run back and forth, and wasted endless lives?

Thrown them aside as if they, every last man and woman, were worthless? Her Blades were dying, her city was being destroyed, her people torn to screaming pieces.

And then, she heard the boom.

She'd heard the sound once before, from the single battery at the cathedral, at the Ceremony of Coming Conjunction – had that only been days before? Then, it had been a test, the great cannon clearing its throat, getting ready for the festival. Now it was a reverberation that she felt in her very chest – the final, bass bellow of holy Opal's funeral hymn.

Our saints laid down their lives for you…

The batteries were opening fire.

A cold flame rose in Kozma, then; a chill white blaze like the ring-light of Opal herself. Her aide with her, she barked for her shuttle and stamped up the ramp like she was the last of the shrine world's warrior saints. Her world was dying, her soldiers, her people. She was their commander. They were her responsibility. She had been overruled and undermined at every turn.

And she had had enough.

In the palace, the governor still prayed. He was cold to the bone, his knees numb, but he had not relented. With the same passion and ardour as the deacon had bawled from the pulpit, Vass Mihaly prayed for his world.

He should have known – he should have *known!* He could see his own errors, now; see the mess that he had made. In trusting the deacon, in refusing to listen to the Sisters, he had abandoned his precious Opal to blood and acid and death.

As the first booms rocked the Capital, he raised his head. Outside the window, open as ever, he could see the sky above the Saints' Cathedral, see the shuttles, the incoming bulk landers, the first wave of the burning meteors, the twisting spiral of clouds that was steadily gathering, obscuring the ring-light. *If only there really was a Saint Veres,* he thought, in a moment of foolishness. *If only he would come and save us now!*

A shudder went through him, pain and guilt and shame. He was the governor of Opal, and he had presided over so many empty parades, so much pompous noise. So much arrogance... Staggering with the stiffness in his bones, he came to his feet with a lurch. He would not die on his knees like a weakling. He would die as befitted a–

The hiss and the scrape behind him were his only warning. With a sudden, sick surge of terror he started to turn, got an impression of gleaming teeth...

But it was already too late. Lashing out with three sets of claws, the monster tore him in half.

Incoming at speed, Augusta's Aquila met the cloud-vortex. Tumbled this way and that, the vehicle fought to gain headway, grit and smoke both streaming past its nose. Below it, the Sister Superior could see the Saints' Cathedral – now a mote of light at the heart of the storm, its glassaic glinting. Its bells still rang, clamour and clatter and noise. The inhuman scream of the deacon had not faded. It called to the skies, and beyond, laden with need and anticipation.

Saint Veres comes!

The shuttle lurched suddenly sideways, sending the Sisters and Kamilla clattering to the floor.

'The batteries!' The pilot's words were sharp.

Raising her head, the Sister Superior heard the first, deep thunder of the orbital defences. Her heart hammered, sick with adrenaline and prayer and she swore, vicious enough to put Viola to shame.

'Get us down as close you can. We *will* succeed.'

'Sister.'

The shuttle dropped, and Augusta could hear the nose cannon firing, trying to clear enough of a landing space... Then something impacted against the vehicle's shell, and then something else. Little things, hurling themselves upwards.

'By the Throne,' the pilot said. 'They're *jumping.*'

'Then so can we,' Augusta returned. 'If we're that low, clear us a path.'

Kamilla blinked, looking at her with a spark of fear.

'You will jump, cadet.'

The girl nodded, her expression setting to sternness.

'Good. Pilot, drop the–'

The hiss of hydraulics buried her words. The ramp was coming down, dirt swirling through the gap. Augusta could not see how high they were, but figures were already throwing themselves at the Aquila's interior. Viola, riding the floor with feet placed apart, sent them back with the thrice-blessed heavy bolter.

'Now!' Augusta shouted.

Leaving Rhene but taking Kamilla with them, the four of them ran, jumped. The shuttle, engines screaming, flattened the air as it lifted off again. As she hit the ground, rolling with the impact, Augusta saw it turn and open fire, tearing holes in the cathedral's sacred grounds. Bodies flew. Cultists? Opal's fallen faithful? It did not matter – all were xenos now.

Outside the vehicle, the deacon's scream was even louder and the battering of the wind was growing. The daylight was starting to fade and the storm was turning faster and faster, a mighty bank of twisting clouds that sucked up dirt and rubbish, and that made the cadet stagger. She still looked resolute, though, and she still had her rifle, her knuckles white with the tension in her grip.

'Run!' Augusta shouted.

They ran. Shooting stark five-round bursts to keep the people back, praying aloud, skidding in the wind, their boots sliding every which way, they ran.

'Be with us, O Emperor!'

The scream was growing louder, far louder than could come from any human throat. It filled the Sanctum, the Capital. It was part of the thundering storm, part of the writhing, turning clouds, the vortex whose very heart was opening, now, opening to a centre of pure darkness. Opal's afternoon sky, the holy halo of her ring-light, the swarms of shuttles, the falling meteors... all had gone. Even as Augusta ran, the glassaic roof of the cathedral shattered, exploding under the sheer power of the scream. Sparkling shards were picked up by the winds, and they whirled in a blizzard of deadly edges.

'Guard us, guide us, stand beside us! Grant us your holy wrath!'

Over the vox, the Sisters prayed. Augusta could hear Kamilla echoing the words, made no attempt to stop her. As best she could, she kept the cadet in the lee of her armour. Whirling glassaic fragments started to shatter against the ceramite.

Around them, more and more figures were appearing through the storm, shadows at first, resolving as they came closer. The deacon's congregation were everywhere, carrying whatever weapons they could bear. Some still had their simulacra from the festival, some had broken pews. Whatever they carried, they brandished it with a wild-eyed, wild-haired frenzy and they came at the Sisters with murder in their every movement. Glass shredded their clothing, their flesh, and they did not even notice.

'A spiritu dominatus!'

Shouting the words of the litany, Viola gunned them down. The fierce wind misted with scarlet spray, the stone grew slick underfoot. Broken figures crawled, still howling Veres' name, dragging their own legs or guts behind them. Augusta heard Kamilla curse, cough, and retch.

'Domine, libra nos!' Drawing her blade, screaming along with its rasp, the Sister Superior surged forwards, cutting and hacking and stamping. This was no tidy firefight, with neat movements and skirmishes and extended lines; this was the teeth of the storm, the brutal hack and slash and roar of warfare – the kind that Opal had never known.

But this world… truly, she knew it now.

Briefly, Augusta thought about Kozma, about her unprepared soldiers. The Sister Superior could almost find concern for them, but there was no space for that here – she could only pray that the *Pride of Faith* and the *Star of Victory* were protecting the skies as best they could, that the loaders and shuttles could still land. Then, suddenly, she was through the madness and the wind dropped like a dead thing.

In the eye of the storm, the air was still. Ahead of them, all the cathedral's doors were open, even as they had been when she and Viola had attended the Mass of the First Martyr. Inside, the deacon stood in the now shattered pulpit, a skeleton of twisting steel. Shining glassaic covered the floor.

Leona, fire!

But Augusta's attention was caught by something else – and for a short moment, she stared. Above her head, she could see an almighty, rotating hololith, a pattern of stars that filled the entire centre of the building, orbiting the deacon's head even as the storm was doing. Here were the three outer planets of the Denar Alpha System, now almost in perfect alignment. And there…

By the Throne.

The light was tiny, no more than a bright speck. It occupied the other side of the sky, the other side of the sparkling, yellow image. But she knew what it was, knew as if He Himself had reached down to touch her heart.

Sol, nine planets orbiting. And the third one… *Terra*.

By His holy light! By the very Golden Throne!

Hope. Blessing. Courage. The Emperor's touch and presence, here, at the very centre of the xenos' power. She heard Alcina choke – a rare display of feeling. Heard Caia say, 'Is that...?'

Viola replied, 'Yes.' Her voice, too, was full. 'Praise Him, for Opal is not alone.'

'We are never alone,' Augusta said softly. She found herself blinking fiercely. 'The shadow in the warp is but a xenos trick. He is with us. Always.'

Beside her, Kamilla had something in her hand, a tiny sphere of interlocking brass rings. Not letting go of her rifle, she held the thing up to the golden, shining holo-orrery that now gleamed under the broken roof.

Augusta wanted to fall to her knees, sing the prayers that rose in her heart. But she was a veteran Sister Superior of the Order of the Bloody Rose, and the prayer in her heart was *rage*.

The deacon, his arms aloft, his head back, was still screaming. The noise battered at them, seemed enough to knock them from their feet, to fill their minds with false hopes, and horrors. With images of the incoming saint. It tangled round the cries of the dying, round the clamour of the bells. Behind them, more people were all calling Veres' name. They had followed the Sisters through the door. Trapped them in the building.

There was no vox from the canoness, no contact from the cathedral's outside. They could no longer even hear the orbital defences. Everything else had been obliterated by the storm. They were unsupported. But they needed no orders, not now.

She shouted, 'We are the Bloody Rose. We stand here by the Accords of Hydraphur – by the word of Saint Mina, by her blade and her courage. By the blessing of the God-Emperor and by His guidance. We are the Adepta Sororitas, and since the Age of Apostasy, our Sisters and we have stood at the gates to hell.

Only we can stand sentinel here. And we say – *enough*.' She felt her Sisters rally behind her. 'Cadet,' she added, more softly. 'Find Akemi. Do not fail me in this. When you have found her, run for the shuttle and Sister Rhene. We pray for His blessing, for the life of our Sister.'

Kamilla, her face and clothes already badly cut, went even paler, but nodded.

'And we, my steadfast Sisters. We finish this. In His name.'

'In His name,' they said, as one.

xxiii

THE SISTERS
AND THE HERETIC

In the roadway, her plasma pistol still executing cultists by the hundred, the canoness had one eye on the sky. She saw the tiny, shining sparks. She saw them detonate, struck by the orbital batteries and filling the sky with fireworks. She saw the very first of those streaking, burning meteors pass the defences, saw it strike the roadway to her left, saw rock and ruin thrown skywards.

The tyranids were landing.

Another, and another, and more, now all across the Capital. Fiery tails of incoming death, of slavering appetite and utter, ravenous destruction. The bulk landers were still hovering, but even as the canoness raised her furious prayer, she saw a meteor strike the closest starport, saw it explode in a blooming flower of promethium. A tumble of shuttles were caught in the convection, tossed aside like so many toys.

'Jolantra!' she shouted into the vox. 'Sister Jolantra!'

It was Roku that responded. *'Her Exorcist was caught in the blast, milady. The spheres now fall all round us.'*

The evacuation was over.

'Go!' she barked. 'Leave the vehicles. Take as many of the pilgrims as you can, and get the bulk landers clear. I will give Adept Kende the final command.'

She tried to reach Kozma, had no response; tried to reach Augusta, had no response. Thousands of aberrants and mutants were surrounding her Immolator, now, crawling over the rubble, howling gleefully as they came. The Penitent Engine stamped its last and toppled, its flamer still running.

Over the vox, Eleni said, *'The spheres, milady…'* There was a quaver to her voice – not fear so much as revulsion. *'They crack as they land. In His name, I have never seen such creatures…'*

'Enough.' She was steel and fire, resolute. 'Sister Aitamah, tell the adept – one Solar hour, beginning now.'

'Milady.'

'We will attain the cathedral, support Augusta and ensure the success of this mission.'

Her hymnal still echoing, defiant over Opal's destruction, the canoness rumbled onwards. The bulk landers, now empty of the Order's vehicles, were filling completely with the last of the fleeing pilgrims. But the roadway ahead of her was swarming with monsters, with tearful people, their faces raised to the meteors.

Witness your Saint Veres, she told them silently. *Witness the final truth of your saviour's arrival. Your world is ending. And this is the price of her heresy.*

The canoness had not reached them.

Before the Sisters, in front of Augusta, the deacon was screaming, still haloed by the shining, golden hololith. Around them, crawling forwards over the broken pews, incoming from every direction, were his followers, his converted – the corrupted pilgrims of Opal. No longer the faithful of the God-Emperor, they had come to greet their saint, and to slay any who got in their way.

Even as Augusta raised her bolter, the deacon ceased the scream. The bells stopped dead too, leaving after-echoes ringing through vaults of sudden quiet. Outside, the storm still raged. The tyranids must be landing, but she could not see them, not here. She would end this, no matter what.

'You foolish, arrogant women!' He leaned down over the pulpit, ringed hands on the rail, his face contorted with heresy and rage. There was pink froth on his lips, and his eyes were alight with some terrible, pale energy. 'This is *Opal!* Gem of the Segmentum Border, Home of the Million Saints! It is a place of warriors, of proud and noble history! It is the place of holy Veres, of his martyrs! And it has been *waiting!* I will not have your false doctrine here! We will *ascend!*'

In Augusta's heart, anger rose like flame – the pure, rose-red rage of Saint Mina herself. She was His faithful, His daughter; she was wrath incarnate. It seemed that every moment in her life, every fight, every victory – every *mistake* – had been leading to this terrible, ultimate confrontation.

The bolter aimed at the deacon's head, she told him, 'We are the executioner. And you, heretic, will *perish.*'

Her Sisters lifted their fury with the holy chiming of the hymnal. 'We beseech thee…'

The deacon snarled, baring bloodied teeth. His eyes flashed with the same sick energy; the storm outside grew wilder, crackling with lightning.

'You are too late! Saint Veres *comes!*'

And Augusta bellowed, 'Fire!'

* * *

Find Akemi.

In that first instant, Kamilla had absolutely no idea where she was supposed to look. The Saints' Cathedral was eye-wateringly huge, its archways and statues towering and massive, its curved pews thick with the slavering faithless. The deacon was leaning from the edge of the pulpit, spitting slaver, his eyes burning.

She had one hand on her rifle, the other still on the compass.

She heard Augusta's command, heard the Sisters open fire. She saw the first flashes of energy that came from the deacon's gaze and fingers, and instinctively she hurled herself aside. They struck Augusta's armour and crackled over her like some electrical charge. Something smelled like burning – her flesh or the thick padding of her underarmour. But the Sister Superior did not flinch; with a snarl, she pulled the trigger. Bolter rounds struck the pulpit's steel, and detonated.

Kamilla had to follow her orders. But that was crazy. How was she to find anything, in all this?

Saint and Emperor! What do I do? What do I do, from here?

There was no one to command her, no unit to offer security. She found herself praying, even in the midst of the madness. Could He hear her? All the way down here? Just one unimportant cadet?

Help me! Help me through the madness!

Certainly, she was unimportant enough for the deacon to have dismissed her. He was intent on the Sisters, raising his hands to blast them with another pulse. Lightning flashed from the vaulted roof, reflected from the shattered glassaic in a thousand, thousand pieces of savage, dancing light.

What do I do? What do I–
Move!

She ducked another blast and started running, though she had no idea to where. Figures saw her, harried her, got in her way. They threw themselves at her, blocked her lines of sight, took swipes at her as she ran past them. The Sisters opened fire, a full suppression. Bodies flew.

Saint and Emperor!

Throwing herself on her belly, she crawled swiftly forwards on her knees and elbows, her rifle held crosswise before her, her compass still gripped in her hand. The stone was slippery, and it stank; blood and fluids covered her already ruined coat. Glassaic shards caught like grit, hurting. She could only pray that the bolter fire, like the deacon, would miss where she now lay.

Go. Now.

Terror clamoured in her heart. *How do I…?*

You are lucky, she told herself. *Lucky – and* blessed.

She came to the end of the curve of shattered pews, peered out into the next aisle. It was completely clear, the corrupted congregation all intent on the Sisters. And…

And the compass in her hand was *shining*.

Staying on her belly, she stared at it. It was not reflecting the deacon's power; it was glinting with the same yellow light as the hololith. The same light as Terra itself, now almost directly ahead of her.

Ice went down her back, sudden and thrilling. She could hear her Uncle Jakob, could see him as clearly as the cathedral itself. She remembered him, curling her little fingers over the compass on the day he had given it to her. A rush of awe and faith and memory and certainty stopped her where she lay. The reflections of the hololith gleamed in the broken glassaic all about her, just like the Capital's reflection had gleamed in the Varadi.

Two cites. Two cathedrals. Two enemy leaders. Her heart in her mouth, her breath balled in her throat, her pulse pounding in her temples, she let the little compass drop from its chain. Watched it turn, settle.

Point.

As if He Himself had reached down through the storm, touching her with His light, she saw what the compass was trying to tell her. Up behind the pulpit, high in the cathedral's nave, flanked by titanic statues, by archways that seemed to reach the very sky, there hung a vast, grey banner, now stained and shredded and flapping. And beneath it, there was an altar, covered in electro-candles, in rich fabrics and shining embroidery.

There, the compass was telling her. *That is where you need to go.*

Carefully, she crawled forwards, hugging the edge of the line of pews, until she could see. The cultists were ignoring her now, throwing themselves at the defending Sisters; the deacon's frenzied energy was slaying countless numbers of them, though he apparently did not care. But she was an eye of stillness. The madness whirled about her, but now her certainly was absolute. Easing forwards further, Kamilla raised her head.

And there, on the altar top, lay a figure like an offering. Like the ultimate gift of this warrior-worshipping world, presented to its incoming saint. Adepta Sororitas.

Akemi.

Unlike Melia, she had no armour, was still lost in her own unconsciousness. And over her, sanguinator in hand – as he had treated a thousand, a million, of the Outskirt's unwell; as he had cared for and fed them for so long – was a figure as familiar as her childhood.

As he had stood in his own cathedral, so now did he stand in this one.

Father Arkas.

'FIRE!'

Augusta and her three Sisters stood like icons amid the seething mass of heretics. Energies flashed at them, the deacon's frothing and shrieking accompanied by bursts of savage, killing power. Pillars blackened; stone exploded and fell, came rattling down in rains of broken pebbles. He was railing, now, crying the name of Saint Veres, the history of Opal, the litanies of her saints and martyrs.

'We will *ascend!*' He was livid with insanity. 'Saint Veres *comes!*' In response, the Sisters *sang.*

They sang like a weapon, they sang like pure faith. Crackling power struck them and fell back, leaving their armour smoking and charred. Enraged at their resistance, the deacon raised his scream and struck at them again, his strange light flashing from his eyes. It tore through the slash in the centre of Augusta's chest-plate, burning her skin and leaving angry flares of pain in its wake. Viola, bawling the battle-prayer, was staggering, but she did not, would not, fall. Roaring, she emptied the thrice-blessed heavy bolter in a full suppression, reloaded it, and emptied it again. Death hammered out from the weapon, slaying heretic pilgrims in their hundreds. Caia was favouring her injured leg, her bolter now held in both hands, but she did not stop shooting. Alcina, still unharmed and her ferocity astonishing, snarled the litany as she cut them down by the dozen.

But the maddened, slaveringly eager pilgrims did not stop. Summoned by the deacon's power and presence, they came on, relentless, waves of them, tearing at each other in their need to get to their foe. Many of them were just people, overwhelmed perhaps by the promises of the festival, by the clarion call of the magus, by the future and the saviours that he offered. As they came closer, Augusta's chainsword rasped and slew, carving limbs and heads. Alcina punched and stamped. Caia called to Melia's name and memory, and wreaked her bloody vengeance upon the heretics of Opal. And Viola...

As the heavy bolter clattered to a halt for the second time,

Viola loosed her full temper at last. Augusta could not turn, but was aware of the young Sister behind her, of the sheer might of her ferocity. The weapon still in her hands, she slammed its butt into faces and chests, and forced the dying hordes away from her.

In the pulpit, the deacon's scream crystallised to words. 'The saint is here! His blessings tumble from the very skies! We will *ascend!*'

Augusta howled back at him. *'Heretic!'*

But he did not hear. Untouched by the Sisters' bolters, defended by his own crackling energies, he lifted his arms once again. Above him, the steadily rotating hololith was growing brighter and brighter, almost dazzling; to Augusta it felt like a clock, counting down to some huge momentous–

It stopped.

'That thou wouldst bring them only death!'

The three gas giants were now in perfect alignment. The deacon was laughing, insane and wild.

'We are saved! Opal is blessed! Come to us, O Veres, saint and martyr! Come to greet your faithful!' His arms rose higher, his robes billowing.

The storm had closed in upon them, descending over the building like a predator. The huge roof rattled. Tiles and stone and archways and buttresses rumbled as they were torn free, crashing down among the pews. More of the cultists were crushed, dying, their assault destroyed in a moment.

'Down!' Turning, Alcina threw herself at the squad. The four of them went over in a tangle of clattering ceramite. A toppling statue missed them, and shattered.

But the pulpit was still there, its steel skeleton rising at the very centre of the madness.

'Behold! I am your prophet, Veres! The Prophet of Holy Opal, the Prophet of the *Stars!* Bless us, O hallowed saviour! Bless us with your presence! Let us *ascend!*'

And even as Augusta came back to her feet, her armour rattling as dust and grit and broken glassaic rattled against her side, she saw Janos pull something from his robes and hold it up, brandishing it like a victory banner. Something small and domed, but plated in pure gold. In the teeth of the gale, the cathedral now collapsing around it, it caught the light of the hololith and it shone like a promise, blinding.

Opal's most holy relic, the thing they had come here to find. The skull of the saint.

From her shuttle, Tamara Kozma saw the light, blazing from the centre of the storm.

She saw the battling canoness, saw the other Sisters and the Exorcists, now closed about the starports and fighting to the last. She heard the echoing boom of the orbital batteries, continuous and terrible. And she saw the burning of the falling, exploding meteors, sparkling in the air as if to celebrate the festival. The cannons took out dozens. But they were not enough, not nearly enough.

In her heart, her anger was still growing, a nausea of frothing and helpless rage – a fury at the Sisters' incompetence, at their arrogance, at their pitilessness, at the sheer *death* that they had caused. Her Blades were failing completely, now, overcome by dread, being torn to pieces by the very people they were trying to defend, and she could not save them. In her grief, her horror, her failure, she needed to fixate on something, something that she could *punish*...

Barking an order, she sent her shuttle towards the heart of the storm.

The pilot said something, but she did not hear, did not care – her reports were telling her that Augusta was at the cathedral. That, even now, the Sister Superior was still failing to save Opal.

And Kozma would find her, would enact vengeance for the Sister's failures, if it was the last thing she did.

But that light – that *light!*

It was pure gold, pure hope. It came in through the front of the shuttle and it touched Kozma's skin like a promise, like the greatest blessing she had ever known. *You are lost,* it said. *You are angry, and betrayed. You feel overwhelmed, and full of fire. Follow me and I will save your world, follow me and I will bless you. Are you not an Opal saint, descended from a line of the same? Are you not a warrior born, a leader? Do you not deserve better?*

The pilot was still talking, his voice crackling in the vox, but Kozma did not hear him. She was staring at the light, caught on the hook of her own pride.

Her shuttle began to lurch as the storm winds caught it. The pilot said something else, but she did not care. In that light, she had found her solution – she had found the way to bless her world. To stop the death, to feel empowered once more. And to punish these damned, betraying Sororitas, who had questioned her every decision!

Clouds and dirt closed over the shuttle, but the light stayed with her, shining in her heart. Without ever knowing that she did so, the commander of Opal let her defences fall before she struck a single blow. Even as the deacon raged and the Saints' Cathedral came down in a hail of broken rubble, even as the governor lay dead upon the floor of the palace, so did Tamara Kozma lose her faith in the Emperor, and her soul to the landing hive.

About the canoness, the eager monsters slavered.

Gold light blazed from the vortex at the Saints' Cathedral. More and more spheres were burning across the skies, leaving searing trails in their wake. Many were exploding, but others were striking the final shuttles, the cable-cars, the still-standing wreckage. They were hitting the ground with massive, rippling percussions, all round the canoness' Immolator, and sending buildings tumbling. They were striking the roadways and wherever they impacted, a great seethe of creatures poured forth – claws and teeth and hunger, darkness and utter devastation.

Screams sounded, but she did not know from where.

Behind her, at the Wall of Diligence, the orbital defences still boomed and roared; she heard the bark and bellow of the Tauroxes and Chimeras as the cultists raged up from the river. One bulk lander rose and turned, striving for the sky. A rain of meteors struck the other, making it slew and veer.

The very last of Kozma's Blades, devoid of both commander and purpose, were scattering, terrified, looking for cover and banding into frantic and soon-doomed groups.

In her Rhino, still rumbling forwards over wreckage and demolishing all in her path, the canoness had only one purpose – to reach the cathedral. To slay the heretic, to retrieve the skull, to not leave Augusta unsupported. Aitamah continued to shoot; Mikaela was still at her side.

And then, with a terrific, resounding boom, a sphere hit the ground dead ahead of her, blowing holes in road and wall. She aimed her pistol, but it split like an egg to spill steaming and liquid content. A great welter of monsters surged forth, turning her belly, but filling her with a bright and holy rage. She shot the largest, and a round from Aitamah's bolter took another. Mikaela's squad shot more of them, exploding their bodies or sending them squalling, or scurrying aside. Yet still, they seethed, endless numbers of them, teeth bared, teeming endless and everywhere.

The Immolator blazed. Twin flamers belching, it ignited monsters to screaming torches, yet there were still more, and still more. As if they understood the threat that the canoness represented, they converged on her location in their hundreds. The driver pressed forwards, crushing them beneath the Rhino's tracks, but the sheer mass of them became too much and before long, the vehicle struggled to make headway.

The canoness said, her voice like a knell, 'We are surrounded.'

Over the vox, Sister Mikaela raised the hymnal, a cry of prayer and determination and holiness, a song from her heart. Aita-mah and the others echoed her. But a welter of horrors was closing all about them now. They were caught, like a single light, at its centre.

And then, the first carnifex rose before them.

Kamilla saw the light, and it dazzled her. On some level, she under-stood it, what it meant – but she was too intent on Arkas, and on Akemi. Remembering to send the vox-message for Rhene and the shuttle, she scrambled to her feet.

And then, she saw the creature. It was only the one, but it was there, right *there* on the altar steps, standing at a corner and half-hidden by a huge stone pillar. Its head was elongated, its mouth full of needle-sharp teeth. It had strange skin, and too many arms. They were tipped in claws, and in a horrific, fleshy flail that seemed to curl from one wrist.

It had heard her. It knew she was there. For a second, they both stopped, staring at each other.

Kamilla, sick with adrenaline, could not move. Some strange, visceral fear was telling her if she moved, the beast would leap like a thing demented, and with a speed and ferocity that she could not hope to match. But she would not run. She had *orders*.

And she had something else.

Carefully, inch by inch, she put the compass in her pocket, put her hand on the stimm. The beast tilted its head, eyed her as if it knew what she was doing.

There was a moment of eternal tension, a tiny mote of stillness.

Roof slates and gargoyles were still hitting the floor and shattering, but here – this was as still as if He had cupped His very gauntlets over the scene. Slowly, gradually, she raised the thing to her teeth, pulled the cap off, and touched its needle to her arm. Gave herself the hit.

A falling buttress smashed into the steps. Pieces flew, cutting Kamilla's cheek. She jumped, her heart roaring to a pounding, violent rhythm. The beast blinked, hissed.

And time snapped back into motion.

Taking two loping paces, it leapt, hurling itself from the steps' vantage. Her ears screaming, Kamilla grabbed her rifle in both hands and fired. She didn't aim; she just kept pulling the trigger. She hit it. Several times. Hurt it. It shrieked, but it did not falter. Snarling, it landed full on her shoulders and buried her.

But the stimm, the rush of heat and movement and *hammering* adrenaline, had cleared her head. Her pit-fighter reflexes took over, left no space for doubt. And there were advantages to being small. She made no attempt to fight the thing, or to throw it off her; it was too big. Instead, she just let herself tumble, then ducked and wriggled downwards, fast as a snake.

Its tongue missed her face, lashing at air.

Still moving, her pulse pounding, she tried to get out from underneath it, but it sprang back up, regaining its feet with astonishing speed. She turned to face it and it circled, its flail-arm lashing, but she did not fear it. All her fears, all her doubts, all her questions – everything was burned away by the purity of combat. It lashed at her again, smacking the rifle out of her hands, sending it flying. She swore. Raised her fists. Bouncing on her toes, she took a gleeful, fierce joy from the stance. If she could land just one decent punch, she might knock it back enough to retrieve the weapon.

Claws slashed; she ducked. The flail coiled and whipped, but she was fast on her feet, bouncing and weaving, and it missed.

And then, like a gift from the God-Emperor Himself, a sudden idea.

In the Capital's death-pits, there were machines. As a cadet, she had never used them for herself, but she knew them, knew what they did. She knew the theories and how you took advantage of the terrain. You used the machines, your surroundings, your opponent's weaknesses, everything you could, in order to win. Just as she had done with Endre.

Beside her, a great stone pillar was carved with prayers. It was already cracked, broken by the storm, but it would do. Still circling, Kamilla put her back to it. The beast moved with her, keeping her in view. It seemed to be enjoying itself, taking its time and assuming she was easy prey.

Come on then, she told it silently, grinning like a fiend. *Come on, monster… You know you want to…*

As if it had heard her, the smaller claws slashed, missed. The flesh-flail flicked again, missed. Kamilla, concentrating hard now, ducked from side to side. And then, it lashed at her with the bigger claw, a thing more like a barb on the end of its arm.

This time, she threw herself sideways.

The barb drove clean into the cracked pillar. Even as the beast realised this, Kamilla spun and kicked its elbow with every bit of strength she had, drove its arm as deep as she could. Got it stuck.

Struggling and hissing, the beast lashed at the stone with its smaller claws, intending to rip itself free. The flail whipped at her, keeping her back. Its tongue tasted the air like a predator's and its eyes burned in its head.

'Got you, you xenos bastard,' she told it, spitting savagely through her teeth.

It bubbled a snarl in response, and then, with a surprisingly human gesture, braced one foot against the pillar and tugged.

Lunging, Kamilla retrieved the lasrifle. *Lucky,* she thought, *and blessed.*

'I don't know what you are,' she told the thing. 'Or where you came from, or why you think this world is yours. But I *will* fight until the end.'

Holding it with both hands, she aimed the weapon right at the creature's hissing and open mouth.

And pulled the trigger.

All but blinded by the skull's glare, Augusta raised her bolter.

'We beseech thee, destroy them!'

In her mind's eye, she could see a terrible vision. She could see the storm vortex like a funnel, leading up through the planet's atmosphere. And she could see, up there somewhere, like darkness within darkness, like some great insect creature, a monstrous leviathan.

And it was *hungry.*

Around the Sisters, the building was starting to shudder. The bell tower was coming down, and the huge brass bells were hitting the stone with massive, dying clangs. The organ loft creaked and tumbled, its pipes like music, a chiming, metallic rattle of dying notes.

The storm had not stopped; it ripped up dust and glass and smaller stones and twisted them into a cyclone, a whorl that had the deacon at its centre. Maddened, the skull still in his hand, he flung demented bursts of lightning. Lashes of illumination roared through the lunacy, brought more stone cascading to the floor. His surviving followers were screaming, tearing at their hair and clothes.

Augusta prayed, but His fire burned in her heart. They were the Sisters of Saint Mina and they would destroy the heretic.

'Sisters! With me! We will achieve our mission!'

Fighting through the gale, they advanced on the pulpit. The deacon's energy was erratic, flashing from him in jagged incoherence, striking at the walls, the pews, the pillars. In the body of the building, more of his followers lay crushed and dying. It was surely His blessing that the squad had not been more badly hurt.

Viola fell; Alcina dragged her back to her feet.

Caia's helm was split and smoking; her eyes burned with grief and faith and fire. 'Death to the xenos traitor! Death!' she cried. Raising her bolter in the teeth of the gale, she aimed the weapon squarely at the deacon.

Understanding, Augusta saw that Caia could feel a great, holy burning of her faith. She knew that Melia's memory was there with them, like His grace, guiding Caia's sight and her aim. Like Kimura, like Jatoya, like Felicity. Like Sister Pia, who had given her life, all those years ago. Like Sister Superior Veradis herself, Augusta's commander and holy inspiration...

Blessed be their memories.

Howling a prayer, Caia pulled the trigger. The round hit the deacon in the forehead, blew his brains from the back of his skull. She screamed as he died, celebration and paean.

But the cyclone did not stop.

'Kamilla.'

Kneeling at the front of the altar, Arkas' face was hidden by shadows. But she could hear him quite clearly.

'Get away from her,' she told him. 'Get away from Sister Akemi.'

The single xenos creature was dead, its brain splattered across the steps. And Kamilla had never felt so alive, so strong, so filled with joy and rage and exultation. She could still feel the deacon, like maggots in her mind, but they were little things now, squiggling pathetically as they died.

The Father was not moving. He'd slumped, both hands wrapped about his belly. As Kamilla watched, he took one of them away, looking down at his own blood-smeared fingers.

'What have I *done?*' he said, his voice shaking.

Kamilla gripped the rifle more tightly. She understood, now, understood that the deacon's power was broken, that Arkas was himself again, freed from the dreams. She understood everything, as if He Himself had shown her.

She understood, too, what would happen to her world. The thought was horrific, churning in her belly like betrayal. Looking at Arkas, hunkered and injured, the horror of full realisation closing over him, she felt that churn increase – a roiling of grief and denial and confusion, of pain and guilt and anger and forgiveness.

He was family. How close she had come to following him!

'It wasn't your fault,' she said, coming up the steps. It was the right thing to say, though the words still tore at her heart. 'The beast in the basement, the power of the deacon's call–'

'You were strong enough.' He was coughing now, bubbles of red on his lips. 'Strong enough to break free. What would Jakob have said? I betrayed my *world!*'

'He wouldn't have judged you, Arkas, you know that.' Something in her knew he was dying, now the energy of the xenos had gone. Her eyes were watering and her nose hurt, but she didn't care.

'I'm sorry,' he said. 'I'm sorry. May the Emperor forgive me.' Sobs wracked his shoulders, pain or sorrow; he cast his gaze to Terra, the tiny light of the hololith. 'All those people, Kam, desperate and poor, starving and diseased, forgotten and discarded. He – *it* – told me that I was helping them. I just wanted to help them. And now...' His face crumpled. 'By the saint. Melia – she tried to *save* me. The Sisters...'

For a moment, the passion in him almost broke her heart – he was the Arkas of old, fuelled by his faith. By his love for both Jakob and the Emperor. His love for her. Now realising what he'd really done, what the xenos had meant for his world.

She reached his side and crouched to grip his shoulder, just as he had done to hers, down through all the years of her life. Her mouth twisted, shook as she fought for control.

'You need to get away from here. Let me take Akemi.'

'It was all so real.' He was still talking, perhaps pleading for absolution. 'The hope. The promises. What I was to do with Melia, and with Akemi. *It* told me, it filled my head. Gave me the strength.'

She realised he meant the monster in the basement. Her hands on her rifle were sweating, she discovered, slipping on the weapon's metal. This man, this man who had been family, her guardian and mentor – he was a traitor. He had fallen to the xenos, helped condemn his world, and Sister Melia, to a hideous death. And yet...

And yet he was still Arkas, the last true holy man on Opal.

'Can you stand?'

He blinked at her, his face streaked in tears, shook his head. 'Take Akemi. I will face my penance, and the fate of my world.'

Arkas!

'You need to leave, try and reach the transports–'

'No, Kam, I won't run away. Henrik was right about one thing – I've been a coward all my life. A lone yellow-belly on a world of warriors. And now, I must find my courage, as much as I can.'

Suddenly, the water in her eyes was no longer just grit.

'I won't leave you for them,' she told him.

'Kam.' He looked up at her, his face streaked with tears. 'I thought we would be *saved*.'

'I know,' she said. 'But I'm still not letting you die like that.'

Her heart breaking, Kamilla raised the weapon to her shoulder. Her eyes meeting Arkas', she said, 'May He bless you, and lead you to the light.'

Even as she pulled the trigger, the tears poured down her face.

Epilogue

THE NEWEST DAUGHTER

Escaping the pull of the planet's gravity, the Aquila banked and slewed, the spirit of its engine screaming with sustained effort. Its windows were covered in filth and fluids, and Augusta could no longer see the dying world below her, but she could feel it in her heart, the loss and pain of its imminent consumption. She sang the requiem for Opal's final moments, for Sister Melia Kaliyan, and for all the people that she had not been able to save.

May your light shine upon them.

May your grace shine upon them.

The shuttle juddered and shook, making her belly lurch. About them, the spores were falling thickly now, a rain of death – there must be thousands of them, eager for the feast below. Her vox was broken, crackling empty, and if she listened, she could no longer hear the orbital batteries, the last defence of the doomed. Perhaps the great towers had been finally overwhelmed, or perhaps the shuttle had just climbed too high, leaving only ruin behind it.

May your glory shine upon them.

May your gaze lift them unto the Throne.

Strapped in her seat, the skull of Saint Veres resting golden in her lap, the Sister Superior felt hollow, drained and exhausted, overcome by grief and by the regrets of her own failures. She had fulfilled her mission, but the *cost...*

Blessed be their memories.

In the seat opposite, Viola had collapsed against the prayer-engraved wall, her face bloodless-pale, her heavy bolter across her lap. Caia was helm off and sobbing and Augusta did not silence her – if left unvoiced, such things placed great weight upon the heart. Alcina sat with her eyes closed and her lips moving, perhaps raising the requiem herself. They had placed Sister Melia in the hold, but kept the injured Akemi with them, stabilised now, and strapped down as best as they could manage. Sister Rhene watched her, and beside the old Hospitaller, Kamilla was head down, her hands over her damaged face. The child's whole world was dying – rubble and debris and ruined buildings, a rampage of monsters loose in the streets. As the Sisters had left, Opal's broken stonework had still shone with its holy glitter, like some last, desperate prayer – but already the larger xenos had been rising amid the shattered buildings. Ravenously, they would even now be dissolving and consuming, digesting the Capital, the people, cultist and pilgrim and Blade.

What was left of Opal's festival.

That they may dwell in your light, now and for always.

'Take courage, Sister Caia,' she said, leaning forward. 'Melia knows no more pain, and stands now in His blessing. By your hand was the magus executed, and her death avenged. This was well done.' Augusta herself had placed a final, lividly furious round through the skull of the heretic deacon, making sure.

'And our youngest Sister is blessed. She will fight another day, another battle, another war.'

Viola had raised her head, blinking with weariness, and Caia quietened, her face still streaked with tears. Kamilla snuffled, wiping her broken nose with one hand.

'But why?' The cadet was shivering; in shock, perhaps. 'Why Melia? She was kind, she did nothing wrong. She even tried to save him. Why did Arkas...? Why did *any* of this have to happen?'

She did not ask the question, but Augusta heard her anyway: *Why did my world have to die?*

The shuttle banked again, twisting hard enough to throw them sideways. Outside, the spores must be blazing close and, in her heart, Augusta continued to pray. Somewhere above them, the *Pride of Faith* and the *Star of Victory* would be coordinating what defences they could, facing the hive fleet, allowing the transports to flee for the Mandeville point and escape the shadow in the warp.

'Easy, little one,' Rhene said. She had removed her gauntlets, and one thin, bony hand patted the girl's knee. 'You have faced a mighty trial, in His name, and prevailed.' She gave Augusta a sidelong look, her expression suddenly sharp. 'He has blessed you indeed, it seems.'

The shuttle lurched back the other way, and the pilot cursed.

'But *why?*' Kamilla said, again. 'Why do I live, while so many of my friends don't? Why does He permit such atrocity? Betrayal? Why do people... good people... my whole *world*... Why do they perish in agony? Endre, and Petra, and Benedek, my friends. Takacs, and Mezei...' She sobbed. 'And *Arkas*. I'm sorry. My uncle used to say... I asked too many questions.'

'Do not apologise for your questions, child.' Rhene patted her again. 'Do not apologise for seeking Him, or for seeking meaning. Many of my Sisters Hospitaller have come to their faith through their questions, found understanding and compassion.'

Kamilla's gaze dropped, and a flush spread through her cheeks. She took out a tiny brass compass, letting it turn and settle. 'All I've done is question,' she said. 'Right from the beginning. Maybe, if I'd been more sure of myself, I could have... could have saved him. Them. Could have done more.' Fresh sobs broke from her, and her shoulders shook.

'Never apologise for the tests that have made you a warrior,' Augusta said. 'He faces you with your greatest fears, the darkest places of your soul. The deeds and decisions for which you will suffer, in mind and in heart and in body. But without that suffering, you will never find true strength.'

'And without your questions...' The voice was Akemi's, weak and thin. 'Your faith has no knowledge, and you are blind.'

Sudden heat pricking at the backs of her eyes, Augusta leaned over, extending a hand to the youngest Sister. 'It is good to hear you, Akemi. He has blessed us indeed.'

The hymnal echoed in her heart, though she did not give it voice – she did not trust herself to speak without weeping. Akemi's awakening was an unlooked-for joy, a touch of His forgiveness that she was not sure she deserved.

Over the vox, the pilot said, *'The* Pride of Faith *awaits us, Sisters. The* Star of Victory *has moved to defend the final evacuees, and to draw the hive ship's attention.'*

Akemi, pale as parchment, struggled up to one elbow. 'I felt the xenos,' she said. 'Whatever penance He demands, I will perform, but I felt their touch in my soul. We have faced both daemon and witch, the sheer might of their presence and the calls that they utter – the nightmares they can bring...'

Augusta frowned, remembering, but Akemi was still speaking.

'But I heard the call of the false Saint Veres and it was a

powerful thing. It spoke to the people and it offered them... It offered them the hopes that they needed the most.'

Kamilla said, 'But you did not give in to it–'

'And neither did you,' Augusta said sternly. 'Though it filled your mind like song. Arkas – his very idealism was his undoing, I feel. You, child, are made of more strength.' She was starting to understand where Kamilla's questions had led. 'Tell me,' she said, 'how did you come to resist the beast's might?'

Kamilla was looking at her compass. 'It was Melia,' she said, tears trailing down her face. 'Her courage, her strength. Her compassion. She made me remember... remember the Sisters of Battle.'

The Sisters of Battle.

Novices at the schola wear such injuries with pride.

Do not apologise for seeking Him, or for seeking meaning... for the tests that have made you a warrior.

Without your questions, your faith has no knowledge, and you are blind.

Augusta stared at the girl. As if He had blessed her – blessed all of them – with the ultimate answer, she understood fully, now. Understood why Kamilla had been placed in their path, and what her future would be.

Her heart lifted in a sudden, silent song, in a paean of hope. It was the great cycle of holy blessing, of death and of new-found life and purpose, in His name. Even as one Sister knelt at the Throne, so another was called to take up armour and bolter. Augusta would need the canoness' authorisation, of course, but the girl's purpose was clear, as clear as a shaft of light through the clouds.

Blessed be your holy name!

'I heard them...' Kamilla was saying. 'The xenos, in my dreams. Arkas must have fallen when he lost consciousness, when he had no way to defend himself. And you,' she said to Akemi. 'You were so close…'

'It was a test,' Augusta said. 'Not just for you, I believe, but for the whole of Opal. A test given by Him, to a world that gazed only at itself. To see if it was worth saving, to see if its warriors were still truly worthy. You passed that test, Kamilla.'

Her use of the girl's name was deliberate, and it made the child look up, then crumple, her shoulders shaking.

'*Sister Superior, my apologies for the interruption.*' The pilot's voice came over the vox. '*But we have left the upper atmosphere. The canoness commands your presence, Sisters. With His blessing, we will reach the* Pride *in moments.*'

'Thank you, pilot,' Augusta said.

Kamilla was looking from one face to another, her eyes wide. 'Oh, my poor Opal,' she said, hugging her arms to her chest. 'My whole life…'

'Sing with us, Kamilla.' Remembering something, Augusta pulled off a gauntlet, and hooked a finger down the side of her gorget. After a moment, she found what she was looking for and carefully pulled it free. 'Opal may be no more, but you, and many of her people, remain.' She passed it to the girl: a silver chain with a single tiny fetish still hooked upon it. 'The Path of the Thousand Humble,' she said. 'While Opal lives in your heart and memory, she will never be truly lost.'

In the belly of the *Pride of Faith*, Augusta and her squad faced the canoness, Kamilla still with them. Rhene had sent Melia to the Haven of Blessed Rest, Akemi to the hospice, and had come to join them, though the old Hospitaller's tiredness was clear.

Around them rose the heart of the freighter – a great hollow of black stone, carved into a myriad elaborate oriels and pillars, all hung with the banners of the Order. A blaze of battered scarlet, now covered in scratches and fluids, Elvorix Ianthe waited at its centre, Aitamah with her, the skull-faced cherub hovering. Behind them, a huge marble statue of the Emperor stood with chin raised and sword aloft. He watched with judgement, Augusta thought, and she could not look at Him – not for long.

As she faced their final muster, a claw of guilt caught at her heart, but she stood tall, accepting of whatever verdict would come. At parade-ground ease, she offered the holy skull with one gauntleted hand.

'Milady,' she said. 'Our mission is complete. The heretic is dead.'

The words sounded so small, oddly unreal against everything they had seen and fought through. Everything she had done – and not done.

But the canoness offered no judgement. Gesturing to Aitamah to take the relic, she said, 'And Sister Akemi is safe. This is well.' She looked Augusta up and down, the filthy, battered mess of her armour and cloak. 'Many of our Sisters have offered their lives, for Opal and for her fleeing pilgrims – Sister Melia, Sister Jolantra, Sister Mikaela, Mistress Susanti and her charges. Truly, it has been a Day of Martyrs, even as Opal's festival would have celebrated.'

Her face was etched in weariness, in faith and pain and loss, in holy joy at her Sisters' attaining of the Throne – the touches of her own humanity.

'My Immolator was overcome by the carnifex, even as the shuttle of the *Pride* came to find us. Mikaela and her squad gave their lives, that Aitamah and I may escape and issue the very final command of this mission. Blessed be their memories.'

'Blessed be their memories.' Augusta dared say nothing else.

'The bulk landers are docking with the *Pride*, milady,' Aitamah said. 'And the transports are all now in motion. As ordered, they will achieve the Mandeville point, and muster at the Seltos moon. We have three minutes until Adept Kende detonates the Capital.'

Kamilla's breath caught on a sob.

'And blessed be the memory of this lost world,' the canoness said. Her gaze moved, assessing first Kamilla, then one Sister after another. 'Sisters, I am proud of you all. You have made errors, but He tells me you have done well. Overwhelmed, you upheld both honour and courage. You refused your own martyrdom, in order to save as many as you could. You were blessed and guided, by His light, to complete your mission, and to save the life of Sister Akemi. You slew kelermorph, clavamus, patriarch and magus. Be not ashamed, Augusta. To face the full might of a genestealer infestation – that is a task that would test the stoutest heart.'

'Milady.' Her heart full, her eyes stinging, the corners of her mouth wavering as she fought for control, it was all she could manage. An uprush of grief and relief and faith and weakness was churning in her chest and she wanted only to fall to her knees, overcome with all of it, with the fact that it was over. With the canoness' forgiveness of her own failings.

'Milady,' Aitamah said. 'The last of the guardian freighters, the *Pilgrim's Courage*, is no more. The claws of the hive fleet have caused her too much damage and she tumbles from the skies, burning in her final moments. But she has succeeded – the bulk landers are docked and the last of the surviving transports are now out of hive range. The *Star of Victory* is moving to a final defence. She cannot hold, but she will give us time to leave. We have two minutes remaining until the Capital's detonation.'

Daring to lift her gaze to His statue, unable to stop the water that was sliding down her face, Augusta heard the *Pride*'s engines as the great ship began to turn, heard the deep, rattling boom of her gunnery as she fought to clear her path.

'This mission still requires its final command,' the canoness said. 'I must call for Exterminatus, purge the xenos completely, and I cannot do that from here. Sisters, even as we leave the system, we will sing for the death of Opal. You will open your hearts and accept your errors, Sisters. You will accept His grace, allow His light to touch you. You must not permit dark thoughts to poison your souls.'

Gathering a shaking breath, Augusta said, 'Milady, there is one other matter.'

The canoness raised a sharp eyebrow. 'And what is that?'

'I wish to commend this cadet, Kamilla, to His blessing, and to the lessons of the holy schola.'

Rhene was nodding, and her eyes crinkled with her smile.

'This is no small matter, Augusta,' the canoness said. 'You propose this young woman?'

'I second,' Rhene said. 'She is blessed, and has shown great valour. Once we return to the Convent Sanctorum, we will formally complete the *Sancrisstimi Vocationis*.'

The second eyebrow had joined the first, but the canoness nodded slowly. 'Very well. Her age is unusual, but since she has warrior training, I will pray for His guidance, and take the proposal under due consideration. We will return to this fully, once we are back upon Ophelia VII.' She eyed Kamilla, snot and dirt and filthy clothing, her nose and teeth broken and her hands shaking, her silver chain round her neck, her compass still gripped in her fingers. 'It is a significant honour – and a significant responsibility.'

'I... I...' The girl was looking from face to face, cornered, but her eyes filling with wonder. 'They say the Emperor blessed me, when I was a babe. And I have no family, not now.'

'If He has truly blessed you, then you shall have family anew.' The canoness gave a rare, gentle smile. 'Come. You are the heart and courage of your world, it seems, and if He calls you, you will be the first child of Opal to join the Adepta Sororitas in almost three millennia.'

Augusta saw the flush that crept up the girl's cheeks, and felt a sudden wash of warmth. The blessing of a new Sister, a new Daughter of the Emperor, a new voice in their sacred hymnal: in among all her errors, this was something truly blessed.

Stammering, Kamilla said, 'Thank you, your eminence. I... I don't know what to say.'

'Then say nothing,' the canoness said. 'Only join us as we sing the requiem. For you are now a true veteran, Kamilla, a blooded warrior of Opal. And you will carry her banner to the stars.'

ABOUT THE AUTHOR

Danie Ware is the author of the novels *The Triumph of Saint Katherine* and *The Rose in Darkness*, the novellas *The Bloodied Rose*, *Wreck and Ruin* and *The Rose in Anger*, and several short stories all featuring the Sisters of Battle. She lives in Carshalton, South London, with her son and cat, and has long-held interests in role-playing, re-enactment, vinyl art toys and personal fitness.

YOUR
NEXT READ

PILGRIMS OF FIRE
by Justin D Hill

Sister Helewise must follow an ancient route of pilgrimage to rediscover and liberate the shrine world of Cion, a former bastion of the Order of Our Martyred Lady.

An extract from
Pilgrims of Fire
by Justin D Hill

War was already raging on the Obscurus Front the year the pilgrim fleet set off from Ophelia VII. They were to retrace the route of Saint Katherine's first War of Faith, their ramshackle ships chained together in a Gordian knot of piety and hope.

The fate of one would be the fate of all, the pilgrim-chiefs declared, the believers suffering together the travails and privations of their holy expedition.

They were plagued by all the dangers of the galaxy. Millions were lost to sickness and starvation. Attacks by xenos, renegades and pirates took countless others, while those of brittle faith fell by the wayside to lives of penance and prayer.

Empty warp ships were cut free and abandoned to the void. But after a decade, a billion souls yet remained, joined firmly by a tightening bond of belief. Their last ordeal was the desperate crossing, through the Fey Straits to Holy Cion.

This journey had twice repelled Saint Katherine. They all understood the danger, and gave themselves over to days of prayers and sacrifice and self-flagellation. There was an air of mourning as the fleet moved towards the Mandeville point.

The augurs were not good, and the warp was in a state of ecstatic tumult. When, at last, the pilgrim fleet broke into real-space, the tethered craft hung together, too weary and broken and stunned to do anything but offer prayers of gratitude to the God-Emperor, after years of travails, for their safe arrival.

The paean of thanks was heard by the astropaths on the shrine world of Holy Cion. Their tower was set in the upper reaches of the Abbey of Eternal Watch, which sat atop the vast stone out-crop known as the Bolt. A great cylinder of black granite which loomed over the surrounding Pilgrim Plains, the Bolt looked as though it had been fired into the planet's crust from some titanic orbital cannon.

Upon its peak, the Sisters of Our Martyred Lady maintained their guard. A cherub brought the news to the high chamber of Canoness Ysolt, where the venerable warrior was at prayer.

The messenger entered the chamber on fluttering white wings, anti-grav generators humming, the iron skull-face speaking in deep, resonant tones.

'Canoness. Tidings have come. The pilgrim fleet has arrived.'

Cion's output of prayer and faith and devotion was as inte-gral to the Imperium of Mankind as the production of any forge world. But the canoness' mind was concerned with disturbing portents. Shadows seen at night, mad laughter coming from empty rooms, reports of ghosts of sobbing women. And now the population of Cion were approaching a state of starvation. A pilgrim fleet was the last thing they needed, a doubting voice said. But, she reminded herself, faith was like a blade. It was there to be used. The Emperor would provide.

Ysolt steepled her fingers. Her voice was strained. She said a brief prayer of thanks and addressed her cherub. 'Sound the Bell of Ancestral Transgressions,' she said. 'I will take the augurs. The

Feast of Landing must take place. We must welcome the faithful
upon our holy soil.'

There were five hundred Battle Sisters within the Abbey of
Eternal Watch. They exerted a gravity upon the population of
Cion like celestial bodies. In better times the festival had been
a moment of due solemnity. But the better times were now
a distant memory for the serving women who worked in the
bowels of the abbey.

The years of gathering privations had ground the working young
girls down to a state of hunger and exhaustion, and none were
hungrier that evening than Branwen, a maid-of-all-work, scrubbing the abbey stairs. She had scoured all the way from the lower
gallery to the Sisters' refectory, and now her knees were sore, her
shoulders ached and her stomach was as empty as an ogryn's brain.

'Hurry, girl!' one of the serving women said, as she carried a
bundle of dirty sheets down towards the laundry. 'They're serving repast downstairs.'

Branwen nodded, but she saw with horror that the woman had
left dirty footprints across the wet floor, and she said a prayer
of contrition as she wiped them clean again. The trail led her
right across the vaulted space. She paused at the refectory door
and looked up. The gothic arch soared into darkness, statues
of Sisters towering over her. The heavy oak doors were closed.

'You, girl!' a voice said.

Branwen jumped.

'Come away from there! What are you doing? Are you listening in?'

'No, ma'am!' Branwen said, but she looked as guilty as the
hanged.

Tula, the Mistress of Chores, caught her by the ear and slapped
her across the scalp. 'Shame on you! Soiling the sanctity of this

place with your presence. You're just a bastard foundling. Away from that door!'

Tula tutted to herself as she dragged Branwen away. 'What do they say about cleanliness?'

'It brings us closer to the God-Emperor,' Branwen said.

'Indeed,' Tula said. 'And it seems this corridor is a long way from Him, who sits in majesty upon His Golden Throne.'

Branwen had tears in her eyes as she sponged her way along the flagstone corridor, dunking her brush into the bucket of caustic soap and slapping it down onto the dirty steps.

It was true, of course. She was a foundling. Everyone knew the story. An unwanted babe, spat out of the city and left at the abbey gates with just a swaddling blanket wrapped about her and a few hours of life within her hungry frame.

She would have died but for the charity of maid-of-all-work Kolpitts, who had taken her in and raised her as her own. And Branwen had tried so many times to be worthy of the life of servitude and prayer. But it was so very hard... Especially when she was *so* hungry.

'Careful!' a voice said.

Branwen had not heard the Sister approach. And now she had splashed the Sister's armoured boot with filthy water. She did not dare look up. 'Forgive me, holy Sister!'

The Sister knelt beside her and put her hand out. Branwen flinched as the Sister's hand touched her chin and lifted her face. Through her tears the maid-of-all-work found herself looking directly into the Sister's eyes. Her suit of armour was black as night, with a curling tracery of interwoven stems, acid-etched into the ceramite. Her face was fine as marble, her gaze resolute. Branwen was mortified. It was not just any Sister, but Lizbet of the Sacred Sword, the most sublime of the Battle Sisters in the abbey. Stories filtered down to the scullery maids of her skill with bolt and blade. Of terrible foes cut down in their pride. Heretics purged. Vengeance made real.

'Forgive me!' Branwen whispered and tried to pull away, but Lizbet held the maid's hands. They were scabbed and raw. Lizbet pressed them between her own and spoke a prayer of spiritual fortitude. At the end she said, 'For your enemies are brought down and broken, and we are risen and victorious.'

Branwen stared like one smitten. Sister Lizbet rose with the gentle whine of servos, her black power armour gleaming with reflected candlelight.

The refectory door opened and Sister Lizbet passed inside. For a brief moment the sound of prayer spilt out. Branwen could not understand a word, but the sound transfixed her. So pure, so transcendent was the song of angels that a wave of raw emotion swelled within her, filled her heart with fierce joy. She could still feel the touch of Lizbet's hands and as she looked at her own, she saw that the raw scabs were gone.

Tears of joy rose through her as she finished her scrubbing and hurried down to the abbey cellars, bucket in one hand, rag in the other. The edificium was a place of wide walkways, heavy with prayer, but the stairs wound down to the servant quarters. They were dark and narrow, the undressed stone marked with simple icons of faith.

Branwen rushed into the slop hall, tipped the dirty water away, hung her bucket onto its hook, dried her hands upon her skirts and hurried through the wide chambers to the scullery.

It was the only warm room, where the maids sat before the fire in the moments when they could draw breath. There was a long trestle table, with plain wooden benches along either side, and a cast iron candelabra hanging from the stone ceiling, the candle flames guttering in the draughty chamber.

Branwen saw the table was empty, the stacked wooden plates picked clean. The day's single meal had been eaten.

Branwen would not cry, she told herself, not when others were out there on the Obscurus Front, dying in their millions. The God-Emperor suffered for all time upon the Golden Throne, and what was her hunger compared to that?

She lifted her face to the candle flames to stop the tears from falling, and one of the cooks breezed in with a damp cloth and wiped the trestle boards clean.

'What's wrong, girl?' the cook called out. 'Don't you have work to do?'

'Yes,' Branwen said, 'but I have not eaten since yesterday, and I came down and—'

'Then don't be late next time!' the cook snapped.

'But—' Branwen started.

'Throne above! The pilgrim fleet has arrived, girl. We don't have time for your fussing.'